DAMIEN LEONE'S

THE OFFICIAL MOVIE NOVELIZATION

DAMIEN LEONE'S

TERRIFIER 2

THE OFFICIAL MOVIE NOVELIZATION
TIM WAGGONER

TITAN BOOKS

Terrifier 2: The Official Movie Novelization
Print edition ISBN: 9781835413210
E-book edition ISBN: 9781835413227

Published by Titan Books
A division of Titan Publishing Group Ltd
144 Southwark Street, London SE1 0UP
www.titanbooks.com

First edition: October 2024
10 9 8 7 6 5 4 3 2

This is a work of fiction. All of the characters, organizations,
and events portrayed in this novel are either products of the
author's imagination or are used fictitiously. Any resemblance
to actual persons, living or dead (except for satirical
purposes), is entirely coincidental.

Tim Waggoner asserts the moral right to be identified as the
author of this work.

A CIP catalogue record for this title is available
from the British Library.

Printed and bound by CPI Group (UK) Ltd,
Croydon CR0 4YY.

Thanks to Brad Miska for inviting me to play in Art's blood-soaked world. Thanks to Kenneth W. Cain for doing such a great job editing the manuscript. And, as always, thanks to my agent Cherry Weiner, my steadfast guide through the wild world of publishing.

CHAPTER ONE

Dr. Seth Bolton was having one absolutely shit-tastic night.

Being a coroner was never a laugh fest, but today had been especially grim. A family of four—parents in their thirties and their two young children—had died in their sleep the previous night. The wife's mother had stopped by her daughter's house to drop off a batch of ghost-shaped sugar cookies she'd made for the kids to celebrate Halloween. When she found the door locked, she tried calling, but her daughter didn't answer. Mom had a key for emergencies, so she opened the door, went inside, and called out their names, but there was no response. Frantic, she searched through the house, and she found everyone in their beds. At first, she thought they were asleep, but when she couldn't rouse any of them, she realized the terrible truth. They were all dead.

She called 911, police rushed to the scene, and after giving the victims a quick once-over, they called the Coroner's Office. Seth answered the phone.

"Got four cold ones for you," the officer who called had said. Despite his profession—or perhaps because of it—Seth didn't appreciate that kind of dark humor, but he said nothing, just took down the address and waited for the EMTs to deliver the bodies. It took two trips, but an hour later, the entire deceased family was in Seth's lab, lying on gurneys, zipped up in body bags, covered by white sheets. Seth was confident the family had died of carbon monoxide poisoning—the cops on the scene said there were no CO detectors in the house—but he still had to conduct autopsies to prove it, on the kids as well as the parents. That had taken a total of eight hours.

He was looking forward to getting the hell out of here, hitting a drive-thru on the way home to pick up dinner, watching a little TV, and going to sleep early for change. But just as he was about to leave, he got another call.

A middle-aged man had dropped dead at a local bar. He and his friends had been debating the Giants' chances for the season, when he broke off in the middle of a sentence—eyes wide, features frozen—and slipped off his bar stool. Seth figured the poor bastard was probably dead before he hit the floor, most likely from a heart attack or an aneurysm. But since the cause of death couldn't be determined at the scene, the man won an all-expenses-paid trip to the Coroner's Office.

The office was criminally short-staffed at the moment, too. One of the other two docs who worked there was out on maternity leave, and the third had quit to take a job as a pathologist in a hospital, and Seth hadn't had time to replace him. This meant Seth was doing the work of three people, so rather than putting the new corpse on ice until the morning, he decided to stay late and perform the autopsy, so he wouldn't be so backed up tomorrow.

Big mistake.

As he was finishing up with the barfly, yet *another* call came in.

A dead woman had been found in a dumpster behind a nail salon. Her clothes were on backward and inside out, and it appeared that most of the bones in her body had been broken. Another bizarre death, another guest at Chateau de Coroner. By this point, it was almost midnight, and Seth said fuck it, brewed another pot of coffee, and got to work on the woman soon after she arrived.

When he finished, it was around 3:00 a.m. Too late to go home since the day shift would start in a few hours, but maybe he'd be able to catch a few Zs in his office before then, provided no one else in this fucking town died in mysterious circumstances before 9:00 a.m.

He'd settled into his office chair, put his feet on the desk, leaned back, closed his eyes... and the goddamn phone rang again. A number of grisly murders had taken place in an abandoned warehouse on the west side of town. When Seth asked the cop on the line how many a "number" was, she'd said, "A lot—and they're bad, Doc. Really bad."

Seth had sighed as he hung up the phone. So much for sleep.

So now here he was, alone with what the nightshift EMTs—Roman and Elston—assured him were only the first bodies recovered from the warehouse massacre. At least two more would be coming. Seth wished he'd listened to his father and gone to law school. Elston had promised to bring him a breakfast sandwich—with bacon. That was something.

Time to open the presents they'd brought him.

He unbuckled the restraints that kept the victim's corpse secured to the gurney, donned a pair of rubber examination gloves, then unzipped the brown body bag just enough so he could get a look at the man's face.

"Jesus."

With the exception of the left eye—which remained intact—his entire face had been reduced to ragged, raw meat. There were cavernous holes where the right eye and nose had been, the lower jaw was shattered and hung at an angle, and only a few teeth remained visible in the violated flesh.

Seth remembered what Elston had told him.

You're probably going to have to identify this poor bastard by his teeth—if you can dig them out of the back of his skull.

He'd thought the EMT had been exaggerating. If anything, the kid had understated the severity of the man's injuries.

Seth looked up and stared at the second body bag, lying on a gurney several feet away. The killer was in there. Elston had said the fucker had killed himself rather than be taken into police custody, but Seth thought the man had gotten off too lightly. Anyone who could do something like *this* to another human being—he gazed back down at the victim's red, wet ruin of a face—deserved to be punished, to *suffer*, for a long time. Seth didn't believe in Heaven or Hell, but at times like this, he wished he did. It would be a comfort to know this man's killer was roasting in the fires of damnation for all eternity.

He sighed. At least the maniac could never hurt anyone else.

"Let's have a look at the man of the hour."

He zipped up the victim's body bag, concealing the ravaged face once more. Seth wasn't squeamish—not after twenty-two years on the job—but that didn't mean he enjoyed gazing at mangled meat and crushed bone any longer than he had to.

He walked over to the second gurney, undid the straps, and unzipped the bag. Before opening it all the way, he looked down at the spot where the killer's head was hidden.

"I hope your fifteen minutes of fame was worth it, you sick son of a bitch."

He pulled the bag open—

—and immediately drew back in surprise.

The motherfucker was dressed like some kind of goddamn demon clown. Why hadn't Roman and Elston given him a heads-up? Maybe they'd just forgotten; or maybe they'd decided to treat ol' Doc to a little trick tonight. Jerks. God, he *hated* working on Halloween.

He leaned forward to examine the killer's face more closely.

The killer wore a bloodstained white skull cap that covered his head and ears, and his face was covered with white makeup. Black makeup encircled his lips and mouth, and formed cartoonishly thin crescent eyebrows that reached up to his forehead. He didn't appear to have any actual eyebrows. Had he shaved them? He had a long, hooked, witch-like nose—complete with a small black wart-like dot on the tip—sharp, protruding cheekbones, an exaggerated brow ridge, and a thick, prominent chin. At first, he assumed these features were

11

merely more makeup, rubber appliances affixed to the man's face with some kind of adhesive. And yet, they looked like real flesh, bone, and cartilage. Seth couldn't escape the feeling that if he were to reach out and gently pinch the end of the killer's nose, he'd find it wasn't a prosthetic at all.

The fucker *stank*, too. He smelled of blood—both fresh *and* congealed. And his body odor was so strong, it was like he regularly bathed in sewer water.

The worst part was the killer's teeth. The mouth was stretched in a wide orifice, revealing swollen black gums and rotting teeth, slick with blood. The mouth looked as if it belonged to some loathsome deep-sea creature rather than a man, and it gave him a disturbingly inhuman appearance.

He could only see a bit of the clown's costume—a ruffled white collar (stained with blood, of course) and a tiny black top hat he wore at a jaunty angle on the left side of his head, held in place by an elastic strap that reached beneath his chin. He supposed the hat was meant to add a touch of whimsy to the outfit, but all it did was make the bastard seem even more creepy.

There was something else about the man, too, something Seth couldn't quite put his finger on. Even dead, he exuded an aura of menace, of violence waiting to erupt at any moment, like a powerful thunderstorm on the verge of letting loose. It was an unsettling feeling, and he didn't like it.

Seth had been so fascinated by the man's bizarre appearance that he'd momentarily forgotten to examine his injuries, and he did so now. The right eye was gone, and since he saw no obvious signs of it being cut or pulled out, he assumed it had been *pushed* out by great force.

He blew his brains out before they could take him in, Elston had said.

Seth saw no obvious wounds to the head, so he assumed the clown had jammed the gun muzzle into his mouth and pulled the trigger. The force of the blast could've forced the right eye out of its socket, and the exit wound would most likely be in the back of the head. Shooting himself that way would account for the blood on his teeth, too.

Police found him eating the face off some girl after he ran her over with a truck.

Then again, the blood could be from another of his victims. Or maybe it was his *and* hers, mixed.

Seth reached for the clown's shoulders, intending to raise him a few inches so he could get a look at the back of his head. But before he could touch the man, all hell broke loose. The fluorescent lights flickered on and off rapidly, creating a disorienting strobe effect, and every electronic device emitted loud, harsh static. The office phone warbled, sounding much louder than it ever had before, and there was a rising-and-falling *sssssshhhhh* that resembled a chorus of whispering voices, but if they spoke any words, Seth couldn't make them out. A woman's voice came from the radio, and the words it said rose above the din.

"You're going to like it here..."

Screaming followed, whether from the woman or some other source. It increased in pitch and volume until it felt like hot spikes were being driven through Seth's ears.

And then it stopped.

The lights remained on, and every electronic device fell silent, including the phone. If his ears hadn't been ringing, he would've thought he'd experienced a hallucination, one most likely brought on by severe sleep deprivation. He looked around, half-expecting—or maybe hoping— someone would jump out of hiding and shout "Happy Halloween!" But no one did.

What in the ever-loving fuck was that?

If only the radio had been affected, Seth thought he might've been listening to some kind of messed-up Halloween program designed to freak out listeners. But the lights, the phone...

He slowly turned his head to look down at the dead clown once more. Could he—

No, that was ridiculous. Seth was a man of science. He didn't believe in ghosts.

The clown's right arm shot upward, and his fingerless-gloved hand fastened around Seth's throat and squeezed tight. The clown sat up, and his one remaining eye—his *living* eye—fixed on Seth with white-hot hatred. Holy shit! The motherfucker wasn't dead! Seth didn't know how Roman and Elston could've made such a mistake, and right then it didn't matter. He needed to get away from this bastard before he ended up like No-Face over there.

He grabbed hold of the clown's forearm with both hands and tried to break his grip, but no matter how hard he pulled, it was no use. The killer was unbelievably strong, especially for someone who had been injured so severely that a pair of highly trained and experienced EMTs thought he was dead. Then again, maybe the clown *had* been dead, and the weird energy surge that passed through the office had somehow brought him back. But he didn't really give a crap if the clown was dead, alive, or something in between. Seth had expected to die as a result of his bad habits—eating shitty food, drinking too much booze, never exercising—and he'd long ago made peace with that. But he'd be damned if he let himself die at the hands of a blood-covered, one-eyed killer clown—and on fucking *Halloween*, no less! His obituary would be embarrassing as hell.

Seth wished he had a knife or a gun, but he didn't. What he *did* have, however, was an expert knowledge of human anatomy. He removed his left hand from the clown's forearm, extended his index finger, and jammed it into the clown's empty eye socket as hard as he could. He swirled his finger around in the bloody slop, hoping to cause enough brain damage to turn off this fucker's lights for good. But instead of crying out in pain or jerking his head back, the clown merely grinned, exposing more of his horrible-looking teeth.

He tightened his grip on Seth's throat, and Seth felt his laryngeal prominence of the thyroid cartilage—otherwise known as the Adam's apple—begin to give way beneath the pressure of the clown's cruel hand. Then there was a sickening *crunch*, and Seth screamed. His ears filled with a roaring sound, and gray slid in from the edges of his vision. He knew this meant he was on the verge of passing out, and if that happened, he would be completely helpless. Once unconscious, the clown could kill him easily, and take his sweet time doing it.

Panicking, Seth pulled his finger out of the clown's eye socket with a wet *schlurp* and jabbed it back in. He repeated this maneuver, jabbing his finger in and pulling it out as fast as he could. In-out, in-out, in-out… But all he succeeded in doing was to piss off the clown. He felt the man's fingers cut into the skin of his neck and then plunge into his flesh. Blood gushed from newly created wounds, and Seth tried to give voice to his pain, but all that came out of his mouth was a harsh coughing gurgle.

Acting on instinct, nothing more now than a dumb animal trying to save its life, Seth started shaking his head back and forth rapidly. More blood flowed, coating the clown's hand and making it difficult for him to maintain his grip. Seth then pulled his body backward with all the strength left to him and slipped free from the killer's grasp.

For an instant, he felt a surge of victory, but then he shoved the emotion aside. He didn't have time to do anything except try to survive. He slapped a hand to his throat to staunch the blood flow, turned, and started toward his instrument tray on the other side of the room, hoping to arm himself with something—a scalpel, rib shears—*anything* with which he could defend himself.

He wanted to run, but the best he could manage was a shambling walk. Blood loss wasn't the only problem he faced—he was having trouble breathing too. Not only had the clown nearly crushed his throat, narrowing his airway, but the killer's fingers had penetrated so deeply into his neck that blood was actually pouring *into* his throat, causing him to swallow and aspirate it. Every time he tried to take in a breath, he sucked more blood into his lungs than air, and when he tried to exhale, he coughed a gout of crimson that soaked his white lab coat or splattered onto the tiled floor. His vision blurred, and he weaved, stumbled, almost fell, but he managed to stay on his feet and keep going.

Something hard slammed into the base of his spine as the clown kicked him, and white light exploded behind his eyes. He crashed to the floor, the impact causing his hand to fly away from his throat. Blood gushed freely from his wounds, and he pressed his hand to his neck once more. The flesh was so wet now it was impossible to maintain a decent seal with his examination gloves, so he stripped off the slippery things, tossed them aside, and pressed his bare hand to his neck. The seal wasn't much better than the glove's, but it was something. His lower back felt as if it was on fire, and he thought how easy it would be to just give up and lie here and let the clown finish him off.

He rolled onto his side, injured back screaming in protest, and turned his head enough so he could see the clown standing behind him, mouth stretched into an impossibly wide grin, blood trickling from his empty socket like red tears, his good eye wild with madness.

He could see the clown's entire costume now, and it followed the same black-and-white color scheme of his makeup. The right arm was black, the left white, while the left side of the body was white down to the pants cuff, the left black. Two black pom-poms were attached to the middle of the outfit like giant buttons. A white ruffled collar, ruffled sleeves, fingerless white gloves, and that tiny black hat completed the ensemble.

He had two thoughts upon getting his first real look at the killer clown. One, he couldn't believe how much blood was on the bastard's costume, most of it probably not his. And two, he couldn't believe a skinny fucker like him could be so goddamn *strong*. Seth's gaze then traveled down the clown's body until he came to the man's feet. Of course the son of a bitch was wearing a pair of giant clown shoes. No wonder his back felt like it was broken.

Then it happened again, only worse this time. The fluorescent lights started strobing once more, their blue-white illumination far more intense, the shadows they created sharper, darker, deeper. Static blasted from every electronic device in the lab, regardless of whether it had been activated before or not, the noise absolutely deafening. Added to that was a discordant chorus of disembodied screams, the voices of a thousand spirits suffering agonies beyond comprehension. Despite there being no windows in the lab, a violent wind erupted from some unknown source, snatched papers off his desk, and swirled them around the room in an invisible vortex.

The clown spread his arms wide, turned his face toward the ceiling, and closed his one eye, as if luxuriating in the chaos that surrounded him. His mouth moved as if laughing with delight, but no sound emerged, and Seth thought the killer's silence was, in its own way, equally as disturbing as the powerful forces that had been unleashed in the lab.

This couldn't be happening, not *any* of it, but it was, and if he didn't get off his ass and start moving again, he would die. The clown was still glorying in the storm of insanity that raged around him, and Seth knew this was his chance. He was now too weak to physically fight the clown, but if he could reach the office phone and call for help… He tried to push himself onto his feet using his free hand, but his back screamed at him, so he abandoned that idea. Instead, he crawled across the tiled floor, keeping his right hand pressed to his throat to minimize his blood loss.

He'd only gone a couple of feet when he felt a prickling on the back of his neck, an atavistic warning of danger. Fearing the clown was about to resume his attack, he looked over his shoulder, but the man remained in the same position, head back, arms spread. But Seth saw… *something* appear next to the clown. It was dark, edges blurry, a shadow that wasn't quite there. Its size varied rapidly, taller than the clown one instant, small as a pebble the next. Then the shadow stabilized at around four feet. It assumed a roughly human form, pure dark and featureless. No, not a shadow, Seth realized. A shadow was something. This was *Nothing* with a capital N—a great, endless emptiness in the shape of a child. As frightening as the clown was, as dangerous as he was, he was nothing compared to this… this *blasphemy*, and Seth was filled with an emotion so far beyond terror he didn't think there was a word for it.

A voice on the radio, the one he heard before, spoke again. *"You're going to like it here… I promise."*

The dark thing turned its head and looked up at the clown, who still stood with his arms spread, head back, eye closed. Then it lowered its head to face Seth, waved enthusiastically, and then faded until it was gone.

The chaos continued—lights flashing, electronics crackling, voices screaming in torment—but the shadow thing was gone, and he was no longer paralyzed by fear. He continued crawling across the floor toward the office phone, struggling to breathe, but, for the moment at least, still alive.

CHAPTER TWO

Art lowered his hands to his sides and opened his eye.

The strange storm that raged around him was beginning to abate. The lights flickered more slowly now, the wind was less violent, the noises issuing from the electronic devices were quieter, and the disembodied screams had ceased altogether.

Too bad. He liked the screams.

A memory, as if from a half-forgotten dream, drifted through his mind. Words, spoken in a man's voice.

I hope your fifteen minutes of fame was worth it, you sick son of a bitch.

He fixed his eye on the coroner crawling across the floor, hand pressed to his wounded neck, blood trail smeared on the tile behind him. Time to finish the job. He bared his teeth in a half smile, half snarl, and started toward the bleeding man. But he only made it a few steps before a glint of light caught his attention. He stopped, turned, saw a mirror hanging on the wall above a sink. The coroner could wait. He wasn't going anywhere.

Art walked over to the mirror and examined his reflection. His clothes were a blood-caked mess—always a hazard in his line of work—and his right eye socket was a crimson ruin. He was vaguely aware the coroner had reached his desk and was attempting to grab hold of the phone's handset. But the man's fingers were so slick with blood that he was having trouble getting a grip on it. Art wasn't ready to deal with him just yet, though. He leaned forward and pulled down his lower lid to get a closer look at his empty eye socket. He leaned back, tilted his head, considered. Not a bad look for him, really.

The coroner, still sitting on the floor, managed to finally take hold of the handset. In order to use the dial pad, he would have to remove his other hand from his throat. He did so, and blood streamed from his wounds as he lifted himself into a crouching position so he could see what he was doing. His hand shook as he extended an index finger and stabbed it at the keys on the dial pad. It took him a couple of tries, but eventually he managed to press 9-1-1. He slumped back to the floor, pressed his free hand to his throat once more, and waited.

Art—still standing at the mirror—could hear the dispatcher's voice as she answered.

"911, what is your emergency?"

The coroner tried to speak, but all that came out of his mouth was a choking sputter.

"Hello? 911. Do you have an emergency?"

The coroner tried again, but only managed unintelligible grunts.

Art reached around to the back of his head, lightly touched his fingertips to the open wound there, felt splintered edges of bone and a slurry of blood and spongy meat. He got his fingers good and wet, pulled his hand away, pressed it to the mirror and began to slowly draw letters on the glass.

"Sir, can you speak?"

"If you can't speak, press any button on your phone. Once for yes, twice for no."

"Are you still there? Sir, I want you to stay on the line for me, okay? I'm gonna track your location."

The letters might've spelled *Art*, but the message they were meant to communicate was, *I'm back, motherfuckers!*

Time for the coroner.

Art turned away from the mirror and took a deep breath to help him refocus. The storm was over now, and aside from the coroner's labored, wet breathing, all was silent. Art swept his one-eyed gaze around the lab until he found what he was looking for—a rolling stainless-steel tray with various surgical instruments laid out upon its surface. He walked over to the tray and considered the array of lovely toys before him.

Decisions, decisions...

"Are you still with me? Hello? Are you still there?"

A gleaming steel postmortem hammer caught Art's eye. He picked it up, felt its weight in his hand, considered its heft, imagined the damage such an instrument could inflict. Yes, this would do nicely. Gripping the handle tightly, he turned back to the coroner, and his lips drew back from his teeth in a savage grin.

"Okay, 129 Peterson Drive, Miles County Morgue. Sir, are you still with me?"

Art walked toward the coroner. The man's eyes widened in panic, and he tried to speak again, the sputters coming more rapidly this time, but he remained unable to form coherent words.

"Just sit tight and remain calm. Police and paramedics are on their way—"

Art gently removed the handset from the coroner's grip and replaced it on the base unit, cutting off the dispatcher. The coroner looked up at the clown, fear in his eyes, along with a silent plea for mercy.

As if.

Art raised the hammer and brought it down onto the coroner's forehead. There was a satisfying crack of bone, and a jet of blood flew upward and splattered onto the wall calendar. The coroner slumped to the floor, and Art crouched over him and swung the hammer into the side of the man's jaw. Another crack, and teeth flew through the air, hit the tile with sharp clacks, and skittered to a stop. Art dropped the hammer, grabbed the coroner's damaged jaw with his left hand to hold the man's head still. Then with his other hand, he reached for the man's right eye.

The coroner let out a gurgling scream as Art jammed his fingers into the socket and pulled the eye free. The optic nerve was still attached, and it flopped around like a tail as Art held the eye up to examine it. Then he rolled up the optic nerve and pressed the eye into his empty socket. When he was finished, he turned the right side of his face to the coroner, grinned, and spread his hands in a ta-dah gesture. He pointed to his new eye, then pointed to the coroner's empty socket, and silently laughed.

The coroner was too busy writhing in pain and choking on his own blood to appreciate Art's little prank, however. He shook his head back and forth, as if saying, No, no, no...

Joke 'em if they can't take a fuck. Art picked up the postmortem hammer and continued smashing the coroner's face, striking one blow after another, until the man stopped making noise and fell still. Art continued hitting the man's face until the man's features were utterly destroyed. Then he dropped the hammer once more, removed his new eye, and tossed it aside. He gripped the top of the coroner's head with both hands and pried open his skull as easily as pulling apart a ripe melon. He reached inside, pulled the brain free, and lifted it with both hands, gazing lovingly upon it, as if holding something sacred and beautiful.

Then he shoved it into his mouth and sank his teeth into its sweet, warm meat.

Coming back from the dead sure gave a guy an appetite.

When Art was finished with his grisly repast, he upended a plastic container and dumped its contents onto the floor. Then he put the container back on the floor and removed the now empty garbage bag.

Time to go shopping.

He raided the cabinets and drawers, in search of new instruments of death. He stuffed his bag with knives, forceps, scissors, scalpels, bone saws, chisels, and whatever else he could find that appeared capable of inflicting serious damage on the human body. He might as well have been a kid in a toy store.

On a shelf containing bottles of various chemicals, he discovered one labeled *fluoroantimonic acid*. He had no idea what *fluoroantimonic* meant, but *acid* was just what the (dead) doctor ordered. He added it to his new collection. He spent a few more moments gathering items, mindful of the time. The 911 dispatcher had told the coroner that help was on the way, and he wanted to finish up and leave before they got here. He'd already died once today, and he really didn't feel like doing it again.

He checked the pockets of the coroner's lab coat, then his pants pockets, until he found the man's wallet. He turned it upside down, shook it, and several quarters dropped out and clattered to the floor. The man didn't carry a lot of cash—who did these days?—but Art found a few singles, took them, then tossed the wallet away. He put the money in his garbage bag, then stepped over to the coroner's corpse. He gazed at it without expression, thinking nothing, feeling nothing. And then he cocked his head, grinned, gave the dead man a farewell salute, and headed for the door.

But before he could reach it, he heard someone approaching from the other side.

*

26

"That man is gonna work himself to death," Roman said.

He and Roman took turns driving the medic van, and tonight Elston was behind the wheel. He liked driving. It occupied his mind so he didn't have to think as much about the things they saw on the job. Like tonight. That warehouse had been a scene out of a fucking nightmare.

Right now, they were waiting in line at an all-night donut shop drive-thru to pick up Doc's breakfast sandwich—a bacon, egg, and cheese croissant with extra bacon—as well as some food for themselves. He'd ordered a large soda and a blueberry muffin, while Roman had selected a large ice coffee and a bagel. A *plain* one, which Elston thought was the most boring bagel of all. Then again, he supposed a blueberry muffin wasn't that daring a choice, either.

"Doc *is* kind of a workaholic," Elston admitted, "but the Coroner's Office really could use more staff."

"Budget cuts," Roman said, and Elston nodded.

The car ahead of them got their food and drove away, so Elston pulled up.

"That'll be $21.98," the woman at the window said.

She was an attractive woman with curly brown hair, and she looked like she could barely keep her eyes open. Elston could relate. Working nights could really take a toll on a person.

He smiled as he handed her his debit card.

"Busy night?" he asked.

The woman mumbled something unintelligible, tapped his card, and returned it to him. She then handed him two bags, which Elston took and passed on to Roman, and their drinks, which he put in the van's cupholders. He gave the woman at the window another smile.

"Hope you have a good rest of your day," he said.

She muttered something that might've been "You too," but which could've just as easily been "Fuck you." Elston pulled away from the window, stopped at the parking lot's exit to make sure traffic was clear, then pulled onto the street and headed back toward the Coroner's Office. A good thing about working nights when you were an EMT: a lot fewer vehicles on the road than during the day. If you needed to get a patient to the hospital fast, there were fewer obstacles to slow you down. Elston sometimes wondered how many people had died en route to the hospital during the day who might've survived if they'd taken the trip during the night.

Roman took her bagel from one of the bags along with a small container of cream cheese. She unwrapped the bagel, then peeled the lid off the container and used a plastic knife to spread the cream cheese. She liked a thin layer on her bagels, while Elston saw bagels as cream cheese delivery devices and piled it on.

"You want your muffin?" she asked.

"Not while I'm driving. But I'd appreciate it if you could put a straw in my drink."

"You got it." Roman did and handed the cup to Elston. He thanked her and took a long drink. He sighed as the coolness hit his throat. It was the first time he'd paused to drink something since their shift began.

Roman finished preparing her bagel, took a small bite, and began chewing.

"Good?" he asked.

Roman swallowed. "Tastes like cardboard."

She wrapped up the bagel and tossed it back into the bag.

He frowned. "You usually like their bagels."

"I know, and on any other night, I'm sure it would taste fine. But after what we saw at the warehouse…"

Elston knew what she meant. As an EMT, you needed to get used to seeing some pretty awful shit, or you didn't last long in the job. On his very first shift as a rookie, he and his partner at the time—a long-time EMT named Patty Willis—got a call to go to a house where there'd been a murder-suicide. A father had shot his wife and two oldest children with a handgun, killing them. He then turned the weapon on himself. For reasons unknown, he hadn't harmed his four-year-old daughter. She'd been the one who called 911.

The little girl was sitting on the porch waiting for them when they arrived. She wore only underwear, and her face and chest were stippled with blood. Elston knew instantly what that meant. She'd not only witnessed her father committing at least one of the murders; she'd been close enough when it happened for blood to hit her. Four fucking years old…

When Elston and Patty hurried over to the girl, she looked up at them. He'd expected her to be crying, but she wasn't.

"Daddy didn't hurt me. He said I was his favorite 'cause I played with his thing when he told me to." She'd looked at Elston then. "Do you have a thing? Does white stuff come out of yours, too?"

29

That had been Elston's absolute worst moment on the job, and nothing he'd seen since had come close to topping it. Until tonight.

He was glad he didn't like to eat while driving. If that muffin had been in his stomach right now, it wouldn't be sitting very well. Not at all.

Just a couple more hours, then you can go home, have a couple drinks, crawl into bed, and hope to Christ you don't have any dreams.

The donut shop was only a few miles from the Coroner's Office, and they should be there in—

The dispatcher's voice came over the radio.

"All units, we've received a 911 call from the Coroner's Office. The individual who made the call couldn't speak, and it's presumed they're in serious distress. We were cut off, and I've tried calling back, but there's no answer. Whoever is closest to the Coroner's, get there ASAP."

"That would be us," Elston said.

Roman grabbed the mic. "Unit 62, en route."

"Acknowledged," the dispatcher said.

Roman replaced the mic and turned to Elston. "What the actual *fuck*? We just left the man!"

She sounded as shocked as he felt. "Maybe he accidentally cut himself while he was working. He did say he'd been going almost twenty-four hours. When someone's that tired, they make mistakes, sometimes bad ones."

"Maybe he had a heart attack from all the junk food he eats," Roman said.

Elston hit the sirens and lights and pressed his foot down on the accelerator. Neither of them said anything else as their vehicle sped through the empty streets.

*

Roman didn't like Doc much. She thought he was kind of a dick, but that didn't mean she wanted anything bad to happen to the man. The fact he hadn't been able to speak at all when he'd called 911 was worrisome. Any number of reasons could account for it, none of them good. Maybe his vocal cords had been damaged, or maybe he'd had a stroke. Maybe he'd been weakened by blood loss, or maybe he'd suffered a blow to the head and was barely conscious. Any way you sliced it, it looked like Doc was in big trouble. When he'd first asked them to bring him something to eat, she'd been irritated. Hadn't the asshole ever heard of Uber Eats? But now she was glad he had asked the favor, since it meant they'd still been in the area and could get to him quickly. His craving for bacon might just end up saving his life.

Hold on, Doc, she thought. *We're coming*.

Elston pulled the medic around to the back of the Coroner's Office, where the bodies were unloaded. There was a rear entrance here that was always unlocked, and Roman and Elston grabbed their medical bags, got out of the medic, and ran for the door. Once inside, they hurried down a narrow corridor with a concrete floor and walls, and Elston called out, "Doc! Are you all right? Doc!"

No response.

Roman wasn't sure what she expected to see when they reached the office, but it sure as shit wasn't the scene waiting for them. Doc lay splayed out on the floor, blood all around him and soaking his white coat. His face… Roman almost threw up her single bite of bagel, and she

31

was sure if she'd eaten more, it all would've come up right then. His face was gone, and what remained looked like ground hamburger meat. There were small wounds on his throat, and his head... His head...

Elston gave voice to her thought. "Someone cracked open his head like a fucking egg and removed his brain."

"Jesus..."

She knew Doc was deader than the proverbial doornail—how the hell could you live without a goddamn *brain*?—but protocol dictated they try to find a pulse on him. Body shaking, she walked over to Doc, put her medical bag on the floor, removed a pair of rubber gloves and slipped them on. Then, still trembling, she averted her eyes from Doc's ruined face and placed two fingers on the side of his blood-slick neck. She was not surprised she detected no pulse.

This is a crime scene, she realized.

She rose and carefully backed away from Doc's body until she stood beside Elston again.

"Call the police," she said.

Elston, looking paler than she'd ever seen him before, nodded and pulled his phone from his front pants pocket. Before he could call, Roman sensed movement behind them. She turned and saw a motherfucking blood-drenched clown standing there. She was about to scream when the clown grabbed both their heads and slammed them hard against one another. There was a sickening crunching sound, fireworks exploded in Roman's vision, then everything went black.

32

CHAPTER THREE

Roman woke with the mother of all headaches. She suffered from the occasional migraine—they ran in her family—but the worst migraine she'd ever had was nothing compared to how her head felt right now. Despite the pain, she tried to sit up, but something stopped her. She looked down and saw that she was strapped to a gurney. What the hell had happened? The last thing she remembered was waiting in the drive-thru line to get their order.

Restrained as she was, she looked around as best she could and saw a guy in a black-and-white clown suit kneeling on the floor next to Elston. But there was something wrong with her partner. He'd been taken apart—head, arms, and legs separated from his torso—and there was blood everywhere. On the floor, on him, on the clown—

—and on the circular blade of the electric autopsy saw in the clown's hand.

She recognized the clown then. He was the bastard who'd killed all those people in the warehouse tonight. But he'd committed suicide before the cops could take him in. How could...

She saw the exit wound in the back of his head, and she knew he *had* eaten his gun. With that kind of injury to his brain, there was no way he could be alive. Yet, he was, and while she'd been unconscious, he'd taken Elston apart like he was a life-sized doll. And if she couldn't get out of here, it would be her turn next.

Roman started thrashing on the gurney, trying to loosen the restraints. She knew it was futile, but she had to try.

The noise she made alerted the clown, and he stood and turned in her direction. His black-rimmed mouth was twisted into a smile of insanity, but his eyes gleamed with cold, malign intelligence. He activated the autopsy saw. The blade whirred to life, and he started walking toward her.

She shook her head violently back and forth. "No! You can't do this! Stay back!"

The clown's smile widened, as if to say, *Yes, I can do this. And I am.*

This couldn't be happening! Her sister Adrienne's wedding was next week, and she was her bridesmaid. Roman had just started dating a firefighter named Cherise, and she'd been debating if it was too early in their relationship to ask her to be her date for the wedding. She had asked this morning, in fact, and Cherise had said yes. Roman had been so happy...

The clown stopped when he reached the gurney, and Roman looked up at him, tears in her eyes.

"I've still got so much living to do," she said.

The clown looked at her for a second, then threw back his head and roared with silent laughter.

34

Then he went to work with the autopsy saw, and Roman spent the next five minutes shrieking in agony.

When Art was finished playing, Roman's toes and fingers lay on the floor, along with both nipples, her ears, her nose, her clitoris, and her tongue. By that point, he was starting to get bored, so he rammed the saw into her abdomen just below the sternum and drove the saw upward until it found her heart and pureed it. She spasmed a few times then fell still.

Art switched off the saw, left it buried inside her, then turned away from the table. He retrieved his new bag of toys from the floor where he had left it, and was about to go, when he reconsidered. He returned to Roman, knelt, picked up her severed parts, and dropped them into the bag. You never knew when sweet tidbits like these would come in handy.

He left through the rear entrance, and as he walked past the EMT's medic, he stopped. He sniffed the air, then opened the passenger-side door. He saw a couple of paper sacks sitting on the floor, so he lowered his bag to the ground, reached in, took them out, and inspected their contents. One held a blueberry muffin, but he hated blueberries, so he tossed it over his shoulder. The other sack contained a bacon, egg, and cheese croissant breakfast sandwich. He dropped the sack, unwrapped the sandwich, and discarded the wrapping paper. He took a bite, chewed, swallowed. The process was a little tricky considering the roof of his mouth had been obliterated when he'd killed himself, but he managed.

Not bad, but it was missing something.

He looked down at his new garbage bag and grinned.

A few moments later, he was walking away from the Coroner's Office, garbage bag slung over his shoulder, eating the breakfast sandwich. It tasted so much better now that Roman's tongue lay on top of the bacon. He took another bite and continued on his way. Art walked down a deserted alley, the trash bag with his new toys slung over his right shoulder, breakfast sandwich devoured and gone.

When he'd almost reached the end of the alley, he heard police sirens, and stopped. A trio of cruisers zipped by, one after the other, lights flashing, sirens *whoop-whooping*. He assumed they were heading toward the Coroner's Office. He hoped the cops had strong stomachs. He'd left a hell of a mess for them.

He giggled silently.

He waited several seconds, and when no other cruisers came, he started walking again.

Ten minutes later, he reached his destination—a small business with a neon sign in front, blue letters blazing into the night: *Clean Around the Clock: 24-Hour Laundry.* And in smaller letters beneath that: *We Never Close*.

When Art had woken on the gurney in the Coroner's Office, he'd felt recharged and ready to slaughter the world. But that energy had deserted him during the short walk to the laundromat, and now he felt bone-weary. What's more, the various injuries he'd suffered tonight— some of which were damn significant—were starting to really hurt. So when he pushed open the glass door and trudged inside, he was in no mood for foolishness.

A man sat next to the door in one of the gray plastic chairs lined against the large front window. Forties, shaved head, mustache and goatee, wearing a gray quilted vest over a long-sleeved gray shirt, gray-and-black pajama pants, and brown boots. Art approved of the man's monochromatic aesthetic. He was slumped in the chair, head back, eyes closed, hands clasped around his middle, fast asleep. Art had no idea if the man was an employee or a customer, and he didn't care, just so long as the guy continued sleeping and left him in peace.

He walked over to an empty chair on the opposite side of the waiting area from where the man was snoozing. He dropped his garbage bag onto the chair, and the instruments inside rustled and clanged against each other. He hoped the bottle of fluoroantimonic acid didn't break. It wasn't the sort of thing you came by every day.

Laundry carts stood against the wall near where Vest Boy slept, and Art walked over to one and removed a wooden hanger from its hanging bar. He carried the hanger back to where he'd left his toys and used its metal hook to snag the zipper on the back of his blood-soaked costume. He then used the hanger to pull the zipper down.

He stopped halfway to take off his oversized shoes, then pulled the zipper the rest of the way down, and slipped out of his clothes. He wore nothing underneath his costume, and after the night he'd had, the warm air of the laundromat felt good against his skin. His face and upper body were covered with blood, and he smelled like an overflowing porta-potty in an abattoir, but luckily for Vest Boy, the stench didn't rouse him.

37

Art stripped off his fingerless gloves and wiggled his fingers to get the kinks out of them. He then removed his skull cap and detachable fake collar and tossed the whole mess into one of Clean-Around-the-Clock's front-loading washing machines. Art didn't like old, dried blood. There was no life in it. But fresh *living* blood? *That* was a different story. He fished the quarters and the dollar bills he'd taken from coroner out of the garbage bag. He went to the change machine, inserted the bills one by one, and scooped up the quarters the machine deposited.

He bought a small box of detergent from a wall-mounted vending machine, considered, then bought another. He emptied both boxes into his washer, fed quarters into it, and then started the machine. He tossed the empty boxes into a trashcan and saw someone had left a newspaper behind on top of one of the machines. He grabbed it and headed back to the chair where he'd left his bag. He moved the bag to a top-loading machine next to the chair and sat with a sigh. It was nice to sit down for a change. He perused the paper's front page.

The headline for the top story was printed in bold, capital letters, and the instant Art read it, he roared with silent laughter. *HEAD-ON CRASH KILLS FAMILY OF FOUR.* He laughed so hard tears fell from his one eye.

Suddenly, there was a loud crackle of electricity, and the washing machine with his clothes in it shut down. Like an animal sensing the presence of a threat, he lowered the paper, listened, looked around. Vest Boy was still asleep, and there were no other customers in Art's line of vision. But there was a hallway with dryers behind him on his left, and he leaned forward and turned his head to look around the corner.

A young girl sat three chairs down from him, also leaning forward, head turned toward him, as if she'd known he was going look in her direction. She was in costume, which wasn't so strange given that it was Halloween. What *was* strange was that she wore the same outfit as he did, or at least a version of it. Hers was a dress with a skirt and short sleeves, and the color scheme was reversed. Where his costume was black, hers was white. She also wore a little top hat—white, of course—on the opposite side of her head, only her long hair had been pulled through the hat and it stuck out in a messy ponytail. The hair on the other side of her head hung loose. Her tights were black on the right side, white on the left, and she wore no shoes. Her face was covered with white makeup, and she had black circles around her eyes and lips, as well as the same pencil-thin cartoon brows drawn on her forehead. She even had a little black dot on her nose. Her teeth looked like his, too, but her smile was more of a grimace, and madness danced in her cold blue eyes.

There was something else about her too, an aura of dark power that he'd felt before, and recently. The weird energy storm in the Coroner's Office—that was it! This Little Pale Girl felt exactly like that, only her power was contained and controlled.

Her expression remained frozen on her face, and the rest of her body stayed motionless as she raised her left hand and waved at him. He hesitated a moment, then slowly raised his own hand and tentatively returned the wave. He tried to smile but didn't quite succeed.

39

She continued staring at him, body stiff, eyes unblinking. Black fluid gushed from between her legs then—thick, foul-smelling, chunks of something solid in it—and splattered to the floor beneath her dangling feet.

Art looked at the pool of disgusting muck for a second, unsure what to make of it, then he looked at the Little Pale Girl once more. She remained statue-still, eyes wide, not blinking. After a few seconds, she hopped off her chair—jumping far enough forward so she didn't land in her own horrid discharge—and walked over to stand in front of him. Her smile remained frozen on her face, and now that she was close, he could see her eyes were dry and dull, as if made from plastic.

All in all, she was a creepy little thing.

His smile was genuine this time.

She reached toward Art's face, and he remained perfectly still while she pinched the tip of his nose. Then her hand moved toward the ruin of his eye socket. She touched it with her index finger, gently at first, then inserted the finger inside and swirled it around. Art liked the squishy noises this action made.

He laughed silently, and the girl laughed with him, equally as silent. He put his hand in front of his socket and mimed the eye shooting outward, then he shrugged as if to say, *Waddya gonna do?*

They laughed even harder at that.

His socket started itching then, but he ignored the sensation.

The Little Pale Girl then clapped her hands together and held her right palm out to Art. It took him a moment to understand what she was doing, but when he did, he grinned and nodded. They began playing pattycake, slowly at first, but with increasing speed.

Pattycake, pattycake baker's man
Bake me a cake as fast as you can
Pat it and prick it and mark it with "B"
And put it in the oven for baby and me!

When they reached the end, the Little Pale Girl mimed rocking a baby.

Art laughed with silent delight. He felt much better than he had when he'd walked into the laundromat. Stronger, full of energy.

He felt *good*.

The Little Pale Girl clapped with delight, and Art did the same.

Sherman Maldonado was dreaming his girlfriend Kendra was triplets, and they were having a foursome on stage at Carnegie Hall. At least, they were *trying* to. The house was packed tonight, and everyone in the audience had high-powered binoculars so they could get a close-up view of the action. Sherman suffered performance anxiety under normal circumstances, but with over two thousand people watching, his dick wasn't just soft—it had withdrawn into his body like a turtle pulling its head into its shell.

The audience was thunderously chanting, *Where's your cock? Where's your cock?*

Sherman woke with a start. For an instant, he didn't know where he was, and when he saw a naked, blood-covered clown sitting against the opposite wall, playing pattycake by himself, he thought he was still dreaming. But when the clown finished the game and started clapping excitedly, Sherman realized he was awake. He wasn't startled by the clown's appearance. Sure, he was weird as fuck, but Sherman had been working here most of his adult life. The clown didn't even make the list of the top ten weirdest things he'd seen on the job. Besides, it was Halloween. All kinds of strange shit happened then. He closed his eyes and clasped his hands around his middle and settled in to catch a few more winks.

He hoped he wouldn't go back to his nightmare about Carnegie Hall, but if he did, he'd try to dream up a bottle of extra-strength Viagra to help him out.

One wash wasn't enough to clean Art's costume. He would have to run it through again, and maybe one more time after that for good measure. Since he didn't have enough money to do that, he used the postmortem hammer—its striking surface still sticky with the coroner's blood—and a stainless-steel chisel to break into the change machine to get more quarters. It took only two strikes to crack that piggy bank, *clank-clank!* Quarters poured out of the broken machine, and, while he caught as many as he could in his cupped hands, quite a few fell to the tiled floor—*ting-ting-ting-ting-ting*... Art—still bare-assed—looked over his shoulder to see if the noise had woken Vest Boy.

The Little Pale Girl stood in front of the man, waiting. The instant he started to wake, she moved swift as a striking snake and grabbed his wrist. Vest Boy frowned when her flesh touched his, and he mumbled something unintelligible, as if the contact upset him on a subconscious level. His eyelids twitched a couple of times, but they remained closed, and soon his breathing deepened, became slow and regular. Good trick! Art hoped the Little Pale Girl would teach it to him sometime.

His costume wasn't the only thing that needed washing. Art himself was covered with dried blood—most of it not his—and after he'd cleaned himself, he'd need to reapply his makeup. Except he carried his makeup in his original trash bag, which he assumed was still somewhere in the warehouse where he'd had his fun tonight.

The Little Pale Girl walked over to him, smiling, hands behind her back. When she reached him, she stopped and held out a pair of round makeup containers. Art mimed laughing, then nodded his head once in thanks. He took the containers from the girl, rose from his chair, and went off in search of the restroom. On the way, he found a pile of clean towels someone had left on one of the folding tables, and he grabbed a couple.

The restroom was located in the back of the laundromat, but when Art tried to open it, he found it locked. Not a problem. He leaned back, kicked the door open with one of his big-ass clown shoes, and stepped inside. He was in there a while, but when he came out, he had no blood on him, and his makeup was perfect. Plus, he smelled... well, not *clean*, but clean*er*.

His eye socket itched like crazy the entire time he was in the restroom, but when he exited, the itch was gone. What's more, his vision on that side was restored. Curious, he reached up and touched his index finger to what had been an empty socket but which now contained a healthy

43

restored eyeball. He reached up to touch the back of his head and found the skin and bone there had grown back—and all the other injuries he'd collected during the night were healed as well.

He thought of how the Little Pale Girl had inserted her finger into his eye socket, how she played pattycake with him. He remembered how much stronger he'd felt afterward. It seemed she'd not only infused him with strength but had healed him as well.

Cool.

He walked to the front of the laundromat, intending to check if the latest wash had cleaned his costume enough for him to put it on so he could get out of here before a cop—on alert because of the massacre at the abandoned warehouse—stopped by to make sure everything was all right. *Can't be too careful with a maniac clown on the loose, can we?*

When Art reached the washer, he saw that Vest Boy was still asleep in his chair by the entrance, and no other customers had walked in while Art had been cleaning up. He saw no sign of the Little Pale Girl, though. It seemed she'd gone as mysteriously as she'd come. This saddened him, but he had a feeling the two of them would meet again, sooner rather than later.

He looked forward to it.

When he checked on his uniform, he found it clean—or at least clean enough—but it was still wet. He didn't want to toss it in a dryer and wait around some more. Without his new friend, this place was boring as hell. He wrung out his uniform over one of the sinks, and then he put it on and used a hanger to zip up the back. The damp cloth felt uncomfortable against his bare skin, but he could live with it.

He was about to retrieve his bag of toys and beat feet when he saw a puddle of water on the floor in front of the sink where he'd wrung out his uniform. Looked like he hadn't been as careful as he could've been. Not wishing to be a bad customer, he found a mop and started cleaning up the mess he had made. Compared to the carnage he ordinarily left in his wake, a little water was nothing, and he'd have it literally mopped up in a couple of minutes.

"What the hell are you doing?"

Art looked over at Vest Boy. He was awake and sitting forward in his chair, an angry scowl on his face.

Art sighed. He gripped the top of the mop handle, gave it a vicious twist, and snapped off a foot-long length. He let the rest of the mop drop to the floor, then started toward Vest Boy, lips drawing back from his rotten teeth in a snarl.

Art finished his work and put the broken-handled mop into its wheeled metal bucket. He picked up his bag of new toys, slung it over his shoulder, and headed for the door. He paid no attention to Vest Boy, who sat in his chair, eyes wide, blood running down his face and onto his shirt, the broken length of mop handle jutting out of his skull.

Art opened the door, stepped outside into the cool night air, turned right, and headed down the sidewalk. All things considered, it had been a good night, but it was time to go home.

CHAPTER FOUR

One Year Later

Brendan Poole's grandmother called him at six o'clock in the morning in near hysterics. Her bathroom ceiling had collapsed, and she asked if he could come over and take a look at it—if he wasn't too busy, that is.

"Sure, Grandma, no problem. Don't worry. It's gonna be okay."

He ended the call, dropped his phone on the bed, covered his face with his pillow, and screamed. He'd kept that up for over three minutes, and when he was finished, he felt ashamed. He'd hoped Lindsey hadn't heard him.

Grandma was a lonely woman. Her husband had died of a sudden heart attack when Brendan was a baby, and his father and mother (Grandma's daughter) had moved to Canada when his father—a computer programmer—took a job with a videogame company located in Edmonton. That was seven years ago, and they only came back for Christmas and Easter. Before they'd left, they'd given Brendan their house—the one he'd grown up in—which had already been paid off. Brendan happily accepted, and he moved out of his shithole one-bedroom apartment, and into his new (old) home.

Grandma didn't have any other children, so whenever she felt the need for company, she'd break something around her house and call him to come fix it. Like his mother, Brendan was also an only child, so he couldn't ask his nonexistent siblings to keep Grandma company sometimes and give him a break. Grandma duty fell to him and him alone.

Once, when he'd been working on her dishwasher, he'd tried telling her that she didn't have to break shit to get him to come over; she could just ask him to visit. Grandma had burst into tears, said he was accusing her of lying, said her own grandson—her *only* relative in the whole US of A—didn't trust her... It had taken most of the afternoon to calm her down, and after that, he didn't bring up the subject again. He *had* tried talking to his parents about it, though.

"You know how old people are," his mother had said. "They get needy sometimes, even desperate for a little attention. Visiting her can't take up that much of your time, can it? And you are a professional handyman. Plus, your father and I did give you the house free of charge. Seeing your grandmother once in a while—when you know your father and I can't come home often—is such a small way to pay us back, isn't it?"

And that had been the last time he'd brought up the subject with her.

He didn't bother showering. What was the point? He was only going to get dirty again. He searched among the mound of clothes piled in the corner of his room, found a T-shirt that was more or less clean and a pair of jeans that smelled a little but were good enough for going over to Grandma's. He dressed quickly, went to the kitchen to don his work boots, then grabbed his tool belt, which he'd left on the kitchen table last night, and put it on.

The kitchen was a fucking disaster—not that the rest of his house was much better. He shuddered to think what his parents would say if they saw it in this state—dirty dishes stacked in the sink, used cups sitting on the counter, trash overflowing with empty fast-food containers. Well, maybe not *entirely* empty, judging from the number of roaches crawling on them. He'd stop at a drive-thru on the way to Grandma's and get a coffee, but he was hungry now, and he knew from experience that if he waited too long to eat in the morning, he'd get a terrible headache that could last the rest of the day. That was something he definitely wanted to avoid, especially if he was going to spend the entire morning fixing Grandma's bathroom ceiling.

He went to the fridge, opened it, and immediately wished he hadn't. There was hardly anything in there. A stash of fast-food condiment packets of various kinds stuffed into the compartment where butter should be, an almost empty half pint of milk that had—he leaned forward and squinted to read the date on the carton—expired last week, a couple of shriveled oranges that had white fuzz growing on them, a jar of pickles with only brine in it, and half a bottle of Bud that he'd started maybe two weeks ago and never finished. He wasn't what you'd call a big drinker.

He debated his meager choices. The oranges might be okay. People ate dried fruit, right? But he didn't trust that white fuzz. Sure, he could try to scrape it off, but what if he didn't get all of it and accidentally ate some? He'd watched an old Japanese horror movie once where these shipwrecked people ate some weird mushrooms and then turned into mushroom people. He didn't want anything like that happening to him. So, the oranges were out.

The condiment packets? He looked through them quickly—ketchup, mustard, soy sauce, hot sauce, mayo, relish, and one suspiciously marked *Secret Sauce*. He couldn't remember where he got that one. Could he squeeze the contents of all the packets into a bowl, stir it around to make some kind of goop-soup? He took a quick look in the cupboard, but there weren't any clean bowls. So, no goop-soup this morning. He'd have to try it some other day.

He tried drinking the pickle juice, but it was too salty. He thought about downing the rest of the Bud, but what if he got pulled over by a cop on the way to Grandma's and they smelled the beer on his breath? The cop might make him take a breathalyzer test, and he could end up with a DUI. He already had a lot of unpaid parking tickets. If he got arrested for drunk driving too, they might throw him in jail and never let him out.

No beer.

That left only the milk.

He took the carton out of the fridge and shook it. There wasn't much left. He opened the carton and took an experimental sniff. *Kee-rist*, that was foul! He'd watched a YouTube video once that claimed sour milk was perfectly safe to drink, it just *tasted* like shit. Only one way to find out.

He put the lip of the carton to his mouth, tilted it, and drank. He gagged a couple of times, but he got it all down. His belly made an unhappy gurgle, but he didn't immediately projectile vomit, so he counted that as a win. He rinsed his mouth at the tap, spit the water into the sink, and headed for the basement door.

He put his ear to the wood for a few moments, but he didn't hear anything. Satisfied, he took a ring of keys out of his pocket and unlocked the padlock. Then he pulled back the deadbolt and used another key to unlock the doorknob. He opened the door. It was dark in the basement—he'd turned off the lights after coming upstairs last night— and he leaned forward and shouted down.

"Lindsey, honey, I have to go over to Grandma's for a little while. Probably no more than a couple of hours. I hope, anyway. I'm gonna do a quick stop for supplies before I come home. Is there anything special you'd like me to pick up? Some of that dark chocolate you like, maybe? Some pork rinds?"

He listened for an answer, but none came.

"How about I just surprise you then? Okay, gotta go. Love you!"

He shut the door, engaged all three locks, and headed for the garage. He couldn't wait to get back home and go down into the basement and spend the rest of the day with his love.

*

Brendan was in a much better mood when he got to Grandma's house and surveyed the extent of the damage to her bathroom. The "collapsed" ceiling consisted of a couple of small round holes made with what he suspected was a broomstick. He had everything he needed in his van, and it took him less than thirty minutes to fix both holes. He didn't have the right color paint, though, and he told Grandma he'd have to get some and come back another day to finish the job. This made her happy, and he hoped it would keep her from breaking anything else around her place, at least for a little while.

She didn't let him escape then, though. She made him sit at the kitchen table and have a cup of coffee with her. He *despised* drinking coffee with her. She was the *slowest* coffee drinker in the world, and she had to reheat her coffee in the microwave two or three times before she finished a single cup. Plus, he'd listened to a podcast once that claimed too much coffee would ruin your kidneys, so he tried to avoid it whenever possible. But Grandma had made fresh banana bread last night, so Brendan ate a couple of pieces while she ignored her coffee and talked about the various sins her neighbors had committed since the last time he'd visited.

Mr. Ballard *still* hadn't raked a single leaf in his yard, and for some unfathomable reason, Mrs. Frazier had started doing her housework naked *and* she kept the curtains wide open while she worked. Yes, the woman had a good body for someone in her fifties, but that was hardly an excuse! There was more, but Brendan tuned out his grandmother while he finished his banana bread. She might be a lousy saboteur of her own house, but she was a hell of a cook. After using the pad of his index finger to get the last few crumbs, he told Grandma that he needed to go. He had a date with Lindsey this afternoon.

"Why don't you ever bring her with you when you visit?" Grandma asked.

"She's really shy. I've told you that. But I'll keep trying to convince her, okay?"

Before he left, Grandma made sure he took a slice of banana bread for Lindsey. She put it on a small paper plate, wrapped it in plastic wrap, and handed it to him with a smile.

"I'm sure she'll love it," he said.

He went outside, got in his van—black with a white hood—and waved at Grandma one last time as he started the engine, put the van in gear, and started forward. He ate half of Lindsey's banana bread before he reached the end of Grandma's driveway, and he finished off the rest before he could accelerate to the speed limit.

Brendan made his living as a handyman—that was true—but it wasn't like he had his own official business or anything. The only advertising he ever did was tack business cards with his name, phone number, and email address below the words *I FIX STUFF* to every bulletin board he could find in Miles County. And when he ate at a restaurant, he'd leave a card on the table for someone to find after he left. But he didn't have a website or a social media presence, and he didn't buy commercial time on the radio.

He'd thought about having *I FIX STUFF* and his contact information painted on the sides of his van, so his vehicle would serve as a traveling bulletin board. But he was no artist, and if he tried to paint the letters himself, he knew they'd look like shit. He'd considered hiring someone to do the painting for him, but in the end he decided against it. He got his cards fairly cheap at a local business supply store, but he didn't want to spend any additional money on something as unnecessary as advertising. Sure, he might not get a ton of jobs, but he got enough. Working that way wouldn't make him rich, but it did leave him plenty of free time to spend with Lindsey.

He stopped at a QwikMart and topped off the gas tank, then he pulled up to the store, parked, and got out. A guy in a clown costume and full makeup stood next to the entrance, leaning back against the wall, arms folded over his chest, face expressionless, staring off into the distance.

Fucking weird.

Brendan was afraid the clown would try to talk to him before he went inside the store. Maybe he'd give Brendan a spiel about donating to some charity or just simply ask for a handout. *Can you spare some change for a clown down on his luck?* The clown ignored him as he walked to the door, took hold of the handle, and started to open it. Then the clown's head swiveled toward him, tilted to the side, and grinned. He reached up and lifted the small top hat he wore, as if to say, *Good day to you, fine sir*, then he released the hat and it snapped back onto his head with a soft *thump*. The clown's features went immediately slack, and he faced forward once more, arms crossed. It was as if Brendan had ceased to exist for him—which was fine with Brendan. The less he had to do with that spooky motherfucker, the better.

Some people took Halloween way too seriously.

Brendan opened the door and stepped inside. The first thing he did was breathe in the faint scent of bleach. This QwikMart always smelled as if its floors had been recently mopped, and he liked that. He might be a slob at home, but out in the world, he appreciated cleanliness. Plus, the smell reminded him of Lindsey, as this was where they'd first met. There was a stack of plastic shopping baskets on the floor just inside the entrance, and Brendan took one and stepped into the first aisle.

He knew the items in the store were way overpriced, the idea being that people would pay extra for the convenience of being able to dash into a small store, grab what they needed, and then get the hell out quickly, the process so much faster than if they stopped at a grocery store. And Brendan did like that aspect of it. He didn't want to spend any more time away from Lindsey than he absolutely had to. But nostalgia was the main reason he shopped here.

As he moved through the aisles selecting items—a couple of bags of cashews, various snack cakes, a fresh carton of milk—he remembered seeing Lindsey here for the first time. Her long red hair had caught his attention first, then the freckles on her cheeks, then her beautiful green eyes. He had judged her to be in her early thirties, around the same age as him. Then he trailed after her around the store, trying to be subtle about it, but she glanced nervously at him several times anyway.

He hadn't been lying to Grandma when he'd said she was shy. He had lingered near the register when she paid for her items, and then he followed her outside without

54

getting anything himself. She got into her Sentra and pulled out of the parking lot, and he had tailed her in his van. When they reached her apartment building, he got out of his van at the same time as she got out of her car, and he had hurried over and introduced himself.

They'd been together ever since.

He gathered a few more items then went up front to pay for them. As the clerk behind the counter was scanning his purchases, Brendan turned and, through the store's front window, saw the clown standing in front of his van. The man had his hands on his hips, and he tilted his head from one side to the other, as if he was a buyer on a car lot and Brendan's van was a vehicle he was thinking of purchasing.

Brendan didn't like that.

He paid for his items, and the clerk put them into a white plastic bag with the QwikMart logo on the side. Then Brendan hurried outside to see what the hell that goddamn clown was up to.

The man still stood in the same position he'd been in when Brendan had spotted him from inside, and he was still turning his head from one side to the other, the motions mechanical, as if he was one of those life-sized Halloween mannequins with moving parts. Brendan had always hated those things. They creeped him the fuck out.

"Can I help you, buddy?"

The clown didn't respond, but his head stopped moving.

"It's a little early to be so dressed up, isn't it? You should save it for tonight."

55

The clown didn't turn to look at him, but his arms fell to his sides.

Brendan was starting to get angry now. He wanted to get back to Lindsey, and this bastard was slowing him down. "Look, I need to get going. Why don't you take your freak show somewhere else?"

That got the clown's attention. He turned to face Brendan, his black lips stretching into a slow smile. His eyes were narrowed, though, and Brendan saw the man's own anger smoldering within them.

Brendan wished he'd kept his goddamn mouth shut, walked past the clown, gotten in his van, and driven off without interacting with the son of a bitch. Too late for that now.

But then the clown's eyes brightened. He pointed to the van, then to himself, then mimed taking a wallet from a back pocket, opening it, removing bills, and holding them out to Brendan. It took Brendan a moment to understand what the man was trying to communicate. He wanted to buy the van, and he was asking Brendan how much he wanted for it. Why the fuck he didn't just come out and *say* this, Brendan didn't know. Clowns, right?

"Sorry, it's not for sale," Brendan said.

The clown brushed his hand down the front of his black-and-white costume, then pointed to the van again. This time Brendan understood what the man was saying right away. He wanted the van because it was black and white and matched his outfit. Of all the craziest fucking reasons to buy a vehicle…

"Once more, it's not for sale."

The clown smiled wider and batted his eyes, as if to say, *Pretty please? With sugar on top?*

Brendan was done.

"Have a good day," he said stiffly, then moved to walk past the clown.

But the clown grabbed the back of his shirt and stopped him. Brendan turned around, and the clown fell to his knees, clasped his hands together as if begging, and pretended to cry.

Jesus! This wasn't creepy anymore. It was downright pathetic.

"Leave me the fuck alone, or I'm gonna call the cops!"

The clown held his begging position, but his gaze grew cold as arctic ice, and his lips twisted into an expression that was as much a snarl as it was a smile. Then the clown bounded to his feet, grabbed Brendan's hand with both of his, gave it two hardy shakes, then released it. He threw Brendan a quick salute, then turned and walked briskly away, a jaunty pep in his step.

What the hell was *that* all about?

Shaking his head, but glad to be rid of the clown, Brendan got in his van, put his sack of groceries on the passenger seat, and started the engine. He heard a soft *thump*, felt the van rock slightly. He checked the sideview mirror, but he didn't see anything. Probably his imagination. The encounter with the clown had really stressed him out. But that was all right. He knew he'd feel better once he was home and he could hold Lindsey and stroke her beautiful red hair.

He put the van in reverse, backed out of his parking spot, put it in drive, and pulled onto the road.

CHAPTER FIVE

The trip home was strange.

Other drivers kept waving and honking at Brendan, some looking concerned, some laughing and giving him a thumbs up, while others pointed index fingers upward, as if they wanted him to look to the sky. He peered out his windshield to determine what they were going on about, but he didn't see anything special, just sky and clouds.

People lose their goddamn minds on Halloween, he thought.

He kept his eyes focused on the road and tried to ignore the honking, laughing, and pointing. Before long, he reached his house—a ranch with a black roof and ugly yellow siding—and he pulled into the driveway and up to the garage. He pressed the remote and watched as the garage door rose. Its movement was a bit jerky, and he told himself he'd have to take a look at it and see if something needed adjusting. Then he pulled in, turned off the engine, and shut the garage door. He got out while it was still closing, QwikMart bag in hand, and he decided to give the van a quick once-over to see if he could figure out why all those drivers had been gesturing at him.

He walked around the vehicle once, but he didn't see anything out of the ordinary. He shrugged, then went into the house. He walked by the locked basement door — *Soon, Lindsey* — and carried the bag to the kitchen counter. He pushed some cups aside to make room, then put the bag down. The only thing he'd bought which needed to go in the fridge was the milk, so he removed it from the bag, carried it over to the refrigerator, opened it —

— and something hard and heavy slammed into the back of his head.

Pain flared bright behind his eyes, and he fell to his hands and knees, dropping the milk as he did so. The carton hit the floor, burst open, and milk spilled onto the tile. He struggled to rise, but he felt too dizzy, weak, and nauseated to move. A hand grabbed the back of his shirt and roughly hauled him to his feet then spun him around.

Brendan saw the clown from QwikMart standing there, a cast-iron skillet in his hand. Did the clown get that from here? Brendan didn't cook, so he had no idea what sort of kitchen stuff his parents had left behind when they'd moved. The clown smiled, then swung the skillet at Brendan's head a second time. Brendan was too out of it to try to avoid the blow, and after it landed, he fell to the floor, landing in a puddle of milk. The clown yanked him to his feet again, and this time when Brendan looked at him, he saw a faint double image overlapping the man.

Probably got some brain damage. He hoped it wasn't too serious.

He thought of the *thump* he'd heard back in QwikMart's parking lot as he was preparing to leave, the way the van rocked for a moment, and he understood what had happened. The clown had climbed onto the top of the van, and the crazy fucker had held on the entire way while Brendan drove home. *That* was what all those drivers had been making such a fuss about. They were trying to say, *Hey, do you know you've got a fucking clown on your roof?*

The clown grabbed the front of his shirt and pulled him over to the kitchen counter. There was a butcher block filled with knives that Brendan had never touched, and the clown dropped the skillet on the counter and selected a knife with a long, lean, and very sharp-looking blade. The clown pressed the tip of the knife to Brendan's throat, and then pulled him over to the basement door. Brendan hadn't been scared up to this point, mostly because he was only semiconscious after being hit in the head twice with the skillet, but the clown dragging him to the basement door gave him a jolt of terror that shocked him back to full awareness.

He shook his head, the motion setting off a wave so intense that he puked a little. It fell onto the front of his shirt and began soaking into the fabric, reeking of stomach acid. "No... please..."

The clown grinned and nodded slowly, as if to say, *Oh yes!* He pointed at the padlock with his free hand. This message was abundantly clear: *Open it.*

"B-but there's nothing down there."

This sounded lame even to Brendan. If there was nothing important in the basement, why triple lock it?

He had to do *something* to keep the clown from going down there, but he was so frightened, he couldn't think of anything.

The clown gave the knife a flick and Brendan felt a stinging pain in his neck, followed by warm blood flowing down his skin. This fucker was *really* good at getting his point across without speaking.

Brendan knew then there was no point in resisting. If he tried, the clown would simply kill him, take the keys from his pocket, and unlock the basement door himself. He'd still get down there, but Brendan would be dead. And if he was dead, he couldn't protect Lindsey.

He removed the keys from his pocket, and a moment later the door was unlocked. The clown grinned, bowed, and gestured to the door. *After you, good sir.*

Brendan pulled the door open, reached in, turned on the lights, and then started down the wooden steps. The clown followed, the knife point pressed to Brendan's side, his large boots clomping on the steps as they descended. When they reached the bottom, Brendan's secret was revealed.

It was a rec room.

Couch, easy chair, coffee table, throw rug, big flat-screen TV on the wall, videogame console, bathroom... and in a corner a large cage with a red-headed woman wearing a brown blouse and blue jeans standing inside.

Lindsey.

The clown looked at her for several long seconds, then he began laughing without making any sound. He gave Brendan a sly look and elbowed him in the ribs, as if to say, *You old dog!* Then he stuck out his free hand for Brendan to shake, as if now that he knew Brendan's secret, they could be friends.

Confused, Brendan took the clown's offered hand—god*damn*, the flesh was cold—and then shook. The clown put an arm around Brendan's shoulders and made a circling motion with the knife. *Let's hear it.*

The clown smelled awful this close, like he'd bathed in congealed blood and rotting meat this morning. Brendan did his best to ignore the stench as he spoke.

"I saw her in QwikMart one day. She was so beautiful, I was mesmerized." He smiled at the memory. "I knew then that if I could make her love me, I could finally turn my life around. Be someone, you know?"

The clown nodded and motioned for him to continue.

"I followed her to her apartment complex and tried to introduce myself in the parking lot. I guess I scared her because she started screaming for help. I panicked. I grabbed her, put my hand over her mouth, and forced her to get into the van with me. I couldn't hold onto her the whole ride back to my house, so I... I had to hit her. It took a couple tries for me to knock her out, but I finally did."

Brendan looked at Lindsey. "Sorry, sweetie."

Lindsey looked back and forth between him and the clown, as if trying to decide which was the bigger threat.

"When I got home, I carried her into the house, brought her down into the basement, and duct-taped her wrists and ankles, then put a strip across her mouth. I felt awful doing that... treating her like a prisoner, but I knew it was temporary, just until I could find the right words to explain what I was doing.

"Eventually, I fixed up the basement and made it into a cozy little home for Lindsey. She... has trouble behaving herself sometimes, so I built that cage for her. She spends more time in there than I'd like, but we're working on it, you know? Love—*real* love—takes time." He looked at Lindsey once again. "But we'll get there, won't we, hon?"

Lindsey pressed herself against the back of the cage, and with her gaze fixed on Brendan, shook her head. Brendan pretended not to notice. Sometimes you had to make allowances for the people you loved.

He looked at his new friend. "So what's your name?"

When Lindsey heard the basement door open then saw the lights come on, she knew she was in for more "special time" with Brendan. She didn't want him coming anywhere near her, but if she didn't cooperate, he wouldn't give her any food or water, and it had been a couple of days since she'd had either.

But when she saw him come down the stairs followed by a *clown* of all things, she didn't know what to make of it—especially because the clown was holding a knife to Brendan's side. Brendan scared her, but that was because his mind was screwed up, and she never knew what he might do. The clown scared her more, and for an entirely different reason: his makeup and costume were a disguise, sure, but she sensed the man underneath was a disguise as well. At the clown's core lay something so dark, twisted, and debased that she wasn't certain there were words to adequately describe it. Brendan was

63

just an idiot playing at being evil, but the clown *was* evil, pure and unadulterated—and he terrified her.

The clown got Brendan to explain about her, not that it took much coaxing. Brendan *loved* to talk, and much of their "special time" was spent with her listening to him babble on about one thing or another. The more Brendan talked, the chummier the two of them seemed, but Lindsey wasn't fooled. She knew the clown was putting on an act, and when Brendan asked the clown what his name was, the clown cut Brendan's throat with a single, practiced motion. He then shoved Brendan to the floor, and while Brendan gurgled blood and tried to breathe, the clown lifted up Brendan's shirt and starting carving lines into his stomach with the knife. When he was finished, he'd spelled out A-R-T.

Art.

Brendan's gurgles stopped.

Lindsey wondered if Brendan had any idea that the clown had answered his question before he died. Probably not, she decided.

Art wiped the knife clean on Brendan's pants leg, and then fished Brendan's keys out of the dead man's pockets. He stood and turned to face Lindsey, his features blank. She had no illusion that he would free her. A creature like him did things *to* people, not *for* them.

After a few seconds, a sly look came into his eyes, and he grinned. He started walking toward Lindsey's cage, keys in one hand, knife in the other. She imagined him unlocking the cage door and blocking the way with his body so she couldn't escape. She imagined him walking toward her, gripping the knife handle harder, eyes dancing with delight as he pictured all the things he planned to do to her before he finally allowed her to die.

But when he reached the cage, he made no effort to unlock it. He simply looked at her for a second, and then stretched his knife hand between two bars and dropped the blood-slick blade. It clattered on the concrete floor, and the sound made her jump. The clown then turned and headed back toward the stairs.

What the hell had just happened? Why hadn't he killed her? Why—

And then she realized the awful truth. The clown wasn't going to release her from the cage, and no one but Brendan knew she was down here in the basement, with no food or water. The clown was leaving her to die, but he'd given her a choice about how it would happen. She could wait to die of thirst, which would probably occur within ten days or so, or she could use the knife to slit her wrists and die within a few minutes. Slow or fast, it was up to her.

"You can't do this!" she shouted. "Wait! Come back!"

The clown clomped up the steps, turned out the lights, shut the basement door, and locked it. Lindsey heard his muffled footsteps as he walked across the kitchen and into the garage. A moment later, she heard the garage door opening and the van start. She listened as the clown backed out of the garage, then pressed the remote to close the door. She listened to it ratcheting downward and then stop.

She was alone.

With Brendan's corpse.

And the knife.

CHAPTER SIX

Sienna Shaw—seventeen, pretty, with long, straight brown hair—sat at the worktable in her bedroom, spraying gold paint on her right forearm guard.

Go slow, she cautioned herself. *Don't screw it up.*

She wore a short-sleeved white top with three monarch butterflies on the front, along with cozy light-brown joggers. She had a horseshoe nose ring and helix piercings in both ears, and her deep brown eyes shone with fierce intelligence as she worked. The admonition to herself to be careful was unnecessary, for her hands moved with grace, dexterity, and confidence as she finished the paint job. She set aside the forearm guard on a sheet of newspaper to dry, then picked up the right spiked shoulder guard and painted it gold as well.

Synth wave music played from her phone—"The Equaliser," her favorite song by The Midnight. She liked all kinds of music, but there was something about synth wave that inspired her like nothing else. It created the exact vibe she needed to focus and be productive.

Her main worktable—she had three of them, arranged in a U shape—was covered with old paint splotches, as well as a scattered collection of tools and materials: scissors, pencils, markers, leather strips, electrical tape, duct tape, masking tape, foam rubber, glue, tubes of acrylic paint, cans of spray paint, staplers, paint brushes, loose white feathers... and several prescription medicine bottles. To a visitor, there would seem to be no rhyme or reason to the way Sienna's workstation was organized, but she knew precisely where everything was, and she could always lay her hands on what she needed without looking.

One glance at her room would tell anyone that it clearly belonged to a creative person. The worktables were a dead giveaway, of course, but the décor added to the story. The pillow and comforter on her bed were white with sparkly dots on them, with matching curtains. Purple wallpaper with black trees on it; strings of white lights hanging down; lit candles and burning incense on one of the side tables to establish atmosphere; a collage of images on the wall in front of her—pictures she'd clipped from magazines or printed from the Internet, her version of a vision board: dragons; pop stars; some artwork by famous painters and sculptors, and then some by newcomers; anime characters; superheroes; cute animals; but most of all, various depictions of angels.

Speaking of angels, a pair of large, white-feathered wings hung on a torso mannequin on the side table near—but not *too* near—where her candles flickered. They were the centerpiece of her costume, and they looked damn good. She couldn't wait to put them on when the rest of the costume was finished and finally see how everything looked together. She'd been working on her outfit for three months now, and while she could picture the finished costume in her mind, imagining it and seeing it were two very different things. Having a dream was wonderful, but making a dream come true in real life… that was downright *magical*. It was why she loved being an artist. That, and—

—her father.

She turned toward the right side table and looked at the gleaming metal object displayed there. It was a high-end replica of a medieval short sword, with an ornate design carved into the handle, resting on a wooden stand. Dad had given it to her before… well, *before*, and it was the single most precious object she owned.

She went back to work, and when she finished painting the shoulder guard, she laid it on the newspaper next to the newly painted forearm guard. Spray paint could take anywhere from five minutes to twenty-four hours to dry, and she'd wait several hours—at least—before even *thinking* about touching the pieces she'd just painted. But yesterday, she'd finished the left forearm guard, and it was surely dry by now. She touched the tip of her index finger to the surface of the left forearm guard, then brought her hand to her face and examined the finger. No paint.

Excited, she picked up the guard, thumbed the catch that opened it, and pressed it to her right forearm.

Please fit, please fit, please fit…

She snapped the forearm guard closed and was relieved to find it fit her arm perfectly.

Then, despite her better judgment, she gently touched her finger to the shoulder guard. She only needed one, since it was designed to protect her—or rather her character's—sword arm, and she was righthanded. She was thrilled to discover the paint was already dry, mostly. She decided to try it on, too, and if she smudged the paint a little, she could always touch it up. To get the proper feel of it, she should probably take off her shirt, bra too, since her shoulders would be bare when she wore the finished costume. But her mother was downstairs making dinner, and she had a habit of coming upstairs to randomly check on her kids, with no warning whatsoever. Sienna wasn't self-conscious around her mother when it came to her body, but she feared Mom wouldn't be pleased once she realized how much of her daughter would *not* be covered by the costume. Better to show the finished product to her, so she'd get the full effect. Maybe then she'd see how awesome it was and wouldn't freak about how much skin it showed.

Maybe.

The shoulder guard seemed a bit loose, but she hadn't attached the foam rubber padding to it yet, and she was sure it would fit better once she had. She removed both guards, put them back on the table, then looked at the can of gold spray paint. She supposed it was time. She shook the can, stood, and began carefully applying a strip of gold paint across the tips of the wings' feathers. She'd been putting this off, afraid of making a mistake. These wings weren't something she could easily recreate if she screwed them up, certainly not in time for Halloween. But her hand was steady, and when she finished, she stepped back, examined her work, and grinned with relief.

Beautiful.

Her "studio" time finished for now, she blew out her candles. She had no idea how long she'd worked—she never kept track of time when making art—but she suddenly realized she was *starving*. She decided to go downstairs and see what Mom was cooking. She hoped it was something good.

Or at least edible.

When Sienna walked into the kitchen, she was not surprised to find Mom "multitasking," as she called it. Sienna called it *Trying to do too many things at once*. Mom stood at the stove, using a metal fork to move a chicken cutlet around a sizzling frying pan. Sienna thought it looked long past done, but she wasn't going to say anything. Mom hated anyone criticizing her cooking, especially while it was still in progress. Mom was wearing her wireless headset—which she seemed to have on 24/7—and talking to someone on the other end, voice raised to be heard over the sound of the stove fan.

"Ma'am, I understand, but we're not allowed to give out this information. Your husband is the only one listed on this policy."

Barbara Shaw was in her forties, pretty, with shoulder-length brown hair that was thicker than Sienna's. She wore a long-sleeved salmon-colored top and jeans, and her wedding band still encircled her left ring finger. Sienna felt a pang of sorrow whenever she looked at the ring, so she usually did her best to pretend it wasn't there.

Mom stabbed her fork into the cutlet, lifted it, and checked the underside. It looked like a charcoal briquette.

"Bitch!" she shouted, then into the headset mic, "No, not you, ma'am. Not you."

She glared at Sienna as she said this last bit. Then she dumped the burnt chicken onto a plate next to the stove, a look of disgust on her face. Mom was a decent cook, but she was always being pulled in too many directions to fully focus on what she was making. Dad used to share meal preparation duties with her—it was one of the ways they'd enjoyed spending time together—but now she had to do it alone.

Sienna had offered to help numerous times, but Mom said she "worked better on my own." Sienna wondered if Mom simply couldn't stand the thought of anyone taking her husband's place in the kitchen at her side—even her daughter. And since Mom was the sole breadwinner now, she worked all the time, taking calls for the insurance company that employed her, starting early in the morning and not ending until almost bedtime.

She said the job sucked ass, but the fact she could do it remotely and be home all day for Sienna and her brother was a big plus. Sienna didn't think constantly talking to people on the phone counted as "being present" for your children, but Sienna would never say this to her. Mom was under too much pressure as it was. She didn't need her daughter riding her about the lackluster job she was doing as a parent.

Having a conversation with Mom while she was working could be awkward, though. You were never a hundred percent sure if she was talking to you or a customer.

71

Sienna had come downstairs because she was hungry, but since dinner wasn't ready, she thought she'd go back to her room and get a little more work on her costume done. Halloween was tomorrow night, and she knew she could finish her costume in time—if she didn't slack off.

She opened the kitchen junk drawer, peered in, moved items around, but didn't see what she was looking for. She closed the drawer and looked at her mother. "Mom, don't we have a tape measure?"

"I dunno. Check the drawer by the microwave." Mom returned her attention to the customer she was helping. "Yes, ma'am, but in the future, your husband really needs to call on this policy." She dropped the fork on the counter and went to the small table near the stove to check her laptop. "The only thing I can tell you is that it's still active."

Sienna closed the junk drawer and walked to the counter on the other side of their cramped kitchen. She opened the drawer her mother had indicated, and sure enough, there was the tape measure. She picked it up, closed the drawer, and was about to leave when a thought occurred to her. If she was going to head back upstairs to work, she could use a little something to tide her over until dinner was officially ready. Can't be a creative genius on an empty stomach, right? She sneaked past Mom and examined the blackened chicken she'd deposited on the plate. Time for a taste test. She snagged a cutlet, blew on it a couple times, and took a bite. Extra well-done, but not too bad.

Mom saw what she did, scowled, and smacked her on the side of the head—harder than necessary, Sienna thought.

"Can you wait five minutes?" Mom said. "Go tell your brother to come down, please." She returned to the stove, stabbed a piece of raw meat, and dropped it into the skillet. "Ma'am, my manager is just going to tell you the same thing."

It was Sienna's turn to scowl, but Mom was no longer paying attention to her and didn't see. Probably a good thing. She just would've gotten more irritated. Taking another bite of her stolen cutlet, Sienna walked out of the kitchen and headed for the stairs.

Jonathan's room was across the hall from hers, thank god. Sienna loved her brother—even if he was a weirdo and a pain in the butt sometimes—but she needed complete control of her environment when she created. Hearing Jonathan's videogame noises on the other side of her bedroom wall if his room had been directly next to hers would've made it impossible for her to concentrate.

She finished the last bite of the cutlet before she reached his room. His door was open a crack, but she knocked anyway—more as a courtesy than because Jonathan expected her to—and stepped inside. She never liked going into his room. The walls were decorated with artwork depicting sinister, disturbing images, some of which he'd drawn himself—skulls with green flames coming out of their sockets, sharp-toothed ghouls gnawing on severed limbs, laughing demons with ripped-open abdomens holding their own internal organs in their clawed hands... Seeing them always made her feel a little queasy, and she regretted eating that chicken cutlet before coming up here.

Jonathan sat at his desk over by the far window, reading an article from the *Miles County News* website on his laptop screen. Sienna could see the headline, all caps, blood-red letters: *HALLOWEEN MAYHEM*. She knew exactly which incident he was reading about.

Sienna kept her voice calm as she spoke. "Jonathan, come on. Let's eat."

No response. He was too caught up in what he was reading to pay attention to her.

She raised her voice. "Jonathan!"

He spun his chair around, startled. "What?"

Jonathan didn't look like a particularly morbid kid, although he *was* wearing a black hoodie over a gray T-shirt. He was twelve, with short brown hair and black-framed glasses that seemed a bit large for his face. He was skinny and a bit awkward looking, but Sienna knew this was due to his age. His body would fill out in the next few years, as puberty worked its magic. She saw a lot of Dad in him, and that made her feel both happy and sad at the same time.

"Dinner's ready," she said.

He started to look back over his shoulder, as if he'd just realized Sienna could see what was displayed on his screen. But he stopped himself and kept his expression neutral. "I'll be down in a minute."

"Don't keep Mom waiting, please. She's in a decent mood for once."

He gave her a skeptical look. "Define *decent*."

"Just get down there ASAP."

Sienna turned and headed for the door, trying to hurry without *looking* like she was trying to hurry. She kept her gaze focused straight ahead so she wouldn't have to see Jonathan's dark artwork, but she still felt the creatures in those pictures were following her with their eyes as she passed.

She shivered, and when she made it to the hallway, she changed her mind about getting more work done on her costume. She hurried down the stairs, taking them two at a time, still seeing those blood-red letters in her mind.

HALLOWEEN MAYHEM...

"So, did you figure out what you're dressing up as tomorrow?" Mom asked Jonathan.

The three of them were sitting at the dining table—Mom at the head, Jonathan on her left, Sienna on her right—eating dinner. The last few cutlets Mom had cooked weren't burnt, at least not much, and were actually fairly tasty. Mom had made mashed potatoes as well as a salad, and both of those were fine. Sienna and Jonathan were drinking tall glasses of water, while Mom had a glass of red wine. Jonathan had once asked Mom why Sienna and he couldn't have wine too.

"When you have two kids, a stressful job, and a house to keep up, then you can have some wine with dinner," she'd said.

"The Miles County Clown," Jonathan said in response to her question as if it was perfectly normal costume to wear for Halloween, like a ghost or a space alien.

Sienna shouldn't have been surprised, she supposed, but she was. "Don't do that," she said.

"Why not?"

Jonathan sounded perplexed, as if he honestly didn't know why Sienna was upset at his choice.

"Because that's *beyond* disrespectful," she said.

Mom looked back and forth between the two of them. "What are we talking about?"

Sienna turned to their mother. "He wants to dress up as a real guy who murdered eight people last year." She faced Jonathan once more. "Do you have any idea how *insensitive* that is? Not to mention sick?"

Mom gave Jonathan a stern look. "Oh, you're not doing that."

Jonathan looked even more puzzled now. "It's just a costume. What's the big deal?"

Mom paused for a moment, as if she couldn't believe he'd just said that. "How would you feel if, god forbid, he attacked someone in our family and people celebrated him? That's basically what you're doing."

"You don't see people dressing up as Jeffrey Dahmer or Charles Manson," Sienna added.

Jonathan looked down at his plate and started moving food around with his fork. "I think you're both overreacting."

"Do you?" Sienna challenged.

"Charles Manson *technically* never killed anyone," Jonathan pointed out.

Mom had officially run out of patience. "All right, enough. I said no and that's it."

Sienna and Mom started to eat again, but then Jonathan said, "Did you know the Nazis used to inject dye into children's eyeballs to see if they would change color?"

Mom dropped her fork on her plate. "*Jonathan!*"

Sienna glanced at her mother. "Thank you." Then she gave Jonathan a look that said, *See? Even Mom thinks you're acting weird.*

The three continued with their meal, and after a few minutes, Mom started a new conversation. "Sienna, I need you to pick up some candy on your way home from school tomorrow. I forgot to buy it last weekend. And you're helping us hand it out this year. I'm *not* running to the door every five minutes."

Shopping for candy only a few hours before the trick-or-treaters came sounded awful to Sienna. All the good stuff would be gone, and she'd be stuck buying off-brand chocolate that tasted like wax and cheap peanut-butter-cup knockoffs that tasted like sawdust. Kids would *love* coming to their house this year.

"Why can't you just leave a bucket on the porch like everyone else?" she asked.

"Absolutely not. We tried that one year, and some goddamn kids took the whole thing. You know what? 'Yes, Mom.' That's all I wanna hear for the rest of the night. Understood?"

Sienna nodded.

Jonathan gave Sienna an evil grin. "You were right. She *is* in a decent mood for once."

Mom glared at her, and Sienna sighed.

CHAPTER SEVEN

After dinner, Jonathan returned to his room, and Sienna helped Mom clean up the kitchen. Sienna used a dish towel to dry a pot, and Mom wiped down the counter with cleaning spray, when she asked, "So, what are your plans tomorrow?"

"Megan Melanie's throwing a Halloween party," Sienna replied.

"Oh, Megan. The girl from your Little League team? That's nice. I didn't know you two were still friends. Who you going with, Allie?"

"And Brooke."

Mom stopped wiping and looked at Sienna. "She's not driving, is she?"

Sienna smiled. "I'm gonna take an Uber."

"Why? So you can get shit-faced? What do you think I am, *stupid*, Sienna?"

Sienna was beginning to get angry, but she knew it would only make things worse if she showed it, so she tried to keep her tone even as she spoke. "Do we have to do this every time I go out? You know I don't drink."

Mom gave her a skeptical look. "So you say."

Sienna held her tongue as she put the dish towel and pot on the counter. She saw a spice shaker that had been left out, so she picked it up and opened an upper cupboard to put it away—

—and a box of open cereal slipped out and fell before she could catch it, scattering multicolored sugary bits shaped like tiny rainbows, hearts, and flowers onto the floor. The box had fallen face down, and on the back was a maze printed in black ink, above it the words *Get Wacky to the Circus on Time*, printed in orange. Wacky the Clown—the cereal's mascot character—stood at the beginning of the maze, and a red-and-white striped circus tent was placed at the end. Sienna thought Wacky looked kind of creepy, especially considering what Jonathan had been looking at on his laptop before dinner.

HALLOWEEN MAYHEM.

"Your brother never closes these goddamn boxes," Mom said, exasperated.

Sienna opened the door to a lower cupboard and took out a whisk broom and dustpan, intending to sweep up the mess. Before she could start, Mom walked up to her and spoke in a gentle voice. "Give me that. I got it."

Sienna stepped back as Mom crouched down and went to work. Mom had always had a bit of a sharp tongue, but it had gotten a lot worse this last year. She wasn't the kind of person who apologized for what she'd done—Sienna thought she might be too ashamed to—but speaking kindly and offering to do something for someone after snapping at them was her way of saying *I'm sorry*. And Mom usually insisted on being the one to clean up any messes. She liked restoring order in her house. Sienna realized then that Mom had been trying hard to clean up a very different mess over the last year, the mess their lives had become, and it had taken a toll on her.

That made Sienna more nervous than she already was. She needed to talk to Mom about something important, but she didn't want to add to her stress and worry. Sienna picked up a mug and began drying it with the dish towel to give her hands something to do as she spoke.

"Mom, do you ever... *wonder* about Jonathan?"

Mom didn't look up as she continued sweeping cereal into the dustpan. "What do you mean?"

"You know."

Mom looked over her shoulder at Sienna. "He's an oddball. So what?"

"He was looking up serial killers when I went in his room before. Now he's talking about Nazis and the Holocaust. I mean—"

Mom picked up the cereal box and stood. "It's just a phase. The psychiatrist said this might happen. He'll grow out of it."

She dumped the cereal bits in the trash, put the whisk broom and dustpan back in its place, then closed the cereal box and returned it to the cupboard.

"You said that a year ago," Sienna said.

"Yeah, well, he lost his father."

"And I didn't? You don't see me crying out for attention."

"Yeah, well, I wish you would from time to time. I never know what you're feeling. You keep everything bottled up inside. It's not healthy."

"All right. Just don't act surprised when you find a dead animal in his room."

"You know what? Watch your mouth, huh? And what about you? When you were nine years old, your daddy took you fishing... You remember what you did to all those poor little middows or... macos?"

"Minnows."

"Whatever they're called. He found you cutting their heads off with a pair of scissors. Didn't think I remembered that, did you?"

"I was a lot younger than Jonathan."

"Well, you were old enough to know the difference between right and wrong. Your brother's fine."

Sienna didn't want to leave it there, but it was clear Mom was done talking about Jonathan. Sienna knew if she continued pushing the matter, she'd only make Mom mad, and she might not listen the next time Sienna wanted to bring up the subject. She'd try again some other time.

She just hoped it wouldn't be too late then.

As soon as Jonathan got back to his bedroom, he closed his door, and this time he locked it. His Halloween costume hung on the back of his door, a black-and-white outfit exactly like the kind the Miles County Clown had worn. He brushed his fingers against the smooth, satiny fabric, and the sensation made him shiver. He was glad that when Sienna had come to get him for dinner, she'd pushed the door open far enough that she hadn't seen the costume hanging there. She'd have lost her shit bigtime if she had.

He went to his dresser, pulled out one of the drawers, and removed a leather-bound journal from beneath the clothes where he'd hidden it. He closed the drawer, walked over to his computer desk, sat, put the journal on his lap, and then logged back onto the Internet.

He returned to the article he'd been reading when Sienna had interrupted him. It was a reporter's blog post on *Extra Miles: The Miles County News* website detailing the murders last year. He'd read the article before—lots of times—but he read it again now.

HALLOWEEN MAYHEM

Miles County Police Department has just released the names of two of the victims of last night's gruesome events on the west side of town. College students Tara Heyes and Dawn Emerson, both Miles County residents, were killed by an unnamed suspect who was also removed from the property after police answered a manic 911 call last night.

Details are trickling in, though we have confirmation that the scene was deliberately grisly. We don't have any information in terms of how Heyes and Emerson might be connected to the suspect, but some sources are commenting that this was a case of being in the wrong place at the wrong time.

We haven't had any confirmation from the Miles County PD just yet, but sources are confident that the deaths of Heyes and Emerson are directly connected to reports earlier of the murders of two gentlemen who owned a local pizza parlor...

He stopped reading and scrolled back up to look at a picture of the two women that accompanied the article. Tara had long black hair and red lipstick, and she wore a Halloween costume—a black dress with a skeleton pattern on the front, like you were looking at an X-ray of her bones. Dawn had blonde hair, and she wore a green dress with straw-like fringe that he figured was supposed to be a feminine version of the Scarecrow from *The Wizard of Oz*. The picture was a selfie of the two women together, a silly one where they were sticking out their tongues and trying to look goofy. Why the author of the post had decided *that* was a good photo to go with an article about the women's horrible murders, he didn't know. It was, as Sienna might say, *beyond disrespectful*.

They were both pretty, and while they were ten years older than him and looked very adult to his eyes, he knew they really had been young when they'd died. They might've lived another sixty, maybe even seventy years— if it hadn't been for the Miles County Clown.

He took the journal off his lap and set it on the desk in front of the computer. He flipped through its pages—most of which were devoted to sketches and drawings—until he reached a newspaper article that had been clipped and pasted into the journal. It was a different story about Tara and Dawn's murders, and he'd read this before too, a lot of times. It didn't really give much more information than the blog post, though. Still, he read it one more time.

The headline for this story was *HALLOWEEN HORROR*, and there were separate photos of Tara and Dawn. He thought they might be their senior high school pictures since they were looking straight at the camera and smiling in stiff, fakey poses. He touched his hand to the photos, as if by doing so he might make some kind of connection with them, gain some insight into what had happened to them and—most importantly—*why* it had happened. After a moment, his hand began trembling, and he quickly removed it from the photos and clicked to another web article he had bookmarked, this one written by a different reporter.

MASSACRE IN MILES COUNTY

Warning: Graphic Content

"No shit," he whispered.

There was a grainy photo of Tara, beneath which were the words *Heyes' body propped up postmortem.* The photo showed Tara, clothes ripped, blood on her face and neck, a black bar across her eyes, in front of her a wooden sign with the word *CIRCUS* painted in white capital letters.

He scrolled down to the next picture. The caption below this one said, *The suspect known as "Art the Clown."*

It showed Art—the Miles County Clown—lying on his back, head turned, black bar over his eyes, blood all over him, his black-ringed mouth open and slack.

Looking at the photo of Art, who appeared dead but evidently hadn't been, made his stomach roil with nausea, and he wished he hadn't eaten so much at dinner.

What was it with the black bars over their eyes, anyway? The bars didn't help conceal anyone's identity. Tara and Art were named in the article! If anything, the eye-bars made them look extra-creepy, especially the clown.

He started reading.

I've been working on putting together a comprehensive file on the Miles County Massacre, including some rare crime scene photos that were printed and then pulled from a few of the local papers. I was very lucky to have temporary access to the hard copies so I could scan some of the more graphic pics. Readers, be warned.

Jonathan scrolled down to a photo of a mirror with *ART* written in blood on the surface.

Who is "ART THE CLOWN"? The letters were blood-red, beneath them: *A Madman's Signature.*

Art had done this at the coroner's office, after killing the man and two EMTs and then escaping. Jonathan tried to imagine what it must've been like for the coroner, to see the killer he thought was dead suddenly get up and bash his face in with a hammer. He shuddered and continued reading.

Tonight I took a long, deep dip into the murky cesspool that is the "Art the Clown" mystery. The information we have so far is sketchy at best, but we have been able to collect a fair amount of it and, ultimately, can form some semblance of a narrative, including some theories about our prime suspect (who remains at large... let that sink in).

Do we have a serial killer on our hands? Technically, yes, the body count checks out, but is this chap following the stereotypical route of the "traditional" serial murderer? This remains to be seen, unfortunately for us.

A police sketch of Art the Clown accompanied the article. Jonathan scrolled down to it, then stopped.

Jonathan had seen lots of scary clowns in movies, videogames, and YouTube videos, and in some ways Art looked like a typical representative of the type. But the thing that set Art apart from all the others was his *eyes*. Jonathan knew this was just a drawing, someone's *interpretation* of Art, but if it was a police sketch, that meant it was based on eyewitness testimony, right? So he assumed the eyes were an accurate depiction. Jonathan had never been especially afraid of clowns—unlike some people who practically shit themselves whenever they saw one— but he'd never seen eyes like Art's before. They were cold, empty, dead. They said, *You're nothing to me but a piece of moving meat, and I can make you stop moving anytime I want.*

Whenever he looked at this drawing, he became transfixed, as if those eyes grabbed hold of him and refused to let him go. He felt the eyes pulling at him, as if they were trying to suck him through the screen and directly into Art's mind. What would it be like in there? Jonathan wondered. A black void of absolute Nothingness? A raging inferno of white-hot hate for all living things? A vast subterranean cavern where the spirits of his victims wandered for eternity, their cries of despair echoing off the stone walls? Likely it was worse than he could imagine, than *anyone* could.

Looking at this drawing was like looking at the face of Death itself. Cruel, random, meaningless... a mindless, hungry beast that killed for its own pleasure, because killing was the only thing it understood.

He'd spent the last year since his father died trying to come to terms with death. Trying to figure out what was the point of living at all if Art—or something more mundane but equally as deadly: aggressive cancer, a rapidly spreading housefire, a bullet fired from the gun of a drive-by shooter—waited for you in the end? *That* was why he spent so much time reading, watching, and listening to true-crime media—websites, podcasts, videos... He had to know *why*. This was why he wanted to dress as Art for Halloween, so he could gain some insight into the killer and what he represented by walking in his oversized clown shoes for one night. Plus, he'd once read that in olden times, people started dressing up like ghosts and demons on Halloween to fool the real spirits into thinking they were just like them. That way, the spirits would leave them alone. It was probably just superstition, but what if it wasn't? It wouldn't hurt to have some camouflage tomorrow night.

Jonathan wished he could find the words to explain all this to Mom and Sienna. He knew they thought he was weird, maybe even mentally ill, knew they worried about him. But every time he tried, all that came out was stupid stuff like the comment he'd made about Nazi experiments on children at dinner. Besides, Mom and Sienna had both gone through their own struggles in the last year—were still going through them, just like him—and he didn't want to burden them with his issue. He'd deal with it in his own way, in his own time. At least, he hoped he would.

Snatches of lines from the two articles echoed in his mind.

…including some theories about our prime suspect (who remains at large… let that sink in).

…a case of being in the wrong place at the wrong time.

Could you ever know what the wrong place and wrong time were? Or was it always a matter of random chance? And could Art the Clown still be in Miles County somewhere right now, getting ready for Halloween?

With a trembling hand, Jonathan logged off the Internet and closed his laptop. He decided to doublecheck his costume and make sure it was good to go for tomorrow night. If Art *was* out there, maybe the costume would protect him.

Then again, maybe it wouldn't.

CHAPTER EIGHT

Sienna sat at her worktable, synth wave playing again, airbrushing color onto the belt buckle for her costume. She'd put her hair in a ponytail to keep it out of the way as she worked. Spray painting was more practical for larger pieces, but she really enjoyed the precision of airbrushing.

Allie and Brooke told her all the time what a great artist she was, and they encouraged her to make it her profession. *It's destiny*, Brooke once said. *Your dad named you after his favorite color, right?* Sienna wasn't sure she was good enough, though. Yes, she really enjoyed her art classes at school, and she loved helping the theater department with scenery, costumes, and makeup for their productions. But she did those things because they were *fun*. Could she really make a living at any of them? She didn't know.

Both her door and windows were open a crack. Mom didn't like her working with paints in a closed space. *The last thing I need is for you to pass out from inhaling a bunch of chemicals while working on one of your projects.*

There was a knock at her door, and she looked over to see Jonathan standing there, holding a small black top hat in his hands. "Do you have any superglue?"

She tapped her phone screen to turn off the music, then rummaged around on her table for a couple of seconds before finding a container of superglue and examining it.

"A little." She looked at Jonathan. "Why, what happened?"

He walked over to her and held out the small hat. "The string came off."

Sienna realized then that the hat was part of Jonathan's Miles County Clown costume. She frowned. "I thought you weren't gonna wear this tomorrow."

"I won't paint my face then."

"Jonathan…"

"Come on. It's too late to get another costume."

Sienna pursed her lips as she considered. On the one hand, she didn't want to support him dressing up like a real-world serial killer. On the other, he was her brother, and he'd come to her for help. She remembered what Mom had said downstairs: *It's just a phase. The psychiatrist said this might happen. He'll grow out of it.*

She sighed and held out her hand. "Give me."

He handed the hat to her, and she took it. As she started working on repairing the string, her hands moving automatically, she glanced up at Jonathan and smiled. "Jesus, did you grow another foot since dinner?"

He smiled back. "Tallest kid in my class."

"Yeah, well, I can still kick your ass."

"Not for long."

She glanced up at him. It was true. In just a couple years he'd probably be as tall as her, if not taller, and likely stronger too. It was weird, realizing that her *little* brother was not so little anymore.

While she repaired the hat, Jonathan looked at the finished pieces of her costume lying on her worktable. "That is *sick*. How much do you have left?"

"Just finishing up the skull."

"It looks just like Daddy's character." He picked up a sketch Sienna had drawn of her in the finished costume, one she used as a guide as she worked. He looked at it a moment, then said, "You know, you draw almost as good as him now."

Sienna wasn't sure how to take this. She knew Jonathan was sincere. They got along well for the most part, and one thing they never did—okay, *almost* never did—was lie to each other. But Dad was incredibly talented, and there was no way she'd ever be as good as he was. She imagined Allie and Brooke telling her to shut up and take the compliment.

"Thanks."

Jonathan walked over to the side table, picked up the short sword, and turned back to face Sienna, the weapon held out before him. He grinned. "Is this a part of your costume too?"

Sienna laughed. "No. I could *not* walk around the street with that thing. I'd get arrested in like two seconds."

Jonathan held the blade to his face, turned it from side to side, watching the way the metal reflected the light. "Yeah, but nobody would mess with you. That's for sure."

Sienna was starting to feel uncomfortable. She didn't like Jonathan playing around with the sword, considering how much he read about serial killers. She didn't want him getting any bad ideas. "Just be careful, please. That blade's like razor sharp."

Jonathan looked at the sword once more, this time with newfound respect, and then carefully replaced it on its display.

Sienna finished with the hat and held it out to Jonathan. "There. Should be good now."

He took it from her and gave it a brief glance. "Awesome."

Sienna picked up the buckle and the airbrush nozzle and started work again.

Jonathan turned to go, stopped, turned back, hesitated, and then said, "You think that guy's still out there?"

Sienna continued airbrushing the buckle and didn't look at Jonathan as she asked, "Who?"

"The Miles County Clown."

She lowered the airbrush nozzle and turned to look at him. A moment ago, she'd thought how grown-up he was becoming, but the way he answered her question—his tone, the way he swallowed afterward—reminded her that at least part of him was still a boy.

"What's up with you and this clown all of a sudden? You're like obsessed."

"They never found his body. What if he decides to come back here?"

"Is that why you wanna dress up like him? You think if he sees you wearing his costume, he'll be all cordial with you?"

"Cordial?"

She thought for a moment. "Friendly."

"No." But he looked to the side as he said this, and Sienna thought she'd hit on the truth, or come close to it.

"I wouldn't worry about it. On the off chance that he *is* still alive, I'm sure he's gone far away from here."

He nodded, but she didn't think he looked convinced. "Thanks again for the hat."

"You're welcome."

She watched him as he left her room and stepped into the hallway. She hoped she'd reassured him, at least a little, but she didn't think she had. Kids at school liked to talk about Art the Clown as if he were some kind of boogeyman who had risen from the dead. But she thought he'd been *almost* dead when he'd killed the coroner and escaped. She figured he'd died of his injuries soon after.

She remembered what Jonathan had said: "They never found his body."

She didn't want to think about that, so she turned her music back on and resumed her work.

CHAPTER NINE

Jonathan walked along the sidewalk, carrying the pillowcase for a trick-or-treat bag. He wore his Miles County Clown outfit, along with white and black makeup to replicate the clown's face. He'd told Sienna he wouldn't wear the makeup, but he thought he looked stupid without it, so he put it on anyway. He wore a white skullcap to hide his hair and the small top hat secured with the strap beneath his chin.

Since the clown didn't wear glasses, he'd left his at home. Everything was a little blurry, but he could see well enough. He'd tried to copy the clown's nose and chin, but his attempts hadn't been successful. He'd bought a pair of foam latex prosthetic face appliances—the kind used in movies—from a special effects website, but when they arrived, he'd been disappointed. The material they were made from was thin and rubbery, and he couldn't get them to look right on his face. The nose flopped around when he moved, and he couldn't get the chin piece to go on straight.

He'd thought about asking Sienna for help, since she did the makeup for the school's theater department, but he knew she wouldn't approve of his costume choice—and worse, that she'd tell Mom about it—so he'd decided not to use the appliances. He was bummed about it. He felt incomplete, unfinished, not scary enough. And if there was one thing the Miles County Clown was, it was *scary*.

At least the night was perfect for trick-or-treating. There was a full moon out—which was *awesome*—and it had rained earlier. The way the moonlight reflected off the wet roads, trees, and houses gave everything a slightly unreal look, like the whole world was haunted. The air was cold enough to have a bite to it, but not so cold it was uncomfortable. The wind stirred the remaining leaves on the trees, creating a constant dry rustling that sounded like hard-shelled insects scuttling across the branches. But the truly weird thing about the night was that Jonathan was alone. He'd seen no other kids, no adults, no one. There were no vehicles on the road, either.

Had he gotten a late start? Had everyone else finished trick-or-treating and gone home? And what had happened to Sean and Eric? The three of them were supposed to go out together tonight. They'd probably forgotten about him and were off egging houses or toilet-papering trees, preferring to play pranks over getting candy.

He tried to remember what time he'd left home, but the memory refused to come. It was like he'd just appeared on the sidewalk, already in his costume and makeup, all set to go. The thought disturbed him, so he decided to forget about it for now and focus on having a good time—especially since this was the last Halloween he was going

95

trick-or-treating. He'd be thirteen next year, and while there was no official cut-off for when someone was too old to trick-or-treat, that seemed like a natural stopping point to him. He'd made the decision at the beginning of the month, but he hadn't told anyone. Sienna would tease him about becoming too old for Halloween, and while Mom wouldn't say anything, she'd become quiet and withdrawn, sad that her "baby" was growing up. So, if this was going to be his last trick-or-treat, he was determined to make it a good one.

The owners of the first house he came to had gone all-out with their Halloween decorations, and Jonathan stopped for a moment to admire their commitment to the holiday. They had a number of grotesquely mutilated mannequins posed around the yard in various scenarios, illuminated by landscape spotlights.

Dangling from the branches of an old oak, naked babies hung upside down at the ends of barbed-wire nooses lashed around their tiny feet, skins an ashen gray, heads cracked open like eggs, brains lying in the grass beneath them. They had no eyes.

Near the tree, a family—dad, mom, two kids—sat at a picnic table with a naked woman on it. Her stomach had been cut open, and her intestines were splayed on the table. Each member of the family had a length of intestine in their hands, clearly intending to feast on it. They slumped against one another, heads lolling, jaws slack, swollen black tongues sticking out of their mouths. Their arms and legs had been bound to the table with zip ties to keep them from falling. Patches of the family's skin had been cut away in various places as well—neck, forehead, hands, arms—exposing raw red muscle and white bone.

They also had no eyes, including the girl on the table.

Not far from the dead family stood a mom wearing gardening clothes—sunhat, sundress, flipflops—holding a hose that produced a thin, constant stream of dark liquid resembling blood. A toddler boy lay naked on the ground in front of her, arms and legs splayed, wooden stakes driven through the hands and feet pinning him to the ground. Every inch of his skin had been removed, his hair too, turning him into a red alien thing. The body wasn't fresh, and flies and maggots crawled all over it. The blood from the mom's hose hit the dead boy's belly, washing away the insects there, but doing nothing to get rid of the rest.

Like the family at the picnic table, the mom's head hung loose on her body, tilting far to the left, her throat cut so deeply that only a few shreds of skin and muscle kept her head attached to her body. Blood had run from her throat wound to soak the front of her sundress as well as the grass around her feet. She was bound to a thick wire frame with pieces of black electrical cord to keep her upright, and her right hand was encased in a ball of silver duct tape, the hose running through the middle, her arm propped up by a thin metal rod with a Y shape.

No eyes on either of them.

The last display in the yard was the most inventive—*and* the most disgusting.

It was a conglomerate thing, a nightmarish creature that would've made Dr. Frankenstein puke. Multiple heads, arms, legs, and torsos—harvested from different genders, ages, and races—had been sewn, stapled, nailed, and glued together. Its form resembled the body of an oversized crab—a carapace made entirely of torsos, eight limbs (four arms, four legs), and heads attached to the surface of its "shell." A pair of hugely muscled arms served in place of claws, and numerous sharp objects were embedded in its flesh: knives, screwdrivers, saw blades, scissors, pruning shears—some new and shiny, some old and rusted, fresh blood running from each wound. Like the other mannequins, a metal framework supported the crab thing's body, allowing it to hold its pose.

Also like the other bodies on the lawn, all the crab-thing's heads were eyeless.

These displays were *wicked*, and Jonathan decided to go up to the door and ring the bell, if for no other reason than it would allow him to walk past the mannequins. He wanted to get a look at them up close, see if he could figure out how they were made, how they looked so *real*.

He started walking along the flagstone path that led to the front porch.

The corpses were positioned close enough to the walkway that he was able to get a good look at them as he went by. Unfortunately, this also meant he got a good whiff of them, too, and man, did they *stink*.

Last August, Mom had done a grocery run, and when she got back, she'd asked him to bring the bags in. This was one chore he never minded because he got to see what snacks Mom had gotten, and if Sienna wasn't home, he'd get first crack at them. He'd made several trips to the garage, took paper sacks filled with groceries from the back seat and the trunk, and carried them to the kitchen. This time, Mom had bought some molasses oatmeal cookies, and she told him he could have two as payment for helping her out. (He ate three.) What he hadn't known was on the drive home, a package of raw hamburger Mom had purchased fell out of its sack in the trunk—she'd probably hit a bump in the road or something—and slid toward the back. He hadn't seen it, so it stayed in the trunk. In the car. In the garage. In the August heat.

For the next four days.

A nasty smell began building up in the garage after the first day, and it continued to get worse. None of them could figure out what it was, but on the fourth day, Sienna suggested they check the trunk of the car.

Mom opened it, the stench of rotten meat wafted out, and the three of them started gagging. They fled the garage and shut the door so the stench wouldn't filter into the house. Because Jonathan had been the one who'd brought in the groceries, Mom made him take the spoiled meat from the trunk and toss it in the garbage. He'd done so, making sure to breathe only through his mouth. Afterward, he left the trunk open to air it out, and opened the outer garage door for good measure. Mom had made him strip in the laundry room and throw his clothes in the washer, then she'd ordered him to go upstairs and take a shower. *On second thought, take two—and use lots of soap.* He got most of the stink off his skin and out of his hair, but the smell lingered in his nostrils for a week.

The corpses smelled like that—rotten meat, only ten times worse than that package of spoiled hamburger.

How was that foul odor created? Did the corpses have the opposite of air fresheners concealed on their bodies somewhere? Air stinkeners? Did stores sell that kind of thing for Halloween? They sold fake blood, fake body parts, and fake organs. Why not artificial rot-stink? But another thought came to him then, one that made his stomach feel even queasier than it already did. Maybe the reason the corpses looked so real was because they *were* real. Real dead bodies that were actually decomposing and filling the air with the stench of their rot. In the light of day, such an idea would've sounded ridiculous, but here, on Halloween night, cold wind blowing, dead leaves rustling, full moon glowing yellow-white in the dark sky, it didn't seem ridiculous at all.

Just as he had when he'd cleaned the spoiled hamburger, he breathed through his mouth, and his queasiness became more manageable. He continued on.

As he passed the crab-thing, he saw movement from the corner of his eye, heard a soft *uuuuuuuuhhhh* of effort. Startled, he turned to look at the creature, expecting to see it coming toward him on its multiple legs, heads snarling, muscled arms reaching for him... But the crab-thing remained in its original position, and there was no sign it had moved at all. Jonathan watched it for several seconds, waiting to see if it would move or make more sound, but it did neither.

Maybe it's animatronic, he thought, *and it has sensors that activate it when someone goes by.*

He waved an arm up and down to see if he could set it off again, but the creature remained still. Jonathan was reluctant to turn his back on the thing, but he did and resumed walking toward the house. He thought he detected slight movements from the other mannequins, heard soft groans, but every time he looked, they were motionless.

His heart was pounding, and his skin was slick with sweat despite the cool night air. He almost turned and ran then, and on any other Halloween night, he would have. But this was his *last* trick-or-treat, and he wasn't a little kid anymore. He had no reason to be afraid of yard displays, no matter how creepy or elaborate they were. Feeling a little calmer, he walked the rest of the way to the house and stepped onto the porch.

The porchlight was a skull with a red bulb inside, and a crimson glow issued from the empty eye sockets, nose holes, and open mouth. But this was no cheap plastic skull. Bits of dried flesh clung to the bone in numerous places, and wisps of hair were still attached to the scalp. If Jonathan hadn't known better, he'd have thought it was a real skull. Whoever lived here sure loved Halloween.

He rang the doorbell, expected to hear some sound effect—a scream or an evil laugh—but it chimed like any normal doorbell. Jonathan was a little disappointed by this. If you were going to go all out with your lawn display, why not have a creepy doorbell ring too?

The door opened, and Jonathan's heart started pounding again. Standing in the doorway, holding an orange plastic candy dish, was the Miles County Clown.

Jonathan had only ever seen the clown in news articles on the web, and he'd looked scary as hell then, but those pictures were nothing compared to confronting him in real life. He was tall and lean, and his features—long nose, pointed chin, pronounced brow—were definitely *not* created by cheap prosthetics. They looked absolutely real, as did his nasty teeth. But the worst part was his eyes. They bore into him with laser-like intensity, and Jonathan felt the clown was contemplating which part of his body to cut into first.

It's not the real Miles County Clown, he told himself. *This person just had the same idea you did. Probably thought dressing as the clown would be a good way to scare the kids who came to his door tonight.*

Well, mission accomplished.

Jonathan had been so horrified to see the clown that he hadn't checked out the candy dish yet, but he did so now—and immediately wished he hadn't. Instead of miniature chocolate bars, chewing gum, or lollipops, the bowl was filled with *eyes,* eyes which Jonathan knew at once had come from the lawn corpses. At least, that's the way it was *supposed* to look. Most likely those eyes were made of candy, and despite their appearance, were probably delicious.

Even so, Jonathan wasn't about to say "trick-or-treat" and open his pillowcase to get one of those disgusting things, which was good, because he was so scared he didn't think he could make his voice work right now. The clown's eyes narrowed as he looked Jonathan up and down, and then he tapped his chest and pointed to the boy. Jonathan didn't know what the clown meant, so he shrugged. The clown scowled, tapped his chest harder this time, then aggressively stabbed his index finger at Jonathan. This time, Jonathan understood. The clown was angry that Jonathan had stolen his look.

Sienna's words came back to him: "Is that why you wanna dress up like him? You think if he sees you wearing his costume, he'll be all cordial with you?"

From the angry expression on his face, the clown was feeling anything but cordial right now.

Jonathan managed to speak then, but he sounded much younger than twelve. "I-I'm sorry. I didn't know. I mean, I didn't want..."

The clown reached into the bowl, took an eyeball between his thumb and forefinger, lifted it out, and flicked it at Jonathan's forehead. *Splat!* The eye bounced off his skin and fell to the ground. Jonathan was so stunned by this that, for a moment, all he could do was stand and stare at the clown. The clown's eyes still burned with anger, but his lips stretched into a hideous parody of a smile. He flicked another eye at Jonathan, hitting his cheek this time.

The eye left wet residue behind, and Jonathan quickly wiped off his cheek using his costume sleeve.

The clown was laughing now—or rather, pretending to laugh. He didn't make any actual sound. He flicked a third eyeball, and this one bounced off Jonathan's chin. The clown laughed harder. Jonathan was *done*. Maybe this guy wasn't the real Miles County Clown, and maybe those weren't real eyes in his candy bowl, but this was *messed up*, and he wanted nothing more to do with it.

He slowly backed down the front steps, but before he reached the bottom, the clown flicked another eyeball, and this one hit Jonathan dead on the lips. Like the others, it bounced off without doing any harm, but for an instant Jonathan felt the slick smoothness against the soft flesh of his mouth, and he wanted to scream. The only thing that stopped him was knowing that if he opened his mouth, the clown would try to flick an eyeball inside it, and if one *did* land there and he *tasted* it, he would totally lose his shit.

The clown laughed, pointed at him, made kissy faces, and laughed some more.

Jonathan turned and ran.

And that's when the lawn corpses began to move.

The dead babies started crying and writhing at the ends of their barbed-wire nooses, as if throwing a mass tantrum. The woman holding the hose turned toward him and blasted him in the face with a spray of blood. Spluttering and trying not to trip, he used his pillowcase to quickly wipe the blood from his eyes, then threw it to the grass and kept running. The skinned boy struggled to pull himself free from the stakes that kept him pinned to the ground, but he couldn't muster enough strength, and all he could do was growl in frustration as Jonathan went past. The woman with the blood hose tried blasting him again, but he'd run too far, and she was only able to hit the back of his head. Blood ran down his neck and inside his costume, wetting his shoulders and back. It was warm and sticky and awful, but at least it didn't block his vision like last time.

The cannibal family had the same problem as the skinned boy. They were bound to the picnic table by the zip ties around their wrists and legs, and they struggled fiercely to free themselves from their restraints. Jonathan heard loud *cracks*, saw splintered ends of bones jut out of arms and legs, but despite their frenzied efforts, the family remained stuck.

The crab-thing tore itself free of the framework that held it up and skittered swiftly toward Jonathan, heads shrieking, muscular arms reaching out, thick-fingered hands contorting into claws. He feared he couldn't outrun the monster, that it would grab hold of him, tear him apart, and feed the bloody pieces to the heads on its carapace. Something did grab the bloodstained back of his costume then, and he screamed. He was yanked to a stop and roughly turned around, and he saw it wasn't the crab-thing that had got him. It was the clown.

Jonathan tried to pull away, but the clown held his upper arm tight, preventing him from running off. The clown moved toward Jonathan until their faces were separated only by inches, giving Jonathan his first close look at the clown's features. Jonathan looked into the clown's eyes then, and what he saw there convinced him that this *was* the real Miles County Clown, and he fought even harder to get away. He heard a heavy *thump-thump-thump* drawing toward them, and he glanced to his left and saw the crab-thing was still coming and still out for blood.

The clown didn't seem to notice the crab-thing, or else didn't care about it. But Jonathan *did* care about it—desperately, in fact, as he had only one chance to survive.

God, please let this work...

Jonathan drew back his right leg and kicked the Miles County Clown in the nuts as hard as he could.

The clown's eyes bugged out, he doubled over, and his mouth went wide in a soundless cry of agony. He let go of Jonathan's arm and put both hands to his crotch, as if trying to protect his injured junk from another assault. Jonathan shot a quick look at the crab-thing and saw it had almost reached them. Every instinct he had screamed at him to run, but he forced himself to remain standing there.

Almost… Almost… Now!

Jonathan shoved the clown toward the crab-thing, then turned and ran like hell.

The crab-thing roared with its multiple voices, and Jonathan heard a nauseating tearing sound, punctuated with loud *snaps*. No screaming, though. Not even death could make the Miles County Clown talk, it seemed.

When Jonathan reached the sidewalk, he paused and turned back to see what was happening. He immediately wished he hadn't. The clown's torso lay on the grass, blood all around it, the arms and legs of his costume empty. The crab-thing—blood coating its strong hands and arms—held the clown's head and his left arm. He'd already given the other arm and both legs to the heads on its back, and they were gnawing at the meat and shaking it like starving dogs. Jonathan then focused on the clown's head. For an instant, he thought it was laughing, but then he saw that its eyes were open and staring, its mouth slack.

Jonathan felt dizzy with relief. The clown was dead and couldn't hurt him, couldn't hurt *anyone*, ever again.

Screw trick-or-treat. I'm going home and taking a damn shower.

He intended to turn around and head back the way he'd come, but he didn't take a single step. The door of every house on the street opened, and clowns—all exact duplicates of the Miles County Clown—walked outside and began heading in his direction. Each held a different weapon in his hand—hammer, knife, hacksaw, crowbar, axe, machete, pitchfork… Jonathan did turn around then, and started to run, but he stopped immediately. More clowns had emerged from the houses on that part of the street too, and they were coming toward him. He looked around, frantically searching for a way to escape, but the clowns were running now and closing in quickly, eyes blazing with hate, mouths twisted into evil grins.

Jonathan backed into the street as the clowns drew near, his head whipping back and forth as he tried to keep track of them all. There were *dozens* of them, and as they closed ranks shoulder to shoulder, Jonathan knew there would be no escape for him. When they were within fifteen feet, they slowed to a walk. No need to rush now. They knew they had him.

Jonathan held up his hands in a stay-back gesture, but the clowns ignored it.

"Please… don't…"

They ignored his plea as well.

He smelled smoke, heard a distant *whooping* sound, but he barely registered them. His attention remained focused entirely on the grinning clowns stepping toward him. And as they closed in, he had time for a final thought.

I wish I never bought this goddamn outfit.

Then dozens of weapons were lifted into the air and brought down upon him.

He screamed, but not for long.

CHAPTER TEN

"I'm cold, hon. I'm gonna turn up the heat."

Her husband didn't say anything, so Barbara figured she was good to go. She knew not to turn it up too high, though. How many times had he told her that if he got too hot when he was driving, he started to feel nauseated? She wished she'd worn a heavier coat. It was colder than usual for this time of year. Climate change sucked. If it had been daytime, the sun would've kept the car's interior warm. But it was dark out, and the car—at least to her—felt like the inside of a freezer.

She fiddled with the heat until she got it where she wanted it, then she adjusted the vents so the air blew on her and not him. Within seconds she began to feel warmer, and she sat back in her seat and sighed in contentment. She looked out the windshield, intending to enjoy the view for a while.

When she'd been a little girl, she'd loved looking out at the road when she was traveling in a car with her mom and dad, watching it come faster and faster, getting larger as it rushed toward them until *zip!* It was gone. She'd quickly turn around in her seat and watch through the back window as the road swiftly moved away from them, becoming smaller and smaller until it vanished into the horizon. Then she'd look forward again and start the game over. Her mom had called her game *Zoning Out*, as in *Barbara's zoning out again*, and that's how she'd thought of it ever since.

She'd stopped playing that silly game as she grew older, but she still enjoyed Zoning Out as she watched the road. Not while driving, of course. That was a good way to get distracted and end up in an accident—which she had learned the hard way when she Zoned Out and drove her dad's Chevy pickup into a tree not long after getting her license. Sure, she'd been tempted to Zone Out on occasion over the years, but that was before the kids were born. Once Sienna and Jonathan came on the scene, Barbara was *never* again tempted to Zone Out while driving. But when she was a passenger? That was a different story. Her husband was driving tonight, and that left her free to watch the road all she wanted, and since neither of their children were here to distract her— *Mom, Jonathan won't scoot over and give me more room; Mom, Sienna keeps trying to see what I'm looking at on my phone*—she could relax and enjoy.

Except… there was something *different* about this road.

It didn't have a dividing line of any kind in the middle— no edge lines, either—and its surface was smooth and shiny, more like polished obsidian than asphalt. The headlight beams reflected brightly off the glossy surface, making it difficult to see what was ahead. Plus, there was nothing but darkness on either side of the road. Even if you were driving in the country, you'd pass houses from time to time, and porch lights would be on, and maybe there would be a light shining in a window or two. But there was nothing here—not a single tiny speck of light in any direction.

She looked out the passenger window, glanced up at the sky. No stars, either. Heavy cloud cover could be responsible for that, of course. She tried to remember if she'd checked the weather recently, and if so, what the forecast had been. But she came up blank, so she decided to check with her phone.

She slid it out of her purse and clicked a small button on the side to wake it. The screen lit up, she input her PIN, and the main display appeared. She stopped then and stared at the background image. It was supposed to be a picture of her kids, taken five years ago, when Sienna was twelve and Jonathan was eight. The whole family had gone apple picking that fall, and Barbara had taken a picture of the children standing beneath a tree and grinning as they held up large Golden Delicious apples in both hands. Now that the kids were older, they complained that the picture was cheesy, and they begged her to change it, but she had refused. It had been a good day, and she loved revisiting it, however briefly, whenever she used her phone. Plus, Sienna and Jonathan looked so cute!

But that wasn't the image on her phone now.

A closeup of a pair of eyes—pinpoint pupils, yellow irises, black circles around them, the skin of the face... What little was visible in the picture was chalk white. It was a disturbing image all on its own, but what made it worse was the feeling that this wasn't a photo but instead a *live* feed, and those eyes were staring at her right now. She tried to turn off her phone, but no matter how many times she pressed the button on the side, the eyes remained. They were crinkled at the edges now, and Barbara had the horrible feeling the owner of those eyes was smiling with amusement. The message was clear: *Try all you want, you can't get rid of me.*

She forgot about checking the weather, jammed her phone into her purse, and zipped it closed. She could imagine the display still lit up in there, eyes shaking as their owner laughed at her, and she turned the heat up a couple more degrees.

She waited to see if her husband would ask her what was wrong, and she was relieved when he remained silent. She felt foolish letting those eyes scare her. She'd probably accidentally downloaded a virus or something. When they got home, she'd try doing a system restore and see if that fixed the problem. If not, she'd get a replacement phone. No big deal. And the lack of stars in the sky? She decided to blame heavy cloud cover and let it go at that.

No way she could relax and enjoy the ride now, though.

"How much longer until we get there?" she asked.

He didn't answer. At first, she thought he might not have heard her—the heat was blowing pretty loudly—and she was about to raise her voice and ask him again when she realized something... She had no idea where they were going. And then she realized something even more disturbing... She didn't know where they had come from.

She remembered sitting in the passenger seat while he drove and feeling cold, and that was it. She didn't have

111

amnesia or anything. Overall, her memory was fine. It was her *recent* memory that was crap. Had she had a stroke or something? She was still a relatively young woman, so that seemed unlikely, but it wasn't *impossible*. She felt the first stirrings of panic, and she turned to look at him, intending to ask him to take her to a hospital so she could get checked out. She'd read somewhere that if a stroke victim got treatment immediately, more of the brain could be saved. She opened her mouth to speak, but then she hesitated. Something was wrong with her husband.

He didn't look… right.

The being behind the wheel appeared to have been sculpted out of shadow. It had the basic form of a human— head, body, arms, legs—but there were no discernible details. No facial features, no apparent clothing, not even any fingers. The hands were only rounded nubs, but he seemed to have no trouble steering with them. She couldn't tell if he was looking straight ahead or looking at her. If he turned his head, how would she know?

It's like he's made of the same stuff as this place.

She'd thought her husband was driving the car, but he wasn't. This thing couldn't possibly be him.

She heard her phone vibrate in her purse, and she wondered if the owner of the yellow eyes was laughing at her.

Did stroke victims experience hallucinations? She didn't know, but she sure as shit hoped so, because the alternative was that she was losing her fucking mind. Better to have a chunk of your brain die than to go totally bugfuck crazy. Her pulse was jackhammer-fast, she felt feverish, and she was having trouble catching her breath. *Panic attack*, she thought. She needed to regain control of herself before she could worry about anything else. She turned off the heat—she was the one who felt nauseated now—sat back in her chair, and closed her eyes. She'd never had a panic attack before, and she wasn't sure what to do. She had always been highly strung, and she sucked big time at relaxing. It usually took a glass or two of wine to help her even start to take the edge off. She didn't have any wine, of course, and the only other time she could truly relax was when she Zoned Out while watching the road go by.

Could she do it now, traveling through a world of darkness, with a shadow man for a chauffeur? She didn't know, but she had to try. She opened her eyes—

—and screamed.

A huge deer stood in the middle of the road, mesmerized by their headlights. At least she *thought* it was a deer. The shape was right—antlers, hooves, small tail—but the coloring was all wrong. Instead of being brown, this animal was black and white, with black around its eyes and mouth, and two curving black lines on its forehead that resembled eyebrows. The left antlers were black, the right ones white. And, strangest of all, it had a small top hat on one side of its head.

It's a harlequin deer, she thought.

The shadow driver was going fast and showed no sign of slowing down, let alone stopping. The car was hurtling straight for the deer, and the deer—frozen in place by the headlights—gave no indication that it was going to get out of the way.

"Slow the fuck down!" Barbara shouted. "Turn off the headlights and honk the horn!"

Without the lights dazzling the animal, the sound of the car horn would scare it into hauling ass off the road. She had done it before herself when encountering a deer while driving at night, and it had always worked.

But the driver ignored her, if he heard her at all. She couldn't see any ears on him, so maybe he was deaf. She reached out to touch his arm and get his attention, but when her fingers came into contact with his dark substance, she drew in a hissing breath and yanked her hand away. He was so cold it burned!

She looked out the windshield again. They were still headed straight toward the deer, and in another few seconds, they'd hit it head-on. She'd read somewhere that around two hundred people died each year from collisions with deer, and she did *not* want to add to that statistic. Fuck it. She'd have to take care of this herself. She reached over, grabbed the steering wheel with both hands—being very careful not to touch the driver's shadowy body—and yanked it hard to the right.

The back tires squealed on the road's obsidian surface, and the rear of the car swung around. Barbara could feel the vehicle struggling to keep all four wheels on the road, and she feared they would flip and roll, but then the rear quarter panel slammed into the deer—*whump!* The impact caused the car to spin, slow, and then stall.

Barbara sat for a moment, stunned, listening to the engine ticking as it cooled. She turned to her husband to see if he was all right, and then remembered it wasn't him behind the wheel. The shadow man sat there, perfectly still, as if nothing had happened. She thought he might be looking at her, but she wasn't sure.

"I-I'm gonna go check on the deer."

Barbara was concerned about the animal, but she also didn't think she could spend another moment in the car with the silent dark thing sitting where her husband should be. She undid her seatbelt, opened the door, and got out. She felt suddenly lightheaded, and she held onto the door for several seconds until she was okay again. A reaction to the accident, she figured, unless she'd just had another mini stroke. She started walking, going slow in case another wave of dizziness hit her. It was cold out here, the kind of cold that seeped into your body until your bones turned to ice. She crossed her arms and pressed them tight against her body, hoping it would warm her, at least a little, but it didn't really help. The air had a stale, flat quality, like a room in a house that had been closed for a very long time. She didn't like it.

She also didn't like the way this strange road felt beneath her feet. It vibrated slightly, as if some great machine buried far below was hard at work doing… something.

She walked around the rear of the car, and in the red wash of its taillights, she saw the deer lying on the road, bent and broken—and unfortunately, still alive. As she drew near, the animal let out a cry of distress that tore at Barbara's heart. Its front legs were broken in several places, and bone fragments jutted out from the skin. The antlers on its right side had been snapped off at the base, and blood ran from its mouth, bubbling and frothing as it bellowed in pain and fear. The rear legs were mostly intact, and they skittered on the road's smooth surface as the deer vainly tried to get to its feet and run away. But given the extent of its injuries, Barbara knew this animal was never going to walk again, let alone run.

She heard the car engine start up, and she turned to see her purse fly out of the open passenger door and land on the ground. The door slammed shut, and a second later, the car began moving. Slowly at first, and there was a grinding noise, as if part of the vehicle was scraping the road, but then the vehicle accelerated.

"Stop!" she said. "You can't leave me here!"

Alone.

In the dark.

But if the shadow man heard her, he paid her no mind. He continued to accelerate, and soon the car was nothing but a pair of red dots dwindling in the distance.

When the driver left, he'd taken all the light with him, leaving Barbara in absolute darkness. When she was a kid, her family had gone on a road trip, and one of the least lame places they'd visited was Mammoth Cave in Kentucky. It had been extremely beautiful, but also eerie, especially when they were down deep and their tour guide said she was going to turn off her flashlight so they could experience a darkness "unlike any you've ever known." The guide had been correct. Once the light was off, darkness swept in and surrounded them with almost physical force, and Barbara remembered thinking this was what it must be like to be dead.

The darkness she was in now was worse than that. *Way* worse.

The deer cried out again, and although she knew the animal was suffering, she was grateful she wasn't entirely alone in this horrible place. At least the shadow man had been considerate enough to toss out her purse before driving off and leaving her stranded. If she could find her purse, she could take out her phone and use it as a flashlight. She wouldn't care if those hideous yellow eyes were still on the display, just so long as she could have some light.

She tried to picture where the purse had been in relation to her position when the shadow man drove off. She estimated it had been about thirty feet away, off to her right slightly. She turned her body six inches to the right, which she judged was the correct angle, and started walking slowly, taking small steps. Behind her, the deer continued bellowing.

She'd only gone a few feet when she saw white light flare in the distance, followed by a loud *fwump!* The light became orange then and glowed steadily.

He's done it again, she thought, although she wasn't certain what this meant. Still, she was filled with almost crippling sorrow, and tears began to slide down her cheeks. The glow was far off, but in this world of dark, the light was still enough to dimly illuminate the road, and she could see her purse. She didn't know how long the glow would last, so she hurried toward her purse and snatched it off the ground. She took out her phone and then slung her purse over her shoulder. She didn't turn on the phone, though. The orange light was still strong enough that she could see, more or less, and she didn't want to use any battery power until she had to.

The harlequin deer's cries became higher pitched and frightened, and when Barbara turned back around to look at the animal, she saw why. The deer's bellowing had attracted predators. Small, black creatures that looked like a cross between a rat and a lizard had emerged from the darkness on the side of the road and were attacking the deer, swarming over its black-and-white body and ripping out chunks of flesh with their teeth. The deer was bleeding from a dozen new wounds, and more appeared every second.

She wanted to go to the deer's aid, but she had no idea what she could do to help. The closest thing to a weapon she had in her purse was a nail file, and she doubted it would be enough to drive off the rat-lizards. She could use the purse itself as a weapon, she supposed, swinging it at the rat-lizards and trying to knock them off the deer. She didn't think it would do any good, though. There were just too many of the goddamn beasts, and once she proved herself to be a nuisance, they might decide to have her for dessert. As shitty as it made her feel, she knew the safest move would be to stay away from the deer and let the rat-lizards have their feast. She hoped for the deer's sake that its death wouldn't take too much longer.

More light shone on the scene then, and Barbara turned to see a pair of headlights rapidly approaching. Was the shadow man coming back? She didn't see how that was possible, since he'd caused the explosion of white light and the orange glow that followed. It had to be someone else. As the vehicle came closer, she could see its headlights were higher up than their car's, so probably a pickup, van, or SUV. She didn't give a shit what kind it was. It could be a rickety wooden cart pulled by an elderly donkey, just so long as she could bum a ride home from the driver.

She stepped into the middle of the road, careful to keep a safe distance between herself and the rat-lizards devouring the deer, and waved her hands in the air to catch the driver's attention. "Hey!" she shouted. "Hey!"

The driver showed no sign of slowing, and as the vehicle—a van, she could see now—came closer, she quickly moved off to the side to avoid getting hit. It was hard to tell in the dim orange light, but she thought the van was black, except for its hood, which was white. It looked like there were two people in the vehicle, a driver and a shorter person in the passenger seat. She wondered if it was the driver's kid. She couldn't make out any specific features, but she could tell that they did indeed *have* features, which meant that whoever or whatever they were, they weren't shadow people.

She expected the driver to slow as they approached, but if anything, they sped up. Then she watched in horror as the van plowed into the wounded deer. Rat-lizards were knocked into the air or crushed to jelly beneath the van's tires, and the deer let out an ear-shattering scream of agony as the vehicle rolled over its body, bounced when it hit the road, swerved, then continued onward at top speed. The van's weight had caused the deer's abdomen to explode, and its guts were spread across the road's glossy black surface.

It shuddered several times, and then its head fell to the ground, eyes glassy, tongue lolling from its blood-frothed mouth. It was, mercifully, dead. A number of rat-lizards had avoided being struck by the van, and they swarmed back over the deer's body, many of them attacking the internal organs that were now very much external, while others crawled into the open body cavity to see what sweet, wet treasures they might discover within.

Barbara turned and vomited. When she was finished a rat-lizard scuttled over to inspect the puddle of puke, and she kicked it away as hard as she could. When it hit the ground, three more of its kind rushed toward it and began ripping into it with teeth and claws. If Barbara still had anything left in her stomach, she would've lost it then.

She saw headlights again, this time coming from the direction the van had gone. It seemed this road was busier than she'd thought. She hoped whoever was behind the wheel of this vehicle would stop to help her, and as she did before, she stepped into the middle of the road and waved her arms over her head.

A few seconds later, she recognized the vehicle. It was the van again. The driver had turned around and was coming back. Did whoever it was driving the van want to run over the deer again and make certain they finished the job of killing it? Or this time, were they coming for her? She had a bad feeling she knew the answer to this question. She was about to run when she realized she smelled something odd. Was that… smoke? She'd hesitated only a few seconds, but that was enough. As the van bore down on her, she glimpsed a pair of pale faces through the windshield.

Both of them were grinning.

And then the van slammed into her, and she discovered a darkness even deeper than that which surrounded the obsidian road.

CHAPTER ELEVEN

Sienna always lost track of time when she worked, and her mom—who was usually on her case about one thing or another—never forced her to stop. She'd stick her head into the room to remind Sienna that she really needed to get some sleep or let her know that she'd be late to school if she didn't get her butt in gear, but she never made her stop working. Sienna wasn't sure why this was. She'd asked Mom once. "Because you're going to do what you want anyway," she'd said, and it was true. But Sienna thought there was more to it than that. She thought Mom liked her daughter's devotion to her art, that it reminded her of her husband. Letting Sienna work as long as she wanted was a way of keeping part of him alive and present.

Since Halloween was tomorrow, Sienna was determined to finish her costume before she went to bed, and she finished painting the last piece at 3:07 a.m. and blew out all her candles. She was exhausted, but happy, and while she was tempted to try on the outfit and see how it looked and felt, she was too tired to do anything but crawl into bed. But as weary as she was, she couldn't fall asleep immediately. Her mind raced with ideas for new projects—her body might stop working but her brain never seemed to get the message—so she turned on her TV to give her brain something else to focus on, hoping to distract it enough so it would calm down and let her sleep.

The program that came on was an old black-and-white movie that she'd seen before—*House on Haunted Hill*. Normally, she might've changed the channel instead of watching a horror film before sleeping, but it was Halloween, so she left it on.

A woman in a plain 1950s-style dress held a lit candle as she searched for something in a chamber with stone walls. She nearly bumped into a scary-looking old woman—wild white hair, blind eyes, hands raised, fingers curled into claws, lips drawn back from her teeth in a snarl, an expression of absolute hatred on her face. But what made the old woman even scarier was the fact that she stood absolutely immobile, like she was a wax figure.

The woman in the dress screamed, and then the scary woman suddenly glided across the floor, like she was a floating ghost, and disappeared through an open door. Sienna thought the effect was cool, and she wondered how they did it. Probably had the actor stand on a wheeled platform with a rope pulled by a crew member. Simple, but effective.

She wasn't worried about the creepy images finding their way into her dreams and giving her nightmares. She'd had awful dreams for a couple of months after Dad died, and in desperation she'd hit the Internet and searched for ways to prevent—or at least deal with—nightmares. That was when she'd learned about lucid dreaming, a technique by which the dreamer was fully aware that they're dreaming and could exert a certain amount of control over the dream's events. She started practicing it, and soon she was able to make small changes to her dreams, and as she improved, she could stop nightmares before they became too scary and switch to a more pleasant dream. She hadn't experienced a bad dream since.

She could feel herself starting to nod off and decided she'd better change the channel before one of the characters started screaming again and woke her back up. But the next program was even worse. It was a cartoon that showed three monstrous priests—they were zombies, or maybe demons—devouring the internal organs of a dead human priest in the sanctuary of a church. A blood-splattered nun wielding a machine gun popped up from behind a pew and started blasting the evil priests with a hailstorm of bullets, tearing bloody chunks out of them. Definitely *not* conducive to sleep. She changed the channel again.

This time the TV screen showed a woman playing a banjo and singing. She wore a floppy blue hat, blue vest, and blue shorts. She had a white long-sleeved shirt beneath the vest with dark blue stripes on the arms, and she wore white leggings with the same blue stripes. Curly red hair hung to her shoulders, she had a blue shape of some kind painted around her right eye, and she wore metallic-blue lipstick surrounded by silver paint, all enclosed within a red line.

She stood in front of a brick wall that had some kind of mural on it, and next to her was a metal barrel with a fire burning inside. Children—*big* children—sitting on a wooden playset watched as she sang, swinging their feet and nodding their heads in time with the music as they enthusiastically ate treats like popcorn and caramel apples. *Some kind of kids' show*, she thought, although why it was on so late at night, she didn't know. She listened as the woman—Banjo Blue, Sienna dubbed her—sang:

> *Drop on by the Clown Café!*
> *Drop on by the Clown Café!*
> *The grub is downright gruesome*
> *But your appetite so big*
>
> *'Cause food's a little funny…*
> *Food's a little funny…*
> *Food's a little funny*
> *at the Clown Café.*

The music was simple, the tune catchy—even if the lyrics *were* a bit odd—and the woman's pleasant singing voice soon lulled Sienna to sleep.

Old-fashioned TV cameras, red lights glowing, are stationed at various points around the brightly lit set, operated by silent men with blurry faces. Four teens in brightly colored clothes play on a wooden playset—swinging, laughing, telling jokes, calling each other silly names—acting more like little children than the near-adults they are.

Past the playset, a line of people stand waiting, airline boarding passes in hand, luggage resting at their feet. They range in age from twenties to fifties, some in informal dress, some in jackets and ties. There's even a pilot and flight attendant in the line. They all chat pleasantly with one another, and seem in no hurry to get wherever they're going. The line ends at an orange-and-black trailer with the words Clown Café on the front spelled out in yellow lights. There's a sliding window above the sign, next to it a smaller sign that says Open. To the right of the window, partially hidden by the line of people, the trailer has a stylized black-and-white portrait of Art the Clown's head.

Banjo Blue steps in front of the trailer and resumes her song, facing one of the cameras and walking backward through the set as she sings:

> Drop on by the Clown Café,
> your favorite meals on wheels.
> The menu is disgusting
> and it's full of special deals.

She moves away from the trailer, past a trash can full of scrap metal, a stack of old tires, and a set of croquet mallets. On her right is a metal barrel with a fire burning inside.

> Nothing here is good for you,
> so grab yourself a tray...

> 'Cause food's a little funny
> at the Clown Café.

She stops in front of a fake brick wall, and the camera zooms in on a painted mural of Art dancing in a ring with small, happy children, all of them holding hands. There's a rainbow behind Art, and he only looks a *little* scary.

> Drop on by the Clown Café!
> Drop on by the Clown Café!
> Gobble up your order quick,
> before it runs away...

> 'Cause food's a little funny
> at the Clown Café.

Banjo Blue continues to sing as the view switches to another camera. This one pans across the teenagers on the playset, giving the audience closeups of their almost giddy faces. A boy in an orange shirt and sweater hangs by his hands from the playset's swing beam. Another boy in a yellow shirt and multicolored striped suspenders— who sports a *serious* five o'clock shadow—rocks forward and backward on a horse glider swing. A girl in a red sweater and a blue shirt with colorful polka dots sits on a swing, holding onto the chains, twisting back and forth and laughing as she talks to a boy in a blue-striped shirt next to her. A second girl sits on an elevated platform of the playset, facing the other kids, her legs dangling over the side. She has short hair and wears a blue top covered with strange, colorful shapes, polka-dot socks, and sneakers. She swings her legs back and forth, smiling big, as if she's having the time of her life.

The camera then pans to a third girl. She's sitting on the platform next to the leg swinger, but she's facing forward, legs over the side of the platform, but she's not swinging them. They're perfectly still. Her head—which has colorful berets and two impressive Pippi Longstocking pigtails— is slumped forward, chin to chest. She's asleep. She wears a white shirt with flowers on it beneath blue jean overalls, along with shorts, knee-high orange socks with colorful dots on them, and blue sneakers. The camera lingers on her for a moment, and then her head comes up, eyes wide, a dazed, disoriented expression on her fake-freckle-dotted face.

Sienna is awake.

She sat for a moment, unsure where she was or what was happening. She heard Banjo Blue singing, only now her voice was louder, clearer, stronger. Sienna listened for several seconds, trying to fight off the panic she felt welling inside her.

> *Why not visit after school*
> *and have yourselves a bite?*
> *An appetizing appetizer*
> *certain to delight.*
>
> *We haven't done it right*
> *Unless it makes your teeth decay*

'Cause food's a little funny
at the Clown Café.

Sienna looked down at herself and saw she was dressed in strange clothes. She touched her fingers to her overalls, reached up, gently touched her new pigtails, and found them stiff as wires. There was something familiar about the shapes on her socks, but she couldn't think of what it was. The panic she'd tried to hold off hit her full force then, and she breathed faster, and her heart raced.

Banjo Blue continued singing, and this time the kids on the playset joined in:

Drop on by the Clown Café!
Drop on by the Clown Café!

The grub is downright gruesome
But your appetite so big

'Cause food's a little funny…
Food's a little funny…
Food's a little funny
at the Clown Café.

The song ended, and the other kids on the playset shouted with over-the-top enthusiasm. It might've been humorous if it hadn't been so fucking *weird*. What the hell was going on here?

She realized then that some of the kids had the same strange shapes on their clothes as she did on her socks.

And the blue shape painted around Banjo Blue's eye—
that was another one! But where—

Your brother never closes these goddamn boxes…

Jonathan's cereal! The box of Wacky Jacks that fell
out of the cupboard and onto the floor, spilling pieces
everywhere. The shapes on her socks, the kids' clothes,
around Banjo Blue's eyes were all like those bits of cereal.
What did that mean?

A woman—an older one, Sienna thought—shouted
then, her words accompanied by the ringing of a bell.

"Will you help this man? You, over there! Yeah! Feed
this man!"

Sienna turned toward the voice and saw it belonged
to a woman in a nun's habit. She was ringing a handbell
and pointing at a sad-faced man sitting on a wooden
crate next to her. He had long gray hair, a thick gray
mustache, and wore a dark-blue jacket, blue jeans, and
sneakers that were falling apart. He held a cardboard sign
with *HELP ME* written in black magic marker.

The nun saw Sienna watching and spoke directly to
her. "How about you? He's hungry. Will you feed this
man? He's not invisible! Feed him!"

Everyone else—the kids, the people in line at the
food truck, Banjo Blue—laughed uproariously, as if the
nun had just told the funniest joke in the entire history
of humor. There was a mean edge to their laughter that
turned Sienna's stomach.

She heard the *oooooo* of microphone feedback then,
and she turned toward the sound. A smaller set branched
off the main one, and it held a 1970s-style kitchen with
truly hideous orange walls. A pair of blurry-faced camera

129

operators faced a young boy in a striped long-sleeved pullover who sat at a dining table, a large orange bowl full of cereal in front of him.

The cereal box sat on the table, angled just right so the audience could get a good view of the front. An announcer's voice came from somewhere then, its tone high-pitched, silly, but—like so much in this strange place—laced with an undercurrent of menace.

"New Art Crispies from Sugar Plum! Fun little surprises in every bite!"

The box's design was similar to Wacky Jacks', but a cartoon Art the Clown held a pitcher and was pouring blood into a bowl of cereal. *Art Crispies* was spelled out in large orange letters in a creepy font, below it in smaller letters: *Bloody Rice Cereal with Marshmallows*. There were cartoon drawings of the various marshmallow shapes—one that looked like an upside-down naked woman that had been cut in two, a hacksaw, a bicycle horn.

The cereal pieces in the bowl were red—she assumed this was the Bloody Rice—and the marshmallows were mixed in. There were other objects, too, but she was too far away to make out what they were. Was there a maze on the back of the box like on Jonathan's Wacky Jacks? And was Art the Clown heading for its entrance instead of Wacky, hoping to find his way to the circus tent? She wouldn't have been surprised.

The announcer spoke again. *"Glass, insects, and razor blades! There's no telling what you may find! Special prize included in every box!"*

The announcer cackled like a madman.

Sienna knew what the other shapes in the cereal were now, and she wished she didn't.

Please don't eat any, Sienna thought. *Don't do it!*

But instead of reaching for the spoon protruding from his bowl, the boy picked up the box and stuck his hand inside. Sienna winced, imagining his flesh being shredded by glass fragments and razor blades.

He showed no signs of distress, though. "Wow! Wonder what I got!"

Before the boy could withdraw his hand from the box, Banjo Blue spoke. "Speaking of surprises, kids—we have a *very* special guest with us today. Now, for a guy who doesn't speak, he sure makes a *lot* of noise. All the way from Miles County, please welcome *Art the Clown!*"

Banjo Blue gestured theatrically to the food van. Its window slid open, and a grinning Art leaned out and gave the audience a broad wave. Everyone—the kids, the people waiting in line, even the camera operators— cheered and clapped loudly. Everyone except the nun and the sad man, that is.

And Sienna.

Her eyes widened when she saw the clown—the *Miles County* Clown—and she began trembling.

No, she thought. *Please, no...*

Carnival music—light and cheery—began playing as Art continued waving at the audience, waggling his hands, making funny faces, blowing kisses... But then he looked straight at Sienna, gaze filled with burning malice, his features twisted into a leering mask of hate. He raised a hand and gave her a quick wiggle of the fingers as a mocking greeting. Sienna couldn't move, couldn't even turn her head and look away. She started breathing in short, fast gasps. She feared she might hyperventilate, but she couldn't stop herself.

Art withdrew into the van, and a moment later he came out from around the back riding a tricycle. He waved with one hand while he worked the bike's bell with the other. The audience shouted and clapped as if Art had just pulled off a dazzling acrobatic trick. Banjo Blue didn't clap, but she smiled happily, as if amused by Art's antics. Art rode around the set waving at everyone, and when he passed in front of the playset, the kids all held out their hands, and Art tapped them with his own as he went by. This drove the kids absolutely batshit with excitement, as if they'd just been touched by God.

Art stopped the tricycle on what Sienna thought of as the main stage. He got off, bowed to the audience, then stepped over to a larger, overstuffed trash bag, and hefted it onto his shoulder. Sienna was able to move her head a little now, and she tracked Art with her eyes as he sauntered toward the playset, head thrust forward in way that made Sienna think of a predator approaching its prey. The kids were screaming with delight now, and when Art reached them, he plunked the trash bag onto the floor, untied and opened it. He reached inside, and with a flourish brought out a large rainbow swirl lollipop. He approached the boy hanging from the playset's swing beam and held up the lollipop for his inspection. He eyed the boy menacingly and then rammed the lollipop into his mouth.

Sienna gasped, fearing the clown had thrust the sweet treat down the boy's throat to choke him. But when Art pulled back his hand, she saw the boy held the lollipop between his teeth, and he appeared unharmed and happy to have received his gift.

Art moved on to the boy on the horse glider. This time the clown pulled a caramel apple covered with nuts from his trash bag. He held it out to the boy, head thrust forward, eyes blazing, teeth bared.

The boy went wild. "Whoo! Whoo! Yeah!"

The boy grabbed the caramel apple from Art, and the clown took a step back.

Sienna realized something terrible then—Art would eventually reach *her*. What kind of "present" would he try to give her?

The people in line, as well as Banjo Blue, watched with delight as Art delivered his presents, laughing and cheering. The camera operators were watching too, but it was impossible to tell what they thought of Art's performance since their faces were only blurry smears.

Art gave the girl on the swing a small box of popcorn, and she attacked it like a wild, starving animal. He gave the boy in the blue-striped shirt a caramel apple—this one without nuts—and to the girl sitting on the elevated platform with Sienna, he gave some cotton candy.

Then it was Sienna's turn.

While she'd regained some movement, she was unable to rise from the platform and escape. She could only sit and watch as Art returned to his trash bag and started rooting around in it once more.

This can't be real... It has to be a dream!

And if this *was* a dream, that meant she could try to control it.

She closed her eyes and concentrated on what she wanted the dream setting to look like. A real playset in a park, with real grass, real sky, and a real sun shining down. Kids—normal ones—playing and enjoying themselves, parents or caregivers close by, watching them have fun. No strange airplane passengers lined up at a sinister food trailer. No Banjo Blue playing a tune and smiling happily, no matter what happened around her. And most of all, no Art the fucking Clown.

She opened her eyes.

Art waltzed up to her, carrying something wrapped in newspaper, an object that was round on the sides, flat on the top and bottom. He offered the package to her, eyes locked on hers, teeth bared in a silent snarl.

Sienna shook her head rapidly back and forth.

Art scowled and thrust the package at her, and when she recoiled, he thrust it at her again, violently this time.

The audience laughed.

She didn't want to touch anything that had been in Art's hands, but she took the package. Art backed away, arms stretched toward her, applauding, as if she was a reluctant audience participant and he was showing his appreciation for her deciding to go along with the act. Art encouraged the audience to support her, and they all applauded as well.

Sienna felt sick. The newspaper wrapping was greasy, and a foul, rotten smell came from whatever was inside the package. She wanted to hurl it away from her, but she feared how Art might react if she did. She wasn't obsessed with the Miles County Clown like Jonathan, but she'd read about the murders Art had committed, and kids at school had talked about the killings for weeks after they'd occurred. She knew what he'd done and what he was capable of doing. Dream or no dream, she did not want to provoke Art into attacking her. The last thing she wanted was to end up like those two college girls he'd killed — or worse. So, as disgusting as the package was, she began to open it, slowly peeling away the greasy paper.

Art was beside himself with delight. He returned to his garbage bag, thrust his hands inside, and began sifting through its contents, searching for something. As he did, he kept sneaking glances at Sienna, as if he couldn't wait to see her reaction to his gift.

She let the strips of greasy newspaper fall to the floor as she unwrapped the package. When she finished, she saw it was a pink hat box. She didn't want to remove the lid, feared what she'd find inside, but since she hadn't been able to change this dream, the only way out of it was to go through it.

She removed the lid.

CHAPTER TWELVE

Inside, a diseased, necrotic heart lay on a bed of blood-red Art Crispies. The mottled organ was surrounded by writhing worms, and it throbbed as if it was beating—*lub-dub, lub-dub, lub-dub*—but there was no blood for it to circulate. The heart smelled *foul*, like raw meat that had been left out to rot in the summer sun and then marinated in a mixture of vomit and feces. Sienna's gorge rose, and she was thankful she hadn't eaten a snack before going to bed, otherwise she'd be puking it up right now.

A thick, black liquid began rising from the bottom of the box, covering the heart and the worms that wriggled around it. As bad as the heart smelled, the liquid was worse.

A horrible thought occurred to her. The other teens on the playset had been given treats to eat. Did that mean Art wanted her to *eat* the heart? It *was* lying on a layer of cereal… well, *kind of* cereal. Was that black muck supposed to take the place of milk? Her nausea grew, and she started dry-heaving.

Everyone in the studio laughed at her discomfort.

No! I might not be able to escape this place through lucid dreaming, but I can control myself.

She closed her eyes, concentrated, pictured herself sitting there, her stomach feeling fine. When she opened her eyes again, her nausea wasn't gone completely, but it had subsided to a point where it was tolerable. Score a small victory for her.

Art was still digging in his bag, searching more frantically now, as if frustrated that he couldn't locate what he was looking for. With all the bizarre things happening, Sienna had momentarily forgotten about the nun and the sad man, but the woman called out again, once more ringing her handbell to underscore her words.

"Stop everything you're doing! I see you feeding your faces. Feed *him*!" She gestured toward the sad man. "He's *so* hungry! Feed this man! Feed this man! *Feed this man!*"

The kids on the playset were still gorging themselves on the treats Art had given them, eating savagely, mindless creatures who lived only to fill their bellies.

Sienna had turned toward the nun when she started speaking, but the black sludge in the box had continued rising, and now some of it had reached her hand. It was cold and slimy, and it was the most disgusting thing she had ever touched. She pulled her hand away from the box, but a portion of the gunk adhered to her skin, and she shook her hand to dislodge it. She succeeded, and the black slime dropped back into the box with a disgusting *splat*. She might've gotten rid of the stuff, but she still felt unclean, as if the muck had infected her somehow. She grimaced as she vigorously rubbed her hands together, trying to get the horrid residue off her skin.

The heart box sat on her lap. Vibrations came from it, and when she looked down, she saw the black substance was bubbling, as if it was boiling, and the heart slowly sank beneath its roiling surface.

"Feed this man!" the nun shouted once more. The sad man still didn't react, just stared off into the distance.

Art stopped searching in his bag and an expression of maniacal triumph came over his face. He'd finally found what he'd been looking for. He withdrew his arms from the bag to reveal he held an old-fashioned submachine gun. It was the same sort of gun the nun in the cartoon Sienna had been watching before falling asleep had used to shred the zombie priests into rotting hamburger.

My god…

All expression left Art's face then, leaving his distorted features slack and emotionless. A great dark emptiness came into his eyes, and Sienna thought she had never seen anything so terrifying in her life. Moving with swift, precise motions, as if he were a machine rather than a man, Art raised the submachine gun, aimed it at the men and women standing in line at the food van, and began firing.

Bullets slammed into bodies, tearing out chunks of flesh, breaking bones, drilling through internal organs, shredding genitals, reducing faces to anonymous red pulp. Blood sprayed the air, so much of it that it seemed the airline passengers were caught in a crimson rainstorm. Their bodies shuddered and jerked as bullets continued to slam into them, making them look like rag dolls being shaken by an invisible force.

Art's face remained impassive as he continued blasting his victims. For her part, Banjo Blue didn't appear fazed in the slightest by the carnage. She merely watched the bloody action, her blue-lipped plastic smile never wavering.

Everyone started screaming at once, including Sienna. The people in line for the Clown Café's questionable culinary offerings screamed too, but not for long. They fell silent as they dropped to the blood-slick floor like marionettes whose strings had been severed, many of them so badly chewed up by gunfire that they looked less like humans and more like cuts of raw, bloody meat purchased at a butcher's shop and stuffed into clothes. Most had soiled themselves as they died, and the air was rank with the stink of piss and shit.

When the last airline passenger went down, Art swiveled toward the teens on the playset, squeezed the submachine gun's trigger, and let the bullets fly. The kids' bodies spasmed as rounds of ammunition slammed into them. Blood spurted from freshly created wounds, gushed from mouths like red fountains.

The boy on the horse glider died first, slumping forward, blood streaming from his violated body onto the floor, covering his caramel apple which had slipped from his hand. Next, the boy that had been hanging from the set's swing beam fell, his dead hands no longer able to maintain a grip. His swirly lollipop slipped out of his mouth before he hit the floor. The girl with the popcorn died, blood-stippled kernels leaping into the air as she fell backward off her swing. Bullets stitched a line across the chest of the boy in the blue-striped shirt, taking him down, and a round struck the head of the cotton-candy girl, exploding her skull and splattering Sienna with blood, brain, and bone.

Sienna let out a high-pitched shriek when a bullet struck the outer thigh of her left leg and bore into the muscle beneath. The impact made her jerk, dislodging the heart box from her lap. It hit the floor, upended, and the heart, worms, and black muck spilled out. Art might have finished her off then and there, but the machine gun ran out of ammo.

As if coming out of a daze, he looked down at the weapon, shook it once, then dropped it to the floor. He turned and headed toward the trash can that was filled with metal scrap. Sienna clapped her hand to her wound and lay back on the playset's platform. The corpse of the girl with the cotton candy still sat next to Sienna, arms extended between a pair of wooden slats, half of her head missing. Sienna barely noticed her. She'd never experienced anything like the pain of her bullet wound, and she could barely think, it hurt so bad. She feared she might pass out, but she couldn't let that happen. Once she was unconscious, Art could do whatever he wanted to her, and she would be unable to stop him.

Get moving, she told herself. *Get out of here while he's distracted!*

She rolled onto her side. Her leg blazed with agony, and she bit her lip to keep from screaming. There were wooden steps at the rear of the raised platform, and if she could reach them... She gritted her teeth and began crawling, using her left hand to pull herself forward, while keeping her right hand on the bullet wound to minimize blood loss.

As Art neared the trash can, Banjo Blue played the Clown Café song, slower than before, and maybe a little sadder. She didn't sing this time, though. She was as silent as Art himself. Art ignored her as he reached into the trash can and removed an old-fashioned blowtorch resting on top of the metal scrap. A delighted expression came over his face as he held up the blowtorch and examined it. Then a cold, mean light came into his eyes, and he turned and stepped toward Banjo Blue.

She was still playing the Clown Café song, smiling and swaying back and forth. She made no effort to escape, and she seemed entirely unafraid as Art raised the blowtorch and blasted her with a gout of flame. The woman's clothes caught fire at once, and the flames spread quickly—far faster than they would have in the real world—until she was engulfed in fire. She didn't scream, didn't fall to the ground and flail about in a frantic attempt to smother the flames. She continued playing her instrument, swaying back and forth. Art lowered the blowtorch and swayed along with her, as if the two of them were performing a grotesque routine.

Sienna reached the ladder. Injured as she was, she knew she couldn't climb down, so she rolled over onto her back, shoved herself forward with her good leg, and fell backward. The steps were at an angle, so she didn't fall straight to the floor, but her spine felt every impact as she *thump-thump-thumped* down. When she reached the floor, she lay there for a moment, the fresh pain in her back joining with the agony in her leg. All she wanted to do was lie there until the pain went away, no matter how long that took, but she knew she couldn't do that. She raised her head and saw Art dancing with the blazing form of Banjo Blue, and the sight of the woman engulfed in flame sent a surge of terror through her.

Fire… Dad…

She couldn't bring herself to face these thoughts—not here, not now—so she looked away from the tableau of insanity that was the dancing clown and the burning woman. Bodies lay strewn all over the studio, blood everywhere. She didn't see any of the camera operators, though. Had they managed to escape before Art could mow them down with the machine gun? She looked for the nun and the sad man, but she didn't see them either. She hoped they'd gotten away and were somewhere safe—if anywhere was safe in this hellish place.

Back in the real world, Sienna tossed and turned in her bed, desperately trying to pull herself free from the nightmare of the Clown Café, but it had too strong a hold on her, and all she could do was let it play out to whatever end it had in store for her.

Not everyone in the Clown Café had died from their bullet wounds. Some moaned in pain or wept uncontrollably. Others, like Sienna, were crawling slowly across the floor, fighting for every inch, hoping to escape the maniac who had mutilated them. Art saw them. He approached the

142

survivors one at a time and blasted them with streams of flame from the blowtorch. They shrieked in pain as they burned, writhing in agony, or rising to their feet in an attempt to run. They didn't get far before their legs buckled beneath them and they fell to the floor, where they lay still and continued to burn like small bonfires.

Art laughed uproariously—without sound, of course—and slapped his knee with his free hand. He then began setting fire to those who were already dead, his mad eyes glowing orange as they reflected the light from the flames.

Sienna rolled onto her stomach and began crawling, leaving a trail of blood behind her as she went. She had no destination in mind until she realized she was heading in the direction of the kitchen set where the Art Crispies commercial had been shot. She remembered the announcer's words: "Special prize included in every box!"

She didn't need a goddamn prize! She needed something she could use to defend herself. She needed a weapon! But maybe she could find one—if she used lucid dreaming. She crawled faster, ignoring the pain in her wounded leg and injured back.

She reached the set and pulled herself up until her elbows were on the table. She saw the boy who'd been so excited to search for his own prize sitting in his chair. His hand was covered with cuts, and shards of glass and a pair of razor blades were embedded in his face. He evidently had tried to eat some of the cereal in his bowl. Lines of blood ran from his shredded lips, and his mouth was partially open, and Sienna could see glass and metal sticking out of his tongue. Several insects scuttled around inside, feeding on the blood oozing from his wounds. The boy's eyes stared unblinkingly forward, and she knew he was dead. There was nothing she could do for him now. She had to think of herself.

She grabbed the box of Art Crispies and fell back into a sitting position on the floor. She turned so she could face forward and keep an eye on what Art was doing. He was busy torching the wooden playset, along with the bodies of the boys and girls that he'd given treats to.

Sienna jammed her right hand into the box and cried out. She yanked it free and saw that there were deep cuts on her fingers and palm. Broken glass jutted from her skin, and a razor blade was stuck in the middle of her hand. Maggots and roaches crawled over her bleeding flesh, and Sienna's revulsion upon seeing them was almost as great as her pain.

Art heard her cry when she stuck her hand into the cereal box, and he turned to look at her. It was almost as if he'd been so caught up in the destruction he was creating that for a moment he'd forgotten all about her. That moment was over now. He started walking toward her, moving slowly, taking his time. There was no need to hurry. It was just her and him now.

And the blowtorch.

Sienna saw him coming, and she knew she had only seconds left. She took several deep breaths, summoned what strength remained to her, and thrust her hand back into the box. She cried out again as fresh pain lanced through her hand, but she told herself that wasn't important now. She needed to be calm, to concentrate.

Give me what I need, she thought.

Art continued his slow advance, eyes gleaming with wicked anticipation. Sienna moved her hand through the cereal, enduring more pain, searching, searching... and then her fingers found something solid. Yes!

Art stopped directly in front of her, turned his head to the side, and regarded her for a moment. She met his gaze with newfound fierceness. Whatever happened next, she would not give in. She'd fight this monster to the bitter end. She wrapped her hand around the object she'd found and withdrew it from the box. There was a metallic *shhhing* and she held aloft the short sword her father had given her.

Snarling silently, Art thrust the blowtorch at her and loosed a jet of flame.

Sienna brought the sword in front of her, got a two-handed grip on it, and shouted a war cry as the fire struck the blade and was turned away. She caught a glimpse of Art's eyes widening in surprise—

CHAPTER THIRTEEN

—and then she woke.

No longer was she wearing her strange Clown Café clothes. She had on an orange tank top and black shorts, and instead of Pippi Longstocking pigtails, her hair was loose and straight.

She sat up abruptly and saw that the wings she had worked so hard to complete were ablaze. Adrenaline shot through her, and she jumped out of bed, grabbed a spare blanket off her footlocker, and started hitting the wings with it, hoping to extinguish the flames. But it was no use. The fire had spread to engulf both wings, the flames rising so high they licked the ceiling. She caught a glimpse of her sword sitting on its display stand. It was wreathed in fire, the metal blackening as it burned. That didn't make sense. Metal melted, but it didn't *burn*, did it? Not like this.

She heard the hall smoke alarm go off, and—realizing that there was nothing she could do—she ran out of her room.

*

Jonathan came out of his room, glasses off, dressed in a light-blue T-shirt and plaid pajama pants, still half asleep.

"I had a bad dream," he mumbled. "What's going on?"

Sienna tried to answer, but she started coughing. Gray tendrils of smoke were already slithering across the hallway's ceiling, growing thicker and more numerous by the second.

Mom flew out of her room at the end of the hall, wearing a blue robe over light-blue pajamas, wide awake and completely focused.

"Get downstairs!" she ordered.

Sienna didn't argue. She put her arm around her brother's shoulders and quickly ushered him toward the stairs. Mom ran inside her room, and Sienna shouted, "Mom, what are you doing? Come on!"

Sienna heard Mom shout, "Jesus Christ!"

Mom ran out of Sienna's room, flung open the hall closet, and yanked out a fire extinguisher. She kept one on every floor of the house. Sienna had viewed that as a typical example of her rigid overprotectiveness, but now she was grateful.

An instant later, Sienna heard the *shoosh* of fire extinguisher foam being sprayed.

Sienna kept her arm around Jonathan's shoulders as they headed down the stairs. She felt an echo of pain in her left leg as they descended, but she told herself it was only a faint memory of something that had never happened.

*

"Really, Sienna? You left candles burning on your dresser *all night*? What are you, fucking *stupid*?"

Sienna sat at the dining table, her clothes and hair reeking of smoke. Her head was lowered while Mom paced in front of her, waving her hands dramatically as she spoke. Jonathan was up in his room.

"I didn't do anything. They weren't lit," Sienna said.

"No? Then explain to me how your goddamn *room* caught fire?"

"I have no idea."

"You have no idea," Mom said. "The fire miraculously combusted out of thin *air*?"

Sienna raised her head, a defiant look on her face.

"I guess so."

"*Sienna…*" Mom broke off when she saw Jonathan—glasses on now—standing at the foot of the stairs. "Get back to bed. You have school in the morning."

"You mean I still have to go?" Jonathan asked.

"*What'd I say?*" she shouted.

Jonathan turned and hauled ass up the stairs.

Sienna put her right elbow on the table and rested her head on her hand. She was upset that her wings had been destroyed, furious that Mom wouldn't believe her, and still confused and frightened by her dream visit to the Clown Café. But most of all, she was so very, very tired.

Mom turned back around to face her. "You're gonna kill us one day, you know that? Between your chemicals and your heat guns and staying up to four o'clock in the *fucking* morning, doing god only knows what!"

Sienna wanted to scream at her mother, but she restrained herself. "Oh my *god*, for the hundredth time,

I was *not* using chemicals and I did *not* leave burning candles on my dresser. Why can't you just believe me?"

"*Because!*" Mom paused, and when she spoke again, her tone was softer. "Stay in my room tonight, and I'll sleep on the couch."

"I don't mind sleeping on the couch."

Sienna didn't want to put her mother out. The fire had happened in *her* room, not Mom's. Besides, she didn't like the idea of sleeping upstairs, so close to where that nightmare—the worst she'd ever had—had happened. But Mom was done arguing.

"Go to bed."

Mom left the room, and Sienna put her head in both hands and sat there, numb and exhausted.

Sienna did as her mother wanted and went upstairs to sleep in her room. But once she reached the second floor, she took a detour. She walked to her room, opened the door slowly and quietly so she wouldn't wake Jonathan— or alert Mom downstairs—then quickly stepped inside and closed the door just as silently behind her. The room smelled like someone had built a bonfire in it, and she supposed, in a sense, someone had. She turned on the light, and with a heavy heart, she walked over to her side worktable to assess the damage.

The wings she had worked on so long—three whole months!—were a charred ruin. She reached up, took hold of one blackened feather, and snapped off a piece. It broke easily and crumbled in her hand like a piece of charcoal. She brushed her fingers across her hand, and the black bits fell to her worktable. It had been damaged in the fire as well, candles melted, bottles of paint warped by the intense heat, surfaces covered by soot. The wall behind the wings was scorched black, as was the ceiling directly above where the flames had been. The two other worktables hadn't been harmed at all, nor had the rest of her costume. All its pieces were intact, and she was thankful for this.

How *had* the fire started? She'd told Mom that she'd blown out all the candles before bed, but what if one had been left smoldering, and a flame eventually grew to life, small at first, but soon large enough to catch her wings on fire? It didn't seem likely, but she didn't see any other explanation—unless she'd started setting fires in her sleep. Could her nightmare have had something to do with it? She'd fended off the flame from Art's blowtorch with the dream version of the sword. Had that fire somehow crossed over into the real world, burning both her wings and the actual sword? It seemed ridiculous, but the fire *had* happened, and *something* had caused it.

She had created her costume—especially the wings—to honor her father and bring one of his visions to life. A vision he'd had of *her*, as a strong, confident warrior angel. That was a big part of why the loss of the wings hurt so much. Plus, the wings had symbolized rebirth to her, a physical expression of her finally coming to terms with her father's death and getting on with the rest of her life. Instead of being angel's wings, though, they'd become the wings of a phoenix, burned and useless.

She heard a voice whisper in her mind then. It

might've been hers, probably was. But it might've been someone else's.

Remember, the phoenix always rises from the ashes...

She realized something then. The short sword, the last gift her father had given her, was gone. She'd remembered seeing it covered in flames when she woke, but she'd been so concerned with trying to save the wings that she'd forgotten about it. The place on the table where the sword had been displayed was covered with ash—which was why thinking of the phoenix had reminded her about the sword—but there was no sign of the blade itself. She didn't see how this was possible. However hot the fire that destroyed her wings had been, it was nowhere near hot enough to melt metal. And Mom put the flames out within seconds of the smoke alarm going off. Even if the fire *had* been hot enough, there hadn't been enough time for it to melt the sword. Then again, it hadn't been a normal fire, had it?

She started to turn away from the table, ready to go to Mom's room and try to sleep, although she didn't see what the point was when she had to be up for school in just a couple hours. But before she could take a step, a glint of light caught her eye—a glint that came from within the ashes on her worktable.

Frowning, she stretched her hand toward the table and gently pushed her fingertips into the ash. She felt something solid, and excitement quickened her pulse. She wrapped her hand around the object and lifted the short sword off the table. It was still covered in ash, but when she turned the blade to the side, it all slid off, revealing smooth, undamaged metal beneath. She held the sword up to her face and turned it so she could see the flat of the blade. She looked for any marks on the metal, but there were none she could detect. If anything, the metal looked shinier than before, and the blade felt—not heavier, exactly, but more... substantial. As if before it had been a pretty object to look at, but now it was so much more.

She realized she could see the reflection of her eyes in the metal, and it was almost as if the sword was looking at her at the same time as she was looking at it. More than that. It was like she was *inside* the sword, like they were one and the same. She held the sword in her right hand while she ran the fingers of her left across the flat of the blade, marveling at how smooth the metal was. It felt like running her fingers across the surface of a calm, still lake.

The sword seemed to glimmer then, warm light traveling along the path her fingers had taken, moving rapidly from the base of the blade to the tip. Then it was gone, but the sword seemed shinier now, as if it had been lovingly polished. Sienna smiled. *Not polished*, she thought.

Reborn.

Morning came way too fast. Sienna took an extra-long shower, shampooing three times to get the smell of smoke out of her hair. When she was done, her hair smelled clean. Mostly.

She dressed in gray pants and one of the few sweaters of hers that hadn't been smoke damaged—white with a black-stripe pattern that covered the chest and both arms. It was a little big on her, but she thought it looked okay. She wandered into the kitchen like a zombie and headed straight for the coffeemaker. Jonathan was eating cereal at the small kitchen table. He didn't look up as Sienna entered. Mom was still in her robe and pajamas, kneeling and sorting through a small pile of Sienna's clothes on the floor. She examined each item as she picked it up and slid it into a plastic bag on the floor next to her.

Sienna poured herself a large mug of coffee. Normally, she added cream and sugar, but today she wanted it black. She hoped the harsh, bitter taste would help wake her the rest of the way up.

"I kept whatever you had in the bottom drawer," Mom said. "Everything else is ruined."

Mom sounded as wrung-out as Sienna felt.

Sienna nodded without looking at her. She stepped away from the counter and held her mug with both hands, letting its warmth soothe her.

Mom stood, went to the cupboard to get her own mug, and poured some coffee for herself.

"And make sure you park in the garage when you get home," Mom said. "Those animals next door are always throwing eggs and shaving cream. I don't need them scratching the car."

The Henderson brothers were a perpetual pain in Mom's ass. Fraternal twins, and troublemakers since the moment they slid out of the womb, one after the other. They were the same age as Jonathan, and the three had played together when they were younger. But the Hendersons were always pulling Jonathan into their schemes, and finally Mom had put her foot down and told him he was never to associate with *those animals* again. Mom would go apeshit if she knew Jonathan still hung around with them at school.

Sienna thought about the sword then, the way that, just for an instant, it seemed to glow with some kind of internal power. "You know the sword Daddy got me?"

"What about it?"

"It was on top of my dresser last night."

Mom finished pouring her coffee and looked over her shoulder at Sienna. "Well, maybe it can be restored." She picked up her mug then turned to face Sienna. "Is it bad?"

"It's fine. There's not a mark on it." Sienna took a sip of her coffee and tried not to make a face.

"Well, that's good. Can't say the same for your clothes. Jonathan, hurry up. You got five minutes."

Jonathan nodded but kept on eating.

Sienna sat at the table opposite her brother, lost in thought. She sat like that for a moment, and then her eyes widened. Jonathan was eating cereal—Wacky Jacks, to be specific. The cartoon clown on the box was very different from Art. Happy and cheerful, with sunbeams radiating outward from him. But after last night, the sight chilled her. An image flashed through her mind then—the boy in the Art Crispies commercial, sitting at his breakfast table, eyes unblinking, blood running from his mouth and onto his chin.

She blinked, found herself staring at Wacky the Clown, and heard the commercial announcer from last night's dream laughing like a lunatic.

CHAPTER FOURTEEN

Art slammed the heavy table leg down on his workbench. He'd gotten it from one of the displays in his home, a dining room scene where a group of clawed and sharp-toothed monsters were seated at the table, knives and forks in hand, drooling as they anticipated devouring the hog-tied businessman squirming on a silver platter. It was one of his favorites. Sometimes he'd visit it and stare at it for hours. But this last time he went, it occurred to him what a fine club one of those dining table legs would make, and he took one.

Of course, he planned to add his own unique touches to it before it made its debut tonight.

His workbench sat up against a fake brick wall and was covered with old, rusty tools: hammers, hacksaws, screwdrivers, chisels, pliers... There were also materials he used to build with: nails, screws, eating utensils, butcher knives, chains, and more. He thought he'd go with the utensils this time (maybe with a few nails tossed in for good measure). It was a *dining* table leg, right? He sat on a stool, picked up a hammer and chisel, and started to carve holes into the thick blocky top of the leg, so he'd have places to insert the forks and knives.

There was no organizational pattern to his workbench, tools and materials strewn about, lying wherever he dropped them. Art was a creature of chaos. Organization was not only anathema to him; it was a waste of time. Do what you want, move on, and forget about whatever mess you leave behind. That was his motto.

The injuries he'd suffered the night he'd died—a year ago now—had long since healed. He had two eyes and could see perfectly well with each of them, and the back of his skull had mended. Hard to say if the brain inside had been repaired, but really, what did anybody need with a brain anyway? They usually just got in the way.

The Little Pale Girl sat cross-legged on the floor behind him. She was with him most of the time these days, although he couldn't remember exactly when she'd arrived at his home. Sometime after he'd first met her at the laundromat, he knew that, but precisely when? Not a clue. Not that it mattered. He appreciated her company.

As Art began pounding metal pieces into the table leg, the Little Pale Girl reached for a small, old-fashioned TV sitting on the floor nearby and slid it in front of her. The screen was dark, so she adjusted the set's antenna, but nothing happened. She lightly tapped the top of the TV with her fingers and the set came to life.

It wasn't plugged in to a power source.

Buzzing static at first, but the picture soon became clear, the sound crisp. Talk-show host Monica Brown appeared—green blouse, brunette hair, square no-nonsense jaw. She was looking straight at the camera, her expression serious.

The Little Pale Girl leaned forward, all her attention focused on the screen.

"Welcome back to the program. If you're just tuning in, I'm sitting here live with the sole survivor of the Miles County Massacre, which occurred exactly one year ago today."

Art lit a blowtorch and used the flame to harden the utensils and nails. Baptizing them with fire, you might say.

"I've worked on the show for many years, and I've never sat across from someone who has a story to tell quite like yours. Thank you again for taking the time to sit down and speak with me."

The static returned, and when the camera switched to the guest's face, her features were hidden by white phosphor dots. Her voice—rough, dry, strained—came through the TV's speaker just fine, though.

"It's my pleasure."

"Now, when we left off," Monica said, "we were talking about the moment you woke up from the coma."

Art had been examining his handiwork, but when he realized what he was hearing, he looked over his shoulder and laughed silently.

"Do you remember your initial reaction when you first saw your face?" Monica asked.

"Yes."

"Would you like to share that with us?"

This time when the camera switched to the guest, the image was crystal clear. She had shoulder-length black hair, but her face was a mass of scar tissue. In place of a nose, she had two off-center vertical slits. Her left eye was gone, the socket a wide recessed area covered with

157

more scar tissue, and her right eye looked more like a fish's eye than a human's. She had no lips to speak of, and her front teeth stuck out prominently. It was Victoria Heyes.

"I wished I was dead."

Art laughed harder—if not any louder—and he turned on his stool to watch the interview.

"Do you still feel that way?" Monica asked.

"People are frightened by the way I look, especially children. And it's really difficult for me to deal with that, so isolation is ideal."

Art rose from his stool, walked past the mural with the children and the rainbow, and stood by the Little Pale Girl, so they could watch together.

"Now, what about your attacker—the man only identified as Art the Clown? There's a lot of controversy surrounding his supposed death. The authorities issued a statement from the County Coroner's Office the morning after the attack."

Art was getting angry now. At first, he'd found Victoria's appearance amusing, but now he realized she represented a failure on his part. He'd meant to kill her, and she *still lived*. Sacrilege! Blasphemy! Not to mention *annoying as hell!*

"He's dead," Victoria said. "I saw it happen."

Furious, Art kicked the screen in. There was a *pop* and a flash of electricity, then the TV went dead.

The Little Pale Girl looked up at him with irritation, as if to say, *Hey, I was watching that!*

*

Jonathan—wearing his backpack and dressed in a black-and-gray jacket, a brown-and-gray shirt, jeans, and sneakers—walked onto the middle-school playground. It was chilly out, and there were leaves all over the ground. It was the kind of morning that reminded you autumn wouldn't last much longer. The thought made him sad. Autumn was his favorite time of the year, and Halloween his very favorite holiday. At least, it had been before the Miles County Massacre. And, of course, before Dad…

He supposed he was just out of sorts because of what happened last night. First, he'd had that messed-up dream, then Sienna's wings had caught fire. That had been scary as hell, and it was hard to get back to sleep after all the excitement—not to mention that his room stank of smoke. He tossed and turned, kept drifting in and out of sleep, and he felt as if he hadn't slept at all.

Despite what Mom thought, he found it difficult to believe Sienna had started the fire. She was always so careful with all her stuff—her candles, sure, but also her paints and cleaners. The surfaces of her worktables might be a little messy, but she never spilled anything on her floor, and he'd *never* known her to forget to extinguish her candles. Both of them had a thing about fire after Dad's death. He stayed as far away from it as possible, while Sienna was as cautious as a trained firefighter.

But he couldn't see how else the fire had started—unless it was a case of spontaneous combustion. He'd read on the Internet that there were hundreds of documented cases of spontaneous *human* combustion. Surely it would be a lot easier for a candle to combust on its own than a person. He supposed there was no way they could ever prove it, though.

There were lots of kids on the playground this morning, gathered in small groups, hanging out and talking before the first bell rang. He envied them. He didn't really have friends, not the kind you hung out with regularly. He was introverted and quiet, and yes— he could admit it—weird. He didn't make connections with others easily.

He noticed four girls talking, and one of them was someone he would very much like to make a connection with—Stephanie Nash. They shared a couple of the same classes, and she was smart, kind, and pretty. He'd wanted to ask her to the Homecoming Dance this year, but he hadn't been able to work up the courage. He'd let his fear get the better of him.

Story of my life, he thought.

He saw Sean and Eric Henderson standing between two dumpsters at the edge of the playground. He didn't hang out with them as much these days as he had when they were younger. Mom thought they were a bad influence, and she wanted him to stay away from them. He'd protested at the time, but secretly, he agreed with her. Sean and Eric were always getting into trouble for one thing or another—he'd heard the teachers called them the Terror Twins—and every time he'd been dumb enough to get involved in whatever they were up to, he got in trouble too.

"They're the kind of boys who drag others down with them," Mom had said, and while Jonathan would never admit this to her, he'd come to agree.

His common sense told him to ignore the brothers and continue on into the building, but he changed direction and started walking toward them anyway.

You're a dumbass, he thought. When he reached the boys, he stopped and said, "What are you guys doing?"

Eric turned to look at him, a big grin on his face. "Dude, look what Sean found."

Sean had a stick and was using it to poke something on the ground. He was grinning too. "It's the new school mascot."

Jonathan looked down and saw what the boys were messing with—a dead possum. Its eyes were gone and most of its ears had been chewed off. Every time Sean poked its distended belly, it made moist, squishy sounds.

Jonathan's stomach turned. "Oh, man."

Sean lifted the possum's tail, then let it drop. "Right up your alley, huh, J-Man?" he said.

It was true that Jonathan was fascinated with morbid subjects, but that was because he wanted to understand why humans did such awful things to one another. Seeing a dead animal just made him sad—and a little bit ill.

"I wonder how it died," Eric said.

"Probably had yesterday's meatloaf," Sean quipped.

The brothers laughed.

Jonathan knew the boys were fraternal twins, but they looked and acted so much alike, they might as well have been identical.

Sean prodded the furry corpse again.

What they were doing seemed wrong, Jonathan thought. No, more than that: *beyond disrespectful*.

"I think you should leave it alone," Jonathan said.

"What for?" Sean chuckled. "He doesn't mind."

"It's so *gross*," Eric said. He turned to Jonathan. "Dude, you should've been here. A couple birds were eating its asshole."

Sean laughed. "Yeah." He then turned to face the playground. "Watch this." He raised his voice and called out, "Stephanie!"

She looked in the boys' direction, and her three friends turned to look at them as well. They seemed confused, but curious, and more than a little wary. The Terror Twins' reputation was well known.

Jonathan's stomach dropped. *Please don't*, he thought.

Sean called out again, louder this time. "Stephanie, come here for a minute."

"Sean, come on," Jonathan said.

Sean just laughed. "It's gonna be awesome."

Sean and Eric knew Jonathan liked Stephanie, and they were doing this as much to taunt him as they were to scare Stephanie. Jonathan had never struck another person before, but at the moment he felt like punching Sean in the jaw. He might have, too, if Stephanie hadn't approached. He didn't want her to see him lose his temper like that.

"What's up?" she said.

"Check it out," Sean said, suppressing a grin. "Some cat just gave birth behind the dumpster."

Stephanie smiled. "Really?"

"Yeah," Sean said. "Go look at all the kittens."

Jonathan knew this was the last moment he could intervene, but he hesitated. If he said something, Stephanie might think he'd planned this with the Hendersons.

But if he didn't say anything, she might think the same thing. He waited too long. Stephanie stepped between Eric and Jonathan and gazed upon the dead possum in all its gory glory. Sean used his stick to lift up a section of hide over the animal's stomach to reveal chewed-up red meat crawling with fat earthworms and writhing white maggots.

Sean and Eric laughed.

"Oh my god!" Stephanie shouted, then turned and fled.

"What's wrong?" Sean called after her. "Maggots need love too!"

Stephanie ran across the playground as fast as she could, passing Ms. Principe, who was talking with another of the sixth-grade teachers. Ms. Principe was well known around school for not putting up with anyone's bullshit. She apologized to the teacher she was talking with and turned to look in the direction Stephanie had come from. Jonathan looked miserable, but Sean and Eric were laughing.

That was all the evidence Ms. Principe needed.

"What's going on?" she shouted in a voice that could carry from one end of the playground to the other.

"Oh shit!" Eric said. "Ms. Principe."

All three of the boys quickly looked away, like little children who hoped they'd become invisible if they weren't looking directly at someone. If I can't see you, you can't see me.

Ms. Principe walked straight to the dumpsters, and she did *not* look happy. "What are you boys doing back here?" she demanded. And then she saw the possum.

"Oh Christ."

She looked directly at Sean. She knew he was the ringleader. He always was. "Mr. Henderson?"

"Nothing!" Sean said.

"Really? You go find Mr. Curtis and tell him to get rid of that right now."

She turned to Jonathan and Eric, grabbed them each by the arm and shoved them away from the dumpsters. "You two, get to class."

When Sean continued standing there, she grabbed his arm and shoved him after the other two boys. "*Move it!*" she shouted.

They moved it.

CHAPTER FIFTEEN

Jonathan sat in Mr. Whalen's third period Algebra class—the one he shared with Stephanie. He sat in the row of desks next to the windows, while Stephanie sat two rows over, a few desks ahead of his. They were taking a test, and she was studiously filling in answers with a number two pencil, like all the other students. Except Jonathan. He was too upset by what had happened on the playground—especially by his failure to warn Stephanie about the possum—to concentrate on Xs and Ys.

He watched her as she worked on her test, and he wondered what she thought about him now—not that he couldn't guess. How could he explain to her that what had happened on the playground wasn't like him? Or at least, it wasn't like the person he *wanted* to be. And even if he somehow found the words, would she believe him? Would he believe him if their roles were reversed? Probably not.

As if Stephanie sensed his gaze upon her, she turned and looked over her shoulder at him. He tried to put everything he felt into his eyes, hoping she would somehow get the message. *I know I screwed up, and I'm so, so sorry. You don't deserve to be treated like that.*

She looked at him for a long moment, scowled, and then turned back to her test.

"Jonathan!" Mr. Whalen said, almost but not quite yelling in that way teachers had. "Keep your eyes on your own paper."

Jonathan looked at Mr. Whalen, then quickly looked down at his test. He couldn't make sense of any of the numbers, and he was starting to feel sick. "Mr. Whalen? May I be excused?"

Jonathan didn't need to use the restroom, but he didn't want to go back to Mr. Whalen's class any time soon. He couldn't face Stephanie right now. So, he walked slowly down the halls, carrying a wooden block on a loop of string with the words HALL PASS written on it in black magic marker. He stopped at a drinking fountain, not because he was especially thirsty, but just for something to do. He bent over to get a drink, and while he was slurping water, he saw movement from the corner of his eye, and he heard light footsteps, as if someone was skipping.

He stood and turned toward the end of the hall. Another hall ran perpendicular to this one, and the wooden doors that normally separated the two were open. There was no one there now, but he thought he'd seen a little girl skipping by—a girl too young to be in middle school. She was carrying something that flopped in her arms as she went. Something… gray? He tried to recall more details, but there was nothing else there.

It's just your imagination, he thought.

The therapist he'd seen after Dad died had said that extreme stress could make a person think they see and hear all kinds of things that weren't there. And between the nightmare and the fire last night, his shame over what had happened to Stephanie and his worries about the Miles County Clown, he'd experienced plenty of stress lately. Everything would be okay, though. Halloween would be over soon, he'd try to find a way to apologize to Stephanie, and while Mom might be mad at Sienna about the fire, Mom would get over it eventually. She always did. All he needed to do was stay calm and make it through the rest of the day.

Feeling a bit better, he started walking down the hallway—in the other direction than the one where he'd thought he'd seen the little girl.

Figuring that he'd pushed his luck as far as he could, Jonathan decided to head back to Mr. Whalen's class. He went down a flight of stairs, turned right, walked down an empty hallway, turned right again—

—and stopped dead in his tracks.

Sitting cross-legged on the floor less than twenty feet from him was the Miles County Clown, along with a young girl dressed similarly to him, down to the same face makeup. Was she supposed to be his daughter? A much younger sister? Or something else altogether? The Clown—Art—held a crooked stick, and the girl cradled the dead possum in her lap. Both were grinning hideously.

Jonathan knew at once that the skipping girl he'd thought he'd seen earlier was this girl, and the object she'd been carrying had been the possum. The girl lovingly stroked the dead animal, and Art tickled its torn-open abdomen with the tip of his stick. Both Art and the girl laughed without making any sound, as if the possum delighted them. As sinister as Art was, the girl was worse. Jonathan could feel the profound wrongness she gave off, as if it were a grotesque violation of reality for her to be here.

He stood frozen, unable to believe what he was seeing. What were Art and the girl doing here? And how had they managed to enter the school in the first place? Like so many schools around the country in the era of school shootings, Miles County Middle School had tighter-than-tight security. There was no way for anyone to get inside during school hours without going through the main office. Since these two couldn't have gotten in, that meant they weren't real. His mind had finally snapped and he was hallucinating them. Was the same thing that had happened to Dad happening to him? The possibility scared him far more than Art and the girl ever could.

Art took the possum from the girl, dug his hands into its body cavity, and pulled out blood-slick loops of intestine with a flourish, as if performing a magic trick. The girl—white eyes shining with hunger—tore off a section of the long organ, bit a piece off as if it was a tube of jerky, and chewed happily.

The wooden hall pass slipped from Jonathan's hand and hit the floor.

Up to this point, Art and the girl hadn't noticed him, but now their heads snapped toward him, and their faces twisted into feral snarls. Jonathan wanted to run, but his body refused to move. His heart pounded, and his breathing came in rapid gasps, and he distantly wondered if a hallucination could scare you so much you had a heart attack.

Art and the girl continued glaring at him, not moving, not blinking. Jonathan wasn't sure they were even breathing. Then Art raised the possum and hurled it at Jonathan. It splatted into his chest, and his hands grabbed hold of it out of reflex. He looked into the dead animal's eyeless face for an instant, as Art and the girl laughed uproariously but silently. Then he threw it to the floor, turned, and ran back the way he had come. Hallucination or not, he was getting the hell out of there.

He only ran a short distance before he collided with a tall, bespectacled African American woman wearing a blue suit jacket and slacks. Principal Turner grabbed hold of him in an attempt to stop him, but he wiggled out of her grasp and continued running.

"Hey!" Principal Turner shouted. "No running in the hallways! Jonathan! Get back here!"

Jonathan didn't answer, nor did he slow down. He didn't care if he got in trouble, didn't care about anything except getting away. He ran to a pair of double glass doors with an EXIT sign above them. They wouldn't open from the outside during school hours, but they did open from the inside, and Jonathan slammed his way through them, plunged into the crisp, autumn air, and kept running. And as he ran, something occurred to him. Maybe that hadn't been a hallucination after all.

*

Abigail Turner put her hands on her hips in frustration as she watched Jonathan run outside. What the hell had gotten into the boy? He had a reputation for being a bit odd, and he hung around the Henderson boys, which was a questionable choice at best. But all in all, he was a good kid. This behavior was completely unlike him—and that meant something was wrong. She had been working in education for almost fifteen years, and she knew trouble when she sensed it.

She walked at a fast clip down the hallway where Jonathan had come from. When she reached another hallway that branched off this one, she stopped.

"Oh... my... god."

A dead possum lay on the tile floor, organs sticking out of its open belly, surrounded by chunks of red meat and smears of blood.

Jonathan, she thought, *what have you done?*

Sienna was so happy when lunchtime came that she could've cried. Normally she enjoyed her classes—well, as much as any high school student could—but because of her lack of sleep, today had been a marathon of suck. She hoped that a break, along with getting some food inside her, would give her the recharge she so desperately needed. She, Allie, and Brooke ate outside when the weather was good, and while it was a little chilly out, it wasn't cold enough for them to stay inside. She was wearing her leather jacket; she'd be warm enough. Besides, eating outside gave them a bit of psychological distance from school in the middle of their day. It was like an oasis for them, and she badly needed it right now.

She got comfort food today—pasta, two orders of french fries, and a bottle of water—and she was carrying her tray full of carbs to the door when Allie came up behind her and spoke in an exaggerated witch's voice. "Happy Halloween, my pretty!"

Allie loved celebrating holidays—all of them—and she was wearing a green rubber witch's nose and green clawed rubber fingers on her hands, hence the *Wizard of Oz* reference.

Allie had shoulder-length brown hair and was wearing a jean jacket over a blue top, black yoga pants with a strategically placed hole over the left knee, and white sneakers. She was the most normal member of their trio. Sienna was the moody, passionate, and all-too-often obsessive artist; Brooke was the over-the-top diva with a heart of gold and a penchant for mischief; and Allie kept them both grounded—as much as she could, at any rate. Sienna thought the three of them were the perfect combination. She didn't know how she could've gotten through the last year since Dad's death without them.

Allie wasn't carrying a tray. It seemed today her lunch consisted solely of chocolate on a stick, with a white candy ghost on the front.

Sienna eyed her friend's meal. "A little early for chocolate, no?"

Allie smiled. "You're talking to someone who eats Count Chocula on a regular basis."

The image of the Art Crispies box flashed through her mind.

Fun little surprises in every bite!

"Can we *not* talk about cereal, please?"

Allie looked away and took off her witch's nose. "Oh... kaay."

Allie pushed open the door to the outside and held it for Sienna to go through. "Someone's in a mood this morning," she said.

"Sorry," Sienna said. "Barely slept last night."

They headed for their regular spot—a raised square seating area that was part of a support column for an overhanging roof. Sienna put her tray down, and they both sat.

"Let me guess," Allie said. "You were up until four o'clock in the morning working on that Halloween costume... *again.*"

Reluctant to meet Allie's gaze, Sienna picked up a french fry and took a small bite. "Actually, it was more like six," she admitted. She nodded toward her fries, and Allie took one.

Brooke ran over and sat down. All she'd bought for lunch was a chocolate chip cookie. *I'll start eating here when the food stops tasting like ass. Except for the cookies. They're okay.* As usual, she immediately started talking, her words coming out in a rush.

"Did you guys hear about Monica Brown this morning?"

Brooke had long blonde hair and wore a fuzzy white jacket over a tan vest, along with tan pants and brown boots. While Allie's makeup was minimal, Brooke's was a touch overdone, but the look suited her big personality.

"Ugh," Allie said, "that bitchy talk-show host?"

Brooke took her purse from her shoulder and set it down. "Yeah, that bitchy talk-show host totally got her face torn off." Brooke smiled. She *loved* gossip, especially when it was trashy, lurid, and best of all, bloody.

"What?" Allie said.

Brooke chuckled, enjoying this immensely. "Okay, get this. So, she had that Miles County Massacre survivor on. Do you remember the one in the coma and her face was all mutilated? What's her name? It was like, I don't know, Victoria or something?"

Here it was, another reminder of Art the Clown, when Sienna had been fighting so hard all day not to think about him and last night's dream. "Victoria Heyes," she said softly.

"Yes," Brooke said. "She had a meltdown on the show, right? And then backstage she went full-on psycho and *mauled* Monica Brown in the dressing room with her *bare hands*."

"No way!" Allie said.

"Is she dead?" Sienna asked.

"I mean, if she's lucky," Brooke said. She broke off a piece of her cookie, put it in her mouth, and started chewing. When she noticed her friends staring at her, she said, "What? You ever see those transplant faces, everyone lookin' like Mr. Potato Head. *Fuck* that shit."

"God, is it really that bad?" Allie asked.

"Well, I haven't seen photos, but from what I hear, she kinda looks like the inside of my cookie." Brooke smiled, and her smile grew bigger the more she talked. "Her eyes are all gouged out. And her nose was like falling off of her face. Oh, my god. And I heard that her cheek—like a little bit—was found at the bottom of Victoria Heyes's shoe."

Sienna had only managed to nibble part of one fry, but she suddenly felt like she was going to vomit. She remembered the bodies scattered across the floor of the Clown Café in her dream. Unblinking eyes, gaping mouths, bullet-ravaged flesh, burned and blackened skin, and blood—so much of it—everywhere. Her pulse thrummed in her ears, her breathing sped up, and the place on her leg where she'd been shot in the dream began to throb.

She got up and ran toward the chain-link fence surrounding the area, limping slightly on her left leg.

"You okay?" Brooke called after her, voice filled with concern.

"Sienna?" Allie said.

Sienna reached the fence, grabbed hold of it for support, and raised her other hand to her chest. Her heart was beating fast as a hummingbird's wings, and her breath was coming in short, rapid gasps. *Get it under control girl,* she told herself. *You're at school with your friends. You're safe and everything's okay.*

Brooke and Allie hurried over to join her, both obviously worried.

"Hey, you all right?" Allie asked.

"I really didn't mean to freak you out with that Monica Brown shit," Brooke said. "I'm so sorry."

Sienna turned away from the fence to face her friends. "I'm okay. I'm okay, I'm fine. I just..." She drew in a shuddering breath. "I just need a second to think."

A couple students were watching Sienna, curious about what was happening. Brooke saw them.

"Hey, excuse me!" she said loudly. "Can you mind your business, please? *Thank* you."

The kids turned away, and Brooke sighed. "My god."

"Sienna, talk to me," Allie said. "What's going on?"

"We had—" She took in a deep breath. "We had a fire last night."

"What?" Allie said. "Where?"

"My room. I must've fallen asleep with the candles burning. It was pretty bad."

"Okay, how bad is 'pretty bad'?" Brooke asked.

"Like flames touching the ceiling, entire house could've burned down bad."

"Jesus," Allie said, "is everyone okay?"

"Yeah. My mother put the flames out in time."

Brooke smiled, shook her head in admiration. "Wow, fuckin' Barbara to the rescue. I swear that woman's a superhero."

"Was she pissed?" Allie asked.

"Livid. Berated me for a good hour and a half this morning."

"Well, that's not so bad," Brooke said. "I mean, you *did* almost torch the whole family in their sleep."

Allie gave Brooke a sharp look, then faced Sienna once more. "Look, the important thing is nobody got hurt, right? Seriously, in a few weeks you'll be laughing about the whole thing."

"More like months," Brooke said.

"Okay. A couple months," Allie said.

"Probably a year," Brooke amended.

"It wasn't just the fire," Sienna said. "It... Something really strange happened last night."

"What?" Allie said.

Sienna hesitated. How in the hell could she explain her nightmare to them? Tell them about how the short sword hadn't been damaged in the fire, how it had seemed to glow for a second when she touched it? They'd think she was losing it for sure.

"Nothing," she said. "Nothing, I'm fine."

"You sure?" Allie said doubtfully.

"Yeah, yeah," Sienna said. "Come on, let's—let's go back."

She started heading back to where they'd been eating, but she saw Brooke and Allie exchange a look before following.

"Now that my food's probably ice cold…" Sienna said.

"You want a piece of my Monica Brown cookie?" Brooke offered.

"*Brooke*," Allie chided.

"Sorry," Brooke said.

Sienna couldn't help chuckling. "I hate you."

Brooke laughed.

CHAPTER SIXTEEN

Jonathan sat at the bottom of the stairs, dried possum blood on his shirt, listening as Mom spoke with the man who'd brought him home—middle-aged, bald, wearing a blue windbreaker. She was trying to sound polite, but Jonathan could hear the tension in her voice.

"Thank you, officer. I'm *so* sorry to cause you trouble."

He smiled, but he didn't look in Jonathan's direction. It was like, now that he was home, he no longer existed for the man. "No problem. Have a nice day, ma'am."

"You too." Mom closed the door and turned to look at Jonathan. Her expression became cold, and anger shone in her eyes. "Get. To. Your. Room."

"But Mom, I—"

"Go to your *room*. I don't wanna hear another word out of you until I say so."

Jonathan wanted to explain that he hadn't been the one who'd brought the dead possum into school, nor had he run away to avoid getting caught. He just couldn't stay there any longer after what he'd seen. But Mom was in no mood to listen right now. And even if she had been, how could he expect her to believe his story? It was too bizarre, and she'd probably blame it on his "obsession" with the Miles County Clown. He didn't want to be alone after what had happened—he wanted the comfort of Mom's presence—but obeying her seemed the best option right now, so he stood and ran up the stairs. He didn't know what he'd do in his room, but he knew one thing for certain. He was staying off the damn Internet.

When Jonathan was gone, Barbara ran a hand through her hair and let out a long, weary sigh. What in the hell was happening to this family? Last night she'd had one of the worst nightmares of her life, then Sienna almost burned down the whole house, and now Jonathan had been caught bringing the mutilated corpse of a fucking possum into school.

She remembered something Sienna had said yesterday: "Just don't act surprised when you find a dead animal in his room."

Technically, the animal hadn't been in his room, but otherwise, Sienna had been right. She might have been joking—probably had been—but Barbara wasn't laughing. She'd tried to reassure Sienna, had told her Jonathan was okay, that he was just going through a rough time since Dad died, but now she wondered if she really hadn't been trying to reassure herself. A thought occurred to her then: had Jonathan actually *killed* the poor animal? Despite Jonathan's fascination with the morbid and macabre, she couldn't imagine him committing an act of violence like that. He was such a gentle boy. Sensitive, like his sister.

Like his father.

It was early afternoon, but as the saying went, it's always five o'clock somewhere. She needed a fucking drink. She headed for the kitchen.

She kept a bottle of Jack Daniel's in a cupboard above the refrigerator, hidden behind a set of old ceramic mixing bowls her mother had given her. As a rule, she didn't drink hard liquor often. Her father had been an alcoholic, and although he got into AA when she was a child and remained sober for the rest of his life, she could vividly recall what he had been like when he was drunk. It hadn't been pleasant, to say the least. She supposed that was why she worried so much about Sienna drinking. She didn't want her to take after her grandfather.

After her husband's funeral, Barbara had gotten the bottle, and she'd drank two-thirds of it the following week. After that, she put it in the cupboard and hadn't touched it since. But she'd been saving it in case she needed it again. And damned if she didn't need it now.

She got the bottle, selected a clean glass from the dishwasher, then sat at the kitchen table. She poured herself two fingers, considered, then poured one more. Her laptop sat on the table, her headset next to it. She'd been working when the truant officer rang the doorbell, and she knew she should get back to it, but she also knew she wouldn't be able to concentrate. She'd probably bite the head off the first customer she spoke with.

The way she felt, she wanted to down the entire drink in one gulp, but she forced herself to take small sips. The alcohol's spreading warmth calmed her somewhat, but it couldn't stop the turbulent emotions roiling inside her.

She never thought she'd be a single parent in her forties, and she'd never imagined it would be so hard. Sometimes she got so angry with her husband for dying and abandoning the family that she wanted to scream. She knew that wasn't fair. He hadn't chosen to get sick, hadn't chosen to change as much as he had before the end.

She'd always had a sharp tongue on her, ever since she was a little girl. When Sienna was born, she vowed that she wouldn't snap and snipe at her daughter, and then later, her son. And for the most part, she'd succeeded. But the strain of trying to keep everything together by herself—taking care of the house, paying the bills each month, paying the goddamn mortgage—had worn her patience beyond tissue thin. She'd seen a therapist a couple of times, and the woman had suggested she was avoiding grieving her husband's death by trying to deal with every other problem in her life, keeping herself so busy mentally and emotionally that she wouldn't have the time or energy to think about what had happened and what they'd lost... What *she'd* lost. Maybe the bitch was right, but Barbara stopped seeing her after that.

Barbara had considered selling the house and moving somewhere that the cost of living wasn't so high, but she didn't want to uproot the kids' lives. What they needed most right now was stability, and she intended to do whatever it took to give that to them for as long as she could. Hopefully, long enough to get them through high school—assuming they both didn't have complete meltdowns before then. She was beginning to fear that Sienna and Jonathan had inherited their father's condition and were showing signs of it much earlier than he had. She'd asked her husband's doctor about this possibility soon after he was diagnosed, and he'd assured her that it was highly unlikely. But that didn't mean it was *impossible*.

She didn't know if she could go through that again with one child, let alone two. But she would if she had to. She was their mother, goddammit. But today, she was going to sit here, drink, and try to keep her shit together as best she could.

Barbara was glad she'd sent Jonathan to his room. She didn't want him to see her cry.

She put her face in her hands and wept.

Sienna stood before a mirror, white wings spreading outward from her back. An assortment of costumes and dresses hung on a rack next to her, and creepy sound effects echoed through the store.

"I can't believe I'm reduced to a pair of cheap store-bought wings." She turned from side to side, examining them. "You think these are too small?"

"How big do you want 'em?" Allie asked. "You're gonna be knocking over people's drinks and shit all night." She smiled. "I think they're cute."

Her wings—the ones she'd made—were way better than these artistically, but she hadn't given much thought to what it would actually be like to wear them around other people. Her wings were—*had been*—significantly larger than these, and if she'd worn them out tonight, she'd have trouble moving through crowds. They probably would've gotten damaged, maybe even ruined, and yes,

181

she most likely would've knocked over people's drinks. *These* wings, while nowhere near the level of craftwork that hers had been, were much more maneuverable. And for some reason, she had a feeling that *maneuverable* would be important tonight.

"Well, they're not terrible," she said grudgingly, but with a smile.

"You don't really have a choice," Allie pointed out.

After school, Sienna had driven into the city so she could get a new pair of wings at Abracadabra, and Allie had come with her. Afterward, they'd stop at a bodega so Sienna could get the Halloween candy Mom had asked her to pick up.

Allie's ringtone went off, and she pulled her phone from her back pocket and checked the screen. "Ugh, it's my mom. Where did you tell your mother we were going tonight?"

Sienna gave her friend a sly smile. "Megan Melanie's Halloween party."

Allie smiled and nodded approvingly. "Okay. I'll catch you out front."

She turned and headed for the store's entrance. Allie and her mother didn't always get along, to put it mildly, and Allie always made sure to talk with her mother privately whenever she called so she wouldn't make her friends uncomfortable in the likely event the conversation degenerated into a shouting match. Sienna thought *her* mom was bad at times, but she was nothing compared to Allie's. If she so much as suspected Allie was going to a *real* party instead of a piddly-ass high school one with popcorn balls and fruit punch, she'd ground Allie for a month, confiscate her phone, and barricade the doors and windows so she couldn't sneak out.

Sienna examined her reflection again, trying to imagine what these wings would look like with her costume. She realized she didn't have anything to wear around her neck. Allie would probably be talking to her mom for several minutes. Enough time to shop for an accessory or two.

Sienna turned away from the mirror, forgetting she was wearing her new wings instead of carrying them. They felt so natural, like they'd always been a part of her.

Allie was hurrying toward Abracadabra's entrance, hoping to get out onto the sidewalk before the conversation with her mother could get started in earnest. Plus, being on a New York City street, with all the traffic and pedestrian noise, made a great excuse if she needed to end the call quickly. *Sorry, Mom! It's so loud I can't hear you! We'll talk when I get home!*

"Hey, Mom. No, I'm just in town with Sienna. What time are you gonna be home? Because—"

She'd been so distracted that she hadn't been watching where she was going, and she collided with someone. It felt like she'd hit a brick wall, but when she looked up, she saw the man she'd bumped into was thin. He was also done up as a nightmare clown, and he looked scary as hell.

"Sorry," she said. She checked out his costume for a second, then added, "Nice."

He smiled, displaying some truly disgusting-looking fake teeth, then he performed a half-bow and extended his arm, as if to say, *After you, milady.*

183

She noticed his fingerless gloves were covered with bloodstains. Great touch. There was something in his eyes she didn't like, though, an... emptiness, as if he wasn't really looking *at* her but *through* her. It chilled her down to the bone, and she wished now she hadn't said anything to the man, just kept on going and gotten the hell out of there. Which is exactly what she intended to do right now. She hurried on as he raised his small top hat in farewell then let it snap back down on his head.

Allie nearly ran the rest of the way to the door. When she was outside, her mom asked her what had happened.

"Nothing. I just ran into a man wearing a terrifying clown costume."

She felt foolish for having been afraid of him, but she told herself to shrug it off. She remembered a quote from one of her favorite horror movies: *You know, it's Halloween. I guess everyone's entitled to one good scare.*

Sienna found a cute collar that she liked, and after picking it up, she browsed through a few nearby sections—wigs, makeup, jewelry—and found herself starting to relax for the first time since the fire. One of the things she loved most about Halloween was that it was the only holiday dedicated to the imagination.

Other holidays were bound by rigid traditions and were basically the same every year. And yes, Halloween had its traditions too—costumes, trick-or-treat, jack-o'-lanterns... But the thing about costumes was that you could be anything you wanted, and it didn't even have to be scary unless you wanted it to. You were invited to become someone—or something—else for a night, to live out a fantasy, explore a part of yourself you normally kept hidden, or just have fun and play. Young, old, or in-between, it didn't matter. Halloween was the one time of the year you could step outside the confines of your normal life and transform yourself into something else. It was magical, really.

And that's why she loved places like Abracadabra. It was full of glorious *possibilities*, and she could spend hours going through the store and looking over everything it had to offer. But she knew Allie was waiting for her outside, *and* she still had to buy candy for Mom. Best to get going.

She turned away from the display she'd been looking at—a collection of feather boas—intending to head to the register up front... and stopped dead in her tracks.

Art the Clown was standing in an open doorway less than twenty feet from her, leaning against the side jamb, arms crossed, smiling his nauseating smile, and blocking the way. His black-and-white harlequin costume was pristine, but his fingerless gloves were stained crimson. Images flashed through her mind—a dozen bloody, bullet-riddled corpses littering the floor of the Clown Café, the bloody-mouthed dead boy sitting at the breakfast table, Banjo Blue still playing her instrument and swaying from side to side as flames consumed her flesh...

Sienna found herself suddenly dizzy and unable to breathe. Somehow, the monster from her dream had entered the real world, and now he'd come for her—the only person to escape his obscene killing spree at the Clown Café.

A maniacal laugh came over the sound system then. *Mu-ha-ha-ha-ha…*

For several seconds, Art didn't move, didn't blink, and neither did Sienna. Then Art waggled his eyebrows. A greeting? If so, it was a mocking one. Sienna started seeing spots in her vision. *Breathe, girl! You wanna pass out and leave yourself helpless with him? Hell, no!* She drew in a slow, shuddering breath, and the spots slowly faded. She looked left, then right, seeking another way she could get to the register. But there were none. If she wanted to get out of here, she had no choice but to go through the doorway Art was guarding, and she would have to pass within inches of him to do it. Close enough for him to touch her with his bloodstained gloves.

Tentatively, not taking her eyes off him, she started forward, heart hammering in her chest, each step a supreme effort of will. Art watched her approach, but he remained so absolutely still, he might've been one of Abracadabra's animatronic figures. When Sienna reached him, she turned sideways and slipped by him, expecting him to burst into movement any second and grab hold of her. But while his eyes tracked her progress, he made no move to detain her, and a few seconds later she was past him and into the other room. She hurried up the stairs to the first floor and then to the register, casting backward glances over her shoulder the entire way to see if Art had followed, but he hadn't.

She refused to believe she was in the clear, though. She wouldn't feel comfortable until she was in Allie's car and they were on the road back to Miles County.

"Can I help you find anything?"

She turned to see a handsome African American man with a goatee standing behind the front counter, smiling at her. He wore a black Abracadabra T-shirt with the name RICKY over the left breast and the store's gargoyle logo over the right. The counter was covered with small Halloween decorations—plastic pumpkins, a skeletal puppy, a two-foot-tall mummy, a creepy dolly... last-minute impulse items. She stood there for a moment, trying to decide what to do. If she stopped and paid, it would give Art time to emerge from the lower level. She didn't want to shoplift, but she *really* wanted to get the hell out of there—*now*.

"Need any *help*?" Ricky asked.

From the way he said *help*, she knew he was asking if she was in trouble. His concern made her feel guilty for thinking about leaving without paying, so after one final glance to make certain the coast was clear, Sienna stepped up to the counter and placed the collar on its surface. While Ricky scanned it, she pressed her hands down on the counter as if to steady herself, and she glanced around, searching for any sign of Art.

"Find everything okay?" Ricky asked.

Sienna didn't look at the man as she answered. "Yeah."

"I'm gonna need to scan those."

Sienna's attention snapped back to the clerk. What was he... then it hit her: the wings. "Oh. Um, right. Sorry." She slipped the wings off and handed them to Ricky.

"It's all good," he said. He scanned them and then glanced at the register. "Okay, that'll be $32.25."

Sienna reached for her bag, but it wasn't there. At first, she feared someone had stolen it, but then she remembered. She'd put it on the floor so she could try on the wings. When she saw Art, she'd forgotten all about it—had forgotten about everything, really—except for getting away from the bastard as fast as she could. Her bag was most likely still sitting on the floor by the mirror. No way she wanted to go back down there and get it, not with the possibility that Art was still there. But she couldn't leave it. It had all her important stuff in it— especially her wallet with her driver's license, school ID, debit card, cash…

Could she ask Ricky to go downstairs and get it for her? No, she couldn't ask him to put himself in danger for her like that. She didn't know if this Art was exactly the same one that had been in her nightmare, but she'd sensed how profoundly *bad* he was. He was dangerous, no doubt, but he was also—and she'd never thought she'd say this about another person—*evil*.

"Yeah, um… I think I left my bag down—"

Art *slammed* her bag on the counter as he walked behind her, making her jump. He continued without pausing, heading for a display of novelty eyeglasses on the other side of the counter. Sienna watched him the same way she'd watch a large predator in the wild, alert for the subtlest sign that he intended to attack. She noticed Ricky was now watching him too, and that made her feel less alone. The store clerk might not know how big a threat Art was, but at least he was keeping an eye on him.

Art stopped in front of the eyeglasses display and examined the offerings. One pair caught his attention, and he reached up to take them off the display. Sienna looked away as she searched in her bag for her wallet, but when she turned to look at Art again, he was standing motionless, grinning, sunglasses with frames shaped like yellow flowers covering his eyes. He should've looked ridiculous, but instead he looked even more terrifying.

She looked back at Ricky, searched in her bag some more, then—unable to stop herself—she glanced at Art again. This time the clown was wearing sunglasses with frames shaped like red handprints. He held his own hands up, mirroring the frames' position, his stained gloves matching the frames' color. His mouth was open in a wide, joyous grin, and he once again stood absolutely motionless, as if he were a statue painted black and white—and red.

Sienna felt the first stirrings of panic, and she began withdrawing items from her bag and placing them on the counter, hoping this would help her locate her wallet faster.

Another glance at Art. This time he wore googly-eye glasses, the kind with springs, so that the plastic eyes drooped out when you leaned over. Art moved his head forward and back, then up and down, the eyes flopping around, springs jangling.

Sienna wanted to scream, but at that moment her hand closed around her wallet. She drew it out of the bag, opened it, removed a five, a ten, and a twenty, and handed the bills to Ricky. He took them with a smile and checked them to make sure she'd given him the right amount. She heard a metallic whirring sound then, and she turned to see Art had given up on the sunglasses and was now playing with a spinning ratchet noisemaker he'd taken from a display of novelty items. Then he suddenly dropped his hand to his side and, as if by magic, a blowhorn noisemaker appeared in his mouth. He blew it and the curled paper tube made a loud squawking noise as it straightened.

Ricky had finally had enough. "*Sir!*"

Art stopped blowing and the paper tube curled back up.

Ricky continued. "If you're gonna to put that in your mouth, you gotta *pay* for it."

Art blew more gently this time, and the noisemaker popped out of his mouth and fell to the floor.

Sienna was putting everything back in her purse while Ricky finished the transaction and handed her the change.

"Here you go."

"Thanks."

Ricky started to hand the wings to Sienna, but then he stopped, looked at them, and said, "You know what? I'm gonna get you a big bag."

The last thing Sienna wanted was to remain in this store even one second longer. "Oh, no, no. I don't— I don't need it."

"It's fine," Ricky said. "I got 'em right back here."

Sienna wanted to shout at him. *Do you not* see *the killer clown standing over there?* Instead, she merely said, "Okay."

Art had been looking over the novelty items, trying to find something else to play with. Suddenly his eyes widened in delight as he reached out and picked up a handheld bike horn. Art started creeping up on her with slow, exaggerated movements, as if he was a cartoon character. Sienna held her bag close to her body and resolutely stared straight ahead, determined not to give him the reaction he so obviously wanted from her. But when he stopped at her side and grinned as he ssslllooooowly raised the horn, Sienna could no longer keep silent.

"Please don't," she whispered.

Art brought the bell of the horn up to her ear, then stopped. He held it like that for what felt like an eternity, and just when Sienna began to think he might not squeeze the bulb...

HONK!

Her body jerked, she gasped, but she still didn't look at him.

He began squeezing the horn repeatedly.

HONKA-HONKA-HONKA-HONKA-HONKA-HONKA-HONK!

"Stop!" Sienna begged. "Please stop! Please!"

Ricky returned to the counter, carrying a large shopping bag with Sienna's wings inside. "Hey, buddy!"

Art quickly dropped his arm to his side, like a naughty kid caught doing something he shouldn't.

"You wanna quit causing trouble?" Ricky asked.

Art didn't look at him. He looked at Sienna, eyes narrowed, teeth bared.

Ricky handed Sienna her wings. "Thank you," he said.

"Thank you," Sienna said out of reflex.

She turned and dashed for the door.

"Happy Halloween!" Ricky called out to her.

"You too!" Sienna said as she shoved the door open and rushed outside.

CHAPTER SEVENTEEN

Allie was leaning against Abracadabra's display window, *still* talking on the phone with her mother. This was the reason Allie never wanted to answer the phone when her mom called. Once the woman got you on the phone, she never stopped talking. Allie loved her mother, but oh my *god*, she could just kill her sometimes! They'd long ago moved on from the topic of Megan Melanie's Halloween party—which Allie, Sienna, and Brooke were definitely *not* going to tonight—and were currently arguing about whether Allie should wear a coat with her costume because it was supposed to rain.

When Allie saw Sienna rush out of the store and come running toward her, she was so relieved she could've given the girl a kiss on the lips.

"Mom, I gotta run. Talk to you later." She disconnected and slipped the phone into her pants pocket.

"Wings fit okay, I take it?" she said.

Sienna hurried to the driver's side. "Get in the car," she said, voice tight with tension.

Allie frowned. "What's the matter?"

"Just. Get. In."

"All right, all right. Christ, you must *really* need a candy fix."

Art watched Sienna leave, dark thoughts writhing in his mind like insects crawling across a bloated, rotting carcass. Later for her. Right now, he had work to do here.

He plunked the horn on the counter and headed for the entrance. When he reached the door, he looked outside to make sure no one was about to come in, then he locked the door and turned the OPEN sign to CLOSED. He'd left his bag of toys on the floor next to the entrance when he'd first come in, and now he picked it up, slung it over his shoulder, and headed back to his new friend Ricky.

Time to have some fun.

Ricky *hated* Halloween.

Not only was it the store's busiest time of the year, it brought out all the crazies. Like Clown Boy. The dude comes into the store in full costume and makeup, harasses a nice young woman, and then acts like everyone should find him adorable and amusing. Goddamn psycho.

At least his shift was almost over. The NYC store closed early on Halloween, otherwise teenagers and drunks came and went all night, playing with all the merchandise and not buying a fucking thing. They broke stuff and stole a lot of shit, too. Ricky had let the other staff take off early to prepare for Abracadabra's own Halloween party, which they held offsite each year. Tonight, they were meeting at

Flanagan's, a fun Irish pub a few blocks west. It might've been a better place to celebrate St. Paddy's Day, but it was what the other employees voted on this year, so what the hell. As manager, Ricky volunteered to stay at the store and tend to any last-minute customers before closing up and joining the others. Now he wished he hadn't.

When he'd seen Clown Boy head for the door, he thought the guy intended to follow the girl with the wings, and he'd been about to call the police. But the dude was heading back to the counter now, carrying a full trash bag. Was the guy homeless or something? Ricky had a hard time believing a homeless person would waste money to buy a clown costume, facial appliances, and makeup, but the world was a fucking strange place.

"Yo, we're closin' up. Can I help you find something?"

Clown Boy reached the counter, put his bag on the floor, then stood and pushed the bike horn toward Ricky. The message was clear: *I'll take this, please*.

Ricky scanned the horn's price. "$8.99," he said.

Clown Boy made a show of patting his non-existing pockets, then he bent down and started removing items from his bag and depositing them on the counter.

The first item was a padlock and chain.

The second was a rusty pair of end nipper tongs.

What the fuck?

"Are you serious right now?"

Clown Boy didn't answer. He deposited a handful of nails on the counter.

"Yo, can you pay for that or not?"

An empty beer bottle. A large wooden mallet.

"Sir, what are you *doing*?"

More nails. A rusty metal cleaver.

Aw, hell no!

"All right. Sir, you know what? I'm gonna call the police."

Clown Boy popped up, crumpled bills in his hand. He laid them on the counter then started adding some coins, putting each down slowly and deliberately.

Ricky slammed his palm down on the counter.

Clown Boy's eyes widened in surprise and his mouth made an O of alarm.

"Hey, did you hear what I said?"

Clown Boy smiled.

Ricky did *not* like that smile. It said, *I'm batshit crazy.* Ricky was starting to get a little afraid now. "Get the hell out of here before I fuck you up."

A coldness came into Clown Boy's eyes then. He reached for the beer bottle, grabbed it by the neck, and smashed it against the side of Ricky's head.

Ricky slumped forward and his head hit the counter.

Art dropped the broken beer bottle to the floor. Fun was fun, but it was time to get down to business. He grabbed hold of Ricky's shoulders, pulled him over the counter, and slammed him to the floor. He then grabbed the back of his T-shirt, hauled him up on his knees, picked up the broken beer bottle, and rammed it into Ricky's left eye. The jagged glass tore into Ricky's flesh, and he cried out in pain as blood gushed down his face. Art didn't stop there. He shoved the bottle in farther, putting real muscle behind the effort. Ricky screamed and his body spasmed as agony overloaded his nervous system.

Art loved his job.

He yanked the bottle free, and a long trail of blood came with it. He let go of Ricky's shirt, and the man fell onto the floor, sobbing. When Art had pulled Ricky across the counter, the toys Art had deposited there had been knocked off. He saw his meat cleaver lying on the other side of Ricky, and he grabbed hold of its handle and raised it high. Gritting his disgusting teeth, he swung the cleaver in a vicious downward arc and buried it in Ricky's head, cutting through skin, skull, and into the brain beneath.

Chuk!

Art placed his other hand on the blade and began pressing downward with all his strength, wiggling the cleaver back and forth to help it cut deeper. The wet sounds of blood and meat being violated were a symphony to Art's ears, and he pressed down even harder. Slowly, inch by inch, the cleaver sank farther into Ricky's head. The man wasn't screaming anymore, was only making soft gurgling sounds, and his fingers twitched as his body started turning out the lights.

Closing time.

Art yanked the cleaver free and raised it again, paused to savor the moment, then swung it down and with three swift cuts severed Ricky's head from his body. Art dropped the cleaver, took hold of the head with both hands, and lifted it off the floor. Blood and ragged bits of meat slid out of the open neck hole and onto the carpet.

Art lifted Ricky's head to his face and examined it.

The flesh around the left eye had swollen shut, but the right eye was open and glassy.

He heard Ricky's voice then: "Get the hell out of here before I fuck you up."

He shrieked with silent laughter, and the store's sound system echoed his obscene mirth.

Mu-ha-ha-ha-ha...

Ten-year-old Donnie Weaver's mom held his left hand as they hurried down the sidewalk to Abracadabra. They weren't here to shop for him. He already had his Halloween costume—he was going as Batman this year— but his mom had forgotten to get something to wear to her date tonight. She was going with Victor, a man she knew from her job at the bank, to a fancy Halloween party uptown while Donnie trick-or-treated with the kids who lived in the apartment next to theirs.

Mom and Dad had been divorced for almost two years now, and Mom didn't date much, so she was nervous. He didn't think she should be. He'd met Victor before, on a day when Mom had to take him to a doctor's appointment in the city, so she'd taken him to work with her for half the day. He liked Victor. He was nice.

When they reached the entrance, they were greeted by a CLOSED sign.

"Oh, my. They're closed."

Mom had a genius for stating the obvious. Donnie was sorry she wouldn't be able to get a costume, but he was more disappointed that they weren't going to get to go inside. He *loved* Abracadabra, and it had been a long time

197

since Mom had brought him here. He pressed his face to the glass and cupped his hands to his head to block out the light so he could see inside.

A creepy-cool evil clown display was located just on the other side of the door—a zombie clown with no lower jaw and a bloody ribcage sticking out of his shirt, two clowns playing tug-of-war with a terrified little girl, a clown with a chainsaw in the process of cutting up a guy lying on a wooden slab, and a clown in a black-and-white outfit holding a man's severed head in both his hands. Blood dripped from the man's neck onto the floor. Neat effect!

"Wow, look at that, Mom!"

"Yeah, that's wonderful, honey."

The animatronic clown looked at Donnie, stuck out his tongue, then returned to this previous position and stood motionless.

"Cool."

"All right. Let's go. You can't stay here the whole time. Come on."

Mom pulled Donnie away from the door, but he wished he could stay just a *little* bit longer. He wanted to see what that clown would do next.

When the boy and his mother left, Art dropped the act. He tossed Ricky's head away since he no longer needed the grisly prop, and it thumped heavily as it landed. No point in performing when there wasn't an audience. He regarded the animatronic clowns in the display for several seconds, then sniffed in derision.

Posers.

CHAPTER EIGHTEEN

"That's fuckin' *crazy*," Allie said.

After leaving Abracadabra, Sienna had driven several blocks to find a bodega. During the drive, she started telling Allie an abbreviated version of her dream of Art and the Clown Café, and then seeing him in real life inside Abracadabra. They'd parked and entered the store just as Sienna finished her story.

"I'm telling you it was him, Allie. Right down to the little black dot on the tip of his nose."

Sienna peered at the items on the shelves as they walked down an aisle, looking for bags of candy, but she was still too upset by her encounter with Art to fully focus.

"Sienna, you said it yourself. I mean, there are gonna be hundreds of douchebags dressed up as that psycho tonight. Even your brother was talking about going as him. *Not* that I'm calling your brother a douchebag. It was just a coincidence."

"Then how do you explain the fire? I dreamt it, and it happened."

Allie paused before asking her next question. "Did you change medications recently?"

Sienna felt a flare of anger. "Jesus Christ! I am *not* crazy!"

A man and a woman checking out the ice cream flavors in the cooler by the entrance turned to look at them. Allie saw them, and she spoke in a soothing voice. "Take a breath. I'm just saying, did you ever consider the logical explanation that maybe the fire caused your nightmare and not the other way around?"

"What?"

"I think the fire started while you were sleeping and worked its way into your nightmare. Your body must've felt the flames. You know, shit like that happens all the time."

Sienna hadn't considered this. It actually made a lot of sense.

"Look," Allie said, "are you getting candy or not? I mean, what are we doing here?"

Sienna realized they'd been standing and talking in front of the candy for the last few moments. Just as she'd feared, all the good stuff was gone. The only things left were off-brand copies of popular candy, which—while resembling the original—usually tasted nothing like it. But it was all they had, so she grabbed several bags and hoped the kids in the neighborhood wouldn't hate them for their lackluster offerings this year.

She turned to Allie. "Even if that *is* the case, it still doesn't explain how the fire started."

"You're a thousand percent sure it wasn't the candles?"

"A thousand and one."

"How about some old faulty wiring in the walls?

I mean, your house is kinda old."

Another good point. Sienna supposed it was a possibility, but it didn't *feel* right.

They walked up to the register, and a sixtyish man of Middle Eastern descent rang up Sienna's purchases.

"$16.89," he said with a smile.

Sienna handed the man a twenty, then picked up her conversation with Allie where they'd left off. "Faulty wiring?"

"Better than your psychotic theory," Allie said. "Listen, you wanna know a good rule of thumb…?"

"$3.11's your change," the man said, and handed the money to Sienna. "Happy Halloween."

Sienna smiled as she took the money and put it in her wallet. "You too."

As they walked out the door, Allie said, "If there's even a one percent chance that something can be explained scientifically, bet on that one percent every time."

Was there a one percent chance in her case? Sienna wondered. She didn't know. What she did know was that Allie was, above all else, logical and practical. She intended to become a physician—a cardiologist, specifically—and Sienna knew she'd make a damn good one.

But Allie wasn't the kind of person who thought outside the box, and in Sienna's situation, she wasn't sure there *was* a box in the first place.

Mom was sitting at the kitchen table working when Sienna got home.

"We don't go direct with our insurers," Mom said into her headset. "Okay, but let me get your zip code. I'm gonna find a broker in your area."

Sienna set the bags of generic candy on the counter. She looked at her mother, noted her pale skin, the puffy bags under her eyes, and Sienna knew she had been crying. She wanted to ask if everything was okay, but given how strained things had been between them since the fire, she thought it best not to bother her while she worked. She'd ask later.

After filling the candy bucket, she went upstairs to her room. But when she saw Jonathan's door was open, she peeked in. He was sitting at his desk, but his laptop was closed, and he was looking at some kind of book with a brown cover. Trick-or-treat was going to start soon, and he should be in his costume and out in the neighborhood, ready to collect mounds of candy.

"What are you doing home?"

Jonathan turned around in his chair to face her. He wore a plaid hoodie, unzipped, a smiley-face T-shirt underneath. "He's here, Sienna."

"Who?" She walked into his room and sat on the edge of his bed, next to the desk.

"The Miles County Clown," Jonathan said.

"What are you talking about?"

"I saw him today in my school. Just like in the police photos."

Jonathan grabbed the book, rose from his chair, and sat on the bed next to Sienna and started flipping through pages.

"Slow down," she said.

"It *was* him."

Sienna saw artwork as Jonathan turned the pages: drawings of a fire-breathing dragon, a brutish-looking man in a robe, a group of insect-winged fairies, a shirtless man in a leather kilt, holding a sword at his side and standing before a dark castle, a cyclops...

She recognized the book, but she couldn't believe what she was seeing. "Is that Daddy's sketchbook?"

Jonathan ignored the question. He pointed to a page. "Look here..."

"How long have you had this? Jonathan, *answer* me. You know how long we've been looking for this."

He ignored her question again. He flipped to a news article that had been pasted to one of the pages. "Read this," he said.

HORRIBLY MUTILATED BODY OF 10-YEAR-OLD GIRL DISCOVERED AT LOCAL CARNIVAL

By Wes Torrance

A grim fate was in store for a young girl after a celebration of the town carnival this Halloween.

Ten-year-old Emily Crane (right) was last seen alive cheerfully roaming the carnival grounds earlier Friday evening. As the night progressed and the attractions closed, family members grew concerned as to her whereabouts. Several carnival-goers worked alongside family and friends to search for the young girl, which came to an end shortly after it began. Crane's lifeless, mangled body was discovered in a makeup trailer just outside the main event grounds.

Crane was the daughter of two prominent circus performers, whose family also includes a long list of very popular, well-respected circus acts, mimes, and similar talents.

A black-and-white photo of Emily accompanied the article. It showed a pretty girl with long, blonde hair and a happy smile. Sienna felt sick knowing the death this poor thing had suffered.

"I saw her today," Jonathan said. "This exact girl. Same clothes, same hair. Identical. Only she didn't look human."

He turned to another page.

This one had two articles pasted on it. These were about the murders last Halloween. *MILES COUNTY CORONER IS LATEST VICTIM IN TERRIFYING HALLOWEEN MASSACRE* and *BELOVED MILES COUNTY PIZZA PARLOR BECOMES SCENE OF GRISLY DOUBLE-HOMICIDE.*

The page next to it had an article from the *Miles County Banner* about the two college students who had been killed the previous Halloween—Tara Heyes and Dawn Emerson.

HALLOWEEN HORROR
VICTIM COUNT MOUNTS AS FAMILIES OF TWO SLAIN STUDENTS SEARCH FOR ANSWERS.

"There's some kinda connection between her, the old carnival, and the Miles County Clown. Something really bad is going to happen tonight," Jonathan said. "I *know* it!"

Sienna looked at him. "Did you put these in here?"

"No. But look at this."

He flipped to a page and held up the book for Sienna. She saw a black-and-white portrait of Art the Clown, exact in every detail, down to the bastard's cold, dead eyes.

"It's *him*," Jonathan said.

"Daddy drew this?"

"That's not all."

He flipped through more pages, showing more black-and-white images—a man with beard stubble and curly black hair, a look of horror on his face, blood spatter in the background; a bald man lying on the ground, blood on his face and neck, more blood running from his mouth; a naked blonde woman hanging upside down, hands bound behind her back, mouth sealed with duct tape.

He turned to another page and again held up the book. This time the drawing was of a Sienna—or rather, the winged warrior angel in her battle armor—sword in one hand, the severed head of a horned demon in the other.

"What if you're connected too?" Jonathan said.

Sienna could hear the fear and worry in his voice. "What? Jonathan, you're acting crazy."

She quickly rose from the bed, walked over to stand by the window. Her brother was starting to freak her out.

"He created this character for *you*," Jonathan insisted. "He gave you that sword right before he died. It's like he saw this coming."

Sienna thought about her nightmare of the Clown Café, thought about seeing Art—or someone dressed as Art—in Abracadabra, and she felt herself beginning to panic. "Daddy drew a lot of things for me. He bought me tons of shit. Seriously, what's wrong with you? Do you even hear yourself?"

Mom walked into Jonathan's then and crossed her arms. "What's going on in here?" she demanded.

Sienna turned to her and gestured toward the sketchbook in Jonathan's hands. "Did he show this to you?"

"She doesn't care," Jonathan said. "She's just pissed 'cause I might get suspended."

"Suspended?" Sienna was shocked. "For *what*?"

Mom looked at Jonathan. "Oh, you didn't tell her?" She turned to Sienna. "Your brother brought a dead animal to school this morning."

"What?"

"Yeah. *A dead animal.* Can you believe it? He vandalized the halls. I almost had a fucking heart attack when they told me."

"It wasn't me!" Jonathan protested. "It was the clown! The little girl brought it in!"

"I don't want to hear another word about this goddamn clown! He was covered in blood on his shirt and his hands when he got here. The principal *literally* caught you red-handed."

"That's 'cause he threw it at me!"

Mom pointed at Sienna. "I should've listened to you. You've been telling me over and over again about this kid. I'm calling Dr. Shifren on Monday. I'm putting a stop to this now." She stabbed her finger in the direction of his desk, where an empty cereal bowl rested. "And put your goddamn bowl in the sink. I'm not telling you again."

Mom turned and walked out the room, muttering to herself as she left.

Jonathan looked up at Sienna. "It *was* him. You gotta believe me."

Sienna didn't know what to think. So much information had come at her so fast and she needed time to process it. But she knew one thing: Jonathan was her brother, and he was scared.

She sat down on the bed next to him again and sighed. "Jonathan, it was probably just some kids at school messing around. It's the one-year anniversary of the murders. I already saw some... *jerk* wearing that costume in Abracadabra an hour ago."

"Was he with the little girl?"

"No, I didn't see a little girl."

"What about the drawings? And these articles, then?"

"We both know what happened to Daddy. Okay, none of this was his fault. And all of these ugly things in here..."—she tapped the sketchbook with a finger—"that's not who he was. He loved you... very much." She put a hand on his shoulder, squeezed gently, and gave him what she hoped was a reassuring smile. "It's gonna be okay."

She rose to leave, but Jonathan grabbed her hand to stop her.

"Stay home tonight," he said.

"Jonathan..."

"Please! I'm begging you!"

"Nothing's gonna happen," she said.

"Fine. Just don't act surprised when a bunch of people get killed tonight."

He turned away from Sienna, stood, carried Daddy's sketchbook back to his desk, and plopped into his chair. Sienna felt she should say something more, but she couldn't think of anything, so she left before she made things worse. As she headed down the stairs, she asked herself if she truly believed what she'd told her brother, about how nothing bad would happen tonight.

She didn't know.

Mom was sitting in front of her laptop when Sienna entered the kitchen, but she wasn't working, just staring off into space.

"Have you ever?" she asked, clearly exasperated.

Sienna leaned forward, put her hands on the back of a chair, and thought for a moment. "I believe him," she said.

Mom looked at her as if she'd just sprouted an extra head. "About what?"

Sienna looked at her. "I don't think he vandalized the school."

"Now you believe him. Yesterday he was the Zodiac Killer. What's changed?"

Sienna was going to tell Mom about her dream last night and her encounter with Art in Abracadabra. But before she could speak, the doorbell rang.

"Get the door." Mom sighed and put her hands to her head, as if she was getting a headache.

The moment had passed, but that was all right. Sienna doubted Mom would believe her any more than she believed Jonathan. Sienna grabbed the plastic candy bucket from the counter and headed for the front door. The news was on the TV in the living room, and a reporter was saying something about a recall of romaine lettuce because of an E. Coli outbreak, but Sienna ignored the story. She had enough problems of her own.

CHAPTER NINETEEN

"Trick or treat!"

Allie's first trick-or-treater of the season was a cute little girl wearing a scarecrow outfit. A woman who presumably was her mother—and who wasn't in costume—stood next to her, beaming, as if to say, *Isn't my child the most precious thing in the world?* Allie decided to ignore the mother and focused on the girl.

"Hi. Happy Halloween!"

Allie reached into the plastic bowl—which was black and had a cat's face on one side—selected a few pieces of candy, and placed them into the girl's bag.

"Oh, I love your makeup," Allie said.

"She did it all herself," Mom said, a bit smugly.

Of course the little genius did, Allie thought. Aloud, she said to the girl, "Wow! Great job!"

Mom leaned toward her daughter. "What do you say?" she prompted.

The girl smiled. "Thank you!"

"You're welcome," Allie said.

The mother and daughter waved at the same time, their motions eerily identical, and then Mom put her hand on her daughter's shoulder to turn her around, slid her hand down to the girl's mid-back, and steered her along the walkway. Cute kid, but Allie felt sorry for her. She knew what it was like to have a controlling mother, and it was absolutely no fun. It was possible she'd misread their relationship, viewed it through the lens of her own issues with her mother. But she didn't think so.

Allie heard the sounds of trick-or-treating in full swing—children talking, laughing, shouting, giggling, the parents admonishing them to hush, to not run on the sidewalk, to wait for them to catch up.

Kids moved through the neighborhood in various costumes, some as minimal as a T-shirt that said *This IS My Costume!* and some so elaborate they would've stood a chance of winning a professional cosplay competition. Parents of the younger kids kept a close eye on their progeny, while parents of older kids mostly ignored their offspring and talked to other adults or chatted on their phones.

Earlier, when Allie had spoken to her mother outside Abracadabra—*after* Mom had given her the third degree about where she was going tonight and who she was going with—she'd told Allie she would be a little late coming home from work. The firm was preparing to defend a high-profile client against an embezzlement charge, and they needed to do some "strategizing" since the trial was coming up soon. Would Allie be a lamb and pass out candy to the kids until she got home to take over?

Allie had hoped Mom would be home by *now*, so she'd have plenty of time to do her makeup and get her costume ready for tonight. She couldn't do either of those things if she had to answer the door every few minutes and hand out candy bags. But all she'd said was, *Okay, no problem*. She didn't want to argue with Mom. Allie needed to remain on her good side if she wanted to get out of the house and go to the party tonight.

But standing here, watching and listening to children having a great time, almost made it worth rushing to get ready later. It brought back good memories, times when Sienna, Brooke, and she had gone trick-or-treating together. The three had known each other since kindergarten, and Allie was confident they'd remain friends until they died—or developed dementia and forgot each other existed.

She wasn't naïve. She knew a lot of school friendships didn't make it through college, careers, romantic relationships, and especially children. She didn't know if she wanted a family, and neither did Brooke or Sienna, but that wasn't the point. The point was time had a way of pulling people apart, and she was determined not to let that happen. The Three Amigas, together forever.

Or until death would them part.

She was about to go back inside when she noticed an older-model black van with a white hood parked across the street from her house. She didn't recall seeing that vehicle before. This was an upper middle-class neighborhood. People here didn't drive black vans, especially not old ones. Hell, most of the residents wouldn't venture close enough to the thing to touch it.

It probably belonged to someone who drove their kid here from somewhere less well-off, in hopes of snagging some really good candy. As far as Allie was concerned, more power to them.

But there was something about the van that really bothered her, on like a primal level, but she wasn't sure what it was. Maybe it just appeared extra-creepy because it was Halloween? The vehicle almost seemed like it wasn't a physical thing so much as a nothingness carved into ordinary space, utter and profound emptiness. And was someone sitting in the passenger's seat?

She squinted and tried to make out the details, but all she could see was a child's silhouette—a child with strange, unsettling teeth and glowing yellow eyes.

A chill rippled down her spine that had nothing to do with the cool October breeze. But as soon as it ended, she chided herself. She remembered telling Sienna about letting her imagination get the better of her: *If there's even a one percent chance that something can be explained scientifically, bet on that one percent every time.*

Weird teeth, glowing eyes? Definitely a costume. It *was* fucking Halloween, after all. She hoped whoever had driven the child here didn't stay away from the vehicle too long. She'd keep an eye on the van, and if the driver didn't return soon, she'd go check on the girl, maybe give her a bag of candy.

Her logical mindset firmly back in place, Allie went inside and closed the door behind her.

She placed the cat bowl on the floor near the door and started heading for her bedroom. If she brought some of her makeup downstairs from her room, she might be able to get ready—at least a little—in between visits by little ghosties and ghoulies demanding their tribute.

The doorbell rang.

Allie spun on her heel, returned to the candy bowl, picked it up, opened the door—

—and saw a six-foot clown with serial-killer eyes and the nastiest-looking teeth she'd ever seen staring at her. He held a large trash bag in his hands.

"Aren't you a little old to be trick-or-treating?" she asked.

The clown's blood-stippled face remained frozen.

"Wait a minute. Aren't you the guy from the costume shop?"

The clown smiled and his head bobbed up and down several times in acknowledgement.

"You are? *What* are you doing here?"

The clown opened his trash bag and thrust it toward her. The sudden motion surprised Allie, but she remained calm.

"Seriously, do you live around here or something?" she said.

The clown swiftly lowered his bag, raised his shoulders, and then tilted his head left, then right. She imagined a little kid doing this then saying, "I don't know," in a sing-song voice.

"You're really weird, you know that?"

More energetic nodding. He opened his bag once more.

"Look, I get it, dude. The whole creepy silent mime gimmick. I mean, it's very effective. And the blood is a nice touch also."

The clown leaned his head to the side, as if to say, *Aw, shucks.*

"I can't give you anything."

214

He thrust the bag toward her again, more insistently than last time.

"No, I'm sorry. Really. No candy for grown-ups. Come on."

She went inside, and as she started to close the door, she saw the clown smiling at her… although really it looked more like he was baring his teeth in anger. She closed the door the rest of the way and resumed heading for her bedroom. Christ almighty, that had been all *kinds* of fucked-up.

The doorbell rang.

She had no doubt it was the weirdo clown. She stopped, looked back, raised her voice. "Go away."

This time he knocked.

She turned to face the door, *really* pissed off now. "Seriously, asshole. Go bother someone else."

Now he pounded on the door—four times.

That. Was. It.

Allie rushed to the door, threw it open, and stepped onto the porch.

The clown stood there, smiling, bag held out and open.

"Are you kidding me right now? I said get out of here. I mean it!"

He thrust the bag toward her, and his smile gave way to what looked like a snarl, and his eyes burned with anger. Allie didn't feel threatened yet. Not in this neighborhood, not in her home. But she *was* starting to become uncomfortable with the clown's stubborn presence. What would it take to— Then it came to her.

"Wait. So, if I give you candy, you'll leave?"

The clown nodded three times, but his expression didn't soften.

It hadn't occurred to Allie that all she had to do was give him some candy to get him to leave. He was a grown man. He could buy candy any time he wanted! But whatever, all she cared about was making him go away.

She grabbed a handful of candy from the cat bowl and threw it at his garbage bag. "Fine. Here. Happy Halloween."

Several pieces missed and fell to the porch, but the majority went in. The clown looked down to examine what he'd been given, and without thinking, Allie did the same. That's when she saw what *else* he had in his bag—a collection of old, rusted, and in some cases *blood-spattered* metal objects: screws, forks, pliers, nails, scissors, knives, a hacksaw, and... wait, was that a fucking *postmortem hammer*? Where the hell had he got hold of that? In fact, a number of the items looked like surgical equipment. Since she intended on becoming a doctor, she'd watched a lot of online videos about basic medical topics, and surgical equipment had been among them.

She remembered something she'd told Sienna in the bodega: "...there are gonna be hundreds of douchebags dressed up as that psycho tonight."

This creepy-ass guy wasn't dressed as a random clown. He was dressed as the goddamn *Miles County* Clown. Armed like the motherfucker, too.

She remembered Sienna's description of the bastard from her nightmare, and how the harasser in Abracadabra had looked exactly like him.

Right down to the little black dot on the tip of his nose.

She raised her head at the same time the clown did, and there it was, at the end of the clown's long hooked nose—the little black dot.

The clown grinned at her, his eyes blazing with... hate? Lust? Anger? Some sick combination of the three which didn't have a name? Allie slowly backed through the open doorway. She wanted to slam the door shut, but she feared if she made any sudden moves, it might set off the wacko. So, she forced herself to shut the door slowly—it was the hardest thing she'd ever done in her life—and when it was closed and the latch softly clicked, she slowly engaged the deadbolt. Trembling, feeling like she was going to vomit up all the chocolate she'd eaten before trick-or-treating started, she went to one of the front windows and peeked through the blinds.

The clown was heading down the front walk, trash bag slung over his shoulder.

It was over.

She hurried into the kitchen, where she'd left her phone, and called Sienna. After a dozen or so rings, the call went to voicemail. Allie intended to leave a message, to tell Sienna how the asshole from Abracadabra had showed up at her house, but when the beep came, she just said, "It's Allie. Call back when you get a chance. If not, I'll talk to you tonight." She disconnected and put her phone back on the counter.

She'd had a chance to calm down a bit, and she was starting to think rationally again. What were the odds that the jerk at her door had *really* been the Miles County Clown? Nearly zero. And while the items in his garbage bag might have been real, she was certain the blood on them was not, and neither was the blood on his face or on his gloves. All of it had been just part of the show, a performance by a pathetic loser who got his rocks off scaring people.

That was it, nothing more, and definitely not something to bother Sienna about. She'd already had a panic attack at school today, and she'd had another after the clown tormented her in the store. Sienna needed time to chill out before the party tonight, and once they were at the party, the three of them would have so much fun that Sienna would forget about that fucking clown.

And maybe she would, too.

Sienna closed the door after filling the bags of a small group of trick-or-treaters—none dressed as clowns, thank god—when a reporter's voice on the television caught her attention. She went into the living room, sat on the couch, and watched. A pretty woman in her thirties with long wavy hair was delivering the news in a pleasant but professional manner.

"In other news, talk-show provocateur Monica Brown is still in critical condition this evening following a violent attack which took place at KLA studios earlier today. The TV host was violently assaulted in her dressing room after a live broadcast with guest Victoria Heyes. Heyes is the sole survivor of the Miles County Massacre, which left eight people dead and Heyes in critical condition. The twenty-year-old was arrested at the crime scene and taken into custody by authorities.

"The interview sparked controversy upon its announcement given Brown's exploitative tendencies. Heyes was released from St. Michael's Hospital yesterday evening after months of rehabilitation and psychoanalysis..." The woman paused. "Like you, Sienna."

Sienna's breath caught in her throat. The woman looked directly at her for a moment, and then she looked back at the camera and resumed speaking in her cheery professional style.

"Halloween is officially here, and thousands are lining up for the parade in New York City's East Village. Weather conditions are expected to be cold and rainy, so dress warm if you're planning to attend."

Sienna leapt from the couch, ran from the living room, up the stairs, and into her bedroom. She shut the door—she didn't want Mom or Jonathan checking on her—then rushed to one of the side worktables. She grabbed the Xanax from her array of prescription meds, opened the bottle, shook out two pills, and tossed them into her mouth. She dry-swallowed them, then picked up a cup of water left over from last night and washed the pills down.

She stood there for several moments, doing the breathing exercises Dr. Shifren had taught her. Inhale for a ten count, hold for a ten count, exhale for a ten count, repeat. She did this ten times, then she went to her bed, laid down, and waited for the meds to kick in. If more trick-or-treaters came, Mom or Jonathan would have to deal with them.

The reporter hadn't actually spoken to her, she knew that. It had only occurred in her mind, but that frightened her as much as if the woman *had* addressed her, maybe more. After everything she'd been through in the last year—Daddy's death, panic attacks, months of therapy—she supposed a little hallucination now and then was only to be expected, right?

Add to that the stress of the last day—her worries about Jonathan, the conflict with Mom, her nightmare of Art and the Clown Café, the fire, being confronted by an Art imitator at Abracadabra (at least, she *hoped* he was an imitator), discovering that Daddy had been collecting newspaper clippings about the murders committed by Art, Jonathan's insistence that she was somehow connected to whatever fucked-up shit was going on in this town... Was it any surprise that her mind had slipped a gear?

Her breathing became more relaxed, and she knew the Xanax was beginning to do its job.

Maybe she should stay home tonight. It had been embarrassing enough having a panic attack at school, but having one at a party would be way worse. Plus, she wouldn't just be embarrassing herself. Allie and Brooke would be there too. If she *did* have a panic attack, her friends would only be concerned about her. They wouldn't care what anyone else thought of them.

She'd feel the same way if their positions had been reversed. But she didn't want to spoil the night for them. Why should they miss out on the fun just because *she* had problems? Plus, Jonathan would feel better if she stayed home. She didn't believe all that stuff about being connected to Art and the killings somehow—at least, she didn't *want* to believe it—but he did. Jonathan was clearly struggling, and if her staying home helped him remain calm tonight, then that would be a good thing.

She thought of Daddy's sketchbook then. Where had Jonathan found it, and why had he been hiding it from Mom and her? He hadn't answered her questions about the sketchbook. He was hiding something, but what was it, and *why* was he hiding it? She thought of Daddy's artwork on the pages, especially his drawing of the warrior angel.

He created this character for you...

She sat up and looked at her worktables. The pieces of the costume were finished and ready—all she had to do was put them on. She looked over at the chair where she had put her store-bought wings. She might not have created them, but they represented her persistence and her strength.

It would be a shame to have put so many hours into building the costume not to wear it, and it would be a nice way to honor Daddy's memory, to celebrate him instead of mourning him. And while she didn't believe in destiny, if Jonathan was right and she did have some important role to play in whatever the hell was going on, did she want to run from that, or did she want to confront it head-on?

She got out of bed, took her wings from the chair, and started toward her workbenches.

CHAPTER TWENTY

Allie sat at her makeup table in her room, leaning close to the mirror as she put on mascara. She was going to be a witch tonight, but a much more sophisticated version than the rubber-nose-and-claws witch she'd been at school today. Her pointed hat for tonight sat on a nearby chair, and her black dress with the gray skull pattern hung on her closet door. Last week, she'd bought a pair of killer black boots to complete her outfit, and she was looking forward to wearing them for the first time tonight. There was no way her costume could ever compare to Sienna's, but she liked it, and that was all that mattered. Besides, she'd look damn cute in it.

It had started raining a short time ago, and she'd opened her bedroom window partway so she could listen to the rain and distant thunder. She loved the sound of rain, had ever since she was a little girl, and she enjoyed the feeling of the cool air on her skin. Because of the rain, the trick-or-treaters had thinned out considerably, and if any more came to the door begging, they'd find themselves out of luck. If Mom had wanted to make sure they gave out all their candy, then she should've been home on time to help pass it out. She couldn't expect Allie to do everything.

She tried to concentrate on applying her makeup, but she was having trouble focusing. Her encounter with the Miles County Clown wannabee had shaken her up more than she'd thought. It wasn't so much his angry insistence she give him candy—although that had been bad enough—as it was something less tangible, more difficult to put into words. She didn't believe in psychic powers, but she did believe in instinct. Humans viewed themselves as separate from the natural world, but they weren't. At their core, they were animals, and they still possessed the same finely honed instincts their small mammalian ancestors had millions of years ago. They might not always *listen* to those instincts, but they were there. And Allie's instincts told her that something had been seriously dangerous about that clown, and she'd been lucky the candy had placated him and he departed. Who knew what he might have done if she'd kept refusing his demand? The thought made her shudder. She'd always loved Halloween as much as all the other holidays, but after this year, she thought maybe she would love it a little less.

She heard a sound then, like shattering glass, although the rain masked it enough that she wasn't sure. Had some stupid kid thrown a rock at one of their windows as a Halloween prank? That kind of destructive behavior didn't happen often in this neighborhood, but it *did* happen.

She decided to go investigate—for her peace of mind, if nothing else. She wouldn't be able to concentrate on getting ready for the party if she kept imagining that someone had broken in. Besides, if her mother came home to find a broken window, she'd freak out. If Allie did a little reconnaissance now, she could call Mom and give her a damage report, which would at least prepare her for what awaited her.

Allie rose from her makeup table and left her room.

She went down the stairs cautiously, listening for any sounds that shouldn't be there, but all she heard was the rain. It was louder than she expected, though. Clearer.

She didn't like that.

The house was filled with shadow. She hadn't turned on the lights when she went upstairs to her room and, between the rainclouds and the approaching dusk, it might as well have been full night outside.

She didn't like this either.

The rainfall became louder as she reached the bottom of the stairs. It seemed to be coming from the direction of the dining room, and the animal instincts she'd been thinking about earlier screamed a warning to her: *Do NOT go there!* She knew she should listen, that she should leave through the front door, no matter how hard it was raining, and run to a neighbor's house. That would be the smart move, and if there was one thing Allie was, it was smart.

But the animal part of her brain did more than warn. It also *feared*, and it was fear that drove her to walk toward the dining room. Fear of the unknown. She *had* to learn what had made that sound, because once she knew, the thing would become real, and something real could be dealt with. Three more steps, and she was in the dining room.

224

The patio door had been shattered, and there was glass scattered on the floor. The glass had fallen inward, not outward. That meant someone had broken it from the outside. And that someone could be inside right now.

She heard footsteps then, turned in their direction, saw the clown walk into the kitchen, grab a glass from a cupboard, then go to the sink and pour himself a drink of water from the tap, as casually as if he lived here. He drained the entire glass in one go, then placed it on the counter. Seemingly unaware of Allie's presence, he picked up a pair of objects sitting on the other side of the sink. When he turned, she saw he held a scalpel in his left hand, surgical scissors in his right. They didn't have these tools in the house. Her gut twisted when she realized he'd brought them with him. He saw her then, standing there, watching him, scared out of her mind. He grinned and worked the scissors a couple times. *Shik-shik!*

"No! No!!"

She turned and ran like hell.

Her first impulse was an animal one — *Go to your lair and hide!* So she ran for the stairs. She was almost there when Art—and it was Art, the real one, the murderer, the monster from Sienna's dream; she believed this now— stepped in front of her, teeth bared, eyes wild. He'd gone the other way out of the kitchen to try to head her off.

"No!" she shrieked.

She flew up the stairs, moving faster than she had in her life. She heard the *thump-thump-thump* of Art's large boots on the steps behind her, felt the vibrations in her feet. When she reached the second floor, she dashed into her room.

Her cell phone was on her dresser, but she didn't go for it. Art was right behind her, swiping the scalpel through the air, trying to cut her. She grabbed hold of the white bookcase holding various items of importance to her—a seashell she'd collected from Myrtle Beach when she was seven; a snow globe her father had gotten her for Christmas, the last one he spent with them before leaving; a cross stitch sampler Sienna had made for her that said, *Keep Kicking Ass, Girl!*; a second-place trophy from a spelling bee competition in middle school; and—most precious of all—a framed photo of Sienna, Brooke, and her splashing around in a wading pool when they'd been children. She pulled the shelves down in front of Art, hoping to trip him or at least slow him down for a couple of seconds. She didn't care that her treasures tumbled to the floor when she did this. All she cared about was staying alive as long as she could.

"No!" she screamed again.

The bookcase fell, but Art saw it in time to stop so it didn't strike him.

Allie raced to her window, opened it the rest of the way, and started to crawl through, intending to fling herself out into the open air. She hoped she wouldn't injure herself so badly when she hit the lawn that she wouldn't be able to get up and continue running. She knew it was a crazy idea with almost no chance of success, but it was all she had.

Before she could leap to freedom, Art jumped over the shelves, grabbed the back of her sweater, and yanked her away from the window. He spun her toward the bed, shoved her face down onto the mattress, then grabbed a fistful of her hair and yanked her head back. With a single swift motion, Art drew the scalpel's blade in a straight line down the left side of her face, cutting from her forehead down to her chin, slicing her eyeball along the way. Allie felt as if her face were on fire, and blood streamed from the wound, spilling down the front of her sweater. She screamed and Art held her like that for a moment, as if savoring her pain and shock, before throwing her to the floor.

She rolled onto her side and attempted to crawl away from Art, wanting to keep the clown in sight, needing to know what was going to happen next. How many times had Brooke told her that she thought too much? Even now, one eye destroyed and bleeding like a stuck pig, she couldn't stop thinking.

She couldn't stop screaming, either. Sound came out of her throat of its own accord, providing shrill accompaniment to Art's assault.

When she reached her dresser, she pulled herself up onto her feet. But she heard the *shik-shik* of the surgical scissors, and she knew Art had exchanged one weapon for another. She saw his reflection in the dresser mirror as he approached, and the expression of maniacal glee on his face made him look more demon than man.

"No! No!"

Art grabbed the back of her hair and held her head tightly in position so she was facing the mirror. She got her first good look at her scalpel wound, and it didn't seem real. How many times in her life had she looked into a mirror and regarded her face? Hundreds? Thousands? And always her flesh had been smooth and unmarked—

not counting the occasional zit, of course. But she didn't recognize the face looking back at her now. It wasn't just the deep cut from the scalpel or all the blood smeared on her mouth and chin, either. It was the fear in her remaining eye, wild and unreasoning.

I'm an animal, she thought. *Prey, ripe for slaughter.*

As if Art could hear her thoughts, he slid the scissors into the soft flesh of Allie's scalp and began swiftly cutting. She cried out—"Ah! Ah! Ah!"—as he worked, blood from the new wounds running down her face, getting into her left eye and turning the world crimson, filling her mouth with the coppery tang of her life. When Art was finished, he yanked on her hair with surprising strength. Once, twice... and then her scalp peeled away with a sickening, wet sucking sound.

She caught a red-hazed glimpse of herself in the mirror. The top of her head was hairless, raw, and bloody.

Art threw her to the floor and used the scissors to cut off her clothes, like doctors did for seriously injured patients in emergency rooms. She thought he'd cut off her bra and panties too, but it seemed the clown wasn't interested in *that* kind of assault. Instead, he took hold of her upper arm, pulled her to her feet, and flung her onto the bed once more.

She landed on her stomach, and before she could move, Art placed one hand on her shoulder to hold her down, then began cutting a horizontal line on her back just below her bra strap. Her screaming was nonstop now, and the pain had reached a height she could never have imagined a human body capable of. It was funny when you thought about it. She'd planned to be a doctor, and here she was, being mutilated by surgical tools. Maximum irony. Maybe Art had even planned it that way somehow.

He stopped cutting and stabbed her in the back several times, the blows hard, the cuts deep. He tugged on her flesh, pulled a strip away, tossed it to the side. Then one hand grabbed the upper part of her left arm, the other her wrist, and he pulled, breaking the arm at the joint. He began bending the forearm back and forth, back and forth, pushing it farther than it was designed to go, pushing, pushing...

Then he pulled hard, and the forearm broke away from her body and blood fountained from the wound. She howled with pain, and within herself, in a far dark place where even this amount of agony couldn't reach, she had a single thought.

I'm... sorry... I... complimented... your... fucking... outfit...

Art threw her arm onto the floor, then rolled her onto her back, took hold of her right hand, and raised her arm. He took her ring finger and pinkie in his left hand, her thumb and forefinger in his right hand—and then he pulled in opposite directions. Allie's undamaged eye was filled with blood and tears, but her vision cleared for an instant, and she saw Art's eyes. They were dull, glassy, empty, and utterly inhuman. Lizard eyes. Shark eyes...

Her arm split down the middle to the elbow, and this time the pain reached all the way to the deepest part of her mind. She was sure she was screaming, but she could no longer hear herself.

She looked up at the ceiling and saw a decoration she'd made, something she would see every night before she fell asleep—a golden geometric design with the outline of a heart. There were three things clipped to it: the word *Happy*, a little heart attached to the bottom of the first P; a strip of paper with the words *PRETTY IN PINK!* printed on it; and lastly, a strip of three black-and-white photos—one of Allie, one of Sienna, and one of Brooke—taken in a Coney Island photobooth last summer.

Love… you… guys…

Then Art swiped his scalpel back and forth across her chest six times, each slice sending lines of blood into the air. When he was finished, he jumped off the bed and jogged out of the room like a performer who'd finished his act and was leaving the stage. Allie—her body a flaming pyre of agony—rolled off the bed and fell to the floor. She barely felt the impact. She began crawling, pulling herself forward as best she could with her split-down-the-middle arm and pushing herself with her feet. Every inch of her was covered with blood, and her bedclothes and carpet were drenched with the red, wet stuff.

"No," she breathed, so softly the word was barely audible. "No, no, no…"

She had no destination in mind, no plan. The girl who thought all the time could no longer think, was no longer *capable* of thought. She was just a collection of skin, nerves, and organs—much of it damaged or missing—a broken and malfunctioning flesh machine that moved for a single reason: to try to escape the pain. But that was impossible because she *was* the pain now. There was nothing else left.

She heard a noise then, a series of musical tones she couldn't place at first, but which were vaguely familiar. They continued to play, and sound broke through the pain and jumpstarted a part of Allie's mind. Phone. *Someone calling. Sienna?* Something stirred within her, a small spark akin to hope. If she could reach her phone…

The device lay atop her dresser, and she sat up partway and scooted across the carpet, moving as fast as her injured body would allow. *Don't hang up, don't hang up…*

Then Art came running back into the room, grinning with delight, an open bottle of bleach in one hand, a container of salt in the other.

No!

Art poured the bleach onto Allie, making sure to cover her entire body. When he was finished, he tossed aside the empty bottle, then quite literally poured salt onto Allie's wounds.

Allie understood then that she had only *thought* she'd experienced ultimate pain. Pain was infinite, she realized, and there was always a new level to discover.

It was strange, but even though Art had been completely silent the entire time—she hadn't even heard him breathe hard—she thought now she could hear him laugh…

And laugh…

And *laugh*.

Then he poured salt into his hand and slapped it on the flayed portion of her back and rubbed it around hard. Then he did the same to the top of her head, and to the long vertical cut on the left of her face—the first

231

one he'd made. Then, for good measure, he plunged his fingers into her ruined eye, took hold of the flesh around the socket, and ripped the skin completely off the side of her face.

And Allie experienced yet another new level.

CHAPTER TWENTY-ONE

Mom was sitting in the living room, glass of red wine in hand, watching a movie on TV. She didn't have the volume up high—she never did—but as Sienna came down the stairs, she could tell by the dialogue which movie she was watching. An old favorite: the original *Night of the Living Dead*. Mom didn't like scary movies as a rule, but she enjoyed them around Halloween, especially when the whole family would gather to watch. Daddy had *loved* scary movies, and Mom had loved her husband. Sienna wondered if by watching the movie, Mom was reliving happy memories or sad ones. Probably some of both, she decided.

The best thing about watching *Night of the Living Dead* with Mom was listening to her complain about her namesake in the movie—Barbara.

The woman sees one goddamn zombie kill her brother, and she goes catatonic after that and sits around the house while everyone else does work. And then she ends up eaten by her zombie brother! Idiot!

Sienna wasn't going to watch the movie tonight, though. She was heading out to have some badly needed fun—and debut the creation she'd worked so hard on for so long.

She stepped into the living room and stopped to give Mom a good look at her warrior angel costume, complete at last. She smiled, proud of her work.

"Well?" she asked.

The sections were made of plastic with a thin layer of foam padding inside, the outside painted golden bronze to look like armor. Spiked right shoulder guard, two forearm guards, armored boots that came up to her knees, a chest plate that showed a *little* cleavage and left her midriff bare, short leather armor skirt in front, short chainmail armor skirt around her hips and butt. A V-shaped buckle on her belt that had a design of a bird skull with feathered wings attached to its sides.

Daddy had designed the outfit, including the symbol for the buckle, but he'd never said what meaning the winged bird skull had, if any. Sienna had decided the winged skull was a kind of yin-yang thing, a symbol of necessary opposites. The skull represented death, and the wings represented life. You couldn't have one without the other.

She'd braided the left side of her hair in corn rows and worked in a number of metal objects she'd taken off an old charm bracelet. She'd sprayed blue highlights in the rest of her hair. She'd used makeup to draw three lines above and below her right eye—two gold lines with a red one in the middle—to look like battle scars. She'd even painted her nails the same color as her costume. Last were her wings from Abracadabra, the feather tips spraypainted a soft pink.

She looked every inch a hero from some fantasy realm—except for the cell phone in her left hand. She'd decided not to wear her nose ring tonight. It didn't really go with the costume's vibe, and besides, Daddy hadn't drawn her character wearing a nose ring, and she wanted to look as close to his design as possible.

Mom's eyes widened as she examined Sienna's costume, but she kept her expression carefully neutral as she replied. "It's... revealing."

"Three months of work, and all you can say is 'revealing'?"

As far as Sienna was concerned, her costume was only as revealing as the average two-piece swimsuit. Less, even!

"Your tits are practically popping out," Mom said.

Sienna looked down to check. "They are not!"

"They are. Turn around."

Sienna rolled her eyes, but she did as Mom requested. When she finished her slow pirouette, she said, "You knew what I was making. It's Daddy's character."

"Yeah, well seeing it on paper and seeing it on your daughter are two different things. You look like you're going to a strip club."

"Mom, this is how people dress on Halloween these days. Do you have any idea how much work I put into this?"

"I'm not taking anything away from the artistry. You did an exceptional job. It's just... when did Halloween become synonymous with sex?"

Sienna laughed. "You're such a prude." Her phone dinged and she checked the screen. "Okay, that's my ride. Later."

She went over to Mom and gave her a quick kiss on the cheek.

"Have fun," Mom said.

Sienna headed for the door, but just as she reached it, Mom called her name.

"Sienna."

Sienna turned.

Mom's voice softened. "Dad would've loved it."

Sienna smiled. "Bye."

She opened the door and stepped out into the dark.

Eva Russell entered her house and closed the door behind her. The rain had let up, but there was still rolling thunder in the distance. Good. Allie might love rain, but she hated it—especially when it thundered. Loud noises had frightened her since she'd been a child. She wondered if kids would return to the streets to finish trick-or-treating. Most likely, she decided. That's what she would've done when she was a kid—as long as there was no thunder.

She immediately noticed the candy bowl on the floor, as well as the fact that it was mostly full.

"Allie?" she called. "Have you been handing out the candy?" She walked to a nearby wall and hung her purse on one of the hooks attached to it. "That bowl is still filled to the brim."

She started for the stairs, took hold of the banister, looked upward. "Allie?"

No answer.

Had that girl left before Eva had gotten home? She *knew* she wasn't supposed to do that! Just as she knew she was supposed to stay and pass out candy until trick-or-treating was over, which she had agreed to and had clearly *not* done. Allie had become increasingly disobedient the last few months, and Eva suspected it was because her eighteenth birthday was coming up. She would legally be an adult then, and like all kids who turn eighteen, she probably thought she'd be free of parental authority. Maybe that's how it worked in some households, but not this one. As long as she lived under Eva's roof, she would have to live by Mother's rules.

She knew Allie thought she was too strict—the girl had told her plenty of times—but she didn't understand that Eva did it for her own protection. The world was a dangerous place, especially for young women. It was filled with people who wanted to hurt you in any number of ways. They tried to use you for their own ends, manipulate you, take advantage of you, exploit you, lie to you... leave you.

Like Allie's bastard of a father. Here one day, gone the next, without so much as a note left behind to explain why. *That's* why Eva was so strict with Allie. She wanted to make sure her little girl never experienced a hurt like that. Maybe she shouldn't let her go to that party tonight. There'd be boys there, girls too, and any one of them might try to sidle up to her daughter and try to get their hooks into her. Allie *had* broken her promise to pass out the candy. That would be sufficient pretext for rescinding her permission to go out tonight. Allie would throw a fit, of course, but she wouldn't argue. She'd learned a long time ago that when your mother is a lawyer, you can never win an argument with her.

Of course, if Allie *wasn't* in her room, if she'd already *left* for the party...

She was about to head upstairs and check when she felt a breeze lightly kiss her cheek. She frowned. Had Allie left a window open downstairs? Whenever it rained, she opened windows all over the house and rainwater would soak the curtains, wet the floor. But Allie had *never* left a window open when the house was unoccupied.

She might be a rebellious child, but she was the most responsible person Eva knew—aside from herself, of course. It was the only reason she ever let the girl leave the house at all. Well, there was a first time for everything. Maybe Allie *had* left a window open, to piss off Eva, if for no other reason.

Eva turned away from the stairs and headed in the direction the breeze was coming from. She entered the dining room, stopped, and stared. Blue-white fluorescence from the streetlight outside illuminated the patio door, and Eva could see its glass had been broken, leaving only a few sharp pieces jutting from the frame.

A hand of ice closed around her heart and squeezed. The world *was* a dangerous place, and sometimes you didn't need to leave your safe little home to find this out. Sometimes the world forced its way into your home to remind you.

"Allie?"

She backed out of the dining room, turned, and ran for the stairs.

"Allie, answer me!"

She headed up, and when she reached the second floor, she called out, "Where are you?"

She went straight for Allie's room, grabbed the doorknob, turned it, pushed the door open, rushed inside—

—and froze.

At first, all she saw was blood. It was *everywhere*—the bed, the dresser, the floor, the walls, the full-length mirror, even on the fucking ceiling, for god's sake! Then she noticed the red thing on the bed, and it took her a second to realize it was a human being. It took her five more seconds before she realized it was her daughter.

Allie sat with her back against the headboard, head drooping, legs splayed apart, wearing only panties. One of her arms ended at the elbow, and the other had chunks missing. The top of her head was gone too, half her face had been torn away to reveal the skull beneath, and both breasts were missing. Sitting on the bed next to Allie was... a clown?

He had blood on his face, hands, and clothes—her daughter's blood. He held some kind of sharp instruments, and he was slicing deep cuts into her left leg, as if it was a roast he was carving for dinner. Allie's right leg was nothing but bone from the knee down.

He's already eaten that part, Eva thought.

Her paralysis broke and she began making loud, breathy sounds, part whimper, part scream.

The clown looked at her and mimed roaring with laughter. He slapped his knee, then raised his hands palms up, as if to say, *Sorry! My bad!*

But as horrifying as the clown was, he was nothing compared to what happened next.

Eva had thought Allie was dead. How could anyone survive being so severely mutilated? But then her head jerked up, and her one remaining eye struggled to focus on Eva.

The clown pointed at her and silently laughed some more.

Allie's blood-slick lips parted, and then softly, she said a single word. "*Mom.*"

Eva released a full-throated scream then. She'd had a single, overriding mission in life, and that was to protect her daughter from getting hurt. But she'd failed... Christ almighty, she'd failed.

Her screams continued, one after the other, with only slight gasps for air between. The clown laughed a bit longer, then he rose from the bed and slowly walked toward her, grinning, pieces of Allie's flesh stuck between his blood-smeared teeth.

"What'd I tell you?" Brooke said.

Sienna grinned. "I never doubted you for a second."

People bathed in crimson light danced around brick columns to the thrum of a techno beat. Those who weren't dancing sat at tables or stood in small groups, drinks in hand, talking loudly to be heard over the noise. Most were in costume, and they ranged in age from early twenties to late thirties, and everyone seemed to be having a blast. When Brooke had told Allie and Sienna that she was going to take them to a hot new club near Bryant Park called Eclipse, Sienna actually had doubted her, at least a little. When Brooke got enthusiastic about

240

something, she tended to exaggerate how great it was, so Sienna had learned to keep her expectations to a minimum when Brooke wanted to introduce them to something cool she'd found. But in this case, Brooke hadn't oversold the club.

Brooke's costume fit her personality perfectly. It was fun, light-hearted, sexy, and attention-getting. Her hair was up and elaborately curled, with a dark fabric rose pinned on top. She wore huge golden hoop earrings and several necklaces. Her white long-sleeved blouse was bare at the shoulders, and low-cut without being slutty. A black corset encircled her waist, and her crimson skirt was short in front, revealing her legs, but long in back, reaching down to the backs of her knees. Sexy knee-high black boots completed her outfit. When Brooke had picked Sienna up at her house, Sienna had gotten her first look at Brooke's costume. "Wow," she had said. "You look fantastic! What are you supposed to be?"

"Hot Bitch!" Brooke had said, and they'd both laughed.

Brooke grabbed Sienna's hand. "Come on. Let's go get fucked up!"

She pulled Sienna into the crowd, and the two of them wove between dancers and headed to the bar. It was crowded, but they managed to squeeze their way into an open space and catch the attention of one of the bartenders. The woman came over to them and smiled.

"What can I get you guys?" she asked.

"Vodka and Coke, please," Brooke said.

Sienna was looking down at her phone, checking to see if Allie had called or texted. Allie had opted to drive herself instead of riding with Brooke and Sienna. "That way you guys won't have to leave the club early if my mom freaks out 'cause it's getting late and she wants me to come home," she'd said. But Allie wasn't here yet, and Sienna was starting to get worried. She knew Allie might be late if her mom started having second thoughts about letting her go out, and Allie had to convince her all over again. Plus, you never knew what the traffic would be like coming from Miles County into the city, and parking was *always* a pain in the ass. Still, not hearing from Allie for the last few hours bothered Sienna. It wasn't like her. She was always so good about staying in touch.

Brooke gave Sienna a gentle nudge with her elbow. "Off your phone. What do you want?"

Sienna looked up at the bartender and smiled. "Rum and Coke."

"Also, can we have two shots of whiskey, please?" Brooke added. "Thank you."

"Has Allie texted you back yet?"

Brooke didn't bother to look at her phone before answering. "No."

Irritated, Sienna said, "Well, can you check?"

Brooke smiled indulgently and did as Sienna asked. "Negative."

Sienna was starting to get really worried now. "You know, this isn't like her."

"It's *fine*," Brooke said. "She'll get here when she can. Just relax and have a good time for once in your life, okay?"

Sienna ignored her. "Maybe if I just text her mom, she'll get back to me."

"No," Brooke said sternly. "Off your phone. Phone down!"

"Okay!"

Sienna had added a leather pouch to her belt so she could carry her phone, ID, debit card, and house key, and she reluctantly tucked the phone in with the other items.

"Look," Brooke said, "we're gonna have fun in a stress-free environment."

It wasn't so much a statement as it was a command.

The bartender returned with their drinks. "You wanna open a tab?" she asked.

"Sure." Brooke gave the woman her credit card, and when the transaction was finished, she turned to Sienna. "Okay, let's go."

They left the bar and found an open space near the dance floor where they could stand. Sienna had a newfound appreciation for her substitute wings. Allie had been right. Their smaller size made it much easier to maneuver through the crowd.

Brooke raised her shot in a toast. "To a great night with my girls."

Sienna touched her glass to Brooke's. "To a great night."

"Happy Halloween," Brooke added, and they downed their shots.

Sienna had only partially lied to her mom when she said she didn't drink. The truth was she *rarely* drank, and she'd never had a straight shot before. She wasn't prepared for the nasty chemical taste and the explosion of warmth in her throat.

"Oh god," she said, grimacing.

Brooke grinned. "Aw, you're such an amateur."

"I do *not* know how you drink that shit."

Brooke held up her other drink. "Well, chase it!"

Before she could take a sip, someone wearing a simple ghost costume—a sheet with black-framed glasses worn over cut-out eyeholes—rushed up behind Brooke, grabbed her around the waist, and lifted her off her feet, roaring like an animal. Brooke squealed in surprise, the ghost put her down, and when she spun around to confront whoever it was, the ghost whipped off its sheet to reveal a tall handsome guy. He had thick brown hair past his ears, several days' growth of beard, and he wore a black shirt that had a drawing of a knife with blood on the end of the blade, and the words *JUST THE TIP, I PROMISE* in gray letters surrounding it.

Brooke smacked his chest with both hands. "You asshole!"

He grinned. "Happy Halloween, baby!"

He grabbed Brooke's face and kissed her passionately. At first, Sienna thought the guy was some drunk creep harassing Brooke, but then she saw Brooke kiss him back with just as much enthusiasm. This wasn't necessarily a sign that they knew each other. Brooke didn't sleep around, but she did live for the moment—unlike Sienna, who overthought everything—and if some random good-looking guy suddenly started kissing her, she might say, *Why the hell not?* and kiss him back.

The guy stepped back and admired Brooke's outfit. "You look *hot*," he pronounced.

Brooke beamed. "Oh yeah? You like my hair?"

"I do. How long did that take?"

"You don't wanna know." Brooke looked at his *costume.* "Nice shirt," she said sarcastically.

"Wishful thinking." He moved in to kiss her again, and this time Brooke turned her face so he kissed her on the cheek.

"I bet," she said, and laughed.

Sienna had stood by awkwardly as Brooke and the guy talked—and kissed—and now he stood behind her, put his arm around her just below her neck in a kind of half-sexual, half-friendly way. Brooke looked at Sienna and smiled. Her eyes were practically sparkling, and Sienna knew she really liked this guy. He was obviously older than her, but by how much she wasn't sure. A few years, maybe more.

She hoped he wasn't one of those older guys who liked to prey on younger women. She was probably misjudging him, she knew that, but when you were as attractive and impulsive as Brooke, it paid to be cautious. Although Sienna didn't think *cautious* was in Brooke's lexicon. If she decided she liked you, she went all in, no hesitation. Sienna had seen her friend get her heart broken this way—more than once—and she hoped it wouldn't happen again.

Brooke smiled at Sienna, and an unspoken message passed between them: *He's one of the good ones.* Sienna decided she would take him at face value—for now.

Brooke introduced the two of them. "Jeff, this is my best friend, Sienna."

Sienna smiled. "Hi."

"Wow," Jeff said. "*That* is a bad-ass outfit."

"Thank you."

245

"This girl is unbelievably talented," Brooke said. "You have *no* idea. She made this whole thing herself, head to toe. What did it take you? Like five months?"

"No," Sienna said. "It didn't take that long."

"Yes, it did," Brooke said. "It took *forever*. You're unbelievable."

"You know," Jeff said, tugging the hem of his T-shirt to straighten it, "honestly, I feel upstaged."

Sienna felt her face redden. She never handled praise well. "Okay, could you guys please stop? You're making me feel a *little* self-conscious."

"Oh," Brooke said. "Well, a couple of shots will help that." She and Jeff started chanting then. "Shots, shots, shots, shots!"

"No," Sienna said. "No, no, no. I *cannot* drink any more tonight. My mom will get so *pissed* if I get fucked up."

"No, she won't!" Brooke said. "Your mom is gonna be asleep in a few hours."

"I can't do it," Sienna said.

Brooke sighed and rolled her eyes. "Okay, *fine*." She turned to Jeff. "Take a picture of us."

Brooke and Sienna put their drink glasses down on a nearby empty table. Then Brooke moved over to stand by Sienna, and Jeff took his phone from his back pocket and began taking pictures while the girls smiled and struck several different poses.

Sienna wasn't surprised that Brooke hadn't told her or Allie she was dating Jeff, nor was she angry. You didn't introduce someone you were dating to your two very best friends—who were practically your sisters—until you were fairly certain they were relationship material.

Thinking of Allie reminded Sienna that she and Brooke hadn't seen any sign of her yet. She wanted to check her phone for texts or voicemails, but before she could pull it out of her belt pouch, a techno song with a hard-driving beat came over the club's loudspeakers.

"Let's dance!" Brooke shouted. She grabbed Sienna's hand and pulled her onto the dance floor. Jeff, bobbing his head to the beat, followed.

They found an empty spot big enough for the three of them and let loose. Brooke and Jeff danced together, and Sienna danced close to them, bouncing and spinning in place, not wanting to move around too much and hit anyone with her wings. Her movements were stiff at first, but she quickly began to relax. She gave herself over to the music, and for the first since her father died, she felt something that might have been happiness.

CHAPTER TWENTY-TWO

Art heard the sound of kids approaching the house, and he smiled. He'd been waiting by the front door for over ten minutes, hoping some more trick-or-treaters would come by now that the rain had stopped. His patience was about to be rewarded.

The kids ran up onto the porch and rang the doorbell.

Art paused for a couple of seconds—timing was everything in his business—and then he slowly opened the door.

A pair of mothers wearing thick, warm sweaters had accompanied the children, and one of them said, "Kids, look, how cool!"

Art stepped onto the porch, holding the severed and hollowed head of Allie's mother, her eyes closed, face slick with blood, neck wound dripping the red stuff. He'd removed the top of her skull, scooped out the brain, and then filled the cavity with candy from the black cat bowl by the door. He leaned forward and moved the head back and forth in front of the children, wanting to make sure each of them had a good, close-up look. Art's face, hands, and clothes were covered with blood as well, most of it Allie's, but some was her mother's.

He looked over the treat-or-treaters' costumes—a football player, a bat, a deer, and a couple of generic princesses. None of the outfits were particularly inspired.

The kids had arranged themselves in a line, and he stepped to the deer on the far left—the girl wearing a homemade pair of cartoonish antlers and white painted spots on her cheeks and forehead. Art leaned forward and held out the grisly candy bowl to her.

Deer Girl didn't notice a drop of blood falling from Eva's neck stump and landing on her shoe.

"Oh my god!" she said as she took a piece of candy from the head.

He moved on to one of the princesses. She made a face as she carefully reached into the "bowl" for a piece of candy. When she finally selected a piece, she held it up to look at it. "Ew," she said. "Why is mine so *sticky*?"

"Don't worry," the other mom said. "It's fake blood. They make it out of food coloring and corn syrup. Just put it in the bag."

The girl didn't look so happy about it, but she did as told. Art let the football player choose a piece of candy next. His was covered in "fake" blood too. The boy lifted it to his nose and sniffed.

"Doesn't smell like corn syrup," he said. He touched the candy to his tongue. "Doesn't taste like it, either." He tossed the candy into his bag and licked the remains of the crimson liquid off his fingers.

Art then moved on to the second generic princess. She looked closely at the dead woman's head.

"Ooh, I like it!" the girl said as she got her treat.

"Ew!" said the bat, as she reluctantly took a piece of candy.

The football player had no such reservations. He reached for a second piece of candy, and Art glared dangerously, smacked the greedy boy's hand away from the head, and held up a single finger in warning. *Only one apiece.* He imagined reaching into the kid's greedy mouth, tearing out his tongue, and feeding it back to him in pieces. He might've done it, too, if one of the sweatered women hadn't put her hand on the football player's shoulder and spoken.

"All right, kids," she said. Then to Art, "Thank you!"

Art's entire demeanor changed. He straightened, grinned, and vigorously waved goodbye to his little guests.

"Let's go," the other mother said. Then she smiled at Art. "Happy Halloween!"

"Happy Halloween!" the kids called as the two adults herded them off the stairs.

As soon as their backs were to him, Art lifted up the woman's head, looked at its ridiculous dead, bloody face, and roared with silent laughter.

Jonathan sat at the foot of Sienna's bed, Daddy's sketchbook resting next to him on the mattress. He held the short sword Daddy had given her, and he gazed at it as he thought. The charred wings were still mounted above Sienna's worktable, and the wall and ceiling still had large scorch marks from the fire. Mom had said she'd call someone to come replaster and repaint the burned areas. Jonathan knew Sienna would've probably preferred to do the work herself. He was sure she was capable of it. Building a costume, fixing sections of a wall and ceiling... There wasn't much difference to her. Jonathan had never told Sienna, but he admired her very much, and he was proud to be her brother. She was really special.

Maybe more special than she realized.

Wherever she'd gone tonight, he hoped she was okay.

He held up the sword, turned it back and forth, entranced by the way light moved across the smooth metal like liquid gold. The sword had been caught in the fire, but it showed no sign of it. It looked brand new, the blade highly polished, the wooden handle unmarked. He'd heard a phrase in a movie once: *Forged in fire*. He knew it was a metaphor for how people could become stronger after going through a difficult experience, and that swords were *literally* forged in fire, but it felt like the phrase applied to Sienna's sword too. It was like the fire had destroyed the old sword and then remade it, better than before—the metal stronger, the blade's edge keener. He wished Sienna had listened to him and taken it with her tonight. He had a feeling she was going to need it.

"What are you doing in here?"

He turned to see Mom standing in the doorway. He didn't answer her question. He thought she'd raise her voice and insist he answer, but instead she asked another question.

"You wanna watch a movie?"

He wasn't sure what this was about. A peace offering, maybe? He wasn't interested in making peace. He was still too hurt by Mom not believing him about the Miles County Clown and the Little Pale Girl being responsible for bringing the dead possum into school. His silence didn't put Mom off, though. She tried a different tactic.

"There is a *lot* of candy left over downstairs," she said. "Come on. I'll let you stay up late."

He'd had enough. "Go away."

Her tone became chilly. "Jonathan, I am *sorry* that your plans were ruined tonight. I really am. But you should've thought about this before you pulled that shit in school today. I mean, enough's *enough*."

Jonathan didn't want to raise his voice, knew it would only make things worse, but he couldn't help himself. "I told you the truth!"

"I'm *not* doing this again—"

"It wasn't me!"

"Well, if it wasn't, then I sincerely apologize. But I just don't believe you anymore."

He returned the sword to Sienna's worktable, went back to the bed, grabbed Daddy's sketchbook, then went over to Mom and held it out before him. "What about this?"

"Again with this *fucking book*!"

Jonathan opened the book and began flipping pages. "Why was Daddy collecting these news articles? 'Slain Girl Found at Carnival.' And this? Look at these drawings! This isn't like Daddy."

He was surprised to see the pain in Mom's eyes. She didn't talk about Daddy much, and Jonathan had begun to think that was because she hadn't really loved him.

But now he reconsidered. Maybe she didn't talk about Daddy because it hurt too bad.

"He was *sick*. Why can't you *understand*? He didn't know who he was or what he was doing half the time. And this...!" She snatched the sketchbook away from him and shook it angrily. "This bullshit is nothing but a fucking reminder!"

She opened the book and began rapidly tearing out pages and throwing them to the floor.

"Don't!" Jonathan yelled. He couldn't believe she was doing this to *Daddy's* sketchbook! It was the last thing they—*he*—had of him. The drawings were part of him: his mind, his heart, his spirit. And Mom was destroying them!

"I want this out of my house!" She threw the book to the floor.

Jonathan knelt and began sorting through the torn pages, trying to determine how many of Daddy's drawings Mom had ruined by tearing them out of the sketchbook and how many were still more or less intact. He felt angrier than he ever had in his life.

He found the drawing of the Miles County Clown, looked at it for several seconds, then turned his head upward to face Mom. "You're such a *bitch*!"

Mom's hand was a blur as it came toward his cheek. He felt the pain of the slap before he understood what was happening, and he put his hand to his cheek, as if trying to manually keep the pain from spreading. Or maybe he was trying to protect himself from another blow.

Mom had *never* hit him or Sienna before. She and Daddy hadn't even spanked them. They'd believed that using violence to discipline children taught them that violence was a perfectly reasonable way to solve your problems. They used words instead, and when those didn't work, they used punishments, such as taking away privileges for a certain amount of time. As Jonathan and Sienna had gotten older, Mom's words had become sharper and more hurtful, but she'd never threatened to hit them, let alone done it.

For a second, Mom looked stunned, as if she couldn't believe she'd hit him either. But she recovered quickly. "Don't you *ever* say that to me again!"

Jonathan's cheek throbbed, but that pain was nothing compared to the emotional hurt he felt. He jumped to his feet, ran past Mom, out of Sienna's room, down the hallway, and bounded down the stairs. He heard Mom call out as he ran.

"Jonathan! You get back here! *Jonathan!*"

He kept running until he reached the front door. He threw it open and ran out into the night. He had no idea where he was going. He just knew he had to get away.

From her.

Sienna didn't know how long they'd been dancing. The music seemed to segue from one song to another without any break. She didn't feel tired at all. In fact, she felt more energized than when she'd first set foot on the dance floor. It was hot, though. Her body was slick was sweat, and her hair was wet with it too. She imagined what she'd tell Mom if she was here.

If I wasn't wearing my "revealing" outfit, I'd be dying in this heat. It's beautiful and practical.

She pogoed and whirled and whipped her hair around for a few minutes longer, then she stopped and made her way over to where Brooke and Jeff were dancing.

She leaned close to Brooke so she could be heard over the loud music. "I'll be right back!"

"Wait. Where you going?"

"I'm gonna grab a drink!"

"Okay!"

Sienna headed back to the bar, weaving a bit as she went. Must be more tired than I thought. She got a large glass of ice water, then returned to the edge of the dance floor. She drank the water down in several gulps, and the spreading coolness inside her felt amazing. She put the glass down on a table covered with other empties, then started walking down a narrow passageway.

She passed a bulletin board with posters advertising bands who were coming to the club. She stared at the musicians' faces, unable to believe how clear and sharp their features were.

They looked so lifelike, she wouldn't have been surprised if they'd started to talk to her. She moved down a narrow corridor, trailing her hands along the wooden paneling, luxuriating in the feel of its texture against her fingertips.

She made her way back onto the dance floor, and she moved slowly among the crowd, checking out people's costumes and the people themselves. There were so many interesting-looking people here tonight. Beautiful people, ordinary people, people who some might've found unattractive, but which Sienna found fascinating to look at.

One of those interesting people—a guy in a short-sleeved blue shirt with a cartoon monkey over the left breast and wearing a ballcap backward on his head—came up to her.

"Yo, can I get a selfie with you?"

Sienna grinned. "Sure."

The guy moved next to her and held his phone up at an angle. Sienna looked toward the camera lens—or at least where she thought the lens might be—and the guy took the photo. He lowered his phone and smiled at her.

"Fuck yeah, girl!" he said, then moved on.

Sienna watched him go, amused but happy that he thought her costume was awesome enough to take a picture with her. She thought about what Mom had said about her outfit being too overtly sexual, and she realized the guy might've had a different motive for taking that selfie.

Oh well. He was gone and she still had the rest of the night before her. She promptly forgot him and continued wandering around the dance floor, gazing upon all the different people, and thinking of how, in this moment, she loved every one of them.

CHAPTER TWENTY-THREE

Sean leaned over the back of the couch, parted the curtains, and glanced outside.

"Time to go," he said.

"Aren't we going to wait for Jonathan?" Eric asked.

The brothers had gone trick-or-treating with Jonathan since they were little kids. It felt wrong to go without him.

"Fuck him," Sean said. "The guy's a goddamn psycho. He brought that dead possum into the school and smeared it all over the walls and shit."

Sean and Eric sat on their living room couch, curtains drawn over the picture window behind them, porchlight off so no trick-or-treaters would ring their doorbell. Their dad worked as a second-shift machinist at Champion Manufacturing, so he was never around during trick-or-treat, and their mom had divorced him and moved to California when the boys were eight. They hadn't seen or heard from her since. This meant the brothers were always left to their own devices on Halloween, which was exactly the way they liked it.

Sean said Mom didn't really divorce Dad. He claimed Dad had gotten tired of her shit, killed her, buried her in the backyard, then made up a story about her abandoning the family. Eric knew Sean was full of shit. Sean loved yanking his chain, almost as much as he loved yanking Jonathan's.

Dad had left a couple of bags of candy for them to pass out tonight. Since "You boys are too old to go out trick-or-treating," he'd said. As soon as Dad left, Sean and Eric divided the candy between them, stashed it in their bedrooms, and donned their outfits. Then they sat on the couch and waited for night to fall. They did their best work in the dark.

"Took some balls for Jonathan to do that," Eric pointed out.

"Yeah, *psycho* balls! Now shut up and let's *go*."

Eric sighed. When Sean had his mind set on something, there was no changing it.

Sean and his brother both wore black pants, black long-sleeved pullovers, and black balaclava masks that left only their eyes visible. If anyone asked about their "Halloween costumes," they'd say they were dressed as ninjas, but in reality they were dressed for playing pranks and (hopefully) not getting caught.

They left their house, each carrying a large burlap bag filled with the supplies they needed for tonight's fun — toilet paper, shaving cream, and bars of soap. It had been raining earlier, which was another reason they'd waited to go outside, but the rain had given way to a light drizzle, and it wasn't too hateful out now.

They saw some younger kids back out on the streets, running from house to house as fast as they could, trying to make up the time they'd lost to the rain. Sean knew

Dad was right about their being too old for trick-or-treating, but at the moment, he wished he could be a little kid again, just for an hour or two, and go running and laughing with the others.

When they reached the sidewalk, Sean turned right, and Eric followed. He didn't know where Sean planned to go first, and he didn't really want to ask. He'd find out soon enough.

Eric and Sean might have been twins, but of the two of them, Sean was a more natural leader. Part of this was because he always came up with ideas for things they could do—or more accurately, for trouble they could get into—but a bigger part was because he had a more dominant personality, which was a fancy way of saying he was a bully. If Sean had been an only child—a scenario he fantasized about quite often—he doubted he would get up to even half the mischief on his own that he got up to with his brother.

In a way, he was glad Jonathan wasn't coming with them tonight. Jonathan wasn't comfortable with the shit they pulled, but Sean always manipulated him into coming along, calling him a pussy, telling him to act like a man for once. And Jonathan—looking miserable—accompanied them on whatever mission Sean had dreamed up for them. Tying a string of lit firecrackers to a stray dog's tail, slashing the tires of Principal Turner's Prius in the faculty parking lot during lunch, hiding behind bushes and throwing rocks at passing cars... And the truth was, Eric was starting to get sick of it.

It wasn't that he had strong moral objections to the pranks Sean wanted to play. Sure, they were wrong, but they weren't Wrong with a capital W. They weren't stealing cars, robbing banks, selling drugs, breaking into homes, or killing people. But in the last few months, he'd come to view them as childish and stupid. He was outgrowing them—*and* outgrowing his brother. There would come a time when he'd have to tell Sean he was done letting him be the boss in their relationship, and that he didn't want to do any more dumbass pranks. That day wasn't here yet, though. He'd go along with Sean's program tonight, and he'd do his best to have fun, although he knew he probably wouldn't enjoy himself. He vowed that this would be the last Halloween that the Henderson brothers would go out as partners in crime.

"Are we gonna do Mrs. Shaw's car later?" Eric asked.

Every year they sprayed shaving cream and threw toilet paper on Mrs. Shaw's car, and the next morning they could hear her furious screeching when she discovered what they'd done. She couldn't prove they'd done it, of course, but *she* knew it, and she knew *they* knew she knew it. That was actually the only part of pranking he'd miss—pissing off Jonathan's mom. The woman was always yelling at Jonathan and Sienna about one thing or another, as if she was permanently on the rag or something.

"Nah," Sean said. "We'll skip her this year, let her think we're done messing with her, and then we'll hit her car *next* year, and she'll go totally apeshit. I got a better idea where we can go tonight."

Eric almost asked, but there was something in Sean's tone he'd never heard before, a kind of sick anticipation that made him uneasy. He almost quit right there and then, but he knew Sean would give him shit for wanting to bail. And if he got mad enough, he might start using his fists instead of his mouth. Better to keep his mouth shut and go along, at least for tonight. But after this, he was done, finished, kaput.

They continued walking.

"This is Stephanie's house, isn't it?" Eric asked.

Sean smiled. "Yes, it is."

They stood on the sidewalk, holding their burlap sacks, and examined their target for this evening. It was a nice two-story house, with a green roof, green shutters, and white siding. The yard was immaculate, with neatly trimmed hedges and large stately trees (mostly leafless now). No Halloween decorations, though, not even a jack-o'-lantern on the porch. Maybe Stephanie's family didn't decorate for holidays, or maybe they had some kind of religious reason for not celebrating Halloween, thought it was satanic or something. This neighborhood was a little more upscale than the brothers', and there were no streetlights here. The residents probably thought fluorescent light was garish and uncouth, or whatever words people like them used to say *ugly* and *low-class*.

It was good news for the brothers, however. The absence of streetlights would make their job easier, especially this time of night. The house only had a single porchlight on too, and it was a low-wattage one that barely put out any light. Could Stephanie's family make this any easier for them? There *was* a full moon out tonight, though, so they'd still need to be cautious, but overall, it looked like a sweet setup.

The brothers weren't friends with Stephanie, and after tricking her to take a look at the dead possum this morning, Sean was sure they never would be. But they didn't have anything against her really, not as far as he was concerned. But Sean? He turned to his brother.

"Why?" he asked, knowing Sean would understand the question.

"Because I asked her to the Homecoming Dance, and she shot me down."

Eric was shocked. Sean hadn't said anything about liking Stephanie or asking her to go with him to the dance. She didn't seem like the type of girl Sean would be attracted to. She was quiet, smart, nice—although she wasn't Eric's type, either. She was the kind of girl who was never late to class, never absent, and who always turned her homework in on time. If Sean was chaos, she was order. Maybe that was why he liked her, because on some level he thought they complemented each other.

Sean continued speaking. "After I asked her, she made a face like she'd just bitten into a bug. She didn't even answer me, just turned around and walked away. Like I was nothing."

This morning, Eric had assumed Sean had called Stephanie over to show her the dead possum because he knew Jonathan liked her, and he wanted to make both of them feel bad. Now Eric realized Sean had really done it to get back at Stephanie, not only because she'd turned him down, but because she'd humiliated him in the process. Eric had never seen his brother like this before, had never known him to have... well, *feelings*. Aside from the dark delight he took in making other people feel miserable, that is.

"And this is just the start," Sean said. "I'm going to make her life hell from now all the way through high school, and I'll keep doing it after that, even if she moves out of town. I'll follow her wherever she goes. She'll *never* be able to get rid of me."

Eric was used to hearing his brother talk big about all the things he'd do to people who'd pissed him off. Most of the time, it was just hot air. But this was different. He'd never heard this kind of anger in Sean's voice before, never heard such sheer *hate*, and not only did he believe his brother was serious about his threat to Stephanie, he thought he might actually follow through on it. This had now officially gone too fucking far for Eric.

Eric put a hand on Sean's shoulder. "Dude, forget about it. She's not worth stressing over. Let's go pick another house, okay?"

"Fuck you!" Sean knocked his hand away. "Nobody gets away with treating me like that! No—"

Lights flared to life behind them, and Sean cut off his sentence mid-word. They quickly turned to look and saw a van parked on the opposite side of the street. Someone inside had flicked on the lights, and while they weren't shining directly on the brothers, they were bright enough to illuminate the portion of sidewalk they stood on. The van was black, with a white hood, and there was something about it that made the skin on the back of Eric's neck crawl. There was nothing about the van's appearance that should've bothered him. It looked

263

perfectly ordinary, but at the same time it looked *wrong*. He couldn't think of any other way to describe it.

There was a rhythmic scuffing sound on the sidewalk then, that made Eric think of a child skipping. As the brothers watched, a girl came into view. She wore a Halloween costume and looked scary as hell—pale skin, ugly teeth bared in a bizarre smile, yellow eyes, messy hair, a ponytail on one side of her head that had been pulled through a tiny white top hat. She wore a black-and-white dress, and her movements were stiff and awkward, as if pretending to be some kind of living corpse. The creepy girl was pulling something behind her on the end of a leash. Was she taking a pet for a walk? And what was she doing all by herself out here in the dark?

As she drew near, she didn't look at them, seemed totally unaware of their presence, but when she passed, her head snapped toward them, and she grinned at them with frozen features. She continued on, and a second later the brothers saw what was on the other end of the leash she held—the dead possum they'd found behind the dumpsters at school this morning. She dragged it along the sidewalk, internal organs sticking out of the wound in its belly, sliding on the concrete and leaving a trail of blood. Letters had been burned into the animal's hide, and they spelled a word: *SPLATTY*. Was that supposed to be the goddamn thing's name?

The girl skipped away from them, pulling Splatty after her. For a few seconds, she was illuminated by the van's taillights, but she soon moved out of their range and was lost to the dark.

The brothers stared in the direction she'd gone for several moments, then they turned to look at each other.

"Fuck this," Sean said. "Let's go home."

Eric thought it was perhaps the most sensible thing his brother had ever said in his life.

Too bad it would also be the last.

Someone quickly came up behind the brothers—a tall someone—and leaned over them. He had one black sleeve, one white sleeve, and a pair of fingerless gloves that might've been white once but were now reddish-brown with dried blood. In each hand he held a butcher knife, and before either brother could react, the man plunged the blades into their pubic area, just above the penis, and then began pulling the knives upward. The boys dropped their burlap sacks, screamed, and stumbled backward into the man, who held them steady against his body as he cut, cut, cut...

The pain was like nothing Eric had ever experienced, but that wasn't the worst of it. As the man pulled the butcher knife over his belly, he felt pressure, then release, and he watched his intestines slip out of his body with a horrible wet *schlurp* and spill onto the sidewalk. He looked at Sean and saw the same thing had happened to him. *We're gonna die*, he thought. But quick on its heels came another thought. *No, we're already dead. We just don't know it yet.*

He looked back over his shoulder, wanting to get a look at the man who was killing his brother and him. He a saw a face similar to the little girl's, but male, longer, leaner, mouth stretched into an evil grin, eyes gleaming with the bright light of madness. *We're being killed by a*

265

demon clown, Eric thought. Then he realized *which* clown it was—that motherfucker that Jonathan was obsessed with, the Miles County Clown. Too bad they'd ditched Jonathan tonight. He would've shit his pants if he'd seen the clown in real life. He tried to laugh, but all that came out of his mouth was blood.

When the butcher knives reached the brothers' sternums, the clown yanked them out, pressed the blades against the boys' necks, and with a pair of swift, merciless slices, laid their throats open. Blood poured from the wounds, and Eric could feel himself slipping away. He tried to turn his head toward Sean, wanted to finally tell him exactly what he thought of him, but he died before he could get out a single syllable.

Art stepped back from the boys, and without his body supporting theirs, they collapsed to the sidewalk and lay in a gory mess of spilled intestines and blood. Art gazed down at his handiwork, and his grin grew wider. The Little Pale Girl came skipping back, pulling Splatty along behind her. Art would put the items in the brothers' burlap sacks to good use. But first…

He turned to face Stephanie's yard, saw the trees, and an idea came to him. He looked at the Little Pale Girl, she looked at him, and they both laughed silently.

Art pulled away from the curb, the Little Pale Girl sitting in the van's passenger seat beside him. Splatty was on her lap, and she stroked the dead thing's matted fur lovingly.

Whenever her fingers came in contact with a maggot, she plucked it off Splatty, popped it in her mouth, and chewed with obvious delight. Art understood. Maggots were damn tasty.

The door to Stephanie's house opened then, and her father stepped out onto the porch. Damon Nash was a literature professor at NYU, but instead of the suit and tie he'd worn all day, he was dressed in jeans and a flannel shirt. He held a flashlight in his right hand, the beam off.

"Hello? Is anyone out there?"

Silence.

He turned on the flashlight, walked down the front steps, and headed out into the yard to investigate. Normally, they didn't have much trouble during Halloween in this neighborhood, but with young people the way they were today, you could never—

He stopped. Stared.

His flashlight illuminated the branches of one of the trees in his yard, an elm, and he saw what he thought at first were lengths of toilet paper dangling from the bare limbs. But toilet paper was thin and white, and these things were thick, and coiled, and a kind of greenish-gray, and they were slick with some kind of red substance.

It hit him all at once. What he was looking at were intestines—real ones—strewn over and around the elm, hanging from its limbs, swaying gently in the breeze. There were objects propped up against the tree trunk, and while he didn't want to see what they were, his hand lowered his flashlight as if of its own accord and revealed two boys sitting with their backs against the tree, legs extended outward. They were dressed all in black, and they... they had no heads. No, that wasn't exactly true. Their heads had been removed from their necks, yes, but they were now housed within their hollow abdominal cavities, eyes gone, an orange glow of candle flame shining softly from empty sockets and open mouths, as if they had been made into some lunatic version of jack-o'-lanterns.

Damon stared for several seconds, unable to believe what he was seeing. He *knew* it was real, and yet it was so grotesquely over-the-top that it was, in a decidedly sick way, funny.

A soft giggle escaped his lips. It was followed by a second, then a third, and soon he was laughing hysterically. He was laughing an hour later when the hospital staff strapped him to his bed and pumped his arm full of chemicals to calm him down. They didn't work. He continued laughing, even louder than before, his throat raw and hoarse.

Laughing and laughing and laughing...

CHAPTER TWENTY-FOUR

Barbara stood at the kitchen counter, holding a prescription bottle in a shaking hand. She pried off the lid, dumped several white pills into her hand, and threw them into her mouth. She washed them down with a bit of red wine left in her glass, then she grabbed the bottle off the counter and refilled her glass. She tried to fight the tears she felt coming, but she lost that battle, and began to cry.

She'd.

Hit.

Jonathan.

Her son. Her *baby*.

She felt like the biggest piece of shit that had ever walked on the face of the Earth. How could she have lost control like that? It had been months since she'd seen a therapist, but she could imagine what one might say. *Unresolved grief trauma. Feelings of abandonment and inadequacy. Trying to do it all on your own for too long. Bottling up your feelings—just as you advised Sienna not to do. Like mother, like daughter. And most of all, fear that you're going to fail your children, that no matter what you do, no matter how hard you try, you'll never be good enough to be their mom.*

It was so much easier when her husband was alive. They'd loved each other, supported each other, worked well together. They were a good team. But his illness had taken a toll on their relationship, and on the family as a whole. And after his… death, she'd kept her shit together and helped get the kids through those first few horrible weeks. And she'd continued to take care of them as best she could, and overall, she thought she'd done a decent job. But these last couple days… Christ, what a shitshow. Sienna's obsession with her costume, the fire in her bedroom. Jonathan's own obsession—the goddamned Miles County Clown—and today the sick prank he'd pulled at school. She hoped the possum had been roadkill that he'd picked up somewhere. She didn't want to think about him finding a live animal and killing it just to have a disgusting prop for his little "joke."

Barbara wasn't religious, but she prayed right then.

Please, don't let anything else fucked-up happen tonight. I don't think I could take it. I just need a day—a single goddamn day—where nothing goes disastrously wrong. Can I have that? Just one day.

She was about to take a drink of wine when she heard a noise. A *thump*, to be exact, like something heavy colliding with something else. And she thought it had come from the garage.

Had Jonathan come back? If so, what was he doing in the garage?

Hiding from you, of course.

Carrying her wine, she left the kitchen and headed slowly down the hall toward the garage. She listened intently, straining to hear even the slightest sound. She hoped it *was* Jonathan in the garage, but it might not be. They lived in a safe area of town, yes, but was any place *truly* safe these days?

She reached the door to the garage and found it open. Not a good sign.

Barbara knew she should go upstairs to her bedroom, lock the door, and call for help. But she was tired of feeling like her life was out of control, and one thing she could do was check out the garage before she panicked, called 911, and was embarrassed when the police showed up and found nothing.

Barbara stepped into the garage and smelled menthol and... pumpkin? What the fuck?

She switched on the light and saw the car was covered with shaving cream and toilet paper. Pieces of a smashed pumpkin were scattered across the hood, and the word BITCH had been written in the shaving cream smeared on the windshield.

The wineglass slipped from Barbara's hand, fell to the concrete floor, and shattered.

She walked around the front of the vehicle in shock, unable to believe what she was seeing.

"Oh... my... god!"

It was those goddamn Henderson brats! Every *fucking* year... She looked at the windshield once more.

BITCH.

No, not the Hendersons.

Jonathan.

*

Sienna continued moving through Eclipse, determined to explore every inch of the club. Everything she encountered was beyond amazing, and she didn't want to miss anything. She stopped at a stone pillar that had a plastic skeleton bound to it with wire. There was an orange light inside its skull, and a beautiful warm glow shone from its sockets.

Hello, Mr. Bones, she thought, and giggled.

The texture of the pillar caught her attention, and she began running her hands across the stone.

"Sienna!"

Brooke came running up, and Sienna had never been so glad to see someone in her life.

"Hey!"

"Hi!"

Sienna smiled broadly, hugged Brooke, touched her forehead to hers. Both girls laughed with delight, happy to be reunited.

"I missed you, girl!" Sienna said. "Feel this!"

Sienna took hold of Brooke's left wrist and pressed her hand to the pillar. "How amazing is that?"

Brooke laughed.

"No, no, wait. You don't understand. I *want* it. I wanna, like, *live* in it."

Brooke laughed harder. She took Sienna's hand and led her to an alcove away from the dance floor, where it was quieter.

"How are you feeling?" Brooke asked.

"Good."

"Yeah?"

"*So* good, actually."

"Okay."

"I feel like… that shot's *really* starting to hit me."

Brooke smiled. "Well, whiskey will do that to you."

"I needed this."

"Yeah."

"You were right," Sienna said. "You were *so* right. I needed to just, like, get out and stop thinking. Worrying about every little thing in my life. Like this costume. I mean, it should be a happy thing, you know? It reminds me of my dad. He used to… He used to draw this character for me when I was a little girl. And he used to tell me I was gonna grow up to be like her one day. And I really believed it."

"Well, look at you now. You *are* her."

"I am *nothing* like her," Sienna said. "I'm not courageous. I'm not brave. I mean, I *literally* had a panic attack in school in front of everybody."

Brooke looked down at the floor for a second, then met Sienna's gaze once more. "I put molly in your drink."

Brooke gave her a big but uncertain smile. Sienna had seen this smile numerous times throughout the years. It was the expression Brooke used when she confessed to doing something that might make Sienna or Allie angry.

"What?" Sienna said.

"I did. I put half a tablet in your drink and half in mine. Not even, really; it was kind of nothing. But it's fine, 'cause I'm also on it. You and me. And that is why you feel like… you're on molly. 'Cause you are. Right now."

Sienna eyes widened in disbelief, then she laughed. "You fuckin' bitch! That is *so* messed up!"

"I did it! I made you feel better, didn't I?"

"I'm fuckin' *pissed*."

"No, don't be pissed. You're smiling. You can't be pissed."

"No, bitch, I'm not smiling." Sienna fought to suppress a laugh and failed.

Brooke laughed too. "You're *totally* smiling!"

They laughed together some more, then Brooke grabbed Sienna's hand.

"Now we gotta get back out there, and we gotta dance," Brooke said.

As Brooke pulled her toward the dance floor, Sienna *was* pissed, extremely, but she also felt like she was having the greatest night of her life, so screw it. She should be happy now, *live* now, while she could. After all, tomorrow wasn't a given.

She'd learned that from Daddy.

Jonathan ran down the sidewalk, no destination in mind, just running so he wouldn't have to stop and think. The streets were deserted, and he was alone, which was exactly what he wanted. Trick-or-treat was over, and the kids of Miles County were in their homes, gorging themselves on candy. He'd expected to be one of those kids this evening, but he didn't care about candy now. He wasn't sure he'd care about anything ever again.

He slowed then, stopped, bent over to catch his breath,

skin slick with sweat, heart pounding in his chest. Now that he was no longer moving, his mind kicked into gear again.

He saw Mom thrusting Daddy's sketchbook toward him. *This bullshit is nothing but a fucking reminder!*

Saw her tearing pages, throwing them to the floor...
Don't!

I want this out of my house!

You're such a bitch!

He hadn't meant to say those words. They'd just come out of him, and he wished he could somehow take them back. He was old enough to understand that he and Sienna weren't the only ones who missed Daddy. Mom was hurting too, and she had nobody to lean on for support. Seeing Dr. Shifren had helped him some, but he and Sienna had grown closer since Daddy's death, and that had helped a lot more. He wished Mom...

A horn honked nearby, interrupting his thoughts. He turned and saw a black-and-white van with a white hood parked on the other side of the street. Black and white... just like the colors of a certain clown. Jonathan's heart started beating faster, and this time it had nothing to do with physical exertion. The van's engine wasn't running, and its headlights were off. The driver's-side window was down, but it didn't look like anyone was behind the wheel.

Something slammed into his shoulder, startling him, but it was just a girl running by with a group of her friends, laughing and whooping, thrilled to have scared an older kid. Not *all* the kids in Miles County were done having fun tonight, it seemed. Little jerks.

He looked back at the van, and this time he thought he saw the silhouette of someone sitting in the passenger seat. He knew he shouldn't, knew it was stupid as hell, but he started walking across the street toward the van. He couldn't stop himself. For better or worse, he had to *know*. Moth to the flame.

As he got closer, he saw that both the driver's seat and passenger seat were empty. He'd been certain he'd seen someone, but maybe he'd just been imagining things. But, if that was so, then who'd honked the horn? He stopped a yard away from the vehicle, reluctant to go nearer. The radio was on, the volume low, but all that came out was static mixed with strange words that he didn't recognize. A non-English station, one broadcasting from the city? Maybe, but it didn't sound like any language he'd ever heard before, and there was something about the words that made his head hurt to hear them, as if they were *bad* words. Not swear words, but words that were literally bad.

Evil words.

He no longer wanted to be alone, and he looked to his right to see if the kids were still around. But they were gone.

The horn sounded again, louder and longer this time.

Trembling, Jonathan slowly turned his head to look at the van once more.

This time he saw the shadowy form of what appeared to be a child sitting in the passenger seat—face white, eyes a glowing yellow, long frizzy ponytail sticking out from the right side of its head. He knew at once who it was— Emily Crane, the girl who had been killed at the carnival two years ago on Halloween, and who'd somehow been resurrected as the Little Pale Girl he'd seen at school. Except... it wasn't her, exactly. She looked different than she had at school, and it wasn't just those horrible eyes. Her face looked artificial, as if it was a mask, concealing something else—something far *worse*—underneath.

A voice speaking English came over the radio then. His mom's voice.

"Jonathan, come back! Jonathan!"

He looked into those eerie yellow eyes a moment longer, then turned and ran like hell.

Sienna and Brooke walked upstairs to Eclipse's main level, planning to step outside for a couple of minutes and get some air. It felt as if they'd been dancing for *hours*, and the thought of cool air on her skin sounded delicious to Sienna. She thought of Allie then. By this point, it was clear she wasn't going to make it tonight. Her mom must've found some pretext to keep her home. Maybe she'd texted to explain? Sienna took her phone from her belt pouch and checked. No texts, but there were a number of voicemails.

"Oh shit."

"What?" Brooke asked.

"My mom called me like six times."

"Do *not* call her back."

"I'm gonna see—"

"Don't call her back!" Brooke tried to take the phone out of Sienna's hand, but Sienna turned away.

"Sienna!" Brooke said.

Sienna ignored her and called her mom. She didn't want to take the time to listen to the voicemails. Mom might call to check up on her once or twice, but six times? She wouldn't call that many times unless it was *really* important.

Mom answered, and Sienna said, "Hey!"

"He's dead, Sienna! I can't deal with him anymore!"

"Wait, what?"

Brooke tried one more time to get the phone from Sienna, but she stepped away, and Brooke gave up.

"Wait, Mom, I can't hear you."

Sienna found a small hallway that was deserted. It was still noisy here—it was noisy *everywhere* in Eclipse—but it was a little quieter. She covered her other ear with her hand to block out as much sound as possible.

"Sorry. What'd you say?"

"He covered the entire fucking car with shaving cream!" Mom was practically screaming into the phone.

"What?"

"Yeah, the whole fucking thing. Shaving cream, toilet paper, eggs! He's dead!"

This didn't make any sense. "He… Jonathan wouldn't do that."

"Yeah, he didn't do this. Just like he didn't vandalize the school this morning!"

Mom's voice echoed now, and Sienna assumed she'd gone into the garage. She heard a plastic *thump* that she assumed was a bucket being dropped to the floor. Mom couldn't stand to let a mess sit for any length of time, and Sienna was certain she'd carried cleaning supplies into the garage to clean up the car.

"Look at this. No, no, no, no, no, no, no! This is crazy now. He's going to that psychiatrist immediately. I cannot deal with him anymore!"

Sienna suddenly found her mom's rant funny. Part of it was the molly and the alcohol, but it was also the realization that Mom let every little thing get to her. She blew small stuff way out of proportion and made herself—and everyone around her—miserable. It was so *unnecessary*.

"Really, Mom? You're gonna send him to a shrink because, what, he put a little bit of shaving cream on your car?"

"I'm glad you think this is funny, Sienna."

"It's just shaving cream. It's not like he took a baseball bat to your windshield. It's Halloween. I mean—"

"Are you drunk?"

Uh-oh.

"No."

"Yes, you are. I can hear it in your voice. How many drinks have you had?"

"I— I thought we were talking about Jonathan."

"Sienna, so help me, if you come home plastered on top of everything else I'm dealing with tonight—"

"No. I swear to god I'm not drunk. I'll even take a breathalyzer."

"You're killing me! You know that? You and your brother both! I have had it!"

Sienna could feel the worry beneath Mom's words, feel the fear. Mom was terrified of losing control of her family. More than that, she was terrified she never had any control in the first place. She felt a wave of warmth for her mother that had nothing to do with the various substances she'd ingested this evening.

"I love you," Sienna said.

"Yeah, Sienna. I am warning you."

"No, really, Mom. I love you. I don't say it enough."

Mom was silent for a moment, and when she spoke again, her voice was much softer.

"I love you too. Go and enjoy your party. I'm— I'm sorry to bother you."

"And listen, everything will be okay with Jonathan. I promise."

Sienna didn't know how, but she had faith in her brother. He was a good kid, and he'd figure things out eventually. And she'd be there to help him when and if he needed her.

"Just remember what I said. Be careful getting home, all right?"

"I will. Bye."

Sienna disconnected and put her phone away. When she returned to Brooke, her friend was having a cigarette.

The DJ yelled, *"Happy Halloween, motherfuckers!"* over his mic, and the crowd cheered.

When Brooke saw Sienna, she said, "How'd it go?"

"Fine."

Brooke lowered her cigarette.

"Let me give you a little molly etiquette here. Rule number one: you never, *ever* call your mother when you're rolling on molly. Okay? *Your* mother, never. All right?" Her voice softened, and she smiled. "Rule number two: you don't let it fucking go to waste. Come on."

Sienna smiled as Brooke took her hand and once again hauled her toward the dance floor.

CHAPTER TWENTY-FIVE

Talking with Sienna had tempered Barbara's rage somewhat, but it hadn't eliminated it. She crouched beside a bucket of water, dipped a large sponge in it, squeezed out the excess water. Then she carried the sponge and bucket to the driver's side of the car, lowered the bucket to the floor, and crouched down again. Barbara looked at the mess on the hood—toilet paper, shaving cream, the fucking smashed pumpkin. She avoided looking at the word—*that* word—written on the windshield. She was ashamed her slapping Jonathan was what prompted him to use that word, and while she hoped it was spoken in hurt and surprise, she feared it was what he really thought about her.

"Look at this," she said to herself. "Did he *really* think he was gonna get away with this?"

She pulled wet toilet paper off the driver's-side door, threw it in the bucket, then began wiping away shaving cream with the sponge.

"He is in for a *rude* awakening."

She stood.

"Things are gonna change."

She wiped a smear of shaving cream from the driver's-side window and revealed a bloody-faced clown sitting behind the wheel. He was looking at her, eyes burning with hatred.

She couldn't believe it! It was the goddamn Miles County Clown! Jonathan had been right!

The clown didn't take his baleful gaze off her as he raised a hand and placed the barrel of a sawn-off shotgun against the window. Barbara barely had time to understand what was going to happen to her before the clown pulled the trigger. Glass shattered, her head exploded, and she fell away into endless darkness.

Sienna, Brooke, and Jeff were dancing, but this time the music was softer, the beat less frantic, the dance floor less crowded. It was later in the evening and people needed a chance to rest and regain their energy. Some were taking a break to get more to drink, use the restroom, or continued dancing, just more slowly. Sienna wasn't worried about Jonathan or Mom anymore. Everything would be fine. As long as they loved each other—and they did—they'd find a way to fix things and move forward, together.

A couple moved off the dance floor then, walking hand in hand. With them gone, Sienna could now see a young girl—nine, maybe ten—standing where the couple had been. Sienna's first reaction was surprise that they'd let a little girl into Eclipse. Then she realized the girl was wearing the mirror image of Art's costume, hers black where his was white, and vice versa. She was struck next by the inhuman expression frozen on the girl's face. White makeup, weird-looking teeth surrounded by a ring of black, same for her unblinking eyes. Her head was tilted at a slight angle as she looked at Sienna, and for some reason this made her ten times creepier than she might've been otherwise. Dirty matted hair hung down from the left side of her head, while the hair on the right side had been worked into a ponytail and pulled through a tiny white top hat on the left side of the girl's head.

This was the Little Pale Girl Jonathan had told her about, the one that had been at his school with Art, who'd helped that sick fuck mutilate the possum and who'd used it to frame Jonathan. Jonathan had said the Little Pale Girl resembled the girl who had been killed at the amusement park a couple years ago. Emily... something. *Crane*, that was it. Emily Crane. Was she seeing a hallucination right now, or was she looking at an honest-to-god ghost?

Some dancers blocked Sienna's view for a couple of seconds, and when they moved out of the way again, the girl was gone.

Sienna scanned the dance floor, looking for her. She wanted to find her, wanted to prove to herself that she wasn't having a complete mental breakdown in Eclipse on Halloween night.

She found the girl standing over by the bar, still frozen, same expression on her face.

Sienna pointed. "Do you see that?" she said, but too softly for Brooke or Jeff to hear.

Same as before, someone walked in front of the Little Pale Girl on their way to get a drink, and when the view

283

was clear again, she was gone. Sienna looked around for her again, and this time she found her more quickly. She was sitting on a set of stone steps near the dance floor, looking exactly the same as she had the last two times.

Sienna pointed again and spoke more loudly this time. "There! That little girl!"

"What is she saying?" Jeff said.

"What are you talking about?" Brooke asked.

The girl was gone again.

"I-I swear to god, she was right there!" Sienna said. "I-I saw her! Right *there*!"

Brooke stopped dancing, walked over to Sienna, and took both her hands. "Okay, come with me. It's bathroom time."

She started to pull Sienna, but then suddenly the Little Pale Girl was standing right next to Sienna, looking up at her, eyes wide. Instead of whites, her eyes had outer circles of red and inner circles of yellow around pinpoint pupils. She didn't *look* any scarier than before, but up close, Sienna saw something in those small pupils, something dark, cold, strong, and unimaginably old. Something filled with hatred for all forms of life, but most especially for *her*.

She screamed.

She flung herself to the floor facedown so she wouldn't have to look at the girl anymore, and she screamed and screamed and screamed.

"Sienna? Sienna?" Suddenly Brooke was on the floor beside her. "Okay. Sienna, look at me. It's okay. Shh, shh, shh. Sienna, *please*, breathe. *Breathe*. You're gonna be okay."

Brooke helped Sienna onto her hands and knees. Sienna stopped screaming, but she was unable to get control of her breathing. She kept taking in fast gasps that didn't seem to draw any air into her lungs. She was going to die—she was certain of it—and when she was gone, the Little Pale Girl would appear, take her hand, and lead her away to a land of blood and shadow.

Jonathan ran the whole way home, and when he reached his house, he bounded up the steps, and opened the front door, grateful that Mom hadn't locked it. He didn't understand why he had heard her voice on the black-and-white van's radio, or why she'd been calling for him to come home. But he knew something was really wrong, knew she needed him, and that was all that mattered. Forgotten was the fight they'd had earlier, along with the slap. All that mattered to him was getting to Mom in time.

Once inside the house, he ran for the stairs, calling, "Mom!"

But then he realized light was coming from the dining room, and he stopped. He slowly turned toward the light, a sinking feeling in his stomach.

The table was set for three, a pair of candles were lit, a plate of chicken cutlets in the center, a bowl of tossed salad prepared and ready to be served. Mom sat at the head of the table—her usual place—glass of red wine on her right. The other two places—his and Sienna's—were empty. There was something not right about Mom, and he wanted to ask her if she was okay, but something told him that she wouldn't answer him if he did. *Look at her face*, he told himself. He did *not* want to do this, though, and he shook his head no. If he looked at her face, that would make this real, and he didn't want that to happen, didn't think he'd be able to handle it. He might even lose his mind, just as Sienna and Mom sometimes feared.

Look!

He wanted to turn and run back outside, wanted to keep running and never, ever stop. But he knew that other part of him was right. He needed to look, to *see*. He needed to bear witness, for his mother's sake, if for no other reason.

So he looked.

She had no face. Where her eyes, nose, and mouth had been, there was now only a ruin of mangled meat and flaps of skin, raw and bloody. No, that wasn't *entirely* true. Her left eye—closed, thank god—still remained intact. The top of her shirt was soaked with blood, making it look as if she wore a crimson bib.

Numb and not fully comprehending what he was seeing, Jonathan started slowly walking toward the table. His body reacted first, his breathing and pulse quickening, as if it already understood what his mind still struggled to process.

The Miles County Clown—Art—came in from the kitchen then, wearing one of Mom's aprons and ringing a little bell, as if to say, *Dinner is served!* There was blood all over him—on his face, his hands, his collar, and the apron was *drenched* in it. He carried a lidded ceramic bowl, the one Mom used whenever she served mashed potatoes for dinner.

Art smiled with cruel delight, and he kept his gaze locked on Jonathan as he stepped to Mom's side and placed the bell on the table. Jonathan had seen cheesy old-time scary movies where someone found a dead person, their eyes and mouths wide open, and proclaimed that they'd died of fright. He'd always thought that was so lame. How could anyone possibly die of fright? But now he understood.

Art placed the bowl on the table, lifted the lid, and picked up a plastic serving spoon that had already been there. He scooped several servings of mashed potatoes and plopped them onto Mom's plate. When he finished, he gave a chef's kiss, then he raised her glass of wine to Jonathan, as if making a toast, then did the same to Mom.

Then he put the wine down, grabbed a fistful of mashed potatoes, and jammed it into the center of the shredded meat that had been Mom's face. He worked the potatoes solidly into the cavity, and when he removed his hand, they stayed in place.

Art turned to Jonathan, mouth wide with silent laughter. He wiped his hands together to brush off mashed potato residue, then he reached into the apron's front pocket and removed a large hypodermic needle. Jonathan's eyes widened at the sight of the needle, and Art pointed to him, still laughing without sound.

Jonathan sensed a presence on his right, and he turned to see the Little Pale Girl grinning up at him. The sight of her broke his paralysis. He cried out, turned, and ran, Art following close behind in pursuit, one hand holding the hypo, the other reaching for Jonathan.

Jonathan reached the stairs and ran up them, Art's big clown boots thumping on the steps behind him. He felt the clown's fingers brush the back of his shirt, but Art didn't manage to catch hold of the fabric. Jonathan realized he couldn't hear the clown breathing. Didn't he make *any* sound? Was he even breathing at all? What the hell *was* he?

As Jonathan reached the second floor, Art tried again to grab his shirt, and this time he succeeded. Jonathan managed to pull free, though, and ran for his bedroom, instinctively seeking a place of safety and comfort. The door to his room was closed, but Sienna's was wide open, and so that's where he went.

"Help me!" he shouted, although to who or what he sought aid from, he couldn't have said.

He rushed into his sister's room and tried to shut the door, but Art managed to insert his body partway, preventing the door from closing. He reached out and grabbed Jonathan's shirt collar, but Jonathan grabbed hold of the clown's wrist with both hands and pushed it away from him.

Art pushed harder, trying to break Jonathan's grip so he could get hold of him once more, but Jonathan was stronger than he looked—plus he was running on pure adrenaline right now—and he was able to hold the clown at bay. He knew he couldn't keep this up for long, though. Art was strong as hell.

He looked around Sienna's room, searching for something he could use to defend himself—and his eyes fell upon Sienna's sword, resting on the ash atop one of her worktables.

That'll work, he thought.

Art shoved the door open then, the impact so hard it knocked Jonathan to the floor. He banged his knee when he hit, and pain blossomed hot and bright. He didn't think he could stand so he started crawling to the worktable, hoping to reach the sword before Art could get him, knowing he would likely fail.

He got his hand onto the table and his fingers groped around, searching for the sword. He felt the metal and was about to try to pull the weapon toward him when Art grabbed his shirt, flipped him over onto his back, and fastened his hand around his throat.

Jonathan tried to cry out, and Art let go of his neck and slapped his hand over Jonathan's mouth and nose. Jonathan grabbed the clown's wrist, tried to pull the hand from his face, and Art shoved his head to the side and held it pinned to the floor.

Jonathan swatted at the clown with his hands, determined to keep fighting no matter what. Out of his left eye, he saw Art lower the hypodermic needle toward his neck. He fought harder, but the clown was like stone now.

Nothing Jonathan did made any sort of impact on him. Then he felt a sharp prick of pain as the needle entered his flesh. Art injected him with whatever chemical was inside the hypo—was it poison?—and his exertions immediately began to slow. His body fell limp, and his vision blurred, started to go dark.

Sorry I wasn't here, Mom. I'm sorry for a lot of things.

He carried these last two thoughts with him down into nothingness.

*

Art looked down at Jonathan. The boy was out, and he'd remain that way for a couple of hours. He'd been trying to reach for something on the dresser before going nighty-night, and Art was curious what it was. He glanced at the dresser and saw a short sword lying among scattered ash. He picked it up, examined it. High-quality steel, keen edge…

Nice.

This one was a keeper.

CHAPTER TWENTY-SIX

Sienna sat in the back seat of Brooke's SUV, staring out the window. Jeff drove, while Brooke sat in the passenger seat. She did *not* look happy.

Brooke turned to Jeff. "I'm sorry you had to leave," she said.

Jeff smiled. "It's no problem." He looked into the rearview mirror so he could see Sienna's reflection. "You okay?" he asked her.

Sienna didn't respond, and Brooke turned to look back at her.

"Sienna, what the fuck *was* that back there?"

Sienna continued looking out the window. She was furious with Brooke, and she was trying to keep from exploding at her. "I'm fine."

"No! You're *not* fine. You are so completely far from fine right now. You just totally *freaked* out."

Sienna looked at Brooke. "Gee, Brooke. I wonder why."

"Don't blame this on me. I'm on the same shit as you. You don't see *me* freaking out."

"Whoa," Jeff said. "What are we talking about here? What shit?"

"I put a pinch of molly in her drink. It was *nothing*."

"Plus Xanax," Sienna said.

"What?" Jeff said, alarmed.

"I did *not* give you Xanax!" Brooke said. "She was already on Xanax, which I didn't know about. Let's make that perfectly *fucking* clear."

"You could've fucking killed me!"

"I was trying to do something *nice* for you! Jesus Christ, you're like Ms. Morbid all the time."

Sienna was silent for a long moment. That one had really stung. "Thanks," she said softly. "Just take me home."

Brooke spoke again, sounding much calmer now. "Sienna, whatever happened back there was not normal, okay? You could've had like a brain aneurysm or a seizure or something. What if it happens again?"

"Want to take her to the emergency room?" Jeff asked.

Sienna was so frustrated and upset, she was on the verge of tears. "I just wanna go home. Just take me home!"

Sienna's phone rang.

Brooke turned around to face Sienna again. "If that's your mother, do *not* answer it!"

Sienna didn't bother to check the screen to see who was calling. What did it matter? "Hello."

"Sienna, I'm in trouble."

It was Jonathan.

"Oh, you think? Mom told me what you did to her car, you little asshole. I mean, really?"

"No, I need your help. You have to come get me."

Sienna forgot about being angry with Brooke. All her attention was focused on her brother now. "What do you mean? What's wrong? Where are you?"

292

"I'm at the old carnival. Eric and Sean left me here. I'm all alone."

"What's wrong with you?"

"Please. I'm really scared. I don't know what else to do. I can't call Mommy."

That was for damn sure. Mom was already pissed at him. No way would she want to hear that he was stranded and needed her to come pick him up, *and* in the same car he'd vandalized. She'd blow a fucking gasket. "All right. Calm down. I'll come get you, okay?"

"Hurry, my phone is dying!"

"All right. Just wait by the main entrance, okay? Jonathan? *Jonathan?*"

The Little Pale Girl ended the call and tossed Jonathan's phone into the back of the black-and-white van, where the boy lay unconscious on an old dirty comforter. The phone hit his left hand and bounced off, but he didn't stir. He was, as the saying goes, dead to the world.

Art sat behind the van's steering wheel, grinning as he drove toward the carnival. He'd had no idea that his little friend could impersonate voices so accurately.

Was there no end to her talents?

"Goddammit," Sienna said. Jonathan's phone must've died.

"He's bullshitting you," Brooke said.

"No, he's not."

"Yes, he *is*," Brooke insisted. "It's Halloween. Are you really telling me right now that it's beneath your brother to pull something twisted like this? Come on. The *old carnival*?"

"No, I know when Jonathan's lying, okay? I could hear it in his voice. Something's wrong."

"Sienna, like, *dude*!" Brooke said.

"It's only a few miles from here," Jeff pointed out.

Brooke turned around to look at Sienna. The two friends held eye contact for several seconds.

"This is so stupid!" Brooke faced forward once more and slumped in her seat. "Great, fine, whatever, I don't care. It's not like this night could get any worse."

She put a cigarette in her mouth and lit it.

Sienna looked out the side window again and wondered what the hell Jonathan had gotten himself mixed up in this time.

Jeff pulled the SUV up to the carnival's front gate, which was chained and padlocked. The vehicle's headlights illuminated a rectangular white sign hanging on the gate with the words CLOSED, NO TRESPASSING printed in bright red capital letters.

From what Sienna understood, the carnival had already been having financial difficulties when Emily Crane had been killed, and her death resulted in so many people—especially families of young children—staying away that the carnival owners bowed to the inevitable and closed the place. They'd been trying to sell it ever since, but so far there had been no takers.

She was surprised to see there were lights on in the place—not a lot, but enough to see at night. She supposed the lights were meant to deter thieves and vandals, as well as give police a clear view of the grounds whenever they drove by at night.

She was grateful for the lights. She hated to think of Jonathan wandering around alone in the dark. Plus, this way they'd be able to see him waiting for them—except he wasn't. There was no sign of him.

Brooke had the passenger-side window down to keep the smoke from her cigarette from building up in the car. "Well, where is he?" she asked.

"I told him to wait in front." Sienna peered through her window, hoping to see Jonathan walking toward them at any minute.

"How old's your brother?" Jeff asked.

"Twelve."

Brooke exhaled smoke out the open window. "Just the fact that he's out here right now should tell you something. Didn't a little girl get murdered out here a couple years ago?"

"I'm gonna go look for him."

Sienna opened the door and got out.

"What?" Brooke said, surprised.

As Sienna walked past Brooke's window, Brooke said, "Sienna, get back in the car."

Sienna didn't answer.

"*Sienna!*" Brooke shouted.

She kept walking.

She found a section of fencing that had been cut away—probably by kids who'd come out here to party—

and she walked through. It was windy, and she should've been cold in her costume, and she supposed she was on some level, but the temperature didn't really register with her. She was too worried about her brother to think about herself.

"Jonathan?" she called, then again, louder. "*Jonathan!*"

Brooke shook her head. "She's crazy."

"Maybe we should go with her," Jeff said.

"Fuck that. I guarantee you her brother's just gonna scare the shit out of her. He's turned into a complete psycho ever since his father killed himself."

"Ever since *what*?" Jeff said.

"No joke. He had like this giant brain tumor that, I don't know, it just made him do all this fucked-up shit. And he was like seeing things. He got really abusive toward the end. Especially toward Sienna. And then one day, he drank a whole bottle of Jack, and he got in his car and drove straight into one of those transformer things. And the car caught fire, and he got trapped in the wreck, and he burned to death. You could hear him screaming from a mile away."

Brooke lifted her cigarette to her mouth with a shaky hand and took a drag.

"Well, I've only known your friend for a few hours, but... that explains a lot," Jeff said.

"Yeah. All things considered, I think she's doing pretty well."

*

The carnival was creepy as hell at night, and the full moon only added to its sinister atmosphere. The lighting was minimal, so there were still shadows everywhere, any one of which could be concealing something dangerous. That was the thing about the dark, Sienna thought. You could never tell what was on the other side of it.

Why had Jonathan come here? For that matter, how had he *gotten* here? Sean and Eric were his age. None of them could drive, and the carnival was too far from home to walk. Had Jonathan come here because of his obsession with Art and Emily Crane?

She'd told Mom that she believed Jonathan's story about how the clown and the girl—the *dead* girl—had been the ones who brought the dead possum into the school building. And she did believe him... up to a point.

She believed Art was there, or at least some man *dressed* like him, but she didn't believe the girl was Emily Crane's ghost. She'd been a real, living girl wearing clown makeup. It would've been easy for Jonathan to mistake her for Emily, especially if she had some superficial resemblance to the dead girl. His fear of Art combined with his imagination had done the rest. Who knows? The clown Jonathan saw might even have been the same asshole she'd seen later at Abracadabra. *Why* the two clowns had brought the eviscerated corpse of a possum into the school, she didn't know. All she knew was Jonathan hadn't been the one to do it.

Had Jonathan convinced Eric and Sean to go with him to the carnival to investigate? She could see them agreeing to it. They loved morbid shit even more than

Jonathan did. And it would be just like the little bastards to play a cruel joke on Jonathan and leave him alone in the carnival. She decided the specifics didn't matter right now. All she cared about was finding her brother. He could tell her what happened later, once they were safe at home.

Sienna passed a merry-go-round that hadn't been ridden in two years, artificial horses frozen in the same positions they'd been in when the ride had been turned off. She'd always found merry-go-round horses disturbing — waxy dead eyes, mouths opened wide in silent screams, metal poles impaling them through the back and out the stomach... What kind of sadist had decided these nightmarish creatures would be fun for children to ride?

The wind had picked up, and now she was cold. She walked with her arms crossed over her chest for what little protection it gave her, phone in hand, just in case Jonathan's wasn't *entirely* dead and he managed to text or call her.

She decided to try calling him. They were closer now, and maybe his phone would be able to pick up her signal. It rang on the other end, but Jonathan didn't pick up. She held the phone in front her, looked at the screen.

"Come on, answer me!"

Then, as if in response, her phone rang. She answered immediately.

"Jonathan, where are you? I'm searching all over the place."

She heard the crackle of distortion, but she thought she heard Jonathan say a single word: *"Help."*

She felt sick.

"Jonathan, can you hear me? I can't… Listen, I'm gonna wait for you by the merry-go-round, okay? Did you hear what I said? Meet me at the merry-go-round. Hello? Text me back!"

She ended the call and checked her text chain with Jonathan. The last dozen messages were her texting him, without any answer. But he texted now.

I'm stuck.

She immediately texted back: *What do u mean stuck? Where r u?!?*

It took several seconds for his reply to come, and when it did, it was in all caps.

THE TERRIFIER

From the Miles County Historical Society's Website

The Miles County Carnival—originally called Joy Zone—was built in Miles County, New York, in 1973, and quickly became one of the most popular attractions in the area. The Terrifier appeared later that year, but there are no existing records specifying the exact date it opened. As local legend would have it, one morning the Terrifier was simply there and ready for business. According to paperwork filed with the city, the Terrifier was constructed by a company called Pandemonia, Inc., but Internet searches fail to turn up any information on the company, although some Reddit users postulate a connection between Pandemonia, Inc. and a sinister traveling carnival that is reputed to have passed through Green Town, Illinois, in the 1950s.

The original owners of the Terrifier were Elisha Prather and his wife, Fabriola, and while they hired staff to see to the day-to-day operation and maintenance of the Terrifier, they often participated as scare actors themselves. "Where's the fun in owning a haunted attraction if you don't get to scare folks yourself once in a while?" Mr. Prather told a local reporter at the time.

The Terrifier was a dark maze, a haunted attraction with dimly lit rooms and corridors with numerous paths and dead ends. It featured scare actors, frightening sound effects, moving walls, air cannons, strobe lights, hanging props, animatronic figures, and fog machines.

Such attractions began in England in early 1900s as part of the public's fascination with spiritualism and the occult. They took hold in America during the Great Depression, around the same time trick-or-treating did. Families would create scary scenes in their basements and then take their children from house to house to view the ones their neighbors built.

Small haunted houses for Halloween started to become popular in America during the 1950s, and of course, traveling carnivals and fairs had their infamous creep shows. But haunted attractions really took off in America when Disneyland opened the Haunted Mansion in 1969. The public became fascinated with scary attractions after that, and they began springing up everywhere. Local organizations such as the Jaycees and March of Dimes used seasonal haunted houses to raise money in 1970s, and professional haunted attractions emerged at the same time—including the Terrifier.

Unfortunately, the Terrifier has a rather checkered history. Fabriola's husband Elisha was murdered inside the Terrifier in 1975, and she disappeared soon after. Local gossips theorized that Fabriola plotted with a lover to kill her husband and ran off with the man afterward, but this was never proven, and she was never seen again. Ownership of the Terrifier fell to the Prathers' oldest son, Norris, after this.

Norris was not especially business-minded, and he'd disliked the Terrifier since the day it opened. "It talks to me, and I don't like what it says," he once told a former schoolmate. He hired a man named Johnny Lee Johns to manage the attraction, which Johns did quite successfully for six months. Johns had a criminal history, however, and when Norris discovered this, Johns killed him and fled before the police could catch him. Rumor has it that Johns moved to the backwoods of Texas, changed his name, and started his own haunted attraction with family members, but this has never been proven.

The two younger Prather children—Reyna and Lucius— inherited the Terrifier and continued to oversee its operation until 1984, when the attraction caught fire and seven teenagers died. They sold the Terrifier to carnival management and left town. No one knows where they went to or if they're still alive. The fire was a tragedy, but it drew national attention to safety issues in the scare industry, which resulted in stricter safety laws, building codes, and inspections throughout the country.

Carnival management debated whether to rebuild the Terrifier or replace it with a new attraction. Unofficial word was the majority was going to vote to replace it, but when the actual tally was taken, management unanimously voted to restore it, and the Terrifier reopened in 1986. The reason for management's change of heart was never divulged.

There were others disturbing incidents regarding the Terrifier throughout the years.

In 1989, Ron and Darla Erickson and their twelve-year-old son, Doug, entered the Terrifier, but only Darla emerged. "One minute they were standing right next to me, and the next they were gone," she told police. The boy and his father were never found.

In 2012, paranormal investigator Grant Walker, host of the cable television series Midnight Walker, and his camera operator—and boyfriend—Jerry Taylor got permission from carnival management to conduct an investigation inside the Terrifier. Grant and Jerry entered the Terrifier at sunset on Halloween of that year and didn't come back out until dawn. They refused to speak to anyone about what had happened inside the Terrifier, and that afternoon they cancelled their series. Two weeks later, Walker jumped to his death from his high-rise apartment building in NYC. Taylor disappeared that same night. No trace of the footage they shot that night within the Terrifier has ever been found.

In 2016, Emily Crane was horribly murdered inside the Terrifier. By this point, the Miles County Carnival was already on life support. Attendance was way down, thanks to people spending their leisure time browsing the Internet, playing videogames, and binge-watching streaming content.

Rides were not being maintained, and attractions were being shut down one after the other. Management made the decision to close the carnival for good, and it's remained closed ever since.

These days, the carnival is more of a nuisance than a fond memory for the people of Miles County. Teenagers regularly sneak in to party, and vandalism is rampant. Surprisingly, Miles County's homeless residents refuse to enter the carnival grounds, even though there are numerous buildings there that could be used as shelter. "We know better," said a homeless man who would only identify himself by the nickname Cowboy.

The Terrifier still lives on today, but as a dark legend rather than a place people once went to wander around in the dark and scream when something with long claws and sharp teeth came rushing toward them from out of the shadows.

Maybe it's scarier that way.

The first thing Jonathan became aware of was the pain in his throat.

The second thing was that he lay on a cold, hard floor.

The third thing was that he had a massive headache and a weird metallic taste in his mouth.

He massaged his neck with one hand while he pushed himself into a half-sitting position with the other. Then he slowly opened his eyes. He'd lost his glasses, but while his vision was a little blurry, he could see well enough.

He was in a room filled with dolls, not regular ones, but scary ones. An old-fashioned girl doll with glowing blue eyes rested on a shelf in front of him, while three more like her sat on swings nearby, hands holding onto ropes which hung from a round frame that turned at a stately, measured pace, rotating the dolls in an endless circle.

On another shelf stood an animatronic doll with blazing red eyes and a mouthful of fangs, swinging a wicked-looking axe back and forth with clockwork precision. A baby doll with a large human head—bald, bulging eyes, sharp teeth, blood running from the corner of its mouth—was inserted partway into a hole in the wall, hugging the edge, head turned to look outward. Everywhere he looked, there were dolls, each creepier than the last—dozens of them. The tinny sound of wailing children drifted through the air, and he had his first coherent thought since returning to consciousness.

That sounds like it's coming from a speaker.

He rose into a full sitting position, and his throbbing head protested loudly at the move. He intended to make an attempt to stand, hoping he wouldn't vomit, when he saw a vanity table with a lighted makeup mirror in one corner of the room. A large doll sat in the chair before it, one with dirty, matted blonde hair, half of it pulled through a small white hat on the right side of... her... head...

Jonathan felt a stab of fear. That was no doll. It was the Little Pale Girl.

A child's laughter came over the speaker then, and Jonathan saw a collection of steel dental tools sitting on the table. They rested in a pool of blood, and a collection of small teeth lay on the tabletop close by. The Little Pale Girl set down a tool with blood-covered fingers, and then turned her face to Jonathan.

The laughter on the soundtrack grew louder.

The Little Pale Girl had used the tools to tear away sections of her face. Her eyes had been removed, the skin around them cut away in roughly triangular patterns. Her nose was gone, leaving an open bloody cavity, and she'd sliced off her lips. She'd removed all her teeth as well, save for the two front ones.

She resembled a mutilated flesh jack-o'-lantern.

The girl smiled and laughed softly, then reached up to touch the sides of her face, as if presenting her handiwork to him. Then she took hold of a strip of flesh near her left eye and peeled it away with a moist, sticky sound.

Laughter roared from the speaker.

Jonathan no longer cared about his headache, or his aching throat, or where he was or how he'd gotten here. He had to get away from the Little Pale Girl before she decided to use those dental tools on him. He sprang to his feet and dashed toward an open doorway, recorded laughter following him as he entered a hallway, turned left, and continued running.

CHAPTER TWENTY-SEVEN

Brooke was not the type of person who could wait long without doing something, and soon after Sienna left, she grabbed hold of Jeff's face, pulled him toward her, and kissed him. They continued kissing, sometimes gently, sometimes fiercely, sometimes with just their lips, sometimes with tongues, running their hands across each other's bodies. Except for Brooke's hair. She'd worked on it too long to let Jeff mess it up now.

She really liked Jeff, maybe even loved him. They shouldn't have worked, really. He was calm and laidback, while she was impulsive and full of energy. But they *did* work, in an opposites attract kind of way. In early October, she'd decided that she'd grown tired of the boys Miles County had to offer, so she'd downloaded a dating app to her phone. She'd done a lot of swiping left before she came to a profile that caught her attention.

Jeff Fischer, first-year student at NYU, majoring in geology.

That wasn't what had interested her, though. What had was his photo. He was *gorgeous*, with great hair and an even better smile. But then she'd asked herself a question: why the hell was a babe like this majoring in something as nerdy as geology? She scrolled through the rest of his profile, and at the end, he talked about why he'd chosen geology as his field.

I like rocks.

She'd laughed her ass off at that, and so she sent him a message that simply said, *Let's talk.* They started texting, and she found him to be funny, sweet, and charming. Definite dating material. She'd lied on her profile and said she was eighteen. It wasn't a *big* lie, since her birthday was in December. She was glad she'd lied because she *really* didn't want to scare off Jeff. *What's two months?* she told herself.

They started talking on the phone, staying up most of the night, discussing anything that crossed their minds. Well, she did most of the talking, which was okay, since Jeff said he liked listening to her. When they finally met at a coffee shop in the city, it was like they'd known each other all their lives. They'd only gone out a handful of times since, but they always had the best time together.

She'd planned to introduce him to Sienna and Allie tonight, but then Allie bailed on them, and Sienna had a psychotic break on the dance floor. Not exactly the best first impressions. Still, if she kept Jeff around—and she planned to—the four of them would eventually get to know each other better, and Brooke really hoped her besties liked him. She knew her friends' opinion shouldn't matter so much to her, but it did.

Jeff broke away, grinning. He reached into the glovebox and pulled out a clear plastic bag containing white powder and a tiny spoon.

"What is that?" Brooke asked. She already knew, though. Cocaine.

Jeff chuckled. "A little pick-me-up."

"Wow, Jeff, okay. Don't let Sienna see that shit."

Jeff opened the bag and began stirring the powder to loosen it. He didn't look up from his work as he answered. "Well, we'll just have to do it before she comes back."

"I'm not doin' that," Brooke said.

"You ever try it?"

"Yeah, once. I didn't like it."

"Oh sure," Jeff said skeptically. "Impossible. Come on. This will put us right back in the club."

He brought the spoon to his nose and inhaled. He rubbed his finger beneath his nose, snorted, then coughed once.

"Fuck!" He got another spoonful from the bag and held it out to Brooke. "Trust me."

She looked at the cocaine for a moment. It wasn't all *that* much, and besides, something had to salvage this night.

"All right. Fuck it."

Grinning, Jeff held the spoon to her nose, and she inhaled.

She rubbed her nose and grimaced. "Ugh. That tastes weird."

Weird, but good. She could feel the drug beginning to hit her system, and she smiled. Live while you're alive, right?

They embraced and started kissing again, more passionately than before.

Yeah, this was *good*.

Sienna hadn't been to the carnival in years, but she had no trouble remembering where the Terrifier was. What kid could forget where the spookhouse was located?

The building itself was only one story tall, but the painted façade that fronted it was two stories. On the left was a giant Grim Reaper, chains crisscrossing its black robe, one skeletal hand holding a scythe with a blade that stretched the length of the entire roof. *TERRIFIER* was emblazoned on the blade in flashing red letters shaped in a spooky font. The Reaper's other hand pointed to the entrance, which was through the wide-open mouth of a giant clown head with orange hair, glowing eyes, jagged teeth, and a bulbous red nose with a hole broken in the middle, cracks radiating outward from it. Inside the clown's mouth, baleful red light shone through a layer of white fog.

On the opposite side of the building's façade was an equally large devil head, with red skin, horns, and fanged teeth. It appeared goofy rather than scary, with a happy smile and light-up eyes that didn't burn as harshly as the clown's. A barred gate covered its mouth, and the same reddish light and fog was inside. The rest of the façade was covered with monsters, skulls, eyeballs, and mounds of gooey, melting flesh. Speakers were attached to the roof, and they issued haunted house sound effects—eerie moans, maniacal laughter, terrified screams...

If it was daytime, the place wouldn't have seemed anywhere near as scary. In fact, it would look cheesy, and old and kind of sad, paint faded, weeds growing all around it. But at night... well, it looked like it might live up to its name—especially because it appeared to be fully operational and running. Who'd started it up? Jonathan? Why would he do that? Would he even know how? And why had he come here? To find someplace warm to wait for her? No, that didn't make sense. If his phone was low on power, there was no guarantee that he'd get her text to say she'd arrived to pick him up, and he wouldn't have been able to contact her to tell her where he was. But since his phone *was* still working, once she told him to meet her by the merry-go-round, he should've left the Terrifier and come to her. Something wasn't right here.

It's a trap.

She wasn't sure what made her think this—some instinct, maybe?—but once she had the thought, she couldn't shake it. Maybe someone inside was holding Jonathan against his will and had forced him to make those calls and send those texts to lure her to the Terrifier.

She wished she'd asked Brooke and Jeff to come with her. Their presence would've been a comfort. But she was alone, and she had a choice to make. Go inside and look for her brother, or call 911 and wait outside until the police arrived. But maybe Jonathan wasn't in danger, maybe he was just scared and confused, hiding inside the Terrifier because he didn't know where else to go.

There was only one way to find out the truth.

She started toward the entrance.

*

310

There was some light inside, but it was mostly dark, which made sense since it was a haunted house attraction. And what light there was had been designed to set the mood for each part of the place—blue, purple, yellow, orange, and most of all, red. Sienna was in a blue room at the moment, one that wasn't too scary, but it was near the entrance. Things would get worse the farther she went. That's how these things worked.

She used her phone as a flashlight, but it only did so much to illuminate her way. Still, it was better than nothing. It was chilly inside, but she was out of the wind, and that made a big difference. She might not be warm, but at least she wasn't shivering anymore. The place smelled of dust, mildew, and rotting wood, but there was another odor too—one she couldn't identify, a… *foulness* that made her think of infection. This was a Bad Place.

"Jonathan?" she called, her voice echoing hollowly in the Terrifier's narrow corridors. If her brother heard her, he didn't answer. Maybe *couldn't* answer.

She walked into another room, and a giant ghoul with white skin, glowing blue eyes, a bulging red nose, and a bloody fang-filled mouth reached for her with huge, clawed hands. Evil laughter came over the sound system—*Muhahahaha!*—and she jumped back, startled. It was an animatronic monster built to resemble the clown on the front of the building, nothing more, and she felt stupid for letting it scare her. It was just a machine, designed to frighten but not to harm.

But why did it have to be a goddamn *clown*?

She continued walking.

*

The coke was really starting to hit Brooke now, heightening her physical sensations. Kissing Jeff was almost as good as sex—emphasis on *almost*. She wanted to stay in the moment and luxuriate in just feeling, but she couldn't give herself over fully to the moment. She was too worried about Sienna. She broke away from Jeff, glanced out the passenger-side window.

She'd insisted they turn on the SUV's headlights so Sienna could find her way back to them easier, but there was no sign of her.

"Where the hell *is* she?" Brooke said.

"Who cares?" Jeff pulled her close again, and they kissed for several more seconds before Brooke pushed him away.

"Wait," she said. "But seriously, what time did she leave?"

Jeff answered, clearly frustrated. "Well, who *cares*?"

They kissed for a few additional moments before Brooke turned away and picked up her phone.

"I'm gonna call her really fast, okay?"

Jeff groaned. "Just be quick," he said. He opened the driver's-side door and started to get out.

"Where are you going?" Brooke asked.

He turned back to look at her. "I've got to go pee-pee. You wanna hold it?"

"Ew. Leave."

Jeff closed the door and headed toward the rear of the SUV. Brooke called Sienna's number. It rang several times before sending her to voicemail.

"Hi, this is Sienna. Leave a message, and I'll get back to you."

Brooke was about to speak, but a woman's voice—not Sienna's—cut her off.

"The mailbox is full and cannot accept messages at this time..."

She disconnected.

"Unbelievable."

"Rawr!"

Something smacked the passenger window hard, and she squealed with fright. She turned to see Jeff standing there, palms flat against the glass, mouth open in a snarl.

Brooke laughed then shouted, "Asshole!"

Jeff grinned. "That's twice!"

"You're so funny," Brooke said. "You know what's actually really funny? Let me see here."

She reached over to the driver's seat where Jeff had left his bag of coke. With a wicked grin, she lifted it up and displayed it to him.

Jeff was suddenly alarmed. "Oh, hey! Don't fuck around. Come on."

Brooke gave the bag a shake. "You better say sorry."

"I'm sorry," he said.

"And I don't really know if you can snort this out of an ashtray."

Now he looked panicked, and he began pleading. "I'm sorry! I'm sorry! I won't do it again, I promise!"

"Are you actually sorry?"

Brooke held the open bag over the ashtray and started to tip it over.

Jeff's eyes filled with desperation. "Hey!"

Brooke hesitated a moment, then she turned to him and smiled. "Okay, fine. But you're a jerk."

He grinned, blew her a kiss, then rubbed it on the window in a circle.

Brooke laughed as Jeff headed toward the rear of the SUV to do his thing.

She was considering giving Sienna's phone another try when she noticed something written in the dirt on the driver's-side window—three words that hadn't been there a moment ago:

JUST THE TIP

Jeff stood behind the SUV, legs spread apart, dick out, taking the most glorious piss of his life. Pissing always felt good after you'd been holding it for a while, and right now he felt as if he hadn't peed in years. The coke heightened the sensation into something almost orgasmic, and he wondered if it was possible for guys to ejaculate at the same time they were pissing. He didn't think so, but then human anatomy was not his specialty. Rocks were.

His stream was strong, arching up and down, spattering onto the grass a full foot away from his feet. He sighed in contentment. He was a simple man who enjoyed simple pleasures, and while there'd been some rough patches tonight, all in all, he was enjoying himself—mostly because of Brooke. Sienna had looked damn hot in her warrior angel costume, but he thought Brooke was just as beautiful, if not more so. It was her bold spirit that he loved most about her, though. She said whatever was on her mind, did whatever she wanted, took no shit from anyone, and was fiercely loyal to her close friends.

She was amazing.

He had no idea what she saw in him, but whatever it was, he was grateful. He planned to ask her to move into his apartment after she graduated from high school, and then—if things went well—he might even ask her to marry him. He'd once considered marriage nothing more than a useful social construct for people who wanted society's permission to fuck, but with Brooke, he could see it being more than that. Much more. They'd be lovers, sure, but they'd be partners in life as well. But most of all, they'd be friends. Maybe that was the true foundation for a strong marriage—two people who were first and foremost—

The clown emerged out of the darkness like a creature born to it and rammed a butcher knife into Jeff's balls with a meaty *thuk!*

Jeff cried out in pain and looked down to see what was happening to him. The clown yanked the knife free in a spray of blood, then stabbed Jeff again in the same place.

Thuk!

The pain was so great, not even the cocaine in Jeff's system could blunt it. He fell back against the SUV, slid to the ground, then rolled onto his back. The clown knelt next to him and rapidly stabbed him seven more times— *thuk-thuk-thuk-thuk-thuk-thuk-thuk!*

The clown shifted the butcher knife—blade dripping with blood—to his left hand. He thrust his right hand into the red, shredded meat that had been Jeff's pubic area, grabbed hold of Jeff's penis, and pulled hard. There was a tearing, snapping sensation, and the clown held Jeff's cock before his face so he could get a good look at the thing that had been the center of his life since puberty began.

Jeff's scream ripped through the night.

Brooke heard Jeff's first scream, and she turned around to look out the rear windshield.

"Jeff!"

She saw him slide to the ground, heard him scream some more. Then, in the red wash of the SUV's taillights, she saw a blood-splattered figure holding a huge butcher knife stand up and look at her, eyes filled with wicked glee, mouth stretched into a hideous smile.

It was the Miles County Clown.

"Oh, my god!" Brooke shouted, then screamed.

The clown continued looking at her for a moment, then he raised the knife high, and resumed attacking Jeff.

Panic took over Brooke, and she slid over into the driver's seat, intending to start the SUV and get out of there, but the key wasn't in the ignition. What the hell had Jeff done with it? Had he dropped it on the floor? She looked but didn't see it. Had he slipped the keys into his pocket before going out to take a piss? If so, she was fucked.

Jeff continued screaming, the sounds louder, more strident now. She didn't want to imagine what the clown was doing to him, but she knew whatever it was, it was horrible.

My poor baby...

Then his screams dribbled away to moans. Brooke continued searching for the keys and spotted them on the floor of the passenger side. *Thank Christ!* She reached down, grabbed them, inserted the SUV's key in the ignition, and turned on the engine.

Before she could put the vehicle in gear, the clown appeared at the driver's-side windshield. She saw him and screamed. Mouth opened wide in a lunatic grin, he swiped a piece of bloody meat across the glass, cutting a crimson swatch through *JUST THE TIP*. With a sick lurch of horror, she realized the meat the clown held was Jeff's penis.

The clown didn't stop there, though. Laughing without making any sound, he held the penis to his forehead and mimed galloping in place, as if he was a unicorn. He stopped, put the blood-slick butcher knife into his mouth, and clenched it in his teeth. Now that both hands were free, he held the penis in one hand while he mimed jacking it off with the other. His hand motions became more rapid, and then he squeezed the cock as hard as he could, and blood jetted from the opening and splattered onto the windshield.

The clown took the knife out of his mouth, threw back his head, and roared with mimed laughter. His expression grew cold then, and—still holding Jeff's penis in his left hand—he made a fist, drew back his arm, and punched the driver's-side window. Glass exploded inward. He dropped both the knife and Jeff's dead penis to the ground, reached into the SUV, grabbed hold of Brooke, and hauled her through the now open window.

Brooke screamed and thrashed, trying to break free from the clown's grip, but he was too strong. He pulled her out of the SUV, in the process dragging her left leg across a shard of glass remaining in the window frame, and she cried out as it bit deep into her flesh. The clown threw her to the ground, then turned away to retrieve his knife.

He knelt, picked up the weapon, and then came toward her, murderous lust in his gaze. Brooke had no time to think, but that was all right. Thinking wasn't her strong suit; acting was. When the clown was close enough, she rolled onto her back and kicked him in the face with the thick heel of her right boot. The clown's head snapped back. He staggered to the SUV, fell against it, then slumped to the ground, stunned.

Brooke didn't waste any time. Jeff was probably dead, and if she didn't haul ass, it would be her turn on the chopping block next. She pushed herself onto her feet, grunting with the effort, then started running, limping on her injured leg, one hand pressed to the wound to try to minimize the bleeding, each step sending violent jolts of pain shooting through her body. She didn't care about the pain, though. She only cared about surviving.

Live while you're alive, right?

Brooke's kick had knocked Art's little top hat out of position, and he readjusted it as he sat with his back against the SUV and watched the girl shuffle away on her wounded leg. He scowled at first, irritated, but then he gave a silent laugh and smiled ruefully. He'd have to be more careful with this one. She might even be as dangerous as Sienna, or nearly so. One thing was certain: her hair looked *fabulous* tonight. It must've taken her *forever* to do it.

Art rose to his feet, gripped the handle of the butcher knife tight, and started walking after Brooke. He heard Jeff moan and writhe behind him, not quite dead yet, but he had no desire to go back and finish him off. The way the boy was bleeding, he'd be dead soon enough.

Art wanted that blonde bitch. Wanted her bad.

He started walking faster.

CHAPTER TWENTY-EIGHT

Brooke entered the carnival grounds through the same makeshift entrance Sienna had, and she called out for her friend as she went.

"Sienna! *Sienna!*"

Ordinarily, she might've dug the carnival's sinister night vibe, but she was hardly in the mood right now. She cried and screamed as she ran, fueled by equal amounts of fear and desperation. She glanced back and saw the clown coming after her, a garbage bag slung over his shoulder, eyes gleaming in the carnival lights. He walked at a deliberate pace, not bothering to run. Maybe he knew he didn't need to run in order to catch her, wounded as she was.

Looking over her shoulder to gauge the clown's progress turned out to be a big mistake, for when she faced forward once more, she stumbled on several bags of old trash and went down. She sat on the ground, watching the clown come closer and closer, his fucked-up mouth stretched into a grin.

She spared a moment to take a look at her injured leg. Deep gashes ran down the outside of her left thigh, and they were bleeding like crazy. She would never get away from that goddamn clown in these boots! They looked super-cute on her, and they worked well for dancing, but when it came to running for your life, they were a fucking liability—but one easily remedied.

Not taking her eyes off the clown, she unzipped her boots and pulled off the left one. The motion set off an excruciating wave of pain in her wounds, and she moaned. As if the sound of her agony excited him, the clown started walking faster. Brooke whimpered as she tugged on her right boot. She knew she had only seconds before the clown used the same butcher knife on her that he'd used to kill Jeff. She gritted her teeth and pulled on the stubborn boot with all her might...

It came off all at once, and she nearly fell over backward. If she had, she knew the clown would've gotten her for sure. She tossed the boot aside and rose to her feet, which now had only ankle-high sheer socks to protect them, and she started limping away as fast as she could. Her left leg screamed in protest, but she told it to shut the fuck up and pushed herself to go even faster.

Art liked it when they ran. Not only did it make the fun last, but the longer they were afraid, the sweeter it was when they breathed their last. Plus, chasing them was a great way to get in his steps.

He grinned and continued following Brooke, entertaining himself by imagining the atrocities he would commit upon her tender flesh when he caught up with her. Soon, he was giggling. Silently, of course.

He passed a row of abandoned carnival game booths—ring toss, milk bottle throw, balloon and darts, plate break… the classics. As he approached the end of this section, a mass of shadow appeared in front of him and blocked his way.

He stopped, cocked his head, frowned. Was this his friend playing one of her games? It didn't feel like her. As he watched, the wall of darkness separated into smaller individual shadows. Five of them, roughly shaped like humans.

He snorted with derision. He didn't have time for this. He was hunting.

He walked toward the wraiths, and they parted soundlessly to make way for him. He continued following Brooke's blood trail, not giving the shadows another thought.

Sienna entered a room where circus music played and a sign on the wall warned *DANGER CLOWNS* in red letters. Her first thought was that Danger Clowns sounded like a great name for a band. Her second thought was that someone needed to learn how to use a colon.

True to the sign, this room was clown-themed, and it was the last thing Sienna wanted to see tonight. An image popped into her head then—Art and the Little Pale Girl in the hallway at Jonathan's school, playing with the stringy, spongy guts of a dead possum.

Well… maybe not the last thing.

A monstrous animatronic clown stood near the room's entrance, holding the legs of a child in its huge clawed hands, dangling the small mannequin as it swiveled back and forth, eyes flashing, the room's speakers echoing with deep, distorted laughter. Circus posters covered the walls depicting elephants, tigers, lions, and other animals, and various metallic torture implements were displayed throughout the room.

Sienna called out, "Jonathan? Can you hear me?"

The only reply she received was laughter issuing from the speakers.

Frustrated, she checked her phone to see if Jonathan had sent her a new message. He hadn't.

Where the hell was he?

And more importantly, was he all right?

Brooke felt as if she'd been running for hours. She knew it was probably only minutes, but they were the *longest* goddamn minutes of her life. The most painful, too. Her left leg had started to go numb, and she knew that wasn't a good sign. Would it need to be amputated? She almost laughed at the absurdity of the thought. If she couldn't escape this fucking clown, her remaining lifespan could be measured in seconds.

She knew she shouldn't keep looking over her shoulder to check on the clown's progress, but she couldn't help herself. Each time she looked, he was a little closer. Panic gripped her, and she started screaming.

"Somebody please! Help me!"

She had no idea if there was anyone else on the carnival grounds—aside from Sienna and her psycho brother—but if there was *any* chance that someone would hear her, she had to take it. So she kept screaming as she ran, hand pressed to her leg wound in what she knew was most likely a futile attempt to slow the bleeding.

The clown continued following, eyes cold, teeth bared, butcher knife gleaming in the moonlight.

Brooke came to an alley between buildings, and she started down it. *GO BACK* was spraypainted on the brick, but she couldn't have heeded the warning if she'd wanted to, not unless she wanted to feel the deadly kiss of the clown's steel blade. The alley sloped downward and ended at the rear of another building. There was a metal door there—a back entrance, she guessed. But an entrance to what? It didn't matter. It was a door, and she prayed that it would be unlocked. If not, she was a dead woman.

She ran, keeping one hand on the wall to steady herself so she wouldn't slip as she negotiated the alley's slope. Shadows flickered at the edge of her vision, and she feared she was on the verge of passing out. She *was* lightheaded, most likely due to blood loss. She heard whispering then, faint, unintelligible, but then it became clearer. A chorus of voices spoke three words.

Sienna is inside…

She didn't question the message. She could *feel* it was true, and she screamed as loud as she could as she continued running for the metal door.

"Help! Sienna!"

Sienna was about to leave the Danger Clowns room and search for Jonathan elsewhere, when she heard a familiar voice—and it was screaming her name.

324

"Brooke?!"

Sienna started running back the way she'd come, moving at full speed.

I'm coming! she thought. *Hold on!*

The metal door *was* unlocked, and Brooke opened it and rushed inside. She didn't know where she was, but the power was on in here, and the halls were narrow and covered with scary decorations. Was this some kind of fucked-up Halloween party? There was no one else around, so—

Brooke turned a corner and a gigantic rat with huge fangs and glowing white eyes lunged at her from a large hole in the wall, roaring loudly. She screamed and threw herself backward, fully expecting to feel the monster's sharp teeth sink into her flesh and crunch her bones within the next few seconds. But the rat didn't come any closer. Instead, it waggled its head back and forth, still roaring, and slowly withdrew back into the hole.

The sound hadn't come from the rat, she realized, but rather a speaker attached to the ceiling near the hole. The goddamn thing was a fake! And that's when she realized where she was: The Terrifier. She'd come here often when she was a kid. It was one of her favorite places in the carnival. In fact, now that she had time to think, she remembered that stupid monster rat.

She ran on, and when she reached the end of the hall, she turned the corner, but her bad leg buckled beneath her, and she stumbled forward into another room, fell, and hit the floor hard. Her numb leg was numb no longer.

Agony blazed from her wound, her entire body felt on fire, and she cried out in pain.

She was in a bathroom, at least a replica of one. A crude cardboard sign hung on the open door that said, *Sorry! Out of Order!* The tiled walls and floor were covered with streaks of fake blood and bloody handprints, a plastic trash receptacle overflowed with blood-soaked paper towels, a grotesque tumorous mass with eyes and teeth embedded in its disgusting flesh sat in the sink, alongside a long block of wood with nails stuck in each end, points facing outward. The words *ART WAS HERE* were written in blood on one of the walls.

Shaking, sobbing, Brooke pushed herself into a sitting position. She heard the sound of plastic sliding across a smooth surface, and she turned to see the clown enter the bathroom, dragging his garbage bag across the floor behind him.

"Stay away from me!" Brooke shouted.

The clown stopped and looked down at her, grinning, eyes burning with menace.

Brooke pushed herself backward to get away from the clown. "Oh my god! Please! No!"

She got to her feet and tried to run away from the clown, but she took only a few steps before encountering a wall. She screamed in frustration and terror as she realized she had nowhere to go. She spun around, pressed her back against the wall, and faced the clown.

His grin widened and he started walking slowly toward her.

Brooke's eyes darted to the left, and she saw the long block of wood lying in the sink next to the tumor-thing.

She reached out, grabbed the block, and held it before her as a makeshift club.

"Stay back. Stop. Please stop. *Stay away from me!*"

The clown walked up to Brooke, stopped only a foot away from her, and released his grip on the garbage bag. He bent down, reached his right hand into the bag, and withdrew his own club—a table leg with knives, forks, nails, and screws driven into its blocky square top. The clown kept his eyes fixed on hers, watching her reaction as he displayed his weapon.

"Wait, wait! No!"

She sobbed as she begged for her life. The clown's eyes narrowed and his smile widened. He liked seeing her afraid. Maybe… Maybe that meant he only intended to scare her. Maybe this was just some fucked-up prank that had gone too far. Or maybe someone was operating an extreme haunted house in the old Terrifier attraction. She'd read about such things, experiences where the scare actors pushed their willing customers to the edge of their emotional and physical endurance, and beyond.

He ripped off Jeff's dick and showed it to you, then he broke the SUV's window and dragged you outside, slicing your leg on broken glass in the process.

But she hadn't actually *seen* Jeff get hurt, had she? Maybe his earlier attempts to scare her were only warm-ups, and *this* was the main event. The clown could be a friend of Jeff's she hadn't met yet, or maybe someone he'd hired to play the part. As for her leg, that might've been an accident. In the dark and in all the confusion, the clown might not even have realized she'd been hurt. Was Jeff somewhere in the Terrifier, watching what was

327

happening on closed circuit TV? She had a hard time believing he could be so cruel, but she'd rather it be true a thousand times over than be facing the real Miles County Clown. Hell, she'd be so relieved that all this bullshit was fake, she might even forgive Jeff—*after* he took her to the ER to get her leg stitched up.

She knew this was desperate, wishful thinking, though. She could feel hatred radiating from the clown like heat from a blast furnace, and she could see long, agonizing death in his eyes. *Her* death. What she *didn't* see was that the clown was holding something in his left hand behind his back: an open jar of clear liquid.

The clown's fingers tightened on his club, and he took a half step toward her. Only six inches separated them now.

Brooke was so possessed by unreasoning terror that she forgot about her club, and she made no effort to defend herself. All she could do was sob and babble weak pleas that she knew would go unheeded. "No, no, no, no! Stop it! Stop! Please!"

The clown whipped his left arm forward and hurled the contents of the jar in Brooke's face.

The girl screamed as her flesh began to bubble and burn, and she slapped her hands to her face, as if trying to keep it from falling off. Art thought it was one of the funniest things he'd ever seen. He laughed uproariously as wisps of chemical fumes began to rise from her rapidly disintegrating face. He was glad he'd taken that bottle of fluoroantimonic acid from the Coroner's

Office. He'd waited a year to see it in action, but it had been worth it!

Brooke pulled her hands away from the ruin of her face, her fingers coming away with large pieces of her skin. Her eyes were gone, the sockets filled with clumps of liquefied flesh. She shrieked like a mortally wounded animal, and Art decided it was time for the fun to really begin.

He got a two-handed grip on his club and slammed it into Brooke's back. She howled as the metal implements shredded her flesh and cracked her bones. Art hit her again, and again, and Brooke—screaming constantly now—collapsed to the floor and writhed in agony. Art bent down, dropped his club to the floor, grabbed hold of Brooke's ankles, and dragged her toward the middle of the bathroom, her mangled back leaving a wide bloody smear behind her. When he got her where he wanted her, he bent down to retrieve his club, gripped it with both hands once more, raised it high, and brought it down on her right knee. Skin tore, blood spurted, and bone shattered.

He raised the club again, and this time he slammed it into the center of her chest, breaking her sternum and her ribs. Blood fountained upward from the wound and spurted from Brooke's mouth. As if this was a signal, Art began wildly swinging the club into her chest, yanking it out, and slamming it right back down. He did this a total of six times, then he staggered backward, momentarily winded. He lowered the club to the floor, then straddled Brooke's body. The girl's lips quivered, and Art knew that she still lived. Good.

He reached into her open chest cavity, forced the edges farther apart, then grabbed hold of her heart and tore it from her body. He held it up to his face and watched it quiver with its last beats. Before the organ could fall still, he brought it to his mouth and bit into it. He sank his teeth deep into the tough muscle just as it beat its last, and a final stream of blood shot from the heart and jetted out the side of his mouth.

Art closed his eyes and savored the coppery taste. There was nothing like fresh heart straight from the body...

Just like mother used to make.

CHAPTER TWENTY-NINE

Sienna raced through the Terrifier's halls, searching everywhere for Brooke, calling her name, receiving no response.

Please let her be okay, please let her be okay…

She came to a small door that she hadn't noticed before. She shoved, it opened, and she dashed through. The door closed behind her, and on this side was what looked like a tiled bathroom wall. A secret entrance, she realized. She ran around a stall and stopped.

Brooke lay on the floor, her face a mass of raw, red meat, eyes and lips gone. Her chest had been caved in, and broken ends of ribs jutted out. She was covered in blood—*her* own blood—and more of it puddled around her on the floor, dripped from the sink, slid in thick lines down the wall. Sienna was an artist. She could tell painted blood from the real thing, and there was a lot of the real stuff all over.

She brought her hands to her mouth in shock and began shaking. Whimpering, she fell to her knees next to her friend's ravaged corpse and struggled to understand what she was seeing. Had her fucking *heart* been torn out? Oh, sweet Jesus…

She sensed the presence of someone else, and she looked up to see Art leaning against the side of the bathroom's entrance, arms crossed in a casual, relaxed pose. She gasped as she beheld the creature from her nightmare, her tormentor in Abracadabra, the Miles County Clown, the drawing in Daddy's sketchbook… She now knew for certain that they were all one and the same.

Art leered as he watched Sienna, and she knew he was drinking in her grief like it was the finest of wines. He raised his right hand—stained dark crimson with Brooke's blood—and slowly waggled his fingers at her in greeting.

He'd done this. *He'd* killed one of her best friends, torturing her in the process, inflicting unimaginable pain. How Brooke—sweet, brash, loving, wild, impulsive, sarcastic, loyal Brooke—must have suffered before she'd died. Sienna had never felt true hatred in her seventeen years, but she felt it now. Art was an abomination, an obscenity, a foul, diseased *thing*, and he needed to be stopped before he could hurt anyone else.

An awful thought occurred to her then. What if Art had found Jonathan before her and had already hurt him? Was her brother dead, too? She'd arrived too late to help poor Brooke, but was it also too late to help Jonathan?

Art started walking slowly toward her then, as if savoring each step. She scooted back to keep some distance between them, the move instinctive rather than conscious. He stopped next to Brooke's body and gazed down at Sienna. He drew in a deep breath and let it out, arms at his sides, hands curling into fists, then relaxing. The hatred that burned hot within Sienna only a moment ago was gone, replaced with paralyzing fear. Her entire body shook with terror as Art continued breathing heavily—without sound, of course—shoulders rising and falling, hands curling into fists and uncurling again, over and over.

Sienna caught movement from the corner of her eye, and she flicked her gaze toward the bathroom entrance. Jonathan stood there, without his glasses, eyes wide as he stared at his personal boogeyman, his body trembling just as hard as Sienna's. He looked unharmed, at least physically, and Sienna felt an overwhelming wave of relief that he was all right. For the moment, at least. But when Art saw him—

"Jonathan! Run!"

But Jonathan didn't move, didn't give any sign that he'd heard her. He continued shaking and staring at Art, mesmerized by the killer clown.

Art grinned at Sienna, then turned his head to look over his shoulder at Jonathan. She knew he would kill her brother first, making him suffer just as Brooke had suffered before he'd ended her life, all to torture Sienna emotionally and maximize *her* suffering before it was her turn to die.

She wasn't going to let that fucking clown hurt her brother, no matter what it took.

Or what it might cost her.

She saw a long wooden block lying on the floor close by. Nails had been embedded in each end—one apiece— their sharp metal points sticking outward.

That'll do, Sienna thought.

"Jonathan, *RUN!*"

She yelled this time, and that did the trick. Jonathan shook his head as if coming out of a trance, turned, and darted out of the room.

While Art watched him go, Sienna—still kneeling—grabbed the club and shoved it nail-first into Art's lower back and then gave it a vicious twist. Art spun toward her, mouth open in a soundless roar of pain. He grabbed Sienna's hair, and she released her grasp on the club, reached up to grab Art's wrist, and tried to dislodge his grip. But he was much stronger than he looked, and she wasn't able to get free.

He yanked her to her feet, slammed her against one wall, then the opposite one. Sienna cried out in pain, but before she could try to fight back, Art grabbed the back of her head and shoved her face into the door of one of the stalls, tearing it from its hinges. White light exploded behind Sienna's eyes, and while she was stunned, Art grabbed the back of her head again and pushed her into the mirror. Her head crashed into the glass, breaking it, and she fell to the floor, bleeding from her nose—which she feared might be broken—as well as deep cuts on her forehead.

She rolled onto her back and lay there a moment, eyes closed, her entire body wracked with pain. Art then slammed one of his oversized boots into her ribs, and she thought she felt a couple crack. The kick's impact rolled her onto her stomach, and she remained motionless for several seconds, gathering what strength remained to her, and then weakly tried to rise. With swift, vicious motion, Art slammed his boot into the side of Sienna's head, and she went limp, hit the floor, and this time she didn't move. Only the fact that she still breathed indicated that she wasn't dead.

Art breathed hard as he gazed upon Sienna's unconscious body. It had been a while since he'd exerted himself like this, and he was surprised by how much resistance the girl had put up. He was tempted to finish her off now, while she was out of it, but that would be letting her off lightly. He wanted to make her *suffer* for daring to resist him—and for slamming a nail into one of his kidneys— which meant she'd get to live a little longer.

Sienna hadn't fought for herself when she was threatened. But she'd fought like hell for her little brother. That meant torturing *him* would also torture *her*. Art loved a two-fer.

He stepped over her still body and stalked into the corridor, determined to find Jonathan before the little bastard could get too far.

Jonathan ran through the narrow halls of the Terrifier, feeling as if he was trapped in a living nightmare. Spooky sound effects followed him everywhere he went, and animatronic ghouls jumped out at him as he passed. He barely paid them any attention, though. They were just machines made to look like monsters. Jonathan had seen *real* monsters this night.

In his mind, he kept seeing Sienna sobbing as she knelt on the bathroom floor, the mutilated body of another girl lying next to her. The corpse had been so badly damaged that he couldn't be sure, but it had blonde hair, so he thought it might be Brooke. He saw Art standing there, his back to Jonathan, watching Sienna as she cried for the loss of her friend. Saw Art turning to look at him, bloodlust in his eyes, a wicked grin on his face, heard his sister shout, "Jonathan! Run!"

And he had.

He felt like a coward for abandoning his sister, even though she had told him to. Had Art attacked her after he'd fled? Was she now lying on the bathroom floor next to Brooke, her body broken and bloody? Was Art looking down at her right now, teeth bared in a horrible smile, his hands dripping with her blood?

He refused to believe that. Sienna was smart and she was strong—far stronger than she knew—and she was wearing the costume Daddy had designed for her. She was the warrior angel, and she would not only survive, she would find a way to stop Art from preying on the people of Miles County... he hoped. Maybe it was a childish belief, but the more he'd pored over Daddy's sketchbook, the more he'd become convinced that it was his sister's destiny to battle and defeat Art. And he was her brother. He should be helping her fight the evil clown, not running blindly through the Terrifier without any idea where he was going. But what could he do? He was only a skinny twelve-year-old with hardly any muscle on him. Art could snap him in two like a twig.

He remembered a piece of advice Daddy had given him, not long before he'd gotten sick.

Do what you can and to hell with the rest.

Had Jonathan done all he could for his sister? No, he hadn't. She'd had his back all his life, especially this last year, after Daddy had killed himself. Now it was Jonathan's turn to have her back, no matter the consequences. He didn't want to die, but more so he didn't want to fail his sister.

He began to grow tired and slowed to a walk. He'd reached a section of the Terrifier designed to look like an old, deserted warehouse—a sign that said *WARNING: HAZARDOUS MATERIALS,* rows of metal drums, rusted boilers, empty crates stacked atop each other, chains dangling from the ceiling, and skeletons with dingy, stained bones located around the room, victims of an apparent chemical spill...

He turned a corner and stopped dead when he saw Art coming the other way. The clown hadn't seen him yet, and Jonathan knew he had only seconds to act.

He quickly backed up, turned, and scanned the area, desperately looking for a place to hide. He saw a thin black curtain hanging in front of a long, narrow crate that looked too much like a coffin, but he couldn't afford to be choosy. He ducked into the crate and hid behind the curtain. This must've been where one of the Terrifier's scare actors had hidden, waiting for customers to come near so they could jump out and surprise them.

Jonathan pulled the curtain aside slightly, making a crack just enough large enough to see through. He watched, scarcely breathing, as Art moved through the hallway, walking in a half crouch, like an animal searching for prey. He held a scalpel in his right hand, and while the blade wasn't as large or intimidating as a regular knife, Jonathan had no doubt that in Art's hands it could easily do as much damage.

Art moved slowly, turning his head from side to side, listening for the slightest sound. Jonathan held his breath and concentrated on slowing the rapid pounding of his heart. He was certain the clown wasn't human, so who knew how keen his hearing was? Jonathan was grateful for the constant sound effects that played throughout the Terrifier, and he hoped they'd mask any sound he might accidentally make.

Art sensed something, and his head whipped around in Jonathan's direction. Jonathan drew his head back and prayed the clown hadn't seen him peeking. The curtain's fabric was thin enough for Jonathan to see through, just a little, and he watched as Art looked around. Jonathan knew the clown hadn't spotted him, otherwise he would've immediately attacked.

Art lingered a few more seconds before finally moving on. When he'd left the room, Jonathan took in a deep breath and let it out. He was still alive, and that was good. He would be of no use to his sister if he was dead. He slipped out from behind the curtain and looked around, wanting to make sure Art was really gone. And then he saw something he'd been searching for the entire time he was running through the Terrifier—a sign displaying a single, beautiful word:

EXIT.

If he could get out of here, he could go for help, call the police, find someone more capable of dealing with Art and saving his sister than he was. He didn't want to abandon Sienna again, but he was in way over his head here. He needed grown-ups to help—preferably well-armed grown-ups who would blow that fucking clown to pieces and rescue Sienna.

He ran toward the sign.

Get up…

Sienna heard someone whisper in her ear. The voice was familiar, but she couldn't identify it. It was a woman's voice, she was sure of that, but whose? At first, she thought it sounded like Allie, but it also reminded her of Mom and Brooke. It sounded like a couple of others, too, women she didn't know but felt she should.

She groaned as she struggled to push herself into a sitting position, her body shaking from the effort. Her head felt as if someone was slamming a sledgehammer into it over and over, and her vision blurred, sharpened, then blurred again. She wasn't sure, but she thought she might have some internal bleeding. She felt faint then, but she fought to hold onto consciousness, knowing if she passed out again, she'd be helpless. Besides, Jonathan needed her.

Sienna saw her phone lying on the floor a few feet away, screen shattered, case broken. It must have fallen out of her belt pouch when Art threw her around the room, and either it had broken upon impact or Art had stomped on it. Either way, it looked like she wasn't going to be calling for help anytime soon.

She saw an object sitting on the floor of a nearby stall, something wooden, with forks, knives, and nails embedded in it. She pulled herself closer to the object, muscles quivering, head pounding. She pushed open the stall door and got a good look at the object. It was a club, made from what looked like a table leg, and blood coated the metal attachments. Brooke's blood, she guessed. She was looking at the object that Art had used to kill her friend, her bestie, her sister from another mister. A single thought crossed her mind then.

I am going to fuck that clown up.

Jonathan almost sobbed with relief when he saw the metal door that led outside. He ran full out for it, but before he could reach it, Art stepped out of the shadows and blocked his way, scalpel in hand. He grabbed Jonathan by the throat and held him fast. The clown's smile said it all: *You didn't really think you could get away from me, did you?*

For a moment there, Jonathan actually had.

Art raised his scalpel in a swift, fluid motion, and a coldness came into his eyes. He pushed Jonathan back until his body hit the other side of a scenery flat, and Art held him there. The clown swiped the scalpel across Jonathan's left cheek, cutting a clean, deep line.

Jonathan cried out as blood started to flow. He tried to break free but only succeeded in partially loosening Art's grip on his throat. He tried pulling away, but Art slashed his scalpel across his back, cutting through his shirt and slicing into the flesh below, once, twice…

Jonathan fell to the floor in agony, hand pressed to his bleeding cheek.

Art laughed silently and pointed at Jonathan, as if he was the funniest sight the clown had ever seen. He clapped his hands several times, almost as if applauding himself, then he made a mock sad face, raised his hand to his eyes, made fists, and pretended to rub them, miming that he was crying, mocking Jonathan's pain.

Jonathan lay on the floor, cheek and back bleeding. He whimpered, feeling completely helpless, while Art continued his silent laugh fest, pretending to play a sad violin. Then Jonathan saw a figure step through an open doorway behind the clown.

It was Sienna, beat-up and bloody-faced, and she carried a club with sharp metal objects driven into its head. He'd never seen his sister look so angry, so determined, or so beautiful. The Warrior Angel had arrived.

She snuck up behind Art, raised the club, and with a cry slammed it between his shoulder blades.

Art stumbled forward, then spun around in surprise. Sienna slashed the head of the club across the clown's abdomen, and he fell to his knees. Before he could rise, Sienna raised the club again, and with a cry, brought the sharp metal implements down on the back of Art's head.

Chuk!

She let go of the club, and it remained stuck in Art's head. The clown's eyes and mouth were wide—with pain, with shock? Maybe both, Jonathan thought. Art grimaced as he reached for the club's handle, clearly hoping to grab hold of it and wrench it free. But his movements were slow and jerky, and his fingers brushed the wood without being able to grasp it.

While Art was busy, Sienna ran over to Jonathan, helped him to his feet, and guided him away from the clown. As they ran, Jonathan looked over his shoulder and saw that Art had managed to get both hands on the club's handle and was struggling to pull it free.

Fuck you! Jonathan thought, and then he concentrated on running with his sister.

CHAPTER THIRTY

Sienna was relieved that Jonathan was not only still alive, but that she'd gotten him away from Art. But even though she'd driven sharp metal objects into the clown's brain, she knew better than to believe they were in the clear. The police had been certain Art was dead a year ago, and he'd gotten up, killed the coroner, and walked out.

And she knew the Art she'd encountered in the dreamworld of the Clown Café was the same one they ran from now. She didn't know what Art was, but he wasn't a normal human, that was for sure. She suspected it would take more than a single bash to the skull to put him down for good—maybe a lot more.

So, she needed to get Jonathan out of here before Art came after them again. Plus, Jonathan was bleeding, which meant he was injured. How badly, she couldn't tell, but she intended to get him to a hospital ASAP. Come to think of it, as bad as she hurt, she could probably use a visit to the ER herself.

But first they had to find a way out of the goddamn Terrifier.

She found a corridor she hadn't been down yet, and she steered Jonathan that way. It led to what looked like a junkyard storeroom—tables and shelves filled with machine parts, metal scrap, coils of barbed wire, lengths of old rope, and tools of every shape and size. One wall was covered with large electric meters, along with a panel containing numerous dials and switches labeled with strips of masking tape. Sienna knew she was looking at the Terrifier's main controls.

"This way!" she shouted.

Jonathan continued running, but Sienna couldn't go any further. It hurt to move, it hurt to breathe, it hurt to fucking *think*.

Sharp pain lanced through her abdomen, so intense that she doubled over, staggered, hobbled to a nearby table, and collapsed onto a wooden stool. Sweat covered her brow, and her breath came in short gasps.

"Sienna!"

Jonathan ran over and knelt in front of her.

"You're hurt bad," he said.

Sienna gave a credible effort at a smile in an attempt to reassure her brother. From the tears glistening in his eyes, she knew she hadn't succeeded. "I'm all right. Let me…" Another pain, this one sharper, and in her chest. She tried to keep the pain from showing on her face. "Let me see you. Are you okay?"

She touched her hands to Jonathan's face and examined the wound on his right cheek. It was nasty looking, but superficial. He'd live. Probably have a hell of a scar there.

"Oh, my god." She drew in a shuddering breath. "You were right. You were right about everything."

"I was right about you, too."

Sienna was having trouble focusing through the pain, and she didn't understand what Jonathan was saying. "About what?"

"They used me to get you here," Jonathan said. "They need you in this place for a reason."

She frowned, confused. "What are you saying?"

"It's what Daddy saw. I think you're the only one who can stop him."

She hesitated before asking the next question, unsure she wanted to know the answer. But she went ahead. "Why?"

"I don't know," Jonathan admitted.

Sienna didn't have time for mysteries and riddles. They needed to get moving again. "Well, we've gotta find a way out of here."

She turned around to look at the mess on the table behind her, hoping to find something—anything— they might be able to use. She found a three-foot metal rod. It looked strong and sturdy, so she picked it up and rose from the stool, trying to ignore her body's strident protests.

"Okay," she said. "Come on."

She put her free arm around Jonathan's waist, he put his over her shoulders, and they supported each other as they moved on from the control room. The next room they came to was designed to look like a nightmarish chapel. Black curtains covered the walls, and robed figures sat on pews facing an altar featuring a large medieval-looking upside-down cross. The congregants were mannequins with rubber fright masks for faces, and in other circumstances they might've looked silly, but here, now, they appeared eerie and sinister.

Another robed figure—a witch—sat before an elaborate church organ, artificial hands positioned on the keys. Thunder cracked over the speakers in the room, followed by strident organ music, creating the perfect dark ambience. The room was decorated with reliefs of skulls, one of them possessing distorted features and wearing a miniature top hat on the left side of its head. No way was that a coincidence, not in this place. She didn't plan on telling Jonathan about the Art skull, though. She figured he'd already had enough of Art the Clown to last him a lifetime. She knew she had.

There was an exit on the far side of the altar, but it curved, and she couldn't see if it was clear for them to proceed.

"Stay here," she told Jonathan and went to investigate, both hands holding the metal pole tight.

As she passed the altar, she saw a lectern, a large leatherbound book sitting open atop it. She knew the book was probably just a prop, but she couldn't see what, if anything, was written on its pages, and she didn't want to. Those pages might be blank, but then again, they might not.

She continued on and saw a narrow hallway with stone walls. An empty *hallway*. She headed back to Jonathan to tell him the good news.

*

Jonathan waited for Sienna in the row between the pews, hand pressed to his cheek wound. The cuts on his back stung like hell, but he wasn't worried about them too much. He figured his shirt would act like a bandage and keep the bleeding to a minimum. At least, that's what he hoped. And if the shirt didn't help the bleeding, there wasn't anything he could do about that right now anyway.

He felt responsible for getting Sienna involved in all this. Maybe if he hadn't been so obsessed with Art and the murders he'd committed, neither of them would be here right now. While he mostly stuck to true-crime sites on the Internet, he sometimes checked out sites that dealt with the occult. On one of those sites, he'd read that evil entities such as demons and other malevolent spirits ignored humans for the most part—until you did something to draw their attention to you.

What if Art and the Little Pale Girl were such creatures, and Jonathan researching the Miles County Massacre was what had alerted them to his presence? And Sienna's. If he'd stopped reading about the murders like Mom and Sienna had wanted him to, maybe neither he nor Sienna would be here right now, fighting for their lives.

Thinking of Mom brought back the image of her dead, faceless body sitting at the head of the dining table, and he immediately banished it. He did *not* want to think about that right now. So, he tucked that awful memory into a box and sent it down into the darkest depths of his mind where he could deal with it later. Or maybe never. Never would be good. Never would be *awesome*.

A new thought came to him then. He knew from going through Daddy's sketchbook that he had collected articles about Art's murders. What if, by doing that, *Daddy* had drawn attention to himself that he shouldn't have? Maybe he hadn't attracted Art himself, but some other evil, one that got inside his mind and manifested as the tumor that changed him and eventually caused him to kill himself? What if by doing these things, Daddy had drawn the evil force's attention to the rest of the family?

Mom was... (*don't think about that don't think about that don't think about that*) and he and Sienna had become targets of Art and the Little Pale Girl. Brooke had died because of them, and who knew how many others? Art, the Pale Girl, and whatever power was behind them both were like symptoms of a malicious, highly contagious, and—worst of all—*fatal* disease. Maybe one for which there was no cure.

Preoccupied as he was by these dark thoughts, Jonathan didn't immediately notice one of the robed worshippers sitting in the pew behind him stand up. He sensed movement, turned, and saw Art pulling back the hood of his robe. The clown's smile was the most horrifying thing Jonathan had ever seen. There was no mirth in it, only bloodlust, hate, and death.

Art shrugged off the robe, grabbed Jonathan's arm, and threw him to the floor. The clown held a chain in his right hand that had a number of sharp instruments attached to its end—scissors, knives, scalpels, nails— and when Jonathan tried to stand and run, Art swung the chain like a whip, and those sharp objects cut deep into Jonathan's back. Jonathan howled in pain, fell to the floor, and Art whipped him again. And again. And again.

Sienna heard Jonathan's shrill scream, and she forgot about her injuries and ran.

When she entered the chapel, she saw Art whipping Jonathan with some kind of chain. She didn't think, didn't hesitate; she *attacked*.

She gritted her teeth and swung the metal pole at Art's face. The weapon hit the clown's jaw with a loud metallic *thud*, and the impact knocked him back a step. Sienna wasn't about to give Art any time to recover. She swung the pole back toward him, striking the other side of his jaw. He was prepared this time, and the blow didn't affect him as strongly.

He whipped his chain toward Sienna, and the sharps on the end sliced into her left upper arm. She let out a cry of pain, and he hit her again, harder this time. She dropped the pole, staggered over to the wall, and fell against it. Art swung his chain once more, and this time a trio of cuts appeared on Sienna's left cheek.

She fell onto a pew, and Art rushed over, grabbed her arm, and hurled her toward the altar. She hit the surface, rolled off, and fell to the floor, landing on her back. She felt something in her right shoulder give, and she cried out in agony. She rolled onto her other side to minimize the pain, but then she heard the jingle of Art's chain, and Jonathan began shrieking again. The clown had returned to flaying her brother.

She rolled onto her elbows and pulled herself across the floor away from the altar. Art had pursued Jonathan toward her, and her brother fell less than three feet away from her position. Art continued whipping him, and she saw her brother's face contort in pain as his flesh tore and his blood flew through the air.

Sienna kept crawling, and when she reached Jonathan, she covered him with her body to protect him. Art was just as happy to torture Sienna as he was her brother, maybe more so. He swung his whip with greater enthusiasm, targeting the parts of Sienna's body her costume didn't cover—her legs, arms, and upper back, leaving crisscrossing red marks all over her.

As much as it hurt, as much as she wanted it to stop, she didn't budge an inch. She'd die before she let this motherfucking clown hurt her brother again.

Art didn't let up. He continued raining blow after blow on Sienna's body, his flail tearing into her wings and sending up a shower of white feathers. Pain became her entire world. She no longer remembered her name, no longer remembered she even existed. All she knew, all she was, was *suffering*.

But then she heard the voice again—or was it voices?—and they spoke three simple words to her.

Fuck.

That.

Clown.

Sienna came back to herself. When Art's next strike came, she twisted at her waist, raised her left arm, and caught the chain in her hand. Art grinned and tried to pull the flail free, but Sienna refused to let him. Art put all

350

his strength into it, but it did no good. With a cry of effort, Sienna yanked the chain out of his hand, and Art's grin vanished. The clown was completely shocked.

Sienna rose to her knees and shoved Art as hard as she could. He staggered backward into the altar, and she jumped to her feet and ran toward him, swinging his chain as if she'd been wielding the weapon all her life. She released a battle cry as she whipped the flail back and forth across Art's body, slicing face, chest, arms, hands, legs... She felt none of her injuries as she gave the clown a bitter taste of his own medicine, only white-hot, incandescent rage.

Art turned his back to her, and she struck him there. Then she rushed toward him and shoved him hard into the wall. He turned around, a look of pure disbelief on his face, and she whipped the flail against the side of his head. He staggered to the altar, pressed his hands on its surface to stop himself, and Sienna swung the flail so hard that the sharp instruments on its end cut deep into his back and released a shower of blood.

Sienna grabbed Art by the arm, dragged him away from the altar, and threw him to the floor. "Motherfucker!" she shouted, and resumed whipping him, determined to tear him apart piece by piece if she had to.

He rose on his knees, and this time when she swung the flail, the scissors struck his face and dug in deep. Art reached for them with a trembling hand, but Sienna tore them free with a vicious yank, and blood jetted from the new wound.

The whip was taking too long, so she dropped it and quickly looked around for a better weapon. A metal fence with thick support rods ending in sharp points ran the length of the room on one side, and she ran over to a section, grabbed one of the rods, and using strength she hadn't known she possessed, she pulled it free with a single swift motion. She spun around to see that Art was still on his knees, stunned.

She raised the rod high, and with a shout, brought it down point first onto Art's head. It penetrated skin and bone and sunk deep into the clown's diseased brain. Blood poured from the wound and streamed down Art's face. Sienna held the rod in place for a long moment before withdrawing it with a single savage motion, bringing up a spray of blood, bone shards, and chunks of gray matter. Bits of Art splattered her, but she barely noticed.

Once the rod was out, Art fell backward and *thudded* to the floor.

Sienna stood frozen, breathing hard from the exertion, but unwilling to lower her weapon until she was absolutely certain Art was no longer a threat. Seconds passed, and the clown continued to lay still, eyes wide and unblinking, blood flowing from the gaping hole in his head. Sienna slowly lowered the rod and released it. It hit the floor with a *clang*, and she stumbled backward, suddenly so exhausted it was all she could do to remain on her feet.

She leaned against one of the room's support beams to steady herself and saw Jonathan lying on the floor in a fetal position, eyes squeezed shut, fists pressed to his ears to shut out all sounds.

"Jonathan…"

She felt a hand grip her throat, and she instantly regretted being stupid enough to ever turn her back on that pointy-nosed, grease-painted son of a bitch.

Art shoved her to the floor, straddled her, then fastened both hands around her throat and started throttling her. She grabbed his wrists and tried to pull his hands away from her, but the strength she'd possessed only a few seconds ago had deserted her, and she couldn't budge him. She couldn't draw in any air, and black spots appeared in her vision. She knew if this kept up for much longer, she was a dead woman.

I'm sorry, Sienna thought, but who this apology was meant for, she wasn't sure.

With a shout, Jonathan leaped onto Art's back. He pounded his fists into the clown, trying to get him to let Sienna go. Art removed his hands from Sienna's throat, but only so he could grab hold of Jonathan and throw him off to the side. Jonathan's back slammed into the floor, and he felt the breath *whoosh* out of his lungs. As he struggled to get his breath back, Art turned away from him and started choking Sienna again.

Jonathan didn't know what to do. He wasn't strong enough to fight Art, but he couldn't stand by and watch the clown kill his sister. If only there was something...

Then he saw it.

The cuff of Art's right pant leg had moved up enough to reveal a sawn-off shotgun bound to his ankle with black electrical tape. Jonathan had read on true-crime sites how police and FBI agents carried handguns as backup weapons in ankle holsters hidden by their pant legs. It seemed Art did the same thing. The whole point of a backup weapon was to get it in hand quickly during an emergency situation. If Art followed this procedure, his gun would be securely taped to his leg, but not *so* securely that it would be too difficult to pull off.

He hoped.

Jonathan lunged for the gun, grabbed hold of it, and pulled. There was some resistance, but not much. The tape parted, and the gun came away in Jonathan's hand. He quickly scooted backward so he'd be out of Art's reach and examined the weapon. He wasn't sure, but it looked like the safety was off.

He'd never held a gun before, let alone fired one, and he wasn't sure he could do it. But he had to. He remembered a video he'd watched once, in which a former soldier turned firearm instructor explained how to shoot a gun in a combat situation.

Always aim for center body mass. It's a larger target, and that means it's less likely you'll miss.

He took a two-handed grip on the shotgun, put his right index finger on the trigger, pointed the weapon at a spot just below Art's sternum, and pulled the hammer back with an unmistakable *click*.

Art froze. He slowly removed his hands from Sienna's neck and turned toward Jonathan. He gave a sheepish smile, as if to say, *Come on, I was just foolin' around. I wasn't really going to kill your sister.* Then he batted his eyes several times, like a cartoon character trying to pretend they were innocent.

The shotgun shook in Jonathan's hands. He was trying to squeeze the trigger, but he couldn't make his finger move.

Art widened his smile and blinked again.

Jonathan remembered the advice the firearm instructor had given in the video about firing a weapon.

Relax, breathe in, breathe out, breathe in again, and this time hold it. Now squeeze slowly… slowly…

The sawn-off shotgun roared and kicked in Jonathan's hand as both barrels discharged.

Pellets flew through the air, struck Art's midsection, and knocked the clown backward as if he'd been hit by a speeding semi.

Jonathan's ears rang. He was shaking even harder now, and he stared at Art's prone form. The front of his costume was shredded, and his stomach was covered with blood. After a moment, Jonathan lowered the gun and then hurried to check on his sister. She was still breathing, but shallowly, and her eyes were closed. He shook her shoulder and tried to rouse her.

"Sienna! Sienna, wake up!"

Nothing happened for a moment, and then her eyelids fluttered. Jonathan began to hope she was okay, but then her eyelids fell still again. Afraid now, he shook her harder.

"Stay with me! Please don't go! Sienna, please don't leave me!"

CHAPTER THIRTY-ONE

Sienna was lost in a universe of darkness, a vast, endless realm where she was the only thing in existence. She wasn't scared, though. It was actually kind of nice here. Cool and quiet, a place where you could drift forever in the blackness and no one would ever bother you, because there was no one else. Only you...

But then a voice came and disturbed her blissful solitude.

"Sienna. Baby, wake up."

Sienna slowly opened her eyes. She was lying on a cold concrete floor, and someone was sitting cross-legged next to her.

"Mom?"

She pushed herself to a sitting position and looked around. They were in the Terrifier, in a room Sienna hadn't seen before. It looked a little like a rundown, decaying version of their living room at home, except for some reason, the light here was blue. No annoying sound-effects were playing—that was a big plus.

Mom smiled and touched a gentle hand to Sienna's cheek. "Sweetie, it's okay. You're safe."

Sienna looked at Mom's face for a moment, unable to believe what she was seeing. Then she threw her arms around her mother and hugged her tight. Mom hugged her back just as hard, and Sienna began sobbing softly.

They rocked back and forth together, and Mom said, "Shh, shh, shh. Everything's gonna be okay."

Sienna's tears flowed freely now. "I thought I was never gonna see you again."

"Oh." Mom broke their embrace and took Sienna's face in her hands. "Jonathan told you, didn't he?" Her tone was sad, but loving.

Sienna frowned. "What?"

She heard Jonathan's voice then, but it was faint, echoing, as if it came from a great distance away.

"Sienna, get away from her! That's not Mommy!"

She turned in the direction of the voice and saw Jonathan standing not ten feet from her. Confused, she turned back to Mom—

—and saw her skin was chalk-white, her eyes yellow, her teeth malformed and dingy, and part of her hair was pulled through a small white top hat to make a ponytail. Mom's lips drew back from her teeth in a snarling smile.

Her hands shot forward and pressed tight against Sienna's eyes... and she *saw*.

Saw Mom—her *real* mom—standing in their garage next to the driver's side of their car. The vehicle was absolutely covered with shaving cream and toilet paper, and the remains of a smashed pumpkin lay on the hood. Saw Mom wipe a sponge across the driver's window. Saw Art sitting behind wheel, saw him grin, press the

357

sawed-off shotgun—the same one Jonathan had used to shoot the clown—against the inside of the glass. Saw Mom's expression of terror as she realized what was about to happen. Saw Art squeeze the trigger...

Saw Mom's head explode in a cloud of red mist.

More images came. Mom's faceless body posed at the head of the dining table, plates, glasses, and food laid out for dinner. Art standing next to her, wearing a bloodstained apron, and laughing without making any sound. The Little Pale Girl standing nearby and watching him with dark glee. And finally, Art, sitting in the car, window glass blown out, smoke curling from the twin barrels of his gun, teeth bared, eyes filled with sadistic satisfaction.

The visions ended, and Sienna understood that Mom was dead, killed by goddamn Art the motherfucking Clown. Grief slammed into her like a tidal wave, and she felt as if she might be washed away on tides of sorrow, her mind and soul forever lost. The pain from all the injuries she'd suffered at Art's cruel hands combined weren't a drop in the ocean compared to the pain she experienced now. She was kneeling in the dark chapel, had never left it, and she wrapped her arms around herself and sobbed uncontrollably.

After a few seconds she began to regain some measure of control. She opened her eyes, looked around, saw she was alone.

Where was Jonathan?

She rose to her feet, staggered toward the corridor she'd seen earlier, started down it, leaning against the stone wall for support and calling her brother's name as

358

she went. She reached the end of the corridor, turned a corner, and found herself in yet another of the Terrifier's rooms, although the theme of this one wasn't apparent at first glance. Walls of gray stone, unpainted support beams, power tools lying on the floor among fragments of old skeletons.

Jonathan lay on the concrete floor, surrounded by pieces of bone, hair matted with blood, streaks of red down the right side of his face. Art—still very much alive after being stabbed through the brain and blasted in the gut—stood motionless at Jonathan's feet, arms at his side, gazing down at her brother. Jonathan's eyes were closed, and he wasn't moving.

"No!"

She rushed toward Art, and he turned to meet her charge, face expressionless. She beat her fists against his chest repeatedly, but he showed no reaction. She hit him faster, harder, shouted, cursed at him, and his mouth slowly stretched into a grin. He wrapped a single hand around her throat and squeezed. His grip was like iron, and although Sienna tried, there was nothing she could do to break it. He pushed her across the room, Sienna choking and gasping, and then stopped. He increased the pressure, cutting off all her air, staring deep into her eyes, waiting to see the spark of life go out.

Sienna managed to draw in a slight gurgling breath. She spit a stream of blood into his face, and then ground out two words. "Fuck... you."

Art's grip loosened a little, and an expression came over his face she'd never seen before—a mixture of amusement, anger, and... respect?

359

He shook his head as if to say, *You're a very naughty girl, Sienna.* He released her throat, put his hand on her forehead, and gave her a hard shove. She fell backward, smashed through old wooden planks covering a square opening, and plunged into the darkness below.

Sienna fell twenty feet and landed on hard, rocky ground in a shower of dust and broken wood. Art stepped to the edge of the opening, squatted, and gazed down at the result of his handiwork.

The chamber was circular—basically a deep tube—and the walls were made of large smooth stones that bore a passing resemblance to skulls fitted tightly together. Uneven steps carved into one section of the wall led upward, but Sienna was in no condition to use them. Her arms were spread out, one leg twisted awkwardly, and she was either unconscious or dead.

Art knew which he preferred.

He looked at her a moment longer, then spit. His saliva fell and splattered onto her bare abdomen. Bullseye! He'd always prided himself on his excellent aim.

Sienna's body convulsed and she drew in a loud, gasping breath.

Her eyes opened. She coughed, groaned, and rolled onto her stomach. She got her arms beneath her and tried to push herself up, but she hurt so much she didn't know if she could do it. She looked around, saw she was in a shadowy stone chamber, likely yet another of the

Terrifier's seemingly endless rooms. Maybe the goddamn place really *was* infinite inside. At this point, she was willing to believe just about anything.

As if taking that thought as a cue, crimson light flared into existence, and Sienna turned her head to see where it was coming from. The light issued from a rectangular opening in the stone floor—one she would've sworn hadn't been there a second ago. Glowing light bulbs marked its border, and white mist curled upward from somewhere inside.

She might've thought the opening was simply another of the Terrifier's exhibits—*Dare You Look Upon the Gateway to Hell!*—except she could feel a strange energy emanating from the opening, and it pulled at her, compelled her to drag herself across the stone floor toward it, despite each movement setting off bright bursts of pain throughout her broken body.

When she reached the edge of the opening, she heard a cacophony of indistinct voices rising from within, moaning, wailing, laughing, screaming. The mingled cries chilled her to the core, and she knew whatever lay down there, hidden by white mist and crimson light, it was *Bad*.

Stiffly, painfully, she rose to her feet and gazed down into the opening one last time. Then she turned, intending to take the stone stairs back up to the floor above. But Art was standing there, grinning, and he held Sienna's short sword, the one given to her by her father, and he thrust it into her stomach. The blade was preternaturally sharp, and it passed easily through Sienna's skin, muscle, and organs, as if they were soft as warm butter.

Her eyes went wide with shock, and she gasped. The pain was so intense that it overloaded her already severely strained nervous system, and for a moment she felt nothing at all.

Art—his blood-covered face looking completely red in the light issuing from the opening in the ground—gave the sword a hard shove. As if a dam burst, agony flooded her body, and her muscles shook like she was having a seizure. Art kept the sword inside her with one hand, while he put the other on her shoulder and almost gently pushed her down until she knelt before him.

She gazed up at the creature that had become her own personal demon, and Art looked at her almost lovingly before withdrawing the sword from her body in a single, swift motion, giving the blade a savage twist as it came free.

Sienna, still shaking, teetered on the edge of the opening, and then she fell backward and plunged down into the mist.

Art raised Sienna's sword and examined it in the crimson light emanating from below. He turned it this way and that, admiring its balance and the exquisite sharpness of its edge. It had done a stellar job of finishing off Sienna—and he *loved* the darkly poetic irony of it being the weapon that killed her—but it really wasn't his style. Too flashy. He was a simple clown, with simple tastes. He dropped the sword to the ground, turned, and trudged toward the steps.

His work here was done.

*

"Speaking of surprises, kids—we have a very special guest with us today."

Sienna woke in water.

She was trapped inside a glass-walled cabinet completely filled with water, the kind magicians and escape artists used in performances. Without thinking, she tried to breathe, drew in water, coughed, panicked, reflexively inhaled, and took in more. Her throat burned and her lungs felt heavy. She pounded the glass with the flats of her hands, trying to get the attention of someone outside, but no one responded. The cabinet was illuminated by a light above her, but outside—where it was *dry*, where there was *air*—it was completely dark. She could be alone, or there could be a thousand people out there watching her. She had no way to know.

She turned herself all the way around, sliding her hands across the glass as she did so, desperately searching for some way out, but she found none. Her body still hurt from the injuries she'd sustained in her battle with Art, and threads of blood issued from her wounds, drifting in the water. But the pain was muted, distant, and not really a concern at the moment, for if she couldn't get out of this cabinet within the next few minutes, she would drown.

She didn't know how she'd gotten here, didn't know where *here* was, didn't know why she wasn't dead. Art had stabbed her with the sword Daddy had given her— she remembered that—had rammed the blade deep into her stomach. Art had withdrawn the blade, she'd fallen backward into the mist and crimson light, into the place where the voices came from—but after that, everything was a blank. The next thing she knew, she'd woken inside this death trap. Was this another of Art's cruel torments? Was she destined to be killed by him over and over, caught in some kind of horrible death loop?

She pounded on the glass some more, shouted, "Let me out!" In desperation, she decided to swim to the top of the cabinet and see if she could find a way to break out up there. She kicked her legs, started to rise, but then a leathery black tentacle rose from somewhere beneath her, wrapped around her left leg, and prevented her from ascending. She reached down and clawed at the tentacle with her hands, tried to pull it free, tried to gouge out chunks of it with her nails and make it let her go, but no matter what she did, the thing held her fast. She screamed, pounded the glass some more—

—and that's when the lights came on outside the cabinet.

She heard the laughter of an unseen audience, then saw the childlike teens on the playset. They appeared to be alive, still holding the treats Art had given them in her dream, but their eyes were a solid white, their bodies riddled with bullet wounds, and they were covered with coagulated blood. The floor beneath the playset was slick with the red stuff as well. Banjo Blue, still burning like a living pyre, swayed in front of the mural of Art holding hands with a circle of children, plucking at her instrument and singing, but the voice that came out of her flame-filled throat was horribly distorted.

Drop on by the Clown Café!
Drop on by the Clown Café!

The undead teens joined in, as did the boy from the breakfast commercial, still sitting at his table, spoon in hand, eyes white, blood dripping from his mouth. Everyone sang happily, while Banjo Blue played and swayed as she burned.

Drop on by the Clown Café!
Drop on by the Clown Café!

The grub is downright gruesome
But your appetite so big

'Cause food's a little funny...
Food's a little funny...
Food's a little funny...
Food's a little funny
at the Clown... Ca-féeeeeeeeeee!

Sienna had continued to pound on the glass throughout the song, thrashing to try to free herself from the tentacle's grasp, but now her exertions began to lessen. Her oxygen-starved body began to convulse, and she looked upward and raised her arms, as if making a last-second plea to a higher power for help. Then her body grew still, her face became slack and expressionless, her eyes slowly closed, and she went limp. She floated in the water, her hair undulating gently as it spread out above her head.

She was gone.

The studio was silent now. The teens lay spread out on the blood-slick floor beneath the playset, eyes closed, dead once more. Breakfast Boy leaned back in his chair, his white eyes normal once more but unblinking, head cocked to the side, motionless. Banjo Blue's fire had gone out at last, and all that remained of her was a charred, blackened husk lying on the floor beneath the mural of Art and the children, her instrument lying next to her, now little more than ashes.

Unseen by anyone, six shadows glided toward the water cabinet and Sienna's floating body. They gathered before it, silent and solemn. Sienna was dead, but her spirit yet lingered, and acting as one, the Six reached out to it.

CHAPTER THIRTY-TWO

Sienna opened her eyes.

She was in water again, but this time it was different. The water was clear, warm, soothing, and she was totally relaxed and at peace as she floated within its gentle current. She had no urge to breathe, and she felt no pain, although she still possessed her wounds, for she could see her blood flowing outward to join with the water. This didn't distress her, though. In fact, it seemed perfectly natural in this place. She was still dressed as the Warrior Angel, but her costume—which had suffered significant damage throughout the night—had been restored to its pristine state. She glanced over her shoulder, saw that she was wearing her original wings, the ones she'd worked so hard on for so long, and they too had been returned to the way they'd been before the fire.

She didn't know what this place was, and she didn't care. It was pure bliss, and she intended to remain here forever.

She continued to drift for a while. How long, she didn't know. She didn't think time was a thing here, and that was okay with her. She was sick of living by the clock. Here, she could just *be*. Since waking, she had seen nothing else in the water—no fish or plants—but now she spotted several dark objects far off in the distance. Six of them, she thought. She felt no fear, but had no desire to go to them either. If the current brought them together, so be it. If it didn't, that would be okay too.

But the current, which up to this point had been slow and easy, suddenly grew stronger, and Sienna found herself picking up speed. She surged through the water, leaving a wake of bubbles behind her, and for the first time since coming to this place, she was afraid. The six dark figures grew larger as she hurtled toward them, and she could see that they were shadows, their forms roughly human but devoid of any distinguishing details. As she drew close to them, the current eased, and she began to slow, and by the time she reached the shadows, she had come to a gentle stop.

What are you? she thought.

Not what. Who.

The shadows took on distinct shapes, and Sienna found herself looking upon six monstrosities.

One was a naked mutilated woman with black hair, left arm missing at the elbow, breasts gone, chunks of meat missing from one leg, the other stripped to the bone, half of her face removed, the skull beneath exposed.

Two wasn't even a full body, just a head, top of the skull cut away, brain hollowed out, empty cavity filled with candy.

Three was a woman in blood-splattered clothes, a pair of rubber gloves on her hands, a mass of swirling blood where her head should've been.

Four was a blonde woman whose face was a mass of melted flesh, and whose chest was torn open and empty inside.

Five was a strange one, even in this company. A naked blonde woman who floated upside down, her body cut in half from her vagina almost all the way through her face.

Six was the most normal, relatively speaking. Black hair, brown eyes, wearing a black outfit with a skeleton pattern, along with a short skirt. Blood slowly leaked from a bullet wound in the middle of her forehead.

Sienna couldn't see them, but she sensed other figures far off in the distance. Jeff, maybe, and others—so *many*—who'd suffered and died at Art's hands. But the Six were the ones who felt the closest kinship with her, and this was why they had come.

One spoke to Sienna without moving her mouth. *You're almost there, Sienna. We've come to help you make it across the finish line.* What was left of the woman's mouth twisted into an approximation of a smile. *So you can keep kicking ass,* she added.

Two spoke next. *You were a good friend to my daughter. Thank you for being there for her in ways I couldn't.*

Then it was Three's turn. *I'm so very proud of you, Sienna. I wish I'd told you that more often. I love you.*

Four. *I know I could be a pain in the ass sometimes, but you helped keep me grounded, and I'm so thankful for that... And sorry about the molly. That was a dick move.*

Five. *We've waited a year for this.*

Six. *And we're more than ready. Are you?*

Sienna had no idea what these apparitions were talking—well, *thinking*—about. She didn't know who

369

they were, and she didn't care. All she wanted was for them to go away so she could continue drifting with the current in peace.

This is the Sea of Self, Five said.

My friend and I spent some time here, Six added. *It's pleasant enough, but it's ultimately an empty experience. You're basically hiding inside your own spirit.*

It's kind of like a metaphysical coma, Five said. *It can give a wounded spirit time to heal.*

But if you stay here too long, you might not be able to leave, Six said.

But I don't want to leave! Sienna said. *It's warm and safe and there's nothing scary here.*

Three—the woman without a head—drifted closer and touched her fingers to Sienna's cheek. As Sienna watched, the cloud of blood resolved into features that she knew as well as she knew her own face, and her memory began to return.

Mom?

Her mother lowered her hand and smiled with red liquid lips. *You have to go back, sweetie. Jonathan's still alive.*

And so's that fucking clown, Four… no, *Brooke* said.

Sienna knew who the rest of them were now. Allie and Allie's mom, Eva. And while Sienna had never met the last two women, she knew who they were, too— Dawn Emerson and Tara Heyes, two of Art's victims from last Halloween.

Sienna still didn't want to leave the Sea of Self, but she knew she had to: Jonathan needed her—and Art had to be dealt with, once and for all.

What do I need to do? Sienna asked.

You've done most of it already, Allie said. *All you have to do now is let us in. We'll take care of the rest.*

It'll be okay, Mom said. *I promise.*

Sienna smiled. *Yes, it will. All right, let's do this.*

It happened so swiftly that it was over almost before Sienna knew it was happening. The women became shadows once more, and they flowed toward Sienna, their forms stretching, lengthening, become thin as black threads. They streaked toward Sienna's abdomen and slithered into her sword wound. It didn't hurt, only tickled a little. One thread remained, and she sensed that it was Mom.

What was that thing that grabbed my leg in the water cabinet?

You don't want to know, Mom said.

And then she passed into Sienna's wound and joined the others.

Every place that Sienna had been hurt tonight—from the slightest scratch on her skin to the deep wound in her gut—tingled as they rapidly healed. Seconds later, it was finished, and Sienna no longer had a mark on her. She heard her mom's voice in her mind one last time.

Time to go back.

And Sienna began to rise, slowly at first, but with increasing speed.

I'm coming for you, Jonathan! Sienna thought.

Her expression darkened, and a dangerous glint came into her eyes.

And I'm coming for you too, Art.

*

Art returned to the room where he'd left Jonathan. He walked over to the boy, knelt next to him, and leaned his head forward to take a good look at him. The rise and fall of the boy's scrawny chest told Art that the kid still lived, but it didn't tell him if he was still unconscious or—he almost laughed at the thought—playing *possum*. He snapped his fingers several times next to Jonathan's ear, but the boy didn't move. Art then clapped his hands loudly, and while the boy stirred slightly, as if he'd heard a sound in his sleep, that was all.

Art lightly slapped Jonathan's cheek next, but again, the boy didn't respond. Art took hold of the boy's left shirt sleeve between his thumb and forefinger, lifted the arm, released it, and watched it fall limply back to the floor. Art turned his hands palm up and shrugged in a *What's a lunatic clown to do?* gesture.

Oh well. Waste not, want not.

He reached for the boy.

Jonathan felt something tugging on his arm. At first, he thought it was Mom, trying to wake him. Had he overslept? Was he late for school? Then he felt the pain.

He opened his eyes to see Art chewing on his left wrist.

He screamed and Art lifted his head and screamed silently back, his mouth and teeth wet with Jonathan's blood.

Jonathan yanked his arm free from Art's grasp and tried to crawl away, but Art grabbed his legs by the ankles and pulled him back. Jonathan continued to struggle, but Art had too tight a hold on him now, and he couldn't get away. Overwhelmed with fear, he shouted his sister's name.

"Sienna!"

Art bent over Jonathan's leg and sank his teeth into the boy's young, soft flesh.

Jonathan screamed again.

Sienna's sword lay on the ground, its blade still wet with her blood. Jonathan's scream echoed throughout the subterranean chamber, and in response, the sword began to glow with golden energy, dimly at first, but then brighter, stronger, until it blazed like a miniature sun.

Sienna's motionless body floated in the water cabinet, blood still flowing from her abdominal wound, the black tentacle still wrapped around her leg. A glimmer of golden light issued from inside the wound, and it grew in intensity, until the water was infused with its energy. Sienna's body convulsed once, twice...

The wound closed, and she opened her eyes.

"*Sienna!*" Jonathan's voice.

She tried to swim upward, but the tentacle kept her from moving.

What was that thing that grabbed my leg in the water cabinet?

You don't want to know.

Sienna no longer cared what the thing was. All she cared about was getting to her brother. She reached down, grabbed hold of the tentacle with both hands, and tore it apart as easily as if it were tissue paper. She let go of the section of tentacle she'd ripped away and pulled the rest of it off her leg. She released it, and it rapidly withdrew, disappearing into the darkness somewhere far below the cabinet. As soon as it was gone, she gave it no more thought. With sure, strong strokes, she started swimming upward.

Jonathan howled with pain as Art gnawed on the meat above his ankle. Blood dripped from the clown's mouth as he chewed, pattered to the floor like scarlet rain.

Sienna, still wet from the water cabinet, raised her sword in a two-handed grip and thrust it into the clown's back. Art stiffened, eyes wide with surprise. He reached around and clawed at the blade, trying to get hold of it and pull it out, but it was no use. Sienna held the blade fast, bearing down on it with her full weight, and Art's body spasmed. She kept the sword there for several more seconds before violently withdrawing it in a spray of blood.

Art crawled away from Sienna, but she followed him, breathing hard, face filled with hatred for this loathsome thing that had killed her mother, her two best friends, and had tried to devour her brother alive. Art rose shakily to his knees, attempting to stand, and with a cry Sienna swung the sword into the juncture between his neck and shoulder.

Thuk!

Blood gushed from this new wound, and when Sienna yanked the sword free, Art—panicked and desperate—

managed to get on his feet. He put a hand to his neck in an attempt to staunch the bleeding, and he staggered forward, stepping awkwardly through the debris littering the floor—pieces of wood, bits of metal, scattered tools, and skeletal remains. When Sienna had first seen this room, she'd assumed it was just another of the Terrifier's exhibits; but after seeing what Art was doing to her brother, she wondered if the bones littering this room weren't fake but rather the leftovers of the clown's past meals.

Sienna swung her blade into the other side of Art's neck, then pulled it free. More blood gushed, and the clown's body spasmed with fresh pain. He fell to his knees, and Sienna put her free hand on the top of his head, pulled it back to expose his neck, and then swiped the sword across his throat, not once, but twice. A fountain of blood jetted from the wound, and Art slapped his hand to his throat in a vain attempt to stop the bleeding. His body was shaking now, and he struggled to breathe. Still, he remained silent, as always.

Sienna stepped around Art and stood in front him. The clown looked up at her, his eyes glazed over, as if he was having trouble holding onto consciousness. He had never extended the slightest mercy to his victims, and Sienna didn't expect him to ask it of her now. In this, she wasn't disappointed. His focus sharpened then, and Sienna could see the hatred burning in his gaze. She slowly raised her sword, Art's eyes following her blade as it rose. When the sword reached its apex, Sienna held it there. She wanted Art to feel what his victims felt before he took their lives. She wanted him to feel fear.

Art showed no sign of that emotion, though. He met her gaze, and for several seconds neither of them moved. Then the clown nodded his head, seemingly more to himself than to Sienna, and then he grinned and cocked his head to the side, offering his neck to her. Sienna yelled as she accepted the clown's offer. She swung the sword into his neck, once, twice, three, four times. She put everything she had into the fifth swing, and her blade sliced through the clown's neck. His head tumbled to the ground, and his body quickly followed.

Sienna released a scream of victory. The Warrior Angel had triumphed.

She looked at Art's severed head as her breathing began to ease. In death, his face was utterly devoid of expression, cold, empty, and absolutely inhuman, and Sienna wondered if she was looking upon Art's true face for the first time.

"Sienna!"

Jonathan.

Sienna left Art's corpse and hurried over to her brother. He leaned against a metal beam propped up at an angle on the floor to support himself, as he was unable to stand, thanks to Art taking a bite out of his leg. Jonathan had watched Sienna kill Art, every blood-soaked moment, and his expression was a complex mixture of shock, relief, newfound admiration for his sister, but most of all, love.

When Sienna reached him, she lay her sword on the beam and hugged him fiercely, and he hugged her back with equal force.

"You got him," Jonathan said, tears running down his face.

Sienna broke their embrace and touched her hands to his cheeks. "It's over now, okay?"

"Okay."

Sienna pulled her brother into her arms once more and leaned her head against his.

But it wasn't over.

The Little Pale Girl stood near Art's body, staring at them with her yellow eyes.

Sienna grabbed her sword and pushed Jonathan behind her so she could protect him. She could feel hatred emanating from the girl, so strong it hit with almost physical force. Sienna remembered seeing the girl on the dance floor at Eclipse, remembered getting a glimpse of the terrible dark thing that lay behind her mask. Art had been a terrifying monster, but the Little Pale Girl was something else entirely, and Sienna didn't know if she had the strength to defeat her.

The girl walked closer to Art's body, or more specifically, his head. She regarded it for several seconds, then knelt and picked it up. She held it to her ear, listened as if it spoke to her, then grinned and nodded several times. Then she turned to look at Sienna and Jonathan, smiled and cocked her head to the side in a stiff, almost robotic fashion. Then her smile became a snarl, and her eyes glowed with a baleful yellow light. She turned back to Art's head, and her eyes returned to normal—well, normal for her—and she smiled again.

She stood, cradled the head to her chest as if it was a baby, then turned and began walking away from Art's body. She walked slowly to an open doorway leading to a set of stone steps cloaked in shadow. Without a backward glance at Sienna and Jonathan, she mounted the steps, started upward, and was soon lost to darkness.

Once the girl was gone, Sienna lay down her sword, and hugged her brother once more, receiving as much comfort as she gave. Jonathan wept in her arms, and she thought of what she had told him only seconds before. *It's over now, okay?* But after seeing the Little Pale Girl leave with Art's head, she knew she'd been wrong.

It was only over *for* now.

CHAPTER THIRTY-THREE

One Day Ago

Victoria sat in a wheelchair in a hospital hallway. She was in street clothes, a welcome change from the hospital gowns she'd been wearing for the last year. Her mother and father stood close by, gazing down at her, smiling. Dr. Perez—"Call me Melinda," she'd said at their first meeting—was smiling too. *Her* smile looked genuine, even if it was the result of years of professional training. Her parents? Their smiles were forced, strained.

At least they're trying, she thought.

She gazed up at Melinda and thought for perhaps the thousandth time since they met how beautiful she was. Long, silky brown hair. Perfect facial features. Understated makeup. (When you were as pretty as she was, you didn't need much help to look your best.) Flawless skin. Sometimes Victoria imagined running her tongue across Melinda's cheek, tasting its salt, feeling its smoothness... It was a favorite fantasy, one she often used to help her relax and get to sleep at night. She'd never told this to Melinda, of course. Melinda would've said she had a *fixation*, that it wasn't *healthy*.

What did that bitch know?

Her parents' faces were comforting to her, but she didn't like to look at them long. Partially because their skin was old, thin, and wrinkled, but mostly because of the pity in their eyes, mixed with revulsion that they both tried but failed to conceal. In the last year, she'd become exquisitely attuned to people's reactions to her face, and no matter how much they attempted to act normally when they looked at her, she could always tell how they really felt. And there was one other thing. When she looked in her parents' eyes, she wondered if they blamed her for not getting to the warehouse in time to save Tara.

She'd asked them about it once, about a month into her long hospital stay. Tara had been buried for three weeks at that point. Victoria hadn't been able to attend her funeral and burial, but Mom had taken video to show her.

Wasn't that thoughtful? "Of course we don't blame you!" Mom had said. "The only one responsible is that goddamn maniac," Dad had said. Still, Victoria wondered... Would they tell her the truth if they *did* hate her for not saving their other daughter's life? Probably not, she decided.

"Thanks again for everything, Doctor," her mom said. "You'll be in our prayers."

What good do prayers do? I prayed before every operation that once they put me under, I would never wake up. A dozen fucking times I did that, and I'm still here.

"Please, don't mention it," Melinda said. "We're all gonna miss this one. She's been so cooperative." She smiled at Victoria. "Makes everyone laugh."

Now Mom smiled at her, and this time, she almost looked like she meant it. "Well, she certainly hasn't lost her sense of humor."

"Yeah," Dad said. "Still a wise ass." His smile remained strained, and he looked *near* her face, but not *at* it.

Melinda laughed. "It's a good thing. It's important to stay positive, right?"

"Absolutely," Mom said. "Good spirits."

"She'll be fine," Dad said.

Melinda gave her one last smile. "Well, take care of yourself, Victoria. I'll see you in a couple months."

Victoria couldn't smile, but she tried to make her voice sound upbeat, even cheerful. "Thank you, Doctor."

The hardest part of her rehab was learning to speak intelligibly without having any fucking lips. They'd ended up teaching her techniques that ventriloquists used. It had taken her forever to master them, but she had in the end. Now when she spoke, she sounded almost normal. Almost.

"You're welcome."

"So long, Doctor," Dad said.

"Goodbye."

Melinda turned and started down the hallway. Victoria would bet she was going back to her office to take a few sips from the flask in her desk drawer—a reward for keeping it together while she said goodbye to her prize monster.

Dad looked at her. "What do you say, kiddo? You ready?"

His tone was uncertain, and Victoria knew *he* wasn't ready. She didn't think he ever would be. "Yep."

Melinda stopped, called back over her shoulder. "Oh, and good luck with your interview tomorrow."

She continued onward after that.

Dad pushed Victoria's wheelchair while Mom walked alongside. Victoria could walk just fine, but it was a hospital regulation that patients ride a wheelchair to the parking lot when they were being discharged. Victoria figured it was less about patient comfort and more about the hospital administration not wanting anyone to trip and get hurt on their way out and then sue.

Dad offered to take her out through one of the hospital's side entrances, but Victoria told him the main entrance was fine. For a second, she thought he might argue, but all he did was nod.

When they were outside, Dad said, "You ladies wait here while I go get the car."

He headed out into the parking lot, and Mom took the handles of Victoria's wheelchair to keep it steady. People walked in and out while they waited, and all of them did a double-take when they saw Victoria. Some stared, some quickly looked away, and if they walked with a companion, the two began whispering in hushed voices, shooting her glances as they talked.

Victoria pretended not to be aware of it all. One good thing about having a face incapable of expression was that people could never tell what you were thinking.

Three weeks ago, during one of her daily sessions with Melinda, the doctor had started discussing plans for Victoria to go home. "You've got a decision to make about how you... *present* yourself when you're among people other than your parents."

Victoria had known instantly where Melinda was going with this. "You mean whether or not I hide my face."

"Yes. There are a number of options. You could wear a mask—"

"Like the Phantom of the Opera," Victoria put in.

Melinda smiled thinly, not especially amused. "Or you could wear a jacket with a large hood or a scarf that you can wrap around the lower half of your face. You can wear sunglasses with any of those choices in order to conceal your eyes... I mean *eye*. Sorry."

Victoria thought about the options for several moments. A mask would be safest. As long as it stayed on, she wouldn't have to worry about anyone catching a glimpse of her appearance. The hood or the scarf would look more natural and probably be a lot more comfortable. Wearing sunglasses all the time when she was out would make her feel kind of silly, like she was pretending to be a movie star or something, but she could see the practicality of it.

It was this moment when she first saw the Little Pale Girl.

She stood next to Melinda's desk, as if she'd been present the entire session. Victoria didn't see her appear out of thin air or anything. She was just... *there*. The girl was not what most people—Victoria included—would regard as normal. Pale skin, strange teeth, yellow eyes, stark black-and-white dress. The girl's outfit was similar to Art's except the colors were reversed and she wore a skirt. The resemblance to Art's costume should've bothered her, but for some reason it didn't. Her definition of normal had changed the night she fought Art and lost.

She could still feel his teeth tearing into the soft flesh of her face, had never *stopped* feeling it.

She didn't say anything about the girl to Melinda. For one thing, she wasn't confident the girl was real, and if she admitted seeing her, it could jeopardize her release at the end of the month. If Melinda thought she was having hallucinations, it might be another year before she escaped this place—if she ever got out at all. But there was another reason she didn't want to let Melinda know she was seeing this girl. It was obvious that Melinda didn't see her. The girl stood only a few feet away from the doctor. There was no way Melinda could miss her. But there was something about her presence that felt *real* to Victoria, and she figured if the girl didn't want Melinda to see her, she probably had a good reason.

Melinda kept talking about Victoria's *presentation choices*, but Victoria paid her no attention. She kept her gaze focused on the girl. She mimed putting on a mask, then she frowned and shook her head. Then she walked up to Victoria, put her hands—her cold hands—on Victoria's face, and gently stroked the scar tissue. Victoria had next to no feeling in her face, but she felt the girl's touch as strongly as she would have before the attack. She'd forgotten what it was like to feel someone touch her face lovingly like this, and the sensation was so overwhelming, she almost burst into tears. But she only had one tear duct now, and it only functioned intermittently, so her eye remained dry.

The girl lowered her hands, stepped back, pointed to Victoria's face, and nodded. Her message was clear: mask no, face yes.

"I've come to a decision," Victoria said.

The Pale Little Girl grinned, then she was gone.

That had been the one and only time Victoria had seen her—until now.

She stood on the walkway outside the hospital's main entrance, less than twenty feet from where Victoria sat, waiting for her dad to bring the car around. The girl cocked her head stiffly, raised her hand, and waved it back and forth mechanically, as if she was a child-sized metronome. Victoria waved back. A moment later, a middle-aged man escorting his elderly mother into the hospital stepped between Victoria and the girl, momentarily blocking her from Victoria's view. When the man and his mother had moved on, Victoria saw the girl had vanished.

"Who were you waving at?" Mom asked.

If Victoria still had her old face, she would've smiled. "A friend."

Victoria's interview with Monica Brown was over. It hadn't been a *complete* disaster, but it had come damn close. Toward the end of the interview, which had been broadcast live, Victoria had been admiring Monica's absolutely *gorgeous* face, and imagining what her skin would feel like between her teeth, when she'd been overcome by a seizure of some kind. She'd gripped the edge of the table where she sat opposite Monica, and began shaking all over and making animalistic grunts. Victoria had managed to pull out of it before Monica was forced to cut the interview short and go to clips from past interviews. Monica looked terrified, but she soldiered on, wrapped up the interview, and shook Victoria's hand without looking her in the eye.

Then Monica hightailed it to her dressing room, leaving Victoria standing on the set by herself. Her parents had been in the audience, and they hurried up to check on her.

"You okay, kiddo?" Dad said, concerned.

"I *knew* it was too soon," Mom said,

Victoria assured them she was fine. Too much excitement, that's all. She told them she was going to get a drink from a fountain and use the restroom before they left, and before either parent could ask if she needed an escort, she walked away. She thought Dad would respect her choice, but she wasn't sure Mom would let her poor baby girl go alone—but she did, and Victoria was grateful. She didn't go to the bathroom, though. Instead, she went to Monica Brown's dressing room and discovered the door was open a crack. She opened it a little more, relieved the hinges didn't creak, and slipped in.

Monica was a well-known local celebrity, and Victoria was surprised her dressing room was so small. Evidently, muckraking and sensationalism didn't pay as well as she'd thought. Monica sat at her makeup table, talking on her phone, facing a mirror and touching up her eyebrows. There was a clothes rack in the room behind her, filled with dresses, blouses, suit jackets, and slacks.

Victoria silently moved behind the clothes rack, hoping Monica would be too distracted to notice her. When the woman didn't immediately start screaming for security, Victoria figured she was in the clear. She listened as Monica talked.

"Did you watch it? Oh my god, I thought she was going to *attack* me. My heart was pounding the entire time. Yeah, well, if you think she looks that bad on television, imagine what she looks like sitting two feet *away* from you. I thought I was going to gag at one point. Babe, do me a favor. If I ever look like that, promise me you'll put me out of my misery. You think I'm kidding? I'll do it myself. Yeah, Tom said we won't know until the morning. But he thinks the ratings are going to go up big time."

Victoria felt a small hand take hers, and the unexpected contact startled her, and she inadvertently brushed against some clothes, causing them to move—not much, but enough to alert Monica. The woman turned to look at the clothes rack for a few seconds, frowned, then faced forward once more and returned to her call.

Victoria still held the small hand in hers, and she looked down to see the dim shape of the Little Pale Girl standing beside her, her eyes glowing a soft yellow. She gave Victoria's hand a squeeze, and Victoria squeezed back. It was good to see her friend again.

Monica laughed at something the person on the other end of the call said.

"*Exactly*. We've finally figured out the formula for success—faceless victims and a host in jeopardy. Yeah, watch, next month it's going to be called *Monica's House of Horrors*." There was a beep, and Monica lowered her phone to check the display screen. "Shit. Can I call you back? I have like fifty people calling me. Okay. All right. I love you, too. Bye."

She tapped the screen to accept another call and held the phone to her face. "Hello? Tom?"

This time Victoria rustled the clothes on purpose. She had to suppress a giggle, and the Little Pale Girl put her hand over her mouth.

Monica turned to look once more, this time scowling. She rose from her chair and walked slowly toward the clothes rack. Victoria watched her come closer... closer... Now!

The instant Monica pushed the clothes aside to check behind them, Victoria slipped off to the right, taking the Little Pale Girl with her. They came out from behind the rack and stood next to Monica. Victoria watched as Monica stuck her head between the clothes, looked one way, then the other, saw nothing, drew her head back, and shrugged. Monica started to turn, obviously intending to go back to her makeup table and resume her conversation with Tom, when she saw Victoria standing there.

She paled, and Victoria attacked.

Victoria grabbed the woman's face, and she took a second to appreciate how baby-soft the skin was. Then she plunged her thumbs into Monica's eyes, and the woman screamed as blood spurted from the sockets. Victoria shoved Monica to the floor, yanked her thumbs free of the woman's bloody eye sockets, and began tearing at her face, ripping away chunks of flesh and hissing like a reptile. She continued savaging Monica's face for several more seconds, then she pulled her hands away, blood streaming from her fingers. She gazed upon the red, wet ruin the woman's face had become. Monica lay there weakly, coughing up blood.

Victoria turned to look at the Little Pale Girl, who was grinning, clapping her hands, and jumping up and down.

Victoria began to laugh.

CHAPTER THIRTY-FOUR

Miles County Psychiatric Hospital
Now

Victoria sat on the floor of her new room, legs drawn to her chest, arms wrapped around them, slowly rocking back and forth, back and forth. The light was off, which was good, because she preferred the dark. Besides, it was storming outside, and she loved seeing the flashes of lightning through the window. She liked the shadows the bars over the window made on the floor, too.

She felt a presence in one corner of the room, turned, and saw two yellow eyes glowing in the shadows. It was her friend. And yet, it was something else, too. Something old and powerful. Her friend spoke to her then, not with words or sounds, but with images. She asked Victoria if she could do her a favor. Victoria said yes.

Her friend stepped out of the shadows and walked toward her, carrying something round in her arms, holding it like it was a baby, her eyes blazing with yellow fire.

*

It was raining again, much harder than earlier in the evening. Driving rain, high winds, constant flashes of bright lightning, and loud, sonorous booms of thunder.

Victoria knelt in front of a metal toilet, hunched over the bowl, puking her guts out. Her body was wracked by intense spasms of pain, and every time the agony reached a new crescendo, she vomited again. The spasms didn't lessen—in fact, they became worse—but the urge to throw up diminished and eventually passed. She leaned back on her knees and examined the foul muck her body had expelled. Thick black liquid with unidentifiable bits of something solid in it nearly filled the bowl to the rim. Whatever that shit was, it must smell like death itself, but she had no way of knowing for certain. She hadn't been able to smell anything since she lost her nose a year ago.

She stuck her index finger in the sludge, stirred it around, and giggled, but her merriment was cut short as another spasm of pain overwhelmed her. She lurched to her bare feet and started walking, a stiff shuffle all she could manage. Blood ran in thin streams down the insides of her legs, and she left a trail of crimson behind her.

Her hair was matted with sweat and black puke, her belly hideously swollen, straining the fabric of her gray smock—the words MILES COUNTY PSYCHIATRIC INMATE printed on the back—to the point of tearing. There was no interval between spasms now. The pain was constant, and she knew it wouldn't be much longer before it happened. The blood flow between her legs became stronger, and soon she was practically gushing red. Blood splattered onto the cold, hard floor, and when

Vicky saw it, she thought, *Might as well decorate the room and get it ready for the new arrival*. She would've smiled then, if she could. *After all, waste not, want not.*

She reached between her legs, got her hand good and bloody, and then withdrew it. Then she walked to the wall next to the door and began writing red letters on its blue surface.

As she worked, she hummed a simple tune, and in her mind, she heard the song's lyrics sung by a woman in a blue outfit playing a banjo.

Alyssa Moran—early thirties, curly black hair, short-sleeved white uniform jacket, slacks, carrying a clipboard—approached the nurses' station. It was late, and apart from the storm outside, quiet, which was exactly how she liked it.

Christ, my feet hurt, she thought. Hospital staff of any kind knew the importance of wearing comfortable footwear when they worked, and Alyssa wore an expensive pair of professional running shoes. When you're on your feet all day, you don't cheap out. But *all day* for her had been sixteen hours so far, and she still had a couple more to go. She was off tomorrow, thank god, and she planned to sleep the entire day. She couldn't wait.

A burly man in his forties sat behind the counter, watching *Plan 9 from Outer Space* on a laptop screen. Burke was a good guy, and she liked working with him. He was an excellent nurse, worked hard, loved his wife, never hit on any of his co-workers, and treated them all as equal professionals. That practically made him a goddamn unicorn in this profession. Plus, he was strong, and that came in handy when you worked with the criminally insane. When there was trouble—*real* trouble—you called Burke.

A large jack-o'-lantern with a leering face and a lit candle inside sat on the counter, and a flock of cardboard bats was taped to a nearby wall. The docs didn't like it when the nurses decorated too much for Halloween. *The morbid imagery associated with the holiday might give some of our more volatile patients... ideas.*

Alyssa plunked her clipboard down on the counter, stepped into the station, and headed straight for the coffeemaker. Burke always made sure there was plenty of coffee for the night staff, which was yet another reason that he was awesome.

"Please tell me this is pumpkin spice," she said.

Burke didn't take his eyes off Bela Lugosi and Vampira as he answered. "Not a chance in hell."

She smiled and shook her head. When it came to coffee, Burke didn't believe in adding flavors. *If God had wanted coffee to taste like fruit, He wouldn't have made it so deliciously bitter.*

As Alyssa poured herself a cup, she noticed a paper plate on the lower counter containing miniature versions of body parts—brain, eyeballs, ears, and fingers, along with copious amounts of some red substance that resembled blood.

She wrinkled her nose in distaste. "What is this?"

Burke turned his chair to face her. "Zombie platter. My wife made it."

"That's disgusting. Creative, but disgusting."

"I wouldn't say that before you try it. It's pretty tasty."

"No thanks. As appealing as that brain looks... I don't really have the stomach for it right now."

Burke frowned in concern. "Everything okay?"

Alyssa sighed wearily. "I've been tending to our celebrity patient all day."

"Is that bad?"

"Let's just say her face doesn't stimulate one's appetite."

Burke leaned forward and lowered his voice slightly. "What's she like?"

Alyssa thought about it. "Tame. Pretty cooperative, actually. It's kind of hard to imagine she ripped that woman to pieces."

Burke grimaced and changed the subject. "Pass me one of those eyeballs, huh? And put some of that brain jelly on it too."

Alyssa got a napkin and a plastic spoon. She used the spoon to pick up an eyeball and place it on the napkin. Then she scooped up some jelly, plopped it on the eyeball, and offered the gross delicacy to him.

He took it then patted his belly. "Diet starts tomorrow," he said.

Alyssa would believe it when she saw it. She added sugar and creamer to her coffee, tasted it, and added more of both. It was especially bitter tonight, which seemed only fitting as it mirrored her mood. She took a sip. Better.

She'd finished making rounds on the floor, and she picked up her clipboard and started writing notes on the form it held. As her pen scratched across the paper, she began humming.

"What is that?" Burke asked.

Alyssa kept writing. "Hmm?"

"That song you're singing. What is it?"

"Oh." She lowered the clipboard and looked at Burke. "I have no idea, actually. Victoria's been singing it all day. I can't get it out of my head."

"Huh."

Victoria sang softly as she worked, her words coming out as harsh, guttural sounds, difficult to understand since she had no lips to form them.

"Drop on by the Clown Café…"

The wall was covered with capital letters written in her blood. It flowed from her freely now, and a widening puddle of it had collected around her feet. She paid no attention to it, so intent was she on her work. In the middle of the wall, she'd written her name—*VICKY*—then clustered other words around it. *CUNT, SLUT, BITCH, WHORE, PIG, FILTH…*

The pain in her abdomen was excruciating now, and she thought she was going to explode any second. She paid no attention to this either. As she worked, she made a variety of sounds.

Sometimes she cursed herself.

"You fuckin' cunt."

Other times, she sang.

"Drop on by the Clown Café…"

And sometimes she repeated swear words as if they were a personal mantra.

"Cunt, cunt, cunt, cunt, cunt."

But the sound she made most of all was unhinged laughter.

Then she felt a great tearing sensation deep inside her, and the stream of blood running from between her legs became a torrent. It was time.

She walked to the center of the room, moving with great difficulty due to the pain. She tried to sit down, but her blood-covered feet slipped out from under her, and she fell and landed hard on her ass. Something broke inside her, and she laughed. She felt something *huge* pushing from the inside, trying desperately to get out. She was never going to expel that big-ass thing from her body the natural way.

Time for a do-it-yourself C-section.

The thunder and lightning grew more intense then, as if nature knew what was about to happen and was not happy about it.

Victoria lifted the blood-soaked hem of her smock over her grotesquely distended belly, then jammed her hands into the tight flesh. Skin tore like paper and blood flooded out in a great wave. She took hold of the edges of the opening she'd created and *pulled*. More tearing, and more pain, but this was infinitely worse than before, and a bestial scream issued from her throat. She wasn't tearing only skin now; she was also tearing a hole in her abdominal muscles. When she thought the hole was wide enough, she reached in and began pulling out loops of intestine and tossing them onto the floor. She needed to make sure *he* had enough room to emerge. Then she reached deep inside her and felt around until she found what she was looking for. When she had it, she began to pull.

The scream that came out of her this time echoed throughout the entire hospital.

Alyssa had finished her coffee and was heading down a hallway toward the restroom, clipboard in hand once more, when she heard the scream. It sounded almost inhuman, and she knew at once where it had come from: Victoria's room.

She hurried down the hall, and when she reached the room, she stopped in front of its metal door and listened. The screaming had stopped, but—while it was difficult to tell with all the thunder—she thought she heard Victoria singing that strange song again.

"Drop on by the Clown Café…"

Cold shivered down Alyssa's spine.

All patient rooms had a rectangular observation window built into the door, with a sliding panel staff could open and close. On the other side of this window was a barrier of metal mesh designed to prevent patients from trying to harm whoever was watching them. Alyssa knew from long experience that she would be perfectly safe if she slid the panel open and took a look at Victoria. So why was she so terrified to do it?

You're a professional… You can do this.

With a trembling hand, she slid open the observation panel, then leaned forward to look through the metal mesh. What she saw nearly shattered her sanity.

Victoria sat on the floor in the middle of a massive pool of blood, surrounded by thick coils of what could only be intestines. *Her* intestines. She held a gore-covered object on her lap, and was... *licking it clean*, like a mother cat who had just birthed a kitten. But the nightmarish thing in Victoria's lap was as far from a cuddly pet as you could get. Victoria looked up then, as if she sensed Alyssa watching her, and she began to laugh like a lunatic. The thing in her lap, the... *clown head* opened its eyes, and its black lips contorted into a hideous smile.

Victoria's laughter took on an even darker edge, and her eyes began to glow yellow.

About the Author

Tim Waggoner writes original dark fantasy, horror, and media tie-ins including *Supernatural*, *Kingsman*, and *Resident Evil*. In 2017, he received the Bram Stoker Award® for Superior Achievement in Long Fiction, he's been a finalist for the Shirley Jackson and the Scribe awards, and his fiction has received numerous honorable mentions in volumes of Best Horror of the Year. Tim teaches creative writing and composition at Sinclair College in Dayton, Ohio.

For more fantastic fiction, author events,
exclusive excerpts, competitions, limited editions and more

VISIT OUR WEBSITE
titanbooks.com

LIKE US ON FACEBOOK
facebook.com/titanbooks

FOLLOW US ON TWITTER AND INSTAGRAM
@TitanBooks

EMAIL US
readerfeedback@titanemail.com